Shelby,
Your sweet, faithful encouragement means so much to me in my writing journey. Keep smiling; the joy of the Lord is so evident in your life.
I hope you'll enjoy the continuing adventures of my TeamWork crew!

Blessings Always,
JoAnn Durgin
Matthew 5:16

TORN VEIL BOOKS PRESENTS

Twin Hearts

Book Three of
The Lewis Legacy Series

JOANN DURGIN

TORN VEIL BOOKS
WINNIPEG

This book is a work of fiction. Names, characters, places and events either are products of the author's imagination or are used fictitiously. Any resemblance to actual events or persons living or dead is purely coincidental.

ISBN 978-1-927339-16-9

All Scripture contained within is from the New American Standard Bible.

PUBLISHED BY TORN VEIL BOOKS
www.tornveilbooks.com
Text set in Garamond
Printed and Bound in the USA
COVER DESIGN BY Dino Piccinini

From the Author

My dear friends, even if you haven't read the first two books in *The Lewis Legacy Series*, you can pick right up with this one. I loved writing ***Twin Hearts***, the story of twins Joshua and Rebekah Grant. Forgiveness and redemption are big themes in my books. Josh was my wayward sheep of the TeamWork Missions volunteers, and I needed to bring him back and tell his story. He's not looking for love, but discovers it in a most tender and surprising way, and therein finds his redemption. His twin sister, Rebekah, is torn between two men, and her journey is one we all must make at one time or another—discovering who we are and the values we hold most dear. It's a loving, teasing and protective relationship shared between these two Louisiana siblings, and I hope you'll see the parallels and similarities in their simultaneous love stories.

Twin Hearts has all the elements I hope you've come to expect from one of my books (humor, emotion, drama and heartwarming romance). Please keep in mind that while my main characters are Christians, they're "human" and imperfect, but also forgiven. Like all of us, they make mistakes and errors in judgment—sometimes significant ones—but it's how they ultimately respond to others and their situations in life that can impact others of the love of Christ living in their hearts. We are all called to be servants of that Greatest Love of All, and I'm thankful and blessed to share my characters and their stories with you.

As always, there are those I must thank in the writing of this book:

My Lord Jesus Christ for giving me the inspiration and ability to create these characters and their stories in the hope they'll touch your heart in some way with a truth from His Holy Word;

My family for loving me enough through the storms and also the waves of joy in this writing journey;

A.P. and Roxanne Fuchs at Torn Veil Books, for believing in me and my work (and putting up with me during the long editing process);

My friend, Dino Piccinini, for working with me to create another beautiful cover design which so perfectly represents the stories in this book;

Jamie Eiler, my creative cousin, for penning my wonderful "tag lines" for my books, in this case "*Two Hearts, One God, One Way.*" Jamie's mother, my Aunt Ann, for being such a precious encourager;

Brandi Hebert Sharpton and Kandice Savant Dimaio-Moore, my funny Louisiana "sisters" for educating me about a crawfish boil and all things Cajun;

Linda Phillips of Pennsylvania, Debbie Schurz of Virginia and Noela Nancarrow of Australia for their sweet friendship and support;

My faithful prayer warriors and church family—especially Miss Gladys and Miss Shelby; and

My fellow Christian authors within the American Christian Fiction Writers (national and Indiana chapter), my rocks of inspiration and mentors, as well as my new friends in the Louisville Christian Writers group.

May you continue to read Christian fiction, my friends. It's my prayer you'll enjoy the ongoing adventures with the lively group of TeamWork Missions volunteers . . . and now, ***Twin Hearts***.

Blessings,

JoAnn Durgin
Matthew 5:16

Ephesians 1:7

In Him we have redemption through His blood,
the forgiveness of our trespasses,
according to the riches of His grace.
(Josh's Verse)

Isaiah 40:31

Yet those who wait for the Lord will gain new strength;
They will mount up with wings like eagles,
They will run and not get tired,
they will walk and not become weary.
(Rebekah's Verse)

CHAPTER ONE

Mid-March 2002—Monday Morning

APOLOGIZING FOR PAST behavior wasn't a problem for Josh Grant, but asking forgiveness from his former mentor humbled him like nothing else. *This* apology was way overdue. He passed through the revolving door of the downtown Houston high-rise and did a quick scan of the building directory. *TeamWork Missions, U.S. Headquarters. Suite 412.* Shoving his hands deep in the pockets of his suit pants to quell his nerves, Josh exchanged a nod and a "Good morning" with the security guard and headed toward the bank of elevators. He stared at the elevator doors with tunnel vision and crossed his arms, ignoring the blonde in a business suit eyeing him with undisguised interest. It might have been a good idea to bring his briefcase. Call it a crutch, but at least he'd have something to hold and give him some sense of normalcy. What he faced on the fourth floor wasn't one of his routine merger or acquisition deals—this was far more intimidating. He was here for one purpose alone: to see Sam Lewis.

Impatience took over as he rocked on the heels of his Italian leather shoes and waited to see which of the eight elevators would win the race to the ground floor. Stretching his neck, he loosened his collar and new silk tie, which felt like a noose intent on suffocating him. Sam wouldn't care if he wore tattered clothes, hadn't bathed in a week and not a dime to his name. Heart attitude made the man, not the outward representations of worldly prosperity. Although his dad grilled it into him, and his mind possessed that knowledge, his heart hadn't yet crawled out from beneath the heavy burden of guilt and remorse—its own unique brand of shame.

Instead of waiting, he pushed the door to the stairwell and bounded up the steps two at a time. His workouts must be paying off since he was barely out of breath when he reached the fourth floor landing. Opening the door to the hallway, he spied a sign for TeamWork pointing to the left. Each step on the tile floor sounded like a clanging cymbal announcing his arrival in the otherwise empty hallway. Like a prisoner going to his doom. *Shake it off.* Sam was a godly man, and he'd welcome him back with open arms.

Josh stared at the gold-plated sign mounted on the heavy oak door of Suite 412. His eyes focused. *Samuel J. Lewis, Jr., Domestic Missions Director.* He readjusted his collar and straightened the tie in the reflection of the sign, basking him in a surreal, golden glow. Ironic since they'd nicknamed him "Golden Boy" at his Baton Rouge law firm. Little did they know that gold was more tarnished than silver.

With his hand on the door, he hesitated. Perhaps he should have called first. It wasn't so much the element of surprise inasmuch as wanting to do this face-to-face. Man-to-man. The last time he saw Sam haunted him still. After he'd provoked the TeamWork director into a rare display of aggression, they'd rolled in the mud like wild dogs, throwing punches and pounding each other until Kevin Moore—always the peacemaker—forced them apart. Sam almost broke his nose, but he'd deserved it. The man was more than a close friend—his mentor and brother in the faith, and he'd betrayed him in the worst possible way.

Get on with it. Inhaling a deep breath, Josh turned the heavy brass knob and stepped inside. It wasn't a surprise the TeamWork office was tasteful but sparse in its furnishings: an upholstered blue sofa with two matching chairs, an oak coffee table with scattered magazines, a couple of small tables, lamps and a large, colorful throw rug graced the polished, hardwood floor. A middle-aged woman clicked away on a computer keyboard at a desk in the center of the room, her fingers flying as she hummed under her breath. Involved with her work, she appeared oblivious to his presence until Josh cleared his throat to get her attention.

"Oh, goodness me. Good morning," she said, removing her glasses. They fell to the chain circling her neck. "I'm sorry. I didn't hear you come in. May I help you?" Her accent sounded more Midwest than native Texan, but welcoming all the same as she tucked a dark strand of hair behind one ear and gave him a polite smile.

"Good morning. I'd like to see Mr. Lewis, if he's available." Funny how strange it was to call him anything but "Sam."

Her brow creased. "Is Sam expecting you?" She pulled an appointment book across her desk and glanced at it. "I don't have anything written down, and he's in a meeting outside the office."

Josh shook his head. "He's not expecting me, no. I was in the area and hoped to say hello." Not the complete truth, but not an outright lie either. Now that he was in Sam's office, he wasn't leaving Houston until he spoke with him.

"I see." She retrieved a pen and tapped it against the book. "Would you like to schedule something for later this afternoon or tomorrow?" Her smile was kind, and her appreciative gaze fell on his pale blue silk tie. Score another one for the power tie his sister gave him for Christmas.

Josh noted the nameplate on her desk. "Do you have any idea how long he'll be, Mrs. Franklin?"

"Hard to say, and please call me Bennie."

Bennie Franklin? He couldn't help his chuckle, but it helped assuage the tension in his muscles. Based on the grin curving her lips, she wasn't offended. Somehow it seemed fitting Sam's assistant shared a moniker with one of the nation's Founding Fathers.

"My maiden name was Factor, proving my philanthropic parents had either a clever or warped sense of humor. In retrospect, I'd say both." She paused a moment, watching him.

Bennie Factor. Benefactor. Very nice. Josh nodded for her to continue, his smile still in place. This woman must be fun to have around.

"Then God proved *His* sense of humor by pairing me up with a man named Franklin." She shrugged. "It's broken the ice more times than I can mention, and people don't forget it. Now, back to business. I know Sam's meeting Lexa—that's his wife—for lunch at noon, so I imagine he'll go straight to the restaurant from his meeting." She gave him a sympathetic glance. "To answer your question, I doubt he'll be back before one-thirty or two this afternoon. Tell you what. Leave your card with me. Sam usually calls in for messages, and I can give him your information then." The ringing telephone interrupted, and she held up one finger. "Don't go away. Be back with you in a second."

As she answered the call, Josh canvassed the perimeter of the medium-sized office. Photos of Sam and Lexa and other TeamWork officials in London, South America and Asia lined one section of the back wall. For a domestic missions director, Sam was quite the international traveler. No one deserved his success more, and inner peace and contentment radiated in his expression. The TeamWork leader's deep faith was his anchor, and marriage to Lexa obviously agreed with him. He'd heard she'd given birth to their first son near Christmas this past year.

Photos of various TeamWork missions lined an adjacent wall. Pausing, Josh smiled when he spied one of Amy Jacobsen working alongside his twin sister, Rebekah, in a makeshift schoolroom, with the faces of several children in the background. Stepping closer, he examined the photo to its immediate left, scanning the faces of the volunteers. Sure enough, there he was, with Winnie Doyle beside him as they worked on one of the houses they'd rebuilt during the fateful San Antonio work camp.

Sweet, beautiful Winnie. She looked happy in the picture, probably laughing at one of his dumb jokes. The last four-plus years melted away as he stared at the photo. His pulse picked up speed even as guilt pierced his heart. He stood rooted to the floor, unable to move.

"Okay," Bennie said, hanging up the phone. "As I was saying, why don't you leave your card and tell me which number is best for Sam to reach you." She tilted her head and gave him a curious glance. "You look awfully familiar. Are you a TeamWork volunteer?"

Snapping out of his trance, Josh walked back toward the desk. "I used to be. Bennie, would you mind if I wait here until Sam calls? I won't be a nuisance, and I'll stay quiet and out of your way. Promise." He nodded to the nearest chair. "I'll sit and read a magazine."

"I suppose that's okay," she said, but he detected hesitancy as she checked her watch. The phone rang again and she sighed. "It's been ringing off the hook this morning. A new missions trip is in the works and I'm fielding questions. Busy day." She darted a glance at the small switchboard. "Oh, good, it's Sam.

Great timing." Bennie talked with her boss for a couple of minutes, nodding and answering the occasional question as she jotted notes. "Sam, before you go, I have a young man here in the office who's a former volunteer. He'd like to visit with you. Today, if possible. Right." Bennie lowered the phone. "He said he can meet with you this afternoon at three, if you're available."

"That'll be great. Thanks."

Her brows rose. "And may I give him your *name*?"

Fully aware she hadn't pushed the hold button on the switchboard, Josh cleared his throat and employed his best win-them-over voice he'd used in corporate boardrooms all over Louisiana. "Tell him the wayward sheep has returned to the flock."

Shooting him a curious look, she repositioned the phone and started to repeat his message, but stopped midstream. Her dark eyes widened as they fell on him. "I'll do that. Sure thing. Thank you, Sam." Disconnecting the call, she waved him back over to her desk. "So, I take it you're Josh Grant."

"That's right." He stepped closer.

"In that case, I have a very important message for you."

His pulse raced at a furious pace. "Yes?"

Bennie held his gaze steady, not batting an eyelash. "Sam's exact words: 'Go in my office, park yourself in a chair, and don't move a muscle. I'll be there in ten minutes.'"

~

Winnie frowned at the vibrating cell phone on the kitchen counter. "I don't have time for this today," she mumbled, picking up a tray laden with lemon and cherry tarts and shoving it into the oven with more force than she intended. From her quick glance at the phone, she knew it wasn't Lexa. Everyone—*anyone*—else could wait.

Sipping a cup of tea an hour later, Winnie noted the time. Dottie was bringing Chloe home around seven. The Lord would bless that kindhearted woman for being such a saint, offering to keep Chloe most of the day and giving her supper. That should give her plenty of time throughout the afternoon to chop the vegetables for the salad, make the four types of quiche appetizers and finish the fruit tarts. At least the Red Hat Society ladies specified what foods they preferred and which ones they did *not* want for their event. Made her job that much easier.

Buzz. Buzz. Staring at the phone, she sighed. *Buzz. Buzz.* "Okay, okay. You caught me in a moment of weakness." Moving over to the counter, leaning against it, she opened her phone. Not recognizing the number, she considered not answering. Still, it could be a potential client. "Doyle-Clarke Catering," she said, employing her most professional voice—polite, but noncommittal.

"I'm looking for Winnie Doyle." The voice was deep. Male. Smooth Cajun accent. *Familiar.*

Deep shivers ran from her hairline down to her ballet flats. An urge to close the phone seized her, but she managed to hold it against her ear in spite of her trembling fingers. She stopped her tapping foot and closed her eyes. "This is Winnie." Silence. When more seconds passed, her eyes flew open and she snapped the phone shut, tossing it on the counter as if it was shooting flames. "Sorry. You had your chance."

A stab of guilt rushed through her, but she ignored it. Other than her daughter and co-teaching the Sunday school class, the catering partnership with Lexa was the most important thing in her life. She didn't have time to be distracted by people who couldn't make their point in ten seconds or less. If he wanted to talk with her, it would be on her terms, when she had more time. For now, she needed to get back to her task. As it was, her pulse worked overtime.

As she pulled ingredients from the refrigerator, she couldn't stop the thoughts swirling in her mind. A new pink, heart-shaped note caught her eye and gave her pause. *Mommy: kiss Butterfinger.* No doubt Dottie helped her write it, but the big, rudimentary letters made her smile. With a deep sigh, she headed toward Chloe's bedroom. The kitten was in her customary position—curled in a ball, snoozing in the middle of the bed. Putting her fingers to her lips, Winnie blew the slumbering creature an air kiss. It *was* a kiss, and she'd kept the promise. That was the most important thing.

In between rounds of appetizer preparation a few minutes later, she paused while chopping vegetables. She stared at her cell phone on the counter, not dwelling on the reasons why she hadn't turned it off earlier. He'd been persistent, she'd give him that much. Wiping her hands on her apron, she took a deep breath to steady her nerves. Only one man in Baton Rouge—only one man in the entire state of Louisiana—could possibly have access to her private cell phone number. That distinctive voice made her weak at the thought. She'd know it anywhere.

He's back.

CHAPTER TWO

BENNIE NODDED TOWARD Sam's office. "Go on in. Sam rarely locks it. I'll wait until he gets here, then I'm off to lunch." That statement brought an odd comfort. Heaven forbid a grown woman should hear or see him blubber like an idiot, something he might very well do when he faced Sam for the first time in over four years.

"Thanks." Josh closed his cell phone. He'd blown it with that call, but he'd keep trying. Hearing Winnie's voice again tied up his tongue like a sailor's knot. Water would be good. Spying a cooler along one wall, he poured a cup of the ice cold liquid. Downing it before his shaking fingers could spill the contents on the carpet, Josh crumpled the paper cup, aimed and tossed it in the nearby wastebasket. "Another three-pointer and he scores," he said under his breath. Hearing soft laughter, he turned around to face a smiling Bennie.

"My son does the same thing, and no, his name isn't Ben. Were you a basketball player?"

Josh's twisted nerves relaxed and the corners of his lips upturned. "Baseball."

"Ah, the thinking man's sport. Where'd you play?"

"LSU. Born and raised in a small town outside Baton Rouge."

He'd seen that familiar gleam in a mother's eyes before. "You don't say? My youngest daughter, Amanda, lives near there." The way she sized him up, Bennie might have some matchmaking in mind. "What's your line of work, if I may ask?"

"I'm a corporate mergers and acquisitions attorney." Somehow, that statement didn't infuse him with the pride he thought it would.

His answer might please her—and it did, judging by that unmistakable sparkle in her eyes—but now was the time to end the questions. Before he could change the subject, Bennie waved her hand. "Don't mind me. Do me a favor and don't tell my boss his assistant's an old busybody."

Her tone half-teased, but Josh hastened to reassure her. "I wouldn't think of it. I'm actually here in Houston on personal business." Maybe that would push any blind-date-with-the-daughter ideas to the back burner. If this wonderful Christian woman knew his background, she'd keep her daughter far away.

"Well," she said, replacing her glasses and turning back to her work, "enjoy your reunion with Sam, and I hope I'll see you again sometime."

"Thanks. Likewise." Turning the knob to the inner sanctum, Josh left the door ajar as he walked across the room and sat in one of the two maroon armchairs facing Sam's desk. After three minutes of fiddling and fidgeting, he felt like one of his sister's students with ADHD who'd forgotten his meds. *Lord, keep me calm and give me the right words.*

Rotating the picture on Sam's desk, he smiled when he saw Sam and Lexa's smiling, flushed faces at the San Antonio work camp staring back at him. Lexa was as blonde and petite as Sam was dark-haired and tall, an inch taller than his own six-foot-four. The best thing to come from that eventful work camp was the love that developed between these two people from different backgrounds and perspectives of faith, like his parents, who had one of the most solid marriages he'd ever known. He pulled another photo toward him, staring at the face of a smiling infant. No doubt about it, this was Joseph Lewis. Only a few months old, the resemblance to Sam was undeniable with his dark hair and facial structure. Josh ran a finger over the photo.

Hearing voices, he replaced the photo on the desk with shaking fingers, almost knocking it over. No mistaking that deep, Texas drawl as Sam greeted Bennie. He stared at the wall behind Sam's desk, an immovable lump lodged in his throat. *This is it.* Closing his eyes, he didn't need to look over his shoulder to know the TeamWork director had entered the office and stood behind him.

One large palm clamped on his left shoulder and a black Stetson—classic Sam Lewis—flew past him, landing on the desk. "It's about time, brother." Coming to the side of the chair and hauling Josh to his feet, Sam embraced him in the bear hug of his life. "You've been missed. Welcome home." His voice was hoarse with emotion as he slapped him on the back a couple of times.

Josh blinked back tears and returned the hug. Pulling away, he grunted and averted his gaze. "Aw, man, why'd you have to go and say that?" He swiped at the wetness beneath his eyes, powerless to stop the tears in the midst of attempting a grin.

The familiar smile lines deepened. "Calling you brother or the missing you part?"

"The welcome home part pretty much did it." Josh waved his hand. "All of it, but it's all good." Squaring his shoulders, he met those piercing blue eyes. How he'd missed this man, but didn't fully understand how much until now. "I'm sorry, Sam." It was a struggle, but he managed to get out the words. "Sorry for everything, and sorry it's taken me this long to tell you. I only hope you can forgive me. I was selfish and misguided, and hurt a lot of people I care about." He shook his head and tried to lighten the mood. "In case you missed it, you're one of those people."

Sam handed him a tissue from a box on a nearby table and pulled one out for himself. He shrugged out of his suit coat and wiped his eyes before dropping into the chair beside him. "I knew you'd come back when you were ready. You're too good a man *not* to come back, and you were forgiven a long time ago."

"Thanks for saying that," Josh said, balling the soaked tissue in his hands. "You'd better give me another one of those or I'm going to ruin this overpriced tie Beck gave me."

"Take the whole box." Sam pushed it across the desk. "Your sister tells me you're doing well at the law firm." He shot him a wry grin. "Not bad for a guy who graduated at the top of his class. I'm proud of you."

"Thanks." Sam was proud of him? *After all I've done . . .* "It's what I've always wanted to do. Besides, racking up billable hours keeps me busy to the point of exhaustion and helps me sleep better at night."

"What brought you back, Josh?"

Josh raised his head. "Marc Thompson. September eleventh." Noting Sam's stricken expression, he blew out a breath. "I can't even imagine. Things like that tend to wake you up."

Sam looked away, the muscles in his jaws flexing. "Shook us all up. But, once again, the Lord proved His sovereignty. I thank Him every day for sparing Marc and making it clear He wants him around a while longer. Of course, Marc claims he's sticking around for the express purpose of harassing me." He allowed the hint of a smile. "I don't doubt it for a minute."

"For Natalie and little Gracie's sake, I'm thankful he got off that plane. We both know the Almighty orchestrated that one, but I don't know much else about what happened. What I *know* is I owe the man a whopping debt of gratitude for pulling my sister out of that creek on your TeamWork jaunt to Montana. I hope I get a chance to thank him in person someday."

Sam shifted his position. "You will. I know Marc will embrace the opportunity to get to know you. As far as what happened, you probably know he owns a successful sports advertising agency in Boston. When he married Natalie, he cut back on the traveling, but he was flying out to L.A. that morning to sign one of the Lakers. It was a major coup for his agency, a huge deal that warranted the boss making the trip. He forgot to turn off his cell phone, and Natalie called after he boarded to tell him his mother had a stroke. Nothing serious, but after Natalie's fall and losing her memory—everything they went through—Marc doesn't take chances when it comes to his family. This is where divine intervention comes into play. Flight Eleven was delayed fourteen minutes leaving Logan. He's a persistent man, and they finally relented. To hear him tell it, they practically pushed him off the plane."

"And then the plane took off . . ." Josh hesitated, catching his breath, "and slammed into the North Tower within the hour." He met Sam's gaze. "For once, words fail me."

Sam pushed his fist against the firm line of his lips, not speaking for a moment. He shifted his position and cleared his throat. "Marc's gone through a lot, similar to what returning soldiers face. He saw the hijackers, talked to a number of the crew, obviously, but also some of the passengers while waiting to board the flight. He's strong, and he'll get through it. Marc's doing a lot of good work, organizing inner-city neighborhood projects in Boston, Philly and New York. They're pairing up kids with celebrity athletes, putting together basketball camps in his dad's memory." Noticing Josh's raised brow, he added, "Jumpin' Phil Thompson."

Josh whistled under his breath. "No kidding? The Celtics legend? I knew Marc played for the Pawtucket Red Sox for a few years, but had no idea there was a connection between the two. So, are these basketball camps a new TeamWork ministry?"

The corners of Sam's mouth upturned. "Not yet, but there's definite potential." His smile sobered as he leaned closer, elbows resting on his thighs, fixing him with one of his signature, soul-searching looks. "The most important thing here is whether or not you're straight with the Lord and forgiven *yourself*."

Josh looked away. "It's difficult. Hearing about Marc jumpstarted me, but it's taken six months to get to the point where I could make this trip. I've confessed it all and asked the Lord for forgiveness, but I need time to *feel* forgiven. I'm the one who knows better than anyone the people I've hurt. I can't take back my past actions, can't erase my past. I'm not proud of my behavior a few years ago, but I think the rumors ran a little rampant to the point of the absurd."

"I don't need to know, and neither does anyone else," Sam said. "People talk. Nothing we can do about it. Keep your eyes on the Lord. Confess it to Him, and you'll find your peace. He'll let you know if and when you need to ask forgiveness from anyone else."

"It's really about redemption, Sam."

"I know. Allow Him to work in your heart. Look at some of the characters in the Bible we view as heroes. Many of their personal histories aren't pretty, yet look how God used them to do His work. I have no doubt He'll do the same in you, but the key is *allowing* Him to work."

"I fear your faith in me is displaced." Josh's eyes grew moist. "I'd advise against it if you don't want to be disappointed."

"Ah, that's where you're wrong, my friend. It's not faith in *you*. It's faith that God can take your deepest sin and turn it into your greatest blessing. *That's* where you find your redemption."

He'd need to consider those words. Reaching into the inside pocket of his suit jacket, he pulled out a personal check payable to TeamWork Missions and handed it to Sam. "This is something else I should have taken care of a long time ago."

The TeamWork director barely glanced at it. Shaking his head, he folded the check in half and laid it on the desk. "You owe me nothing."

"I know I don't owe *you* the money, but I took the money from the TeamWork safe in San Antonio to help Sheila. I fully intended to put that money back before you ever knew it was missing. This should be more than enough to cover what was taken. Plus interest for five years."

"Sheila was desperate to get away from an abusive relationship. I've known all along you never would have taken the money without good reason." Sam's eyes were kind. "That debt was paid a long time ago. Keep your money."

"Fine. Then consider it a donation."

Rising to his feet, Sam walked around the desk and sat in the black leather chair. Opening the middle drawer, he retrieved the check and put it inside. "Fair enough. On behalf of TeamWork, thank you. I'll make sure you get a receipt for tax purposes." A hint of a grin tugged at the corners of his mouth.

An overwhelming burst of emotion threatened to overwhelm him. "Sam, I sinned with Shelby. *Your* Shelby. And then I wanted Lexa when I thought your relationship with her was over . . . . *How* can you forgive me?"

Sam turned in his chair, toward the wall behind his desk. Moving his gaze upward, Josh focused on the rustic, hand-carved wooden cross—beautiful and meaningful in its simplicity. He nodded, blinking hard, his lashes wet on his cheeks as he released a shuddering breath.

Sam grabbed his jacket and Stetson. "Come on. Let's get out of here. I'm on my way to meet Lexa for lunch, and you're coming with us."

His heartbeat increased tenfold, and he swallowed hard. "Are you sure she'll be okay with that?"

That big hand landed on his shoulder again. "Josh, I live with the woman, and I pray with her. Trust me when I say you're an answer to a long-held prayer. She'll be thankful to see you."

"Lead the way," Josh said, the words raspy as he followed Sam out of his office.

"How long are you in town?"

"A few days. I need to be back in Baton Rouge early next week."

Sam paused while writing a note to Bennie. "Got a place to lay your head?"

"My secretary booked a room for me at a hotel a few blocks from here."

"Tell you what," Sam said, "you're welcome to stay at the house, provided you don't mind occasional crying in the middle of the night."

That one made him laugh. "I trust you're talking about the pint-sized version of you. Congratulations. I saw the photo."

The smile lines deepened. "None other. My boy's got some healthy lungs."

"That's great of you to offer, but let's make sure it's fine with Lexa first. A lot of women don't like the element of surprise."

Sam grunted. "True enough. To humor you, I'll ask her at lunch, but don't be surprised if she suggests it first. We're meeting her four blocks from here, so let's walk and catch up on the way."

Time to ask the second biggest question of the hour. "Sam, I need to see Winnie while I'm here in Houston. Beck tells me she and Lexa started a catering business together. I was hoping you could tell me where she lives."

Sam hesitated only a second before ushering him through the door and locking it behind them. "I'll do you one better," he said as they headed to the elevator. "The ladies have a catering event tomorrow night, which means Winnie will be at the house in the morning, and probably most of the day." Although Sam didn't ask any questions, he shot him an indefinable look as they stepped inside the elevator together. "Hard to believe it's been almost five years, but I think you'll find that San Antonio TeamWork camp was more eventful than you realized."

They rode to the ground floor in silence.

This time *he* didn't ask, and Sam wasn't talking.

CHAPTER THREE

Monday, Early Evening

"HI, MOMMY!"

"Come see me, Buttercup." Winnie opened her arms as Chloe ran from the front door to the sofa, wrapping her arms around her waist. A mass of pretty blonde curls splayed across her blouse as Chloe nestled against her, close enough to smell the fresh scent of baby shampoo. "Thanks for taking such good care of her today and bringing her home, Dottie." Winnie twirled a curl around one finger and gave a gentle tug as Chloe giggled. Raising her face, the child planted a sloppy kiss on Winnie's cheek. How she wished these moments would last forever.

"You know I love spending as much time with your little treasure as I can," Chloe's nanny said, closing the front door behind her. Dottie's children and three grandbabies lived in Alabama, so she didn't see them as often as she'd like. It was inevitable and only a matter of time before the desire to live closer to her family would lure her away. In the meantime, Winnie would enjoy the blessing since Dottie was the closest thing to a grandmother Chloe had ever known. Opening her purse, Dottie pulled out a book and put it on a chair. "We checked out a new book from the library. I'm sure Chloe will read you the words she learned today. I think she added about ten new ones."

"Yup." Chloe sat up and tugged off her lightweight sweater with her help. She apparently needed to teach her daughter the proper way to say yes, but it was cute and endearing. Listening as Chloe rattled off a stream of words, Winnie raised a brow when she stopped. "Mommy, do you know what a grant is?"

Winnie turned her head, coughing to gain a few precious seconds. *Of all the words in the English language, it had to be that one?* If the Almighty was trying to get her attention, it was working. "Is that a word in your book, sweetie?" Aware Dottie eyed her, she avoided looking her way. Recovering her composure as best she could, Winnie watched as Chloe ran and picked up the book, bringing it to her.

"It's a word at the front. See?" Opening the book and finding the page, Chloe showed it to her.

"It's written by an author who received a grant from a scholastic foundation." Dottie's smile was doting. "You know your daughter. She reads books from cover to cover. Like a little sponge she is, soaking it all up. I tried my best to explain what 'grant' means, but it's a challenge, that one."

Winnie searched her mind. "A grant means you give someone something. Kind of like a gift." No kidding. The irony of it smacked her in the face.

Probably not the best explanation, but it would have to do. Pulling herself up from the sofa, she retrieved Chloe's sweater and went through the motions of hanging it in the small coat closet—anything to keep her hands occupied. Her daughter had no idea she embodied the meaning of her new word.

Dottie headed to the door. "Well, I need to be getting home now. I'll see you ladies tomorrow. What time should I pick her up?"

Winnie forced herself to focus, doing a mental rundown of the next day's schedule. "Lexa and I have to be at the hotel to set up at three, so how about two-fifteen? That should give me enough time to get everything together, meet Lexa and make it to the hotel in time."

Dottie paused with one hand on the doorknob. "You'll be at Lexa's all day, right?"

She nodded. "Yes. I was planning on leaving around one to get Chloe at daycare, and then bring her back here until you can pick her up."

"Then I'll just pick her up at the daycare. They already know me, and I don't have any other plans tomorrow. I'll be happy to do it if it'll make it easier for you."

Relief flooded Winnie's entire being. *Lord, thank you for this angel of mercy.* "That would be great. Have I told you yet today how much of a lifesaver you are?"

"I like Lifesavers!" Chloe said, grinning.

Winnie frowned. "The problem is, I'm not sure how long the event will last tomorrow night, and—"

The sweet woman waved her hand. "Don't you worry about a thing. We'll plan a sleepover tomorrow night, and have ourselves a grand time. If you think of it, just send along an extra bag with a toothbrush and pajamas to the daycare with her. Two o'clock okay?"

Winnie's eyes misted. "Yes, that'll be fine. I'll make sure they know. Thanks so much." She'd miss Chloe something fierce, but knowing Dottie loved her daughter like one of her own was a comfort beyond measure. It seemed a large percentage of her life the past few years revolved around details of transportation and childcare, but she wouldn't trade it for the world. *Not a complaint, Lord.*

"Bye, love!" Dottie called to Chloe, who was sprawled on the living room floor, playing with Butterfinger. Good thing she was in some of her oldest playclothes since they bore the evidence of Chloe's love of all things tomato. Out of necessity, she'd become quite the laundry expert.

"Bye, Dottie!" When Chloe graced the older woman with one of her sweet smiles, it made Winnie's breath catch. With each passing day, she resembled her father a little more. While she inherited the same honey color of her hair and shape of her nose, that engaging smile was all his. Another sharp stab of conscience ripped through her. One day soon, her daughter would start asking questions about her father, and she needed to have answers suitable for a quick-witted, intelligent child. Chloe deserved nothing less. She held a cat toy, dangling it in front of the kitten. Her eyes widened in delight when Butterfinger pawed the air.

Time for their evening tradition of hot chocolate. No matter the season, hot chocolate with a small mountain of whipped cream was Chloe's favorite. Going through the open doorway into the kitchen, Winnie filled a pan with water and turned on the burner. As she pulled out the cocoa, mugs and spoons, she pondered how well the catering business worked into their lives. If there wasn't a catering event the same day, she'd often take Chloe along with her to Sam and Lexa's while they cooked or sampled new dishes, balanced the books, discussed recipes or planned upcoming menus.

Chloe adored helping with Lexa's baby, Joseph. At first she complained all the newborn did was sleep, eat and . . . all manner of disgusting things. Now, at three months old, Joe could roll over and babble with the best of them. Chloe loved calling him Joey since she'd discovered it rhymed with her own name. Winnie observed with a close eye whenever her daughter ate her lunch with Joe in close proximity. She couldn't wait until he was ready for solid foods so she could feed him like her baby doll. The ketchup bottle had already been confiscated more times than she could count amidst Chloe's protests of it being a soft food. No sense in inviting trouble, especially since Joe was already waving his arms and attempting the old reach-and-grab technique. She sensed a lecture on safe versus non-safe foods to feed an infant looming in the near future.

With Joe watching from his playpen, Chloe would dance and make funny faces, eliciting hearty belly laughs from the child. The first time they heard it, Lexa and Winnie looked at each other across the butcher block island—over a tray of stuffed mushrooms and pinwheels—and hurried into the family room. Lexa lifted Joe from the playpen and danced around the room with her handsome son, peppering his chubby cheeks with kisses. Watching her, Winnie remembered the same milestones with Chloe, and how thankful she was for every single one.

Hauling a rocking chair over beside Joe's crib in his upstairs bedroom, Chloe tried to sound out words of a Bible storybook. Joseph and the coat of many colors was her favorite. When Winnie once asked which story she was reading, Chloe gave her a Mommy-you-should-know look. How many times would she see that same look in the future? Hearing Chloe's voice on the intercom always made her smile as she worked with Lexa in the kitchen. Mid-afternoon, she'd often discover Chloe fast asleep, curled in the rocking chair with her head resting on the arm, the storybook open on her lap.

"Mommy, can Butterfinger sleep in my bed tonight?" Lost in thought, Winnie jumped as Chloe padded into the kitchen in her bare feet. She stroked the kitten, raking her small fingers through the creature's soft fur. Gorgeous green eyes flecked with amber—the most striking feature Chloe inherited from her father—stared Winnie down with a steely determination belying that innocent smile. Again, so like her dad.

Pouring the steaming water into mugs—a ceramic TeamWork one for her and an insulated plastic Cinderella one for Chloe—Winnie swirled the hot chocolate before adding a generous dollop of whipped cream in both. "Sit down, and let's talk about it." *Why did I let this child talk me into getting a kitten?* She motioned to a chair and watched as Chloe lowered the kitten into the bed in the corner, handling her like the most precious treasure. *That's why*. Watching over Joe and caring for Butterfinger brought out nurturing qualities she wouldn't think possible in one so young. Scurrying to the table, Chloe plopped into the chair. Heaving a big breath, she blew on the hot chocolate and giggled when whipped cream landed on the table between them.

"I'll let the kitten sleep in your bed on one condition, young lady." Grabbing a napkin, Winnie blotted the melted whipped cream.

Chloe leaned her head to one side. "What's a dition?" Ah yes, another new word. Single parenting a bright child could sometimes be exhausting.

Winnie's smile came from the deepest part of her heart. "*Con*dition, and it means yes, Butterfinger can sleep on your bed tonight as long as *you* understand you're expected to make your bed tomorrow morning after breakfast."

"'Kay. Like a promise." A wet chocolate mustache outlined Chloe's upper lip. Reaching with her tongue, she licked it off and grinned.

"Yes, I suppose it is like a promise." *That was easier than I thought.* Sipping their hot chocolate, giggling together, she thanked the Lord for the privilege. How she loved being a mom. For that reason alone, she'd always love Josh Grant. He'd given her the absolute best gift of her life. The gift of *motherhood.*

CHAPTER FOUR

Monday Night

FOR MORE THAN four years, Rebekah prayed her twin would make amends with Sam. So much personal history, so many hurts needing to be healed. When Josh called a few weeks ago and asked for Sam's contact information, she'd given him everything he'd possibly ever need short of Sam's social security number and thumbprint. It was her brother's latest request that had her puzzled. After listening to his message, she stared at her phone. *Why is Josh asking for Winnie Doyle's phone number?*

Sliding the ponytail holder from her hair, Rebekah glanced at the clock on the nightstand. It was probably too late to call. Still, the overpowering need to know won out. Josh had awakened *her* enough times. Payback time. Pressing the speed dial, she pulled back the light coverlet and sheets.

He picked up on the third ring. "Hey, wombmate. How's life in the world of Rebekah?"

She sighed. "You tell me. Josh, why are you asking for Winnie's phone number?"

"That's one thing I've always loved about you. At least with me, you get right to the heart of the matter. You won't let me get away with anything. Tell me, how *are* the two men in your life?"

Rebekah ignored his barb. "You need a watchdog, and good thing for you, I'm it. And don't pull that 'I'm older than you' line on me." For some unknown reason, her brother loved reminding her of his arrival in the world a full eight minutes ahead of her. Holding the phone cradled between her ear and shoulder, she retrieved her favorite, well-worn, purple LSU T-shirt and sleep pants from the dresser drawer. Catching a whiff of her favorite detergent, she smiled.

"Stop multi-tasking and concentrate so I don't have to repeat everything three times." Josh chuckled under his breath. "And what's with the heavy breathing? Which one inspired that, Adam or Kevin?"

He knows me too well. Scary. She was thankful he couldn't see her smile. "I hope you realize no one else has the unique privilege of insulting me on a regular basis. You should feel special."

"Right back at ya, sis. Are you sitting down yet?"

She snorted. "Just answer the question." She wasn't sitting down, but he had her undivided attention. *Something's up. Wait it out and let him tell you. Don't push.*

"First of all, that message is old. Check the date. It was three days ago."

She frowned. "So, I'm a little behind on messages. It still doesn't negate my question."

"Here's the thing." He hesitated, something he rarely did. "Winnie and I . . . well, we shared a special memory in San Antonio. Leave it at that. I'm asking you to trust me on this."

"Oooh—kay." She checked her clock and set the alarm. "It's been a long time since you've seen or talked with Winnie, so you can't fault me for curiosity."

"I saw Sam and Lexa today."

In the middle of choosing a bottle of nail polish, Rebekah paused. Her eyes welled with tears. "Well, it's about time." Huge answer to prayer, that one. *So, he's finally come around.*

"That's the same thing he said before he crushed me. The man is deceptively strong."

"Where was this?"

"Space City, Clutch City, H-Town, Magnolia City." Josh paused. "Need I go on?"

"You're in Houston. Cut to the chase, please. You need your beauty rest. Tell me what happened." She pulled out her Bible and the novel she'd been reading, putting them on the bed. Maybe it was the teacher in her, but it was difficult to sit and talk without doing several things at once. She'd always been that way.

"We're fine. You know Sam. Within two minutes, it was like we saw each other yesterday. I think the man would forgive Hitler if he showed repentance, humbled himself and asked forgiveness."

"That's extreme, even for you. Does this mean you're coming back to TeamWork?" Her voice caught and she dropped onto the bed.

"In some capacity, I'd love to someday, yes. Not sure how, when or where."

She stared at the pattern in her sleep pants, drawing imaginary circles with one finger. "Josh, that's such an answer to prayer, I can't even tell you."

"That's the same thing Lexa said. It's gratifying to know I've had so many praying for me the last few years." The emotion in his voice was almost palpable.

"Now I have a new direction in my prayers for you. I'm sure Sam is already formulating ideas. So, spill it about Winnie. Have you talked with her yet?"

"I'm actually staying with Sam and Lexa, and she's coming over to the house in the morning. I tried to call her today, but we never connected. I might try one more time tonight, but it's getting late."

She could tell he turned away from the phone, probably to check the time. Her brother was the most focused person she knew. "Well, I hope it goes well for you, and that you two share another . . . special memory." Whatever that meant. Rebekah surrendered to her yawn.

"Your turn. Don't play coy. What's up with the bayou love triangle?"

Rebekah rolled her eyes and slumped back against the pillows. "It's not a love triangle."

"Only because the two guys don't know about each other . . . yet." That last word was well-placed. Josh warned her something might happen to force a confrontation one of these days.

"I've made no commitments to either of them, and you know it. I'm going to the school picnic with Kevin tomorrow afternoon and Adam's taking me to lunch on Saturday, if you must know."

"How difficult it must be to be you, Beck."

"Looked in a mirror lately?"

"That's not what I meant, and you know it. Talk to Kevin."

"Therein lies the problem. If I tell Kevin I'm seeing Adam, he'll back off. It's taken him years to get to this point." She twirled a long strand of hair around one finger. "I don't want to risk losing him. He's too important in my life."

"Answer this question, then: is the Brit too important in your life?"

"Of course, he is. He has a name, Josh."

"I know. I just like calling him the Brit." Amusement danced around the edges of his voice.

"Must you always be my conscience?"

"Someone's got to do it. And that's my cue. Love ya."

"You, too. Give Sam and Lexa my love, and give that sweet baby of theirs a kiss. I hope I meet him before he turns a year old. I'll be thinking of you in the morning, that you'll get your chance to meet with Winnie. And praying, always praying."

"Will do on all counts, and thanks. In the meantime, at least *think* about talking to Kevin, okay?" She smiled as he signed off, always thinking he had the last word. Little did he suspect she planned it that way.

~

After tucking Chloe in bed, Winnie pulled out her phone and glanced at the rundown of phone numbers from the day. Eight times was the current tally. Hanging up on him obviously hadn't deterred his mission. The man she knew was nothing if not single-minded and determined. She suspected he wouldn't give up until he talked with her, at the very least. Leaving the phone on the nightstand, she headed into the bathroom to brush her teeth.

More tired than she realized, she released a long sigh of contentment as she slid under the sheets a few minutes later. Rolling over on her side, she hugged her extra pillow and yawned. Her eyes fell on her Bible on the nightstand. She'd been too tired to work on her Sunday school lesson, but figured the Lord would forgive her one missed day. Her eyes strayed to the phone. "If you really want to talk to me, I'm here now. Ring already." She startled and cried out when it buzzed within the minute, as if on command. Clamping a hand over her mouth, not wanting to wake Chloe, she grabbed the phone.

Same number. "Hello?" She kept her voice quiet.

"Winnie Doyle, is that you?" This time he didn't give her the opportunity to hang up on him. That deep, rich voice resonated in her ears, making her dizzy. She'd always loved it—completely masculine yet capable of being incredibly gentle and tender.

She nodded, but of course he couldn't see. "Yes."

"This is Josh. Joshua Grant." He paused. As if she wouldn't know.

The blood rushed to her cheeks and she brought a quick hand to her chest. *Please, Lord, don't let me faint.* How pathetic was she that hearing his name gave her heart palpitations? She fumbled for her Bible and pulled out last week's church bulletin, using it to fan her flaming cheeks. "Josh," she breathed. *What does he want? Why now? Where is he?* Perhaps more telling, why did she go all soft—like some kind of silly, besotted schoolgirl—at the mere sound of his voice?

"I'm here in Houston." He'd always been good at reading her mind, or else she was way too obvious. Could be a combination of the two. "I'm staying with Sam and Lexa."

Guess some mighty big fences have been mended I haven't heard about yet. Lexa hadn't even hinted, and she thought she'd trained her better than that. But it might also explain why her catering partner hadn't called her all the livelong day. Being the day before a big job and not hearing from Lexa should have tipped her off something was going on. Winnie's thought process halted with the onset of sudden clarity. *I'm meeting with Lexa at the house in the morning.* That last bit of recall had her sitting up, and—swinging her legs over the edge of the bed—she dropped her head between her knees. *Breathe.*

"Uh huh," she mumbled. Her hair, usually tied back in a ponytail, covered her face. Impatient, she lifted her head and sputtered as one long strand brushed across her mouth. She loved the scent of her shampoo, not so much the taste.

"I can't hear you. You sound . . . muffled." The amusement in Josh's voice rattled her even more.

"Sorry." She smoothed her fingers through her mussed hair and stretched out on the bed, flat on her back, one hand over her mouth. She waited, not knowing what to say to this man. What *could* she say? A million things, and yet nothing. *Lord, you've orchestrated this whole thing, haven't you?* She'd always known the Lord had a sense of humor. She'd deal with Him later in their nightly conversation.

"Will you meet with me tomorrow? I'd really like to see you. There are some things I need to tell you."

She buried her face in the comforter, squeezing her eyes tight. Her fist bunched up the fabric, releasing and repeating several times.

"You can just tell me now."

"I can't hear you again," Josh said.

Sitting up cross-legged on her bed, she forced a lightness into her voice. "Is this any better?"

"Much better. I understand you and Lexa are business partners, and it's going very well."

"That's right." She swallowed the lump in her throat. Good. Only two words, but it sounded entirely professional and not in the least like he'd turned her world on its axis in the last two minutes.

"I think that's great. Sounds like you've found your niche."

Winnie sighed. "Did you call me to chat, Josh?" She cringed at how rude it came across.

"I called because I want to talk with you, tell you how sorry I am the way things ended between us in San Antonio, but I'd prefer to do it in person. I hope you'll give me the opportunity."

"Well, uh . . ." She hesitated, chewing on a fingernail, her eyes focusing on the framed watercolor on her bedroom wall. A Chloe Doyle original. A light-colored teddy bear held a bouquet of gorgeous pink roses, and a bright red, oversized heart covered the bear's chest. Winnie's eyes misted as they fell on Chloe's scrawl in the bottom corner—too small to see from the bed, but forever stamped on her heart. *Twin Hearts—Mommy and me.* She'd made it in her nursery school class at church and presented it to her last month for Valentine's Day. Winnie could never look at that teddy bear without it bringing a smile. Even now, she felt her heart softening, her anxiety draining.

"I hope you'll allow me to speak my peace, and then I'm headed home."

She swallowed hard. "Things are kind of busy right now. How long are you here in Houston?" It was a stall tactic, and he probably knew it.

"As long as it takes."

She certainly didn't expect that response. "As it long as it takes . . . for what?" She knew she'd regret asking that one.

"As long as it takes to talk with you. I'm much more patient than I used to be."

Her mind worked overtime. Maybe if she agreed to meet with him, he could ask her forgiveness, she could give it, and then he'd be gone. But it wouldn't be—couldn't ever be—that simple. Josh might have a confession to make, but she couldn't let the man go back home to Louisiana without confessing the secret that slept in the very next room. She'd had enough conversations with God about Josh Grant to know He was behind this one all right. It was *time.*

"I'll meet you at Lexa and Sam's in the morning. Lexa and I need to start cooking at eleven, so I'll be there by nine-thirty. Hopefully, that'll give us enough time to talk."

"Thanks, Winnie. I'm looking forward to seeing you again."

The relief in his voice was obvious. She prayed she'd get a little sleep, but doubted it. "Okay, then. I guess I'll see you in the morning."

"I'll be here waiting."

CHAPTER FIVE

Tuesday Morning

AS SOON AS Lexa opened the door, Winnie knew she was in trouble. Those aquamarine eyes widened and she let out a low whistle. "Winnie Doyle, you are an absolute *vision.*" Reaching for her hand, Lexa hauled her into the kitchen. Closing the side door, she circled her, taking in the full view.

"Stop it, already. You're making me dizzy. It's like watching a Hitchcock movie," Winnie said, laughing. "You can close your mouth now. I know my way around a tube of lipstick and mascara, you know." Even so, it was the rare occasion when she applied more than blush and tinted lip gloss.

Lexa gave her a nod of approval. "I'm loving the look. Gorgeous dress, and it's nice to see your hair down." Her eyes trailed to her feet. "New?"

"Yes, I have feet. It's called nail polish and sandals, Lexa. Get over it."

"Chloe at daycare this morning?"

"Yes, like she always is when we have a catering job the same day."

"Right," Lexa said, "and just like you always dress to the nines before working in the kitchen all day long. If I didn't know better—"

"But you *do* know better," she said, giving her a pointed stare, "so we'll get this little meeting over with, Josh can go back to The Pelican State, and we can all get on with our lives." She almost slipped and used the word apology. Lexa didn't need to know that, although she probably already did.

Hearing a deep grunt, Winnie stared at Lexa, afraid to look behind her. *Please, Lord, don't let Josh be standing in this kitchen.*

"Hello, gorgeous!"

Winnie blew out a sigh of relief as she pivoted to face Sam. "I thought you knew better than to sneak up on two women in a kitchen. Have we taught you nothing?"

Sam planted a kiss on her cheek. "You're going to knock his socks off."

Winnie's cheeks grew warm. "That's not what I'm trying to do and you know it, you evil man."

Catching his wife's eye, he laughed. "Toss me your keys, and I'll bring the trays in."

Winnie obliged his request with a well-aimed toss. "I'll help you." She started toward him, but Lexa stopped her with one hand on her arm.

"We'll bring them in. You have better things to do like march yourself into the living room. Josh is waiting."

Her pulse picked up again as she stared at the swinging door. "Hand me a paper bag. *Now.*" Lexa didn't move although she thought it sounded quite commanding. The corners of Lexa's mouth twisted. Surely the woman wouldn't laugh at her personal angst and emotional upheaval.

"I've never known you to hyperventilate in your life, and it's not going to start now. I understand you're nervous, but this is *Josh.* The same Teamwork friend we all know and love." Lexa pulled her into a quick hug, and Winnie leaned into it. She needed it, especially today. "He's changed for the better—he's solid and strong. The kind of man we always knew he was."

And just like that, their roles reversed. Usually *she* was the one patting hands and whispering words of encouragement, enough to earn her the nickname "Mother Hen" among the TeamWork crew. Even though they'd never discussed it, surely Lexa and Sam suspected Josh was the father of her child. If Chloe's smile didn't tell them, those green eyes were an undeniable Grant hallmark.

Sam approached the side door, balancing two large trays loaded with the result of yesterday's all-day cooking and baking spree. Winnie opened the door, and he maneuvered through and slid the trays on the counter. "One more trip should do it. Anything in the trunk? Got any *peach* tarts in there?"

"A few trays, yes, but the peach tarts will have to wait until the next event. Were you ever a waiter, Sam? The way you handle those heavy trays is downright skillful—" She turned to Lexa. "Which reminds me, did you get the same call I did from the temp agency? We're already down two servers tonight."

"I know, but we're covered, so don't you worry about a thing," Lexa said. "Okay, enough of this. We'll get the rest of the stuff from your car. Now, it's showtime."

Winnie caught the knowing look shared between husband and wife. Her eyes narrowed as Sam headed toward the coffee pot. "You really should play a little harder to get, Mr. Lewis."

"Never." He gave her a wink. "Here you go. Josh needs coffee." He wrapped her fingers around the handle of the carafe. "Put on your best smile and take it out to him."

"Mugs, creamer and sweetener are on the coffee table," Lexa added.

Winnie smirked as she tried to ignore the pounding of her heart. "What about spoons or stirrers and napkins? Gotta have those."

"On the coffee table." The words from Lexa were firm, unyielding. If she didn't keep moving and go through that door soon, her business partner might push her from behind. Lexa was a loving woman, but she only possessed so much patience.

Winnie shot them a look over her shoulder. "You two really *are* made for each other."

It was now or never. Raising her chin, she squared her shoulders and focused on holding the coffee pot steady as she headed toward the door. She prayed she could keep her hand steady. *You're doing this for Chloe.* Pasting on a smile, she pushed through the swinging door to face the man from her past waiting for her in the living room.

CHAPTER SIX

HE STOOD FACING the large picture window at the front of the house, dressed in a perfectly-tailored gray suit, hands in his pockets. Even from the back, Joshua Grant was an impressive man. In the years since she'd seen him, he'd grown broader across the shoulders and filled out his suit coat well. His thick, wavy blond hair was longer than she remembered and curled slightly at the nape of his neck. Winnie's knees felt weak and threatened to buckle beneath her. Ridiculous. *Get over it. You shared a moment with this man more than four years ago and never heard from him again. He's here to say whatever it is, so stop swooning, hear him out and take it like a grownup.*

"Hi, Josh." Her voice was shaky, her hand even more so. Then he turned around. Oh, goodness, the man was gorgeous. Since she'd last seen him, he'd transitioned from a very cute guy into a full-grown, handsome, confident businessman in that suit, a crisp, white shirt and that tie . . . it just wasn't fair. The green in that silk tie was a perfect match for those unbelievable peepers. The heel of her sandal caught on the carpet, and Winnie stumbled forward with a small cry. The modicum of grace she'd acquired from three years of ballet saved her, but she still swayed in precarious fashion, unsteady on her feet.

Rushing across the room to grab the carafe before she spilled the scalding brown liquid onto Sam and Lexa's white living room carpet, Josh somehow managed to rescue it from her hand and put it on a magazine on the coffee table. "Are you okay?" The concern in his voice was gratifying, and his gaze slanted to her hands. "It didn't splash on you, did it?"

"I'm fine, thanks," she said. "Hope *your* fingers aren't scalded. Exhibit A for reasons why *not* to have white carpet with children and clumsy caterers around." She shook her head and rued her fair coloring. The way things were going, she'd be a patchwork of pink, white and red within minutes.

"No harm done. It's great to see you again. Please, come sit down with me."

She didn't want to feel such a strong attraction for him, but her heart and pulse weren't listening. *Don't look at the eyes.* If she repeated it in her mind enough times, would it keep her from succumbing to his charms? Those eyes had been her undoing before and would be again if she didn't watch herself. So much for the self-pep talk. A whole lot of good it did. Why he felt the need to dress in one of his expensive power suits was beyond her, but then again, here she was in a dress costing the equivalent of a monthly car payment for Ladybug. Hypocrisy was highly overrated sometimes.

"It's nice to see the TeamWork volunteers without a veneer of dust and dirt, isn't it?" The appreciation in Josh's glance did not escape her, and made her feel more like a woman than she had since . . . the last time she'd seen him.

Winnie felt an inner tug. Could be her insides melting. *Hospitality would be good.* "Do you want sugar or cream in your coffee?"

"No, thanks. I'm good. You look incredible, Winnie."

"And you look . . . really good, too." *Please tell me I didn't just say that.* She swallowed her pride and dared to look him in the eye as she sat beside him. *Very bad move. Look away now.*

"More beautiful than ever."

"Thank you." Oh, no. The heat was rising again, moving its way from her throat, up her neck and into her cheeks, like a mutinous little army.

"And even prettier when you do *that.*"

She cleared her throat and crossed her legs, clasping her hands over her knee to prevent swinging it back and forth. "Do what, exactly?" Chloe could handle this situation in a more composed manner than her twenty-eight-year-old mother. *Or a more honest manner.*

"Blush."

Smooth talk, yes, but she sensed Josh was genuine and sincere. Nervous as a novice on the high wire without a safety net, she also felt oddly at ease, a jumbled mess of conflicting emotions, to be sure. "Because it's so quaint?" Her voice held a teasing tone, and a dreaded giggle slipped out. They always betrayed her at the most inappropriate times.

"All that and a giggle, too. I didn't know it was still possible." Josh looked like he found it the most refreshing thing in the world. Judging by the tailored suit and obvious sophistication of the man, he must circulate in a world of high society mavens and professional executives. The women in the life of a rising associate in a prestigious law firm would hardly be the type to blush and giggle. How immature and uncultured he must think her.

"I'm nervous, Josh. Thus the giggles. I'm not sure why you're here, what you want to say, and I'm not sure how I'll react." When his eyes widened, she could tell she'd surprised him with her bluntness. Maybe he wasn't used to *that*, either. She diverted her eyes to her fingers dancing in her lap. It brought her TeamWork friend Natalie to mind since that was her trademark mannerism when she was flustered. Winnie forced her hands still and bit her lower lip.

"If it makes you feel any better, I'm as nervous as you, if not more."

This meeting and apology thing was a bad idea. Josh was a nice man, and he'd feel betrayed once he found out the truth. A sinking feeling in the pit of her stomach made her turn her head, the inward changing of the guard transitioning from fear to shame.

With the fingers of one hand, he turned her chin, forcing her to look at him. She should have known he wouldn't let her get away with anything. "I'm very sorry for taking advantage of you in San Antonio. You were vulnerable and needed a friend, nothing more." He shifted on the sofa and took her hands in his. "I was selfish and lost in sin, and what we did—"

Winnie withdrew her hands, and rose to her feet. "Josh, if you're here to apologize and ask my forgiveness, it really isn't necessary. I was a very willing participant, as you might recall. You didn't take advantage of me, and you didn't take anything from me that I didn't freely offer. Rest assured, you can go home to Baton Rouge and know this is one girl who doesn't harbor any resentment or expects anything from you."

He looked at her like he wasn't sure how to react to her diatribe. "Where did all that come from?"

She shrugged and shot him a helpless glance. "I have absolutely no idea."

"You were always the mother of the TeamWork crew, but you were so busy meeting everyone else's needs, you ignored your own."

"So, you thought it was *your* job to tend to my needs?" Little could he understand her anger wasn't directed at him. He was wonderful. She, on the other hand, was a lying, deceitful mess. And he thought *she* was wonderful. *Lord, give me the right words. How can I tell him?*

Standing, Josh reached for her hand. "Please know I'm not implying you're matronly in any way."

"What?" *If only you knew.* "Don't hold my hand. Please," she said, lowering her voice and moving her hand out of range.

"I don't mean to upset you or make you mad," he said. "Based on your reaction, I'm doing a decent job of both. You were the loveliest woman in the TeamWork camp. I only pray you don't hate me."

Winnie swallowed. "I could never hate you." This time she didn't protest when he covered her hands with his. They were warm, protective. Something inside shifted again.

"You want to know my biggest regret?" Josh waited until her eyes traveled a slow, upward path to meet his. "You're an incredible person. A terrific *woman*, and it's to my detriment I never told you how much that night meant to me."

Winnie blinked back her tears, biting her lower lip. "So, the waiting period for such a revelation is four-plus years?" If ever she'd been a hypocrite, that statement defined it. Oh, what a fool she'd been. Still was, based on current behavior.

He shook his head, and there was no disguising the pain in his creased brow, the lines around his mouth. "I regret it's taken me so long to come back and tell you how sorry I am, but I had to work through some things in my life, needed time for the Lord to work on me." He stepped closer. "But I'm here now, and I hope we can start again and move forward. Come to dinner with me."

"Why?" Winnie cleared her throat. *Does he want to try and make me a legitimate, honorable woman?* "You *do* realize I'm almost three years older than you? You don't owe me anything, Josh. Not then, and certainly not now."

"First of all, age doesn't matter. I want you to say yes because you want to catch up with an old friend." He raked a hand through that lush mane of naturally blond hair. "Honestly, Winnie? I didn't come to Houston with the purpose of asking you out. I came here to ask Sam's forgiveness—and *your* forgiveness. To tell you how sorry I am for the way I treated you, the way things were when I left the camp. We never had the opportunity to say a proper goodbye."

"Seems to me it's a little late for that. Being proper, I mean," she stammered, making a total mess of this awkward conversation.

He sighed and looked deep into her eyes. Mesmerized, she couldn't even turn her head, her eyes locked with his. Winnie squirmed and prayed he couldn't tell how fast her pulse was racing. "Then let's make it a proper *hello.*"

The man could be a scriptwriter; he had her hooked all over again.

"I hope you'll believe me when I tell you that you were the last woman I was with . . . in every conceivable sense of the word."

Conceivable? Oh, Josh, you have no idea.

"I want you to know my track record isn't pretty, but I'm also not the evil guy others might have led you to believe. Do you understand what I'm trying to say?"

She nodded. "Yes," she said. "No one thinks you're evil, and your so-called track record is none of my concern." She was still stuck on his sentiment about a proper goodbye. What, exactly, would have been proper in their case? *How am I supposed to process this information? Lord, a little help here, please. Yes, yes, I'll go to dinner with you. That's how you answer.* Since Chloe was born, she hadn't been on an honest-to-goodness date, although she'd been asked. She'd agree to dinner with Josh—for a nice meal and adult conversation, if nothing else. Oh yes, and telling this man he had a child. *Any excuse will do.* When the Lord opened a door, she'd learned to walk through it with her head held high.

"There's something between us, Winnie." He stepped closer. "You can't tell me I'm the only one in this room who knows that."

You're right, Josh, but you have no idea it's a little girl named Chloe. Inhaling a deep breath, she lowered her voice. "You're just remembering that night. Seeing each other brings it all to the surface again. Let the dust settle a little. *Then* we'll talk."

"Not that it in any way excuses what I did, but we're good together. I felt it then, and I sense it now. The timing was wrong and we gave into temptation, but I repented of my bad behavior long ago and asked the Lord and everyone else I could think of for forgiveness. I've pushed certain things out of my life because I didn't know how to handle them." He paused a moment before finishing his thought. "Seeing you here today, I'm finally beginning to understand why."

What in the world is the man trying to say? "Oh, calm down already. I'll go to dinner with you. How long did you say you're in town?" She tried her best to sound nonchalant, but failed miserably. She knew it, but worse, Josh probably knew it.

"I have to be back in Baton Rouge early next week at the latest." He paused, eyeing her closely. Why, she couldn't fathom. "Until then, I'll take it day-by-day."

"Okay, then. One dinner," she said.

"That's all I ask."

"Not tonight. I have a date with the Red Hat Society. It's a dinner we're catering." She glanced at her watch and frowned. "Look, this has been great and all, but I really need to get to work now." Smoothing a hand over the front of her dress, she managed a small smile.

"Let me help you." Josh put a hand on her arm.

She darted her eyes to his hand and then back to his face. Would she never learn? *Those green eyes are big old pools of luscious water, inviting me to drink. It's just not fair.* "Help me how?"

"I can serve, dish out food, pour drinks, whatever you need. Surely you could use an extra pair of hands. Just give me something to do, and put me to work."

"What?" That came out louder than intended. Something fell in the kitchen. Raising an eyebrow, Winnie gestured for Josh to follow. Giving the swinging door a slight push, she heard a muffled yelp.

"Now, why did you have to go and do *that*?" Lexa said, rubbing her nose as they moved into the kitchen.

"That's what you get for eavesdropping." It crossed her mind to be mad, but the expression on Lexa's face was too comical. *How much of their conversation had she heard?*

"I really wasn't eavesdropping." Lexa shrugged her shoulders with a sheepish grin. "I only heard the last part of your conversation. But if I were you, I'd take Josh up on his offer," she said as she returned to a tray of canapés.

Winnie frowned. "You told me you had the staff situation under control."

"It *is* under control. Josh is onboard now, and when Sam knows that, maybe he'll be more agreeable. Up until now, I've tried to persuade him, but nothing's worked."

"I'm sure you'll think of something." Winnie shot a sidelong glance toward Josh. "I guess that means you're hired. By the way, you're grossly overqualified since we don't normally require our servers to have a law degree. And you'll have to live with a much lower wage scale."

Josh's smile was reward enough. *Well, now, isn't this going well?* She darted a quick glance at Lexa, who patently ignored her, busying herself with the canapés again. One thing Winnie knew: if she caught another one of those knowing winks exchanged with Sam anytime again soon, she might just have to smack her, catering partner or not.

CHAPTER SEVEN

Tuesday, Late Afternoon

"AREN'T YOU SUPPOSED to alternate the vegetables with the meat or shrimp?" Rebekah picked up another soaked bamboo skewer. Shaking it, she handed it to Kevin and watched as he speared a row of cherry tomatoes with accurate precision.

"You can, but cherry tomatoes are different," he said. "These little babies only take a couple of minutes to cook, so you need to grill them separately." He pointed to her half-loaded skewer. "It's also good to keep the ingredients about the same size so they cook evenly, and you've done a great job with that. I hereby crown you a certified kabob specialist."

Rebekah grinned in the way only she could, and it reached those beautiful green eyes. He could stare at her all day. So could every man in Louisiana, but he was learning to live with it. She was the type of woman who garnered attention without trying, even though he knew she didn't like it.

"You're pretty handy to have around," she said. "Tell me, did they teach you how to load a kabob in engineering class at A&M?"

He cleared his throat and focused on his task. "Of course. They taught us things besides how to install a light bulb. My mom hoodwinked Tommy and me into helping her prepare kabobs once when we were kids." He shrugged. "Guess I never forgot it."

"Haven't done it since?" Her smile teased, those luscious lips inviting.

"Not once. Until today. Must be like riding a bike."

Rebekah shook her head. "I can't see Tommy having the patience to make kabobs."

"You're right. He'd rather be eating them. By the way, he said to tell the lovely Rebekah hi." Tommy adored Rebekah and kept pushing Kevin to ask her to join him in holy matrimony. He loved her all right, and knew in his heart she was *the one*, but he wasn't ready to confess undying devotion until everything was in place for a permanent commitment—until he'd saved enough for a deposit on a house and a diamond ring. Even though they'd worked a few TeamWork missions together, they'd only dated a little over a year.

Using the back of her hand, Rebekah flipped her ponytail behind one shoulder. He preferred her hair loose and natural around her shoulders, but she looked incredible any way she wore it. It made more sense to wear it pulled back for a picnic and it might be too distracting if she wore it down. He watched as she speared a couple of shrimp.

"Here," he said, handing her another skewer. "Use two for shrimp. It helps cook it evenly." She watched as he demonstrated. "Sorry, Rebekah." He handed it to her. "I'm getting annoying now, huh?" The last thing he wanted to be was annoying, but maybe he shouldn't have left the question open-ended.

She shook her head. "You couldn't be annoying if you tried. You're like the guy next door, the favorite teacher, the cute pizza delivery guy and the crush from high school all rolled into one adorable package."

He looked at her askance, one brow raised. "Thanks?" Adorable. *That* was the last thing he wanted to be called, but coming from her, he'd accept whatever she offered.

"Trust me, that's a *good* thing," she said. "You can call me Beck, you know. After all, everyone else does. I kind of like it."

"Sorry, but I can't. You'll always be Rebekah to me. Beck is too masculine for such a beautiful woman." Maybe that was laying it on thick, but he considered it pretty bold coming from an *adorable* man. He finished loading another kabob and placed it on the platter beside them, catching the flush in her cheeks at his compliment.

"So, how many more of these kabobs are we making?" she asked, leaning closer, bringing a whiff of her light, citrusy perfume. It must be a popular scent for women since the bank officer and a woman in the grocery line also wore it. Of course, it always brought Rebekah to mind. As if he needed much incentive to think about her.

He sight-counted the remaining wood skewers. "Thirty or thereabouts."

"Okay. Let's pick up speed then. I think they're waiting for us, and I'd hate to be accused of dawdling."

"May it never be," Kevin murmured, working faster on the next skewer as he raced her. Looking over his shoulder, he noticed some of the men gathered around the huge pots for the crawfish boil. "Don't they know a watched pot never boils?"

She laughed. "Very funny. Hi, Jason!" She waved at a boy he presumed was one of her students; the child brightened and waved back.

"I imagine all the boys in your class are in love with you," Kevin said. "None of my teachers ever looked like you. Which, in retrospect, was a good thing. It would have been hard to concentrate on math facts with you looking over my shoulder, Miss Grant." He leaned forward to kiss her, but stopped, thinking better of it.

Later, she mouthed. They talked for the next ten minutes as they prepared the remaining kabobs. "There!" She put the last one on the platter. "Race you to the grill!" she called over her shoulder, hurrying across the short expanse to the grill, leaving him with the kabobs.

"Unfair advantage, Rebekah." He shook his head, content to sit and watch the view.

~

Trina Welch caught Rebekah's eye and motioned her over to where she was setting one of the picnic tables. The expression on the school psychologist's face was intriguing—a combination of concern and bemusement as she handed her packages of napkins and plastic silverware.

"What's that look all about?" Rebekah blew out a sigh. "What have I done now?"

"You know very well, young lady." Trina didn't look at her, but moved to an adjacent table, nodding over her shoulder. Michael Harrison, the school's gym teacher, talked with Kevin by one of the big pots. Rebekah grinned when she saw Kevin pull a Saints apron over his head, tie it in back and take the paddle Michael handed to him.

"Please don't make me feel guilty," Rebekah said. "Kevin and I have never said we're exclusive."

Trina nodded. "I know that, but the big difference here is that you've known him a lot longer than Adam. Working those TeamWork missions with him was a great way to get to know each other. Reveals true character and the heart of a person. The way he looks at you, that sweet man's under the impression he's the *only* man you're seeing." She tossed a glance Kevin's way as she moved to another table. "Adam *does* know about Kevin, right?"

"I have no idea what Adam knows," Rebekah snapped. She counted under her breath for a few seconds. Avoiding Trina's scrutiny, she concentrated on her task. "When I turned down Adam's marriage proposal, he accepted that decision on *my* terms. He was fully aware I wasn't ready to make a permanent commitment." She paused. "As a matter of fact, he hasn't pushed for exclusive rights, either."

Trina's expression softened. "I guess the answer to my question is no. And you're still nowhere near ready to make a decision between these two men, are you?"

Rebekah blew out a breath. "Must you always play the psychologist? Haven't you ever seen one of those old romantic comedies with a love triangle? It makes for some intriguing complications, and everyone loves those movies. They're classic. Romance and slapstick fun." She frowned. *What am I saying?* Hadn't she told Josh it *wasn't* a love triangle?

"And do those terms with Adam still apply?"

"Yes, those terms still apply." She sounded snippier than she intended. "I'm afraid Adam's getting ready to ask me to marry him again. All the signs are starting to surface." Slumping down on the bench, Rebekah lowered her head into her hands and groaned. "I don't mean to lead either one of them on, and I love both of them, but for different reasons. It's just so hard." Her fingers started to feel numb; she massaged them, wishing Kevin was beside her. He always sensed when she needed it. Adam, on the other hand, never noticed. *Stop it!* All these questions only prompted mental comparisons, and it wasn't like she had to make a decision right this moment.

"I can just imagine." Trina sat down beside her and put a comforting arm around her shoulders, pulling her close in a quick hug. "Having two gorgeous men vying for your affection must be a hardship and quite exhausting. I don't know how you do it." She lowered her voice and leaned close. "Is it really that hard a choice? They're two very different men, after all."

"Believe me, I know," Rebekah mumbled. "It's like my perfect man is the combination of them, and trust me, I know there's no such thing as the 'perfect' man."

"Do me a favor, and maybe yourself," Trina said, "looks aside, tell me about them—a comparison, if you will."

"I don't know. Is that really fair?"

"It is if it helps you put it all in perspective." Trina shrugged. "I thought it might help, but it's up to you."

"Okay, then, why not?" Rebekah took a quick breath. "Here goes. Adam studies the history of the places he takes me so he can be my own personal tour guide. He loves gourmet dining, and speaks *four* languages. He's started a charity in London for orphans and widows, and he works with various programs for underprivileged kids on a regular basis. I love hearing how he's trying to help others. Adam's well-traveled, intelligent and he always dresses well. Prince William is a 'mate' and he gets invitations to fabulous balls by dukes and earls. He's an aristocrat—not that I'm even sure what that means—but he gets the Royal Family Christmas card!" She ignored Trina's smug expression. "He's a man of quiet faith, but it's there. You know how the British are more reserved. I'd never want for anything with Adam. But he's much too ordered and doesn't know the meaning of spontaneity. Everything has to be just so with him," she said, slicing her hand through the air. "That drives me absolutely crazy!"

Trina sat, arms crossed, observing her with what must be her professional mask of neutrality. "I'm not saying a word. Now, tell me about Kevin."

Rebekah sighed. This *was* good, talking through it. "Kevin's content with the simple things of life. We take long walks, and he writes beautiful songs that come straight from his heart. He's romantic without trying to be. Kevin works very hard at his dad's lumber company, and he's one of the most godly men I know. He amazes me with his knowledge of the Bible and teaches a Sunday school class for the teenage boys. I've seen him sit and read or play checkers with the folks at a senior citizens center for hours. When Kevin spends time with you, he invests himself in your life and lets you know you're important. You come away a better person just for having spent time in his company." She blew out a long, deep sigh. "Kevin's biggest flaw? It's taken him forever to move our relationship forward to this level. At the rate he's going, I'll be almost forty before anything significant happens, and I *do* want children."

Trina leaned back, propping her elbows on the picnic table. It looked like she twisted her lips in an effort not to smile. "I see your point. They both sound wonderful. Not that you asked, but in my considered opinion, you need to try and convince the saint—I mean Kevin—to either get out a bit more or else persuade Professor Higgins—I mean Adam—to stay home on occasion."

Rebekah shook her head. "What exactly would that prove?"

Trina's smile was sympathetic. "Seems to me you need to choose which one your heart wants—and think about your priorities—and then let the rest work itself out. Maybe you're still not ready to make a commitment to either one of them, and that's why you can't choose. Nothing wrong with that, either. Just be careful, sweetie. Someone's bound to get hurt." She patted her knee. "I just don't want it to be you."

"I know you're right, and I hate the thought of hurting either one of them. I just feel . . . unsettled. It's hard to explain. I mean, I have everything I've ever wanted in my life, but it's like there's something missing. Whatever *it* is. Pray for me, Trina." She shot her a sheepish look. "I suppose you think I'm a terribly ungrateful person."

"Yeah," Trina said, "you're a real whiner. A huge pain."

"There you are!" Kevin walked toward them, smiling. "Hey, Trina," he said, dropping down beside her on the bench.

"Nice apron." Rebekah nudged his shoulder. "I see Michael corralled you into helping with the crawfish boil."

"Now he wants me to supervise the grilling of the kabobs. I just came over to grab some napkins and see how you're doing."

Rebekah laughed. "No wonder I like you so much. You're a multi-tasker like me."

"Anything else you ladies need before I go back to my post?"

"I'm sure Beck will think of something." Trina winked as she departed, calling to her daughter to stop pestering her younger brother.

"Kevin, did you bring your guitar?"

"It's in the back of my truck. You know my motto: have guitar, will travel." Leaning toward her, he planted a quick kiss on the tip of her nose. "Play your cards right, and you might get a private performance later. I wrote a new song a couple of days ago."

"Oh?" She closed her eyes when he leaned close. Her eyes fluttered, her lids heavy. "I was thinking maybe you could play and sing some of your songs for the whole group."

"I'd rather play just for you." Another sweet, loopy grin surfaced. "You're getting that look again," he added in a low voice.

"Hmm? What look is that?" She couldn't help it. Kevin was like a drug—addictive and heady.

He chuckled. "The look that makes me want to take you in my arms and never let you go."

"You must feel pretty comfortable around me to say something like that." She grinned and nudged his foot with hers. "After all, it took you years to work up the nerve to even tell me you liked me."

"I *do* feel comfortable with you. Surely you must know that by now."

"You make me very happy. You should know that, too."

"I know something else," he said, standing and holding out one hand.

"What's that?" She put her hand in his and he pulled her up beside him.

"I want to share a kabob with the prettiest teacher on the planet."

She laughed. "Thanks, but is that your way of issuing a new challenge?"

He raised a brow. "Guess so, although I was focusing more on the compliment. You start on one end and I'll start on the other, and the twain shall meet somewhere in the middle. Or something like that." Kevin's smile was infectious.

"Sounds real romantic."

"I'm certainly willing to find out. You might be surprised."

He's getting pretty good at this flirting thing. "Don't forget these." She handed him a stack of napkins.

They talked together as they walked to where some of the parents, staff and students congregated. Soon after, she moved over to help serve the smaller children as Kevin positioned himself behind the grill. Shy as he was, he was so good with people and always had a ready smile and a kind word. She loved how he was willing to pitch in at her school function. He didn't have to help, didn't have to leave the lumberyard early to come. A few times, she felt his eyes on her. When she looked his way, he winked. Kevin had come a long way in the last few months alone. *Maybe there's hope for him yet.*

"So, has he said it?" Hannah Kendrick, her student teacher, asked as they worked alongside one another.

Rebekah dished out some beans and corn for one of her students.

"Thank you, Miss Grant."

"You're very welcome, Kendra." She dished up the same for the next child in line. "Who said what?" She didn't like playing coy, but perhaps she should avoid large gatherings with Kevin where people would ask questions. Well-intentioned or not, it was getting plenty annoying. Thank the Lord Josh wasn't here, but at least he'd be ecstatic she was with Kevin and not the Brit. *Good grief, now I'm calling him that, too.*

Hannah nodded to where Kevin talked with some of the guys. "It's written all over the man's face. He's irresistible, you know. If you decide you don't want him, I have a few willing friends waiting in the wings. On the other hand, the same applies to Adam."

"It's not like they're the prize in a cereal box." *What's with everyone today?* Couldn't a girl enjoy a nice picnic without getting asked at every single turn about her love life?

Hannah put the bowl of macaroni salad on the table and turned to face her when they had a momentary lull in the food line. "I'm sorry, Beck. I know this situation is driving you crazy, and I don't mean to make light of it."

"You can't tell me anything I don't already know. Trust me, I've gone over everything in my head until I'm sick of myself. I've never strung along two guys at the same time, and I've always detested women who did. Tell me something. Does everyone on the school staff know about my juggling act?"

"Not everyone, and most of us would love to feel your pain. I'm sure you'll know what to do when the time comes."

I hope you're right, Hannah.

CHAPTER EIGHT

AS THEY ATE side by side, Kevin periodically applied light pressure to Rebekah's fingers beneath the picnic table. It might be part excuse to hold her hand, but she'd almost lost several fingers—two on her left hand and three on her right—to hypothermia and frostbite during the TeamWork mission in Montana. The lingering numbness and sensitivity was sporadic, with no rhyme or reason. The tiny line that formed between her brows and the tension around her mouth always clued him in.

He eyed her as he finished, releasing her hand. "Okay now?"

She nodded, giving him a sweet smile. "Yes, thanks."

He held up a kabob with a wry grin. "Are you ready for our latest challenge?"

Wiping her hands on a napkin, she took her position on one end as he took the other. "Meet you in the middle."

Out of the corner of his eye, Kevin spied her blonde head moving along the kabob. He grinned when she tugged, making him work harder. It really wasn't a fair race, and not as easy as sharing an ear of corn like they did at her church picnic last summer. He slowed as they neared the middle at the same time.

"Hi," he said. With his nose pressed against hers, her kissable mouth so close, he watched her take the last bite of red bell pepper. What the woman could do with a simple smile was incredible.

Turning away a moment, he reached for his cup. Hearing a choking, sputtering sound behind him, Kevin turned, his eyes widening as Rebekah clutched his arm, motioning with one hand. She grabbed at her throat, her eyes bright with unshed tears. Moving her hand to her chest, she beat on it with her fist.

Slamming his cup on the table, he jumped up and hauled her off the bench. Wrapping his arms around her, he performed a perfect Heimlich and dislodged the pesky piece of pepper on the first thrust. It must have landed on the little girl the next table over when she yelled "Gross!" and gyrated like she had a big red bug in her shirt.

After sputtering and coughing some more, Rebekah gulped down a cup of cold water Hannah handed her. Slumping back down on the bench, looking almost as red as the pepper, she mumbled her thanks. Gasping for air, she avoided looking him in the eye as she deep-breathed a few times. "I feel like my throat is on fire."

Kevin watched her closely for the next few minutes, sitting beside her, not touching her. He hoped his presence was a comfort in some small way. At length, she leaned her head on his shoulder and released a long sigh. "Are you okay?" he asked. She nodded, but didn't look so well. Taking her by the hand, he led her to the nearby playground swings, deserted for the moment since everyone was still eating.

Rebekah stretched out her long legs and took a couple more deep breaths as he dropped onto the swing beside her. "I'm fine," she said with a shaky smile. "Just embarrassed. I can't believe I choked on that silly piece of pepper. I've never choked on anything in my life." Noticing stares directed their way, she settled her gaze on him, ignoring the others. "Seems I always need a hero. Thank you, Kevin. The TeamWork lifesaving training comes in handy yet again." She leaned forward and he met her halfway. This time, *she* stopped. "Sorry," she said, pulling back, "I momentarily forgot your rule against public displays of affection."

"Oh, I don't know. I might just change my rule for a gorgeous woman who choked on a piece of red pepper. A kiss might even be therapeutic for you."

She looked at him sideways. "You're developing into quite the flirt. Tell me, should I be worried?"

"I only flirt like that with you, Rebekah. Feel like going back to the picnic or do you want me to take you home? Whatever you want."

"Oh, no, I'm not letting you off that easy," she said. "Besides, there's a brownie over there with your name on it. Let's go, but let's not race this time."

He smiled and took hold of her hand. "Fine by me." He kept watch over her for the next hour until she assured him she was fine and wasn't suffering any aftereffects. When Rebekah asked him to join her in the potato sack races, it sounded like the best idea of the day. An hour later, they laughed so hard they almost couldn't stop. Both with one leg in a potato sack, they hopped over the finish line ahead of the others before collapsing on the ground. Raising their clasped hands in the air, victorious, Kevin struggled to sit upright and pulled her up with him so they could accept their "trophy" of a fresh-baked peach pie from where they still sat on the ground.

"Where's Sam Lewis when you need him?" Rebekah laughed, showing the pie to him.

"If it's not made by Lexa, it's not the same. But I'll take it and enjoy every bite. Be good, and I might even be persuaded to share it with you." He winked and struggled to stand before his foot got tangled in the potato sack again, and he fell back to the ground. Hard. "Ouch."

Dropping to her knees beside him, out of breath, Rebekah murmured her sympathies. With her so close, he wanted to kiss her so badly he ached. Although he hadn't kissed many women, Kevin knew it didn't get any better than a kiss from *this* woman. His lips formed a slow, lazy grin. She called it his loopy grin and seemed to like it. Maybe it *was* loopy, but he didn't care. She made him dizzy.

"I think it's best if we take our legs out of this sack *before* we try to stand up again," she said, retracting one leg and lowering the bag for him to do the same.

He watched as she ran it over to the group of waiting competitors.

"What's next?" she asked a few minutes later when they added the pie to their other belongings.

Kevin surveyed their options. *Anything to steal a private kiss sounds good.* "Well, there's ring toss or horseshoes. Either of those tempt you?"

Rebekah shook her head. "A bike ride sounds much better. Hey, Trina?" she called, waving to get the other woman's attention where she walked nearby. "Are those bikes over there free for a spin around the trails?" Trina nodded and motioned for them to help themselves.

"Looks like we're taking a bike ride," he said. *Sounds promising.* Kevin walked alongside her to retrieve two bikes that rested against the base of a huge tree. "I like a decisive woman. Saves a lot of time." That comment might have been misguided. Considering he was moving slow in this relationship, she must be thinking of the irony. He figured she might be wondering if he'd make the move to take their relationship to the next level sometime soon. His brothers teased him about it on a regular basis. He didn't pay any attention to them, but prayed Rebekah understood he wasn't being indecisive. Rather, he was building the foundation, preparing for the future. A future that definitely included her. Something along the lines of "To have and to hold, from this day forward. . ." He handed her the water bottle he'd brought along, and encouraged her to take a drink before they started on the trail.

Taking the bottle from him, she swallowed a few gulps. "Thanks. At least a bike ride should be safe enough." She handed back the bottle with a grin and a cute shrug. "Good to know I have a hero if I need one. With me, I guess anything's possible."

Lost in thought, he was vaguely aware when she took off on her bike.

"Kevin, you're dawdling! Catch up!" She stopped and waved to him from at least fifty yards ahead. "First one to the lake wins!"

Snapping to attention, he pedaled in her direction. One thing about Rebekah Grant—she was always up for a competition.

CHAPTER NINE

Tuesday Evening

JOSH WORKED THE room like the smoothest political candidate. Who knew a corporate lawyer could be such a natural at this catering thing? Winnie watched in awe as he served, poured, offered assistance and did everything they could expect of a paid employee, and then some, all the while wearing a Doyle-Clarke Catering smock over his white, button-down shirt with red silk tie and dark suit pants. Had the man brought half his professional wardrobe to Houston? More likely, he'd borrowed some things from Sam, judging by the slightly long pants. Weaving his way through the room of a hundred or so women in red hats of all sizes and shapes—pretty much a reflection of their owners—Josh was a wonder to behold.

After giving direction to a couple of the hired servers, Winnie stood by the coffee table, tapping her fingers on her hips, observing as the men delivered desserts. Sam had an amused glint in his eye and obeyed without question whenever Lexa had a request. Same with Josh. The Red Hat ladies adored them in an astonishing display as close to swooning as anything she'd ever seen. A number of the women looked at the guys as if *they* were dessert, but they smiled and laughed as they went about their jobs, ignoring the middle-aged hormones in overdrive. Based on all the fanning going on, there were enough hot flashes in the room to bake a cake.

It was too easy to tease and banter with Josh like old times—scary almost. He'd stayed out of the kitchen most of the day, but that didn't mean Winnie hadn't thought about him. A lot. *Okay, most of the day.* She knew Sam took him out for a few hours, and the ladies only saw them in passing. Watching him now, she could tell how effortless that Grant charm was. Josh was the kind of guy others admired and wanted to emulate. The kind of person no one could stay mad at for long, no matter how egregious the offense. Not that Josh's sins were all that horrible, but best not to dwell on that. The man had done his time, so to speak, and she certainly couldn't cast any stones. *Enough of this.* How many men would humble themselves to don an apron and pitch in to help, not expecting anything in return? Well, other than the dinner date. But that's not why Josh offered. *Was it?*

Winnie shook her head and started in the direction of the kitchen. Dwelling on the questions swirling in her mind served no purpose. She had to give Lexa credit for not pushing the issue as they'd worked together earlier in the day, although she must be dying to know the details of her talk with Josh. Preparing the food and all the advance work kept them occupied and busy, and their conversations thankfully centered on their cooking. Lexa also knew her well enough to leave it alone.

Plucking a leftover stuffed mushroom from a tray, Winnie nibbled on it, sinking into a chair with a deep sigh. Even though she'd been in her flats most of the day, her feet hurt, and the briefest of respites was welcome. As evidenced by the increased volume in party noise, she knew someone had come into the kitchen. She could tell it was Josh without looking. The man had a presence. *This is getting ridiculous.*

"Mind if I join you?" Following her lead, he picked up a quiche appetizer and sat in the chair next to hers. He popped it in his mouth, smiling as he chewed. "This is great. My compliments to the chef, but ever think about adding a little Cajun spice?"

Winnie slanted him an amused glance and finished her bite. "Not if I don't want EMTs on standby." She giggled at his smirk. "The tastes here in Houston are more . . ."

"Boring?" He grabbed a stuffed mushroom.

"I was going to say refined or normal, but you seem to be enjoying it all the same, Cajun-free or not. The food choices depend on the client and the event, of course. Besides, having you and Sam here tonight, we have all the spice we need."

"I'm having more fun than I could have imagined."

She shook her head. "I hope you realize you're setting a dangerous precedent." Walking over to the counter, she picked up a wet cloth and wiped down an empty serving tray. "Word gets around we have two handsome—two *male* waiters—every female group in the city will want to book our catering services."

Josh settled back in the chair, arms crossed. "Maybe you're onto something. Would that be such a bad thing?"

She stopped wiping the tray, lowering her eyes. "It is when you're only filling in because we were desperate."

"You think I'm handsome?"

She couldn't stop her smile. "What I *know* is you need to get back out there. Ladies in red hats await, and I'm sure at least one of them needs her water glass refilled."

Josh saluted and headed back to the other room, but not before giving her a wink that put her right back in that chair again.

~

Tuesday Night

Josh worked beside Winnie in Sam and Lexa's kitchen as she washed the last few pans and utensils. "That was nice of you to send my hosts upstairs, give them some private time," he said, handing her the next pan.

"It's Joe's feeding time, and I could tell she needed it as much as the baby." Winnie scrubbed the dried, caked-on food rimming the top of the pan. "It's hard for Lexa and Sam to both be away from the little guy for such a long stretch. But tonight," she said, rinsing the pan and handing it to him, "they didn't have much of a choice since their usual babysitter—the six-foot-five, ordained one—was otherwise engaged." A comfortable silence settled between them for a few minutes as she washed and he dried.

"You'll make a wonderful mother someday," Josh said, his voice quiet and thoughtful. "After all, Mother Hen should have a whole houseful of kids."

At that comment, Winnie dropped the last pan, its loud clanging against the edge of the sink making her cringe. She winced and slanted him a sheepish grin. "Sorry, my fingers slipped." She concentrated on her task, scrubbing furiously. *Lord, I know that's an opening to tell him, but I'm tired and no good could come of it tonight.*

After a couple of minutes, he nudged her arm. "I think you've scrubbed that pan enough. It's plenty clean now."

"Right." She put the scrubber on the side of the sink.

"Tell me something. What is it with Sam and Lexa and white Volvos?" Josh leaned back against the kitchen counter, watching her.

Winnie could have kissed him for changing the subject. Putting the rinsed pan on the towel on the counter to dry, she wiped her hands and draped the dish towel over the bar on the bottom of the double oven. "I'll tell you one of their secrets." Untying her apron strings, she crooked a finger and motioned for him to follow her out the side door. It was a lovely evening, not too cool, but not too warm with a soft breeze.

"Where are you taking me?" He followed her out to the building at the end of the driveway. "Is this an extra garage?"

"You'll see." She stood aside, arms crossed, and nodded her head toward the long, horizontal window. "Take a peek." The corners of her mouth upturned.

"Will I turn into a pillar of salt?" Josh laughed under his breath.

"Just look," she said.

Leaning close, he peered through the window. Pulling back, his eyes were wide. "It's dark in there, but is that what I think it is?"

It took Winnie a moment to catch her breath, overcome with unexpected emotion as she looked into eyes so like her daughter's it brought tears to her own. She swallowed hard. "None other."

"No need to get all emotional over it, but the *bomb*? They kept the bomb," Josh said, shaking his head when he saw Winnie's nod. "Why in the world . . .?"

If only he knew the true reason for her display of emotion. "Think about it. It's what Sam was driving when he picked up Lexa for the San Antonio work camp, and it's where the sparks first started between them. Remember, they had a flat tire and encountered a spitting goat before they ever reached the camp. By that time, I think they were already half in love with each other."

"You're telling me they've kept that prehistoric station wagon all this time purely for sentimental reasons?" His voice held disbelief.

She nodded, planting one hand on the garage door and standing on tiptoe to peer inside. "You haven't been around them since they've been married, but they're pretty shameless on a regular basis." She turned to face him, fully aware he watched her every move. "To be honest, I wouldn't doubt their little munchkin was conceived in that car. It's actually surprising his name isn't Volvo." Josh burst out with the deepest, heartiest laugh she'd ever heard from him. Giggling, she put a finger over her lips. Sam and Lexa probably heard them from their upstairs bedroom.

"It's late, and I need to get home," Winnie said, walking back into the kitchen to retrieve her purse. She tried not to make it sound as though some*one* would be waiting for her at home, and Josh didn't look like it was a question in his mind. Then she remembered Dottie was keeping Chloe overnight. As he walked beside her, Winnie wondered why it felt like saying goodbye at the end of a date. This was a case of a TeamWork friend helping them out tonight. That's all it was. Nothing more. Maybe she should back out of the dinner tomorrow night. She should thank him for his selfless service, shake his hand, get in her car and drive away into the sunset.

"Thank you for the most fun I've had in a long time," he said.

She didn't believe that statement for a moment. "You don't get out much, do you?"

"As a matter of fact, I don't. I haven't felt very . . . social in recent years." He brushed aside a long strand of hair the wind had tousled in its airy dance, his fingers lingering for the briefest of seconds on the side of her face. His eyes held something she'd never glimpsed before. Wistfulness perhaps, and maybe something more, but no way would she hazard a guess. "You're a very special person, Winnie, and I'm blessed to know you."

She leaned into his touch, closing her eyes for a few seconds. Snapping out of her trance, she opened the car door. "Right back at ya, Josh." She climbed into Ladybug, backed out of the driveway and took off down the street without another glance.

~

Reclining on Rebekah's sofa, Kevin stretched out and closed his eyes. He'd played his new song for her, wanting her to hear the tune before he put lyrics to it. His guitar was propped against the sofa, and he rested his head on a cushion cradled on her lap. How she loved his lush, dark hair as she finger-combed it. The look of contentment on his face told her how much he enjoyed it. She continued what she was doing, taking advantage of the opportunity to study his face. So handsome. Rugged was a good word to describe this man. The angles of his face were defined, his lips not too full or thin. Classic boy-next-door looks with a chiseled jaw, firm chest, and hard muscle from all his labor. Her gaze slid down to his boot-covered feet crossed on the arm of the sofa.

"That's the most fun I've had in a long time," he said, opening his eyes, interrupting her thoughts. "Thanks for inviting me to the picnic. They're a great group of people, and I can see why you like working with them."

She loved the way he looked at her, knowing he saw her *heart* as well as what the rest of the world saw. "I do. Sometimes I wonder if I should apply at a Christian school, but it's a good school, and I'm very happy there." She released a sigh. "I like to think I'm making some kind of impact on the kids. In some ways, it's more of a challenge since I have to be careful about what I can or can't do or say since it's a public school." Rebekah yawned. "Did that even make sense?"

Kevin straightened up to sit beside her and put one arm around her shoulders. "They're blessed to have you, and trust me, they know it. You bloom where you're planted, sweetheart."

Rebekah's heart thrilled at his use of the endearment, as it always did. He didn't use it often, but when he did—in moments of closeness like this—she knew his kiss was imminent.

Sure enough, he stroked his fingers down her cheek. "Interested in exploring that kiss now?"

"I might be persuaded," she said, her voice quiet, moving closer. She felt a purr of excitement in her abdomen. Whenever Kevin got close like this, she got that little rumble, and it wasn't hunger for food.

"Are you going to think about it all night, or are you going to kiss me?" He had *the look*. Kevin's fingers gently tugged on her chin as he leaned close.

As she settled into the kiss, he wrapped his arms around her. How she loved kissing this man. His jaw felt slightly rough against her skin, but she didn't mind. His mouth tasted salty, minty fresh and sweet all at the same time. Kevin pulled her closer, his hold on the middle of her back firm. Rebekah thought he might deepen the kiss, but he never did. That would be too intimate for him at this stage. By contrast, Adam had been much too forward too soon.

"We're getting pretty good at this," he said, his voice husky. He pulled away, reluctance written in every nuance of his face. "*Too* good. I'd best be getting out of here. The Lord wouldn't be pleased with what I'm thinking right now. I must say goodnight and thank you for a perfect day."

Rebekah watched through hazy eyes as Kevin rose to his full height. He was one of the most masculine men she'd ever known. Physically strong, but his greatest strength was in his quiet confidence, his reliance on the Lord. Kevin *lived* his faith.

"Choking incident aside, it *was* a perfect day. Call me soon?" She walked him to the front door, running a hand over her slightly mussed hair. Looking at him, she grinned. His hair was sticking up in certain sections and it made him look like a little boy fresh from the bath. Stepping closer, she smoothed it down with her fingers, being careful not to get more distracted. "There. That's better."

"I'll call you tomorrow." Kevin kissed her again, his lips lingering. "What are you doing to me, Rebekah?" A smile tugged at the corners of his mouth as he leaned his forehead on her shoulder and released a long sigh.

She smiled when he lifted his head. "I suspect the same thing you're doing to me." Pushing a lock of hair aside, she resisted the urge to kiss the half-inch scar on the right side, the result of a bike accident when he was eight. That scar only endeared him to her more. Remembering his guitar, she retrieved it.

With a murmured goodbye, Kevin departed. She watched as he climbed into his blue Dodge Ram, and waved as he started the engine and pulled away from the curb. Closing the door behind him, she slumped against it. She hated to see him go, but he was right. It would be dangerous for him to stay any longer. Boundaries needed to be kept, and it was important to both of them to honor the Lord in their physical relationship. She jumped as the phone rang, interrupting her thoughts. Still dazed from Kevin's kisses, she didn't pick it up, knowing the machine would.

"*Hello, lovely.*" Adam. "*Wanted to make sure we're still on for lunch Saturday at half past twelve. Talk to you soon, and I can't wait. Love you.*" She could listen to his cultured British accent all day. If nothing else, his message was a reminder she'd need to adjust the volume of the answering machine—and also move it out of earshot of the living room. Her bedroom would be the best choice. She blew out a breath of relief. That was way too close for comfort. *What if Kevin heard that message? Think, Rebekah, think.* She sank into the closest chair in the living room, grabbed a pillow and hugged it against her.

The phone rang again, startling her, but she didn't feel compelled to answer. She smiled when she heard Kevin's voice, but let the machine record his message, too. His voice was deeper than Adam's, with that familiar Louisiana Cajun accent.

"*Hi, Rebekah. Just wanted to say again that I had a lot of fun today, spending time with you and your friends from the school. Talk to you tomorrow, and,*" he said with a quiet laugh, "*you might want to stay away from kabobs unless I'm sitting beside you. I'm glad you're okay.*" Her heart warmed at the sound of his voice, but her smile sobered as she tuned out his words. *Is Kevin in love with me even a little bit?*

Adam told her he loved her all the time. Somehow, it came across more like a casual comment and not indicative of an I-love-you-and-want-to-spend-the-rest-of-my-life-with-you kind of commitment. Her brow furrowed. He'd dropped broad hints lately about wanting to make changes in his life. It was very confusing.

Climbing into bed a half-hour later, her cell phone rang. Had to be Josh. For whatever reason, both Adam and Kevin normally called her on the landline. She grabbed the phone and stifled a yawn. "Josh, do you have any idea what time it is? I hope you realize anyone else would get my voice mail."

He laughed. "In that case, I *do* feel special. Thought I'd see how the school picnic went today. Any interesting developments?"

"Well," she said, sitting up and leaning against the backboard, "did you know there's a fine art to making kabobs?"

"Can't say as I do. Then again, I'm trained in Louisiana law, not kabob preparation. To use your expression, cut to the chase."

"We had a fun time, save for the small matter of me choking on a red pepper on one of said kabobs."

"You what?" She caught his attention with that one. "You okay, honey?"

"Fine. Just embarrassed myself. It seems I always need a hero around to save me from myself. Tell Sam the TeamWork lifesaving training came in handy again today. Kevin took good care of me."

"Well, I'm glad he was there with you. I doubt the—"

"Don't say a word about Adam. Not now, Josh." Her voice was firm, and he took the hint when he urged her to tell him more about the picnic. "I always have fun with Kevin. He's great. Tell me about Winnie. Sorry I didn't call, but I hope you felt my prayers."

"That must have been the sharp pain I kept getting in my gut today. Either that or sympathy pangs for your kabob emergency."

"Funny. So, *did* you share any special moments with her?"

"As a matter of fact, yes. It was a little awkward at first, but believe it or not, your brother donned an apron and helped out the ladies with a catering event tonight. Sam, too. I think our TeamWork friends are getting used to having me around again. They're not running away kicking and screaming, either."

Rebekah laughed. She thought of a couple of things she could do while they talked, but for once, she didn't feel like doing anything other than listen. She was too tired, but it was a *good* tired. "Did you, now? I'd like to see you in an apron. Bribery has its advantages, you know. I hope Lexa or Winnie got pictures."

"I'm taking her to dinner tomorrow night, Beck."

That was a shocker. "Just so we're clear, you're taking Winnie on a date?"

"That's certainly the way I look at it," Josh said, "but I'm not sure she shares that viewpoint."

"You know, the more you tell me about this—whatever it is between you and Winnie—the more I have to wonder what's up. I had no idea you looked at her in a romantic way. I mean, she's gorgeous, but . . ." For all she knew, Josh hadn't looked at *any* woman that way in a long time, namely out of necessity and getting himself on the right track with the Lord. But now he seemed focused. If he was going to try dating again, Winnie would be a perfect candidate save for the fact she didn't live in Louisiana. Knowing Josh, geography wouldn't deter him.

"Let's see how the dinner date goes. You need your beauty rest. Love ya, Beck." Again, her brother had the last word.

"You too, Josh."

CHAPTER TEN

Wednesday, Late Morning

THE STUDENT AIDE tossed Kevin a shy glance as she led the way through several shiny hallways of the elementary school. Hearing the sound of Rebekah's voice, he smiled as he rounded the corner of her classroom. He whispered his thanks and took a seat on one of the small folding chairs at the back, nodding to Hannah where she stood near the window. Leaning forward, elbows on his thighs, chin on one hand, he took a quick survey of the students. Based on how quiet they were, Rebekah had complete command. He knew she preferred teaching the younger grades, getting the kids "while they're still young and impressionable." Before they started thinking they knew more than God, their parents or teachers.

A slow smile crossed Rebekah's face when she spied him. On any other woman, the light blue blouse and khaki skirt with a sweater tied around her shoulders would look plain and school-marmish. But on Rebekah, the outfit looked nothing short of spectacular. Those long, tanned legs that seemed to go on forever were bare and she wore flat sandals. Her naturally blonde hair was down—the way he liked it best—curling on the ends, falling past her shoulders and halfway down her back.

Not as subtle as he should be, Kevin tuned out her words as he leaned back in the chair and enjoyed the view. He'd been half in love with her since they first met on a TeamWork mission a number of years ago. Other TeamWork guys tried to catch her attention, but she'd always been focused on school and the missions. Still, this girl wasn't one to sit home alone on Saturday nights. He kept watching, praying and biding his time. It lit a fire under him at the Montana mission when he almost lost her. He'd owe Marc Thompson the rest of his days for hauling her from that frozen creek, thankful the Lord put him in the wilderness when Rebekah needed him most. Still, every time Kevin heard Marc referred to as her hero, he couldn't help the slightest twinge of jealousy. He wasn't proud of it, but at least *he'd* been the one Sam called to help once Marc got Rebekah back to the main house at the ranch.

He'd never forget the fear in her eyes, the way she shivered as he carried her to the waiting SUV, wrapped in blankets. The way she clung to him, too frozen to cry or speak. Then as now, he wanted to hold her forever. Protect her. *Love* her. In all his days, he'd never forget her sweet looks of appreciation as he fed her in the small Montana hospital when she couldn't move her fingers. The way she snuggled on the sofa and closed her eyes as he played his guitar and sang to her, or listened to him read. The way she clasped his hand as best she could and prayed with him. The way her eyes smiled with what he hoped was deep affection. Her love of the Lord and desire to share her talents with children endeared her to him. Whenever he looked in those mesmerizing eyes and ended up on the receiving end of her breathtaking smile, he was lost.

Kevin snapped to attention when Hannah clapped her hands and called the students to form two lines at the door. His eyes met Rebekah's as she corralled the stragglers before walking to the back. Rising to his feet, he smoothed his hands down the front of his jeans, hoping he wasn't spreading sawdust on the spotless floor.

"Hi, handsome. This is a pleasant surprise. I didn't know you were coming to see me."

"Hi, yourself. I ended up hauling a load of lumber to a house nearby, so I took the chance you might be available to go to lunch." He gave her a hopeful smile and waved bye to Hannah as she departed the classroom with the kids.

"As it turns out, I'm not assigned to lunch duty and you'd be saving me from a very sorry-looking tuna sandwich."

"Great. Grab your purse and let's head out. Your chariot awaits." He crooked an arm.

"Give me a minute to convince the principal the class is covered. Wait here," she said, "and I'll be back as soon as I can."

Walking around the classroom, Kevin paused near the front, studying the bulletin boards. It pleased him she'd used a couple of his ideas on careers. Turning, he focused on Rebekah's desk, organized and free of clutter. The entire classroom looked surprisingly tidy. Her calendar was open, and a date with a notation circled in bright red caught his eye. Curiosity reeled him in like a hungry fish to the bait. *Trip to London Bridge with A.M.*

He blinked and looked at it again, taking another step closer. The British guy—her former boyfriend—his name was Adam something or other. The sudden squeezing of Kevin's heart reminded him Adam's last name started with the letter M. Mosier? Mason? *Martin.* The guy who'd asked her to marry him and the man he blamed—irrational though it was—for Rebekah's fall into the creek. She'd been thinking about Adam's marriage proposal and lost her footing. Kevin shuddered at the reminder and shook his head to clear his thoughts.

Running a quick hand over his furrowed brow, he backed away. Best not to be caught prying into her business if she returned and found him staring at the calendar. Kevin felt a light tug on his arm. Startled, he looked down into the face of a young boy. Must be one of Rebekah's students, or else this kid was his conscience in human form. He *did* look a little like he did at the same age.

"Are you my teacher's boyfriend?" Wide brown eyes stared up at him.

"I am, if Miss Grant's your teacher."

The boy nodded and gave him a half-grin. "Jacob," he said, thrusting out one hand.

"Kevin." They shook hands, man-to-man.

Jacob tilted his head. "I thought your name was Adam, and you don't talk funny like Tristan said you would."

Kevin swallowed hard and shook his head. "Nope. Afraid it's Kevin." He forced a smile and willed his heart to slow.

"Are you going to eat with us in the cafeteria?"

"I'm not sure," he said, glancing toward the doorway. "Maybe." This whole idea of surprising her at the school didn't seem like such a great plan anymore.

"We're having macaroni and cheese. It's really good." The boy's eyes lit with excitement.

"I'll ask Miss Grant. Tell you what, if she wants mac and cheese then it sounds like we'll be eating in the cafeteria, too."

Jacob hurried to a desk near the middle of the classroom. "I forgot my free lunch ticket. Miss Grant gives everybody one for their birthday." Waving a piece of paper, he headed for the door. "See ya later."

"See you. Happy birthday, Jacob, and enjoy your lunch." Crossing his arms, Kevin walked to stand by the long row of windows, lost in thought.

Rebekah breezed back in the classroom not long after, bringing with her that familiar scent. "Good news. Because of today's schedule, I have almost a full hour for lunch. You picked a great day to come." She smiled. "Not to mention Principal Betty is a big fan of yours after meeting you at the picnic."

He couldn't quite muster a smile. He needed to get himself together and drag his negative thoughts off the floor. *Snap out of it.* Time to concentrate on enjoying this unexpected opportunity for lunch with her. "I met one of your students—Jacob. Nice kid. He came back to get his free lunch ticket and said they're having mac and cheese in the cafeteria today. Interested?"

"No." She shook her head and raised a brow. "Are you?"

"Call me selfish, but I want you all to myself." He wasn't only talking about today and lunch, but no way could she know that.

"Sounds good to me."

~

In his customary work uniform—jeans and a work shirt with cuffs rolled on his muscled forearms to his elbows—Kevin looked great. She'd grown accustomed to the smell of sawdust and liked it, especially combined with Kevin's scent—clean, musky and completely male. Her mind wandered to the time she'd surprised him at the San Antonio TeamWork work site. He'd been hammering something into place on one of the houses they'd built that summer. Dripping sweat with his dark, thick hair plastered to his head and shirtless. She'd nearly gasped aloud when he looked her way. Who knew all those muscles lived under his shirt?

Considering the manual, physical labor Kevin did at his family's lumberyard and store, it shouldn't come as a surprise. When he'd caught her staring at him—ogling was more like it—he'd whipped his T-shirt back down over his head, but it was too late. The image was already seared in her mind as was his look of embarrassment and small smile. She hated it when people judged *her* on looks, yet she couldn't shake that image of Kevin. How vain was she? The man was as close to physical perfection as she'd ever seen up close and personal.

As they walked to his truck parked in the school's front lot, Rebekah grew heated at the memory. Conversation would be good or she'd dwell on things she shouldn't. As Kevin opened the passenger door and helped her climb into the truck, she wished he'd kiss her. It surprised and disappointed her when he didn't try to steal one.

"I thought we'd head over to Hanson's since it's not far," he said. "Is that okay?"

She nodded, but her pulse skipped a beat. Adam had taken her to Hanson's not two weeks before. "That's fine."

As they talked on the way to the restaurant, Kevin seemed quieter than usual. She told him about Josh's reunion with Sam and he seemed as thrilled with the news as she was. He'd been praying—like all the TeamWork volunteers—for a reconciliation between their TeamWork leader and her twin. Although she wanted to mention Josh's meeting with Winnie, something stopped her. She'd best hug that one to herself for now. Not that it was a secret, but why mention it unless there was something to tell? It was Josh's private business, especially since he hadn't even told *her* what it was all about yet. She hoped that would change soon, but her brother would tell her when he was good and ready.

Arriving at the restaurant, Kevin pulled up to the front door and, always the gentleman, assisted her from the truck. His mom taught all her boys the value of *please* and *thank you* and how to treat a woman like a lady. It was a lost art, but the Moore boys had it mastered. Waiting outside the entrance as he parked the truck, Rebekah loved how he carried himself without a hint of bravado or swagger. Kevin was comfortable in his own skin, secure in God's will for his life. He wrapped his hand around hers as they walked inside together.

Kevin thanked the hostess as she seated them at a table overlooking a small, man-made lake. When he pulled out her chair, Rebekah spied three long-stemmed red roses, tied together with a red satin ribbon, resting on the seat.

"Look! How beautiful. I wonder if someone left them here . . ." Catching the look on his face, she smiled. "Good thing I didn't sit on the thorns, huh? Thank you. The second most wonderful surprise of the day. Are you trying to take my breath away?"

He didn't smile, but he waited until she was seated before taking the chair across the table. "I want to make you happy, Rebekah. Hopefully, they'll last until you can get them in some water back at the school."

She nodded. "They'll be fine. Thank you. You're doing a great job making me happy."

They ordered and enjoyed casual conversation until her clam chowder and his scallops were delivered to the table. After praying for their meal, Kevin finally gave her a small smile. "Want to share?"

She'd started to worry something was wrong, and when he winked, her heart soared. "Sure." She watched as he moved to the chair beside her. "You have a thing about sharing your food, you know."

"The view and vantage point from here is much improved."

"Flirt." She adored the look of genuine surprise on his face. "You know," she said, sampling his scallops as he took a spoonful of her clam chowder, "when we were out in Montana, if anyone told me we'd be sitting here like this—practically feeding each other—I'd never have believed it."

Kevin seemed to relax even more as they ate. He asked about her current projects at school and laughed when she told him some of the kids' latest antics. Her eyes strayed to the roses on the table beside her several times. He always remembered red roses were her favorite. "This was really fun," she said as they finished, "but I shouldn't have eaten so much. I wish we had time to walk around the lake. Even if it's not made by God, it's beautiful, isn't it?"

"Sure is." From the way he looked at her, she suspected he wasn't talking about the lake.

As Kevin left the tip on the table, one of the waiters passed by. He looked familiar. *He was the server when Adam brought me here.* She avoided his gaze, but he stopped directly behind her. "Say hi to Adam for me," the young man said. "After talking with him the last time you were here, I decided I'm definitely taking a trip to London next year. Thank him for me, will you?"

Rebekah nodded, but her heart slid to her toes when she glimpsed the stricken look on Kevin's face, the flushed cheeks. The waiter's voice had been low, but apparently not quiet enough. Why would he say something like that when she was here with another man? Anyone with eyes could see Kevin was her date. She bristled, but she couldn't blame this one on the waiter.

Not much slipped past Kevin, but he chose to either ignore the comment or push it aside. Like Josh, he'd bring it up when he was good and ready. The short ride back to the school was even quieter than the trip to Hanson's. She stole a glance his way every now and then, but even if he sensed her eyes on him, he kept his focus on the road. Her heart smiled when, a few minutes out from the school, he captured her hand and caressed her fingers. They weren't numb, but she sensed this time he needed *her* touch.

"What's new with Moore Lumber these days? Anything exciting?" she asked.

"Maybe," Kevin said, pulling into the school's front entrance. He turned to face her, but left the engine running. "Unfortunately, I'm not at liberty to say anything yet, even to you." His voice sounded apologetic. "But exciting things are on the horizon."

"Really? That's great!" Glancing at her watch, she frowned. "I need to get back inside." She leaned close and kissed his cheek, pulling back when he didn't take advantage of the opportunity. "Thanks for coming to the school. It's the best surprise I've had in a long time." The look that crossed his face was intriguing, but intuition told her it wasn't all good.

He pinned her with those gorgeous blue eyes. "I hope you know how important you are to me, Rebekah."

She nodded, holding his gaze steady. "I know."

"There's no one else."

"You mean the world to me, too." Somehow, she knew that wasn't what he expected, what he needed to hear from her.

He sighed and stared out the front window. That sigh told her he had something on his mind other than kissing her.

"Thanks again for lunch, the roses, everything, Kevin. I had a great time. Feel free to surprise me here at the school anytime." She gathered the flowers in one hand, her sweater in the other. She waited as he walked around and opened the passenger door. Once he saw both her feet were firmly on the ground, he released her hand. When he smiled, it wasn't the same, but it seemed the best he could offer.

"Bye." She forced a bright smile. "Call me later?"

Kevin nodded, but said nothing. His expression was guarded, the emotional distance between them more than uncomfortable. She shifted from one foot to the other, uncommonly antsy as an unspoken fear wormed its way into her subconscious. Feeling a sudden chill, she shivered and waited until his eyes met hers. With one last glance, she turned to go.

A few steps closer to the entrance, Rebekah paused, turning to look behind her. Kevin stood on the sidewalk, hands on his hips, watching her. Pivoting, she walked toward him—wanting to run—forcing slow, steady steps even though her feet were weighted with an invisible burden. He met her halfway, drawing her into his arms. She moved her hands around his powerful shoulders, felt the hard muscles beneath his shirt. His kiss was gentle, tentative almost. Probably wasn't the best idea to kiss him in full view of any impressionable students, but common sense couldn't dictate her response. Not now. She was surprised Kevin didn't seem to mind, but something passed between them. What it was, she didn't know, but it was there, strong and real.

"Please don't go, Rebekah." It was barely more than a whisper against her cheek. Resting one hand on the side of her face, his features drawn, his eyes held a pervasive sadness she couldn't understand. Kevin dropped his hand and walked back toward his truck. Climbing inside the cab, he pulled away without waving as he usually did.

Rebekah shook her head, one hand moving to her lips. "Go where?"

CHAPTER ELEVEN

Wednesday, Early Evening

"YOU LOOK BEAUTIFUL, Mommy." Winnie cherished the look in Chloe's eyes—the same as when she stared at the angel or a star atop a Christmas tree. Full of wonder. Breathtaking innocence. How she wished she could preserve it for the future when the world with all its sorrow and heartbreak would one day spoil her daughter's childlike wistfulness. It was inevitable, but she hoped she'd be spared as long as possible. With one finger, Chloe traced an exquisite, embroidered pink blossom on the hem of her light green shantung silk skirt. Winnie's breath caught as eyes which glistened like beautiful, pale emeralds traveled to her face, drinking in her features. "You look . . . like a princess." That comment made her swallow the sudden urge to burst into tears. Chloe motioned with her hand. "Twirl, please."

Winnie obeyed, repeating the same ritual as when Chloe modeled a pretty new dress for church. Twisting back and forth so the skirt swirled around her knees and then turning full circle, she kissed the top of her child's head, thankful her daughter was blessed with the natural curls she'd always coveted. "*You* make me feel pretty, sweetie. Thank you."

Buying this designer outfit made more sense now than it did a few months ago. It was priced obscenely low at a sample shop she'd visited with Amy Jacobsen. Always fashionable, it was amazing Amy knew where to shop in Houston since she lived in Manhattan and flew in for the occasional long weekend. The moment Winnie slipped on the outfit, Amy grinned like a satisfied cat. "That's the one you *must* have. Sleek. Sophisticated. Understated elegance. It's perfect!" When Winnie questioned why and when she'd ever need something so fine, Amy's smile was sly, as though privy to a delicious secret. "For when your prince comes to claim you."

She hadn't encouraged that train of thought. Lexa and Amy were the only ones present at Chloe's birth, and Amy was the only person with whom she'd openly discussed her daughter's paternity. Earlier in the day, she'd called her friend at her office in the New York publishing house to tell her about the dinner with Josh.

"So, he's finally come back," Amy said. "This is great, and we knew it was only a matter of time. Have you told him yet?" Her enthusiasm came through loud and clear. She'd always adored Josh and stuck by him even when the rumors were flying fast and furious in the San Antonio camp, especially after Sam threw him out.

"I'm working my way up to it," Winnie assured her. "It's not like I can say, 'Hi, Josh, nice to see you again. Thanks for the best night of my life back in

San Antonio—the biggest error in *judgment* of my life—but, um, guess what?'" During their conversation, she'd gone into the bathroom and turned on the faucet. No way could Chloe hear any part of *this* discussion. "I'll tell him before he goes back to Louisiana. Promise."

"Make sure you do. He sounded really good, by the way."

Winnie balanced herself on the edge of the tub, trying not to chew on a fingernail. "What do you mean?" That comment was nothing if not calculated. "Spill it."

"Okay, I have a confession, and I hope you're not mad. Josh called me a few days ago and asked for your cell phone number. Beck hadn't returned his call and he hadn't been to see Sam yet. I had to practically sit on my hands to stifle myself not to mention I was dying to burst into a rendition of 'Someday My Prince Will Come,' and you *know* my singing voice isn't one of my better attributes."

Winnie shook her head, but couldn't stop her slow smile. "I couldn't be mad at you, sweetie, but I think our TeamWork crew is a bunch of hopeless romantics. Just blame it on Sam and Lexa. That's what I do since they started it all. I just figured either they or Beck gave Josh my private number. Didn't you think it was strange when he called you out of the blue after all this time?"

"Of course not."

Winnie's brows raised. "Not at all?"

She could hear the amusement in Amy's voice. How she missed her and wished she was there now to give her one of her encouraging hugs. "It's all in God's hands. He's brought the two of you together again, and it's time to let Him work, okay? Promise me that."

"All right. I promise." Winnie never entertained the fantasy Josh would someday return, sweep her onto his white horse and carry her off into the sunset for the fairy tale happily-ever-after—not that she hadn't ever thought about it, especially when reading a princess bedtime story with Chloe. Too much of her life was full of broken dreams and promises. Besides, it wasn't as if she and Josh shared any kind of relationship other than their special TeamWork friendship and one night in San Antonio almost five years ago. Albeit one passionate and incredibly tender night. She wasn't proud of it, but it wasn't like she could snap her fingers and make it go away. Not that she'd even want to, God help her. Otherwise, she wouldn't have Chloe. She'd confessed her lapse of judgment to the Lord and she was forgiven, but the Lord also knew her struggles.

Smoothing her hand over the matching, sleeveless top, Winnie drew in a deep breath and rested one hand over her stomach. A sudden case of nerves might prove her undoing tonight. Or was it excitement at seeing Josh again? The man was too handsome for his own good, but he'd changed in subtle yet noticeable ways. His smile was incredible, as always, the planes of his face more defined and mature. More than his physical looks, he struck her as being more serious and grounded. The years had been kind, but she knew the Lord had also blessed his work and rededication to following His will. It could also have something to do with repentance, hard work and a lot of soul-searching thrown into the mix. They were growing up, the TeamWork crew. That thought made her smile.

"Mommy, are you going to a birthday party?"

Winnie hesitated, biting her lower lip before thinking better of it. Since she'd bothered to put on lipstick, she didn't want to bite it off or smear it all over her teeth. Chloe had rarely seen her wear anything other than lip gloss and never witnessed her with a man, much less a date.

"I have an appointment with a very nice man tonight, Buttercup." Although Josh made it sound like a date, she wasn't altogether sure. The events that transpired in the next few hours would tell, but it also had her twisted in tight little knots. Her normal, ordered life had suddenly become *much* more complicated.

Chloe tilted her head. "You mean like a doctor?" Immediate concern sprang into her eyes. "You're not sick, are you?" Stepping closer, Chloe touched her cheek with the back of her hand, the same way Winnie did when she suspected a fever.

"Oh no, honey," she said with a reassuring smile, squeezing her daughter's hand. Perhaps "appointment" wasn't the best word choice, but not many others were at her disposal. "He's not a doctor. I knew him before you were born, but he lives in Louisiana and I haven't seen him in a long time. You remember hearing about Mommy's friend, Rebekah, from TeamWork?" Blonde curls bobbed. "His name is Josh and he's Rebekah's twin brother."

Those green eyes grew big. "A boy and girl twin? I only know girl twins." With her nose scrunched and her lips curled, Chloe was such an adorable imp.

Dottie emerged from the kitchen where she'd started a light supper.

"Thanks again, Dottie," Winnie said, hoping she understood the depth of her gratitude. "You're putting in double time for me these days and I hope you know how much I appreciate you."

The older woman gave her an understanding smile and lowered her glasses to get a better look. "I do, and it's very nice to see you going out. My, don't you look lovely! You work way too hard and spend too much time on your own. You deserve this. I just hope this man appreciates you." She nodded at a nearby chair. "Don't forget your pretty new sandals."

"His name is Josh," Chloe announced in a matter-of-fact tone. "He's a *twin*." Amazing what impressed a child her age.

"Is he now?" Dottie smiled, a new book balanced on her lap as she motioned for Chloe to join her on the sofa. Winnie's eyes misted. The dear woman invested herself in Chloe, reading and playing games with her instead of parking her in front of a television or allowing her to play computer games.

Winnie pulled a high-heeled gold sandal on one foot and then the other, holding onto the chair to keep her balance as she slid the back straps around her ankles. They really did look pretty—another spectacular Amy find—and were a nice complement to the outfit, but she prayed she could stand up in them let alone walk. Otherwise, she'd be like Chloe, a little girl playing dress-up and trying to look like a grownup.

"I shouldn't be out too late, but I'll call if it'll be later than ten," Winnie said.

Dottie waved her hand. "Don't you worry about a thing, sweet girl. I'm here for the duration. After this little one goes to bed"—she put her arm around Chloe and nestled her closer—"there's a movie I'd like to see and it won't be over until eleven. You stay as long as you want. If need be, I'll fall asleep right here on the sofa. You just concentrate on having a good time. We'll be fine."

Winnie grabbed her purse, a dainty little evening bag she'd dug out from the back of her closet, and dusted off the sad neglect. "You're too good to me. I've got my phone so please call if you need anything. Love you."

"We love you, too. Have a great time." Dottie smiled as Winnie blew a kiss to Chloe, but she was already turning the pages of the book, eager to learn more words. Winnie sighed as she headed out the door. Chloe was such a bright child and Josh Grant could afford to send her to the best schools and . . . . She shook her head. Now was not the time to map out the future. It was one dinner, not a plan book for her daughter's life. *Their* daughter's life.

Climbing into Ladybug, Winnie closed her eyes and lowered her head to the steering wheel. *Lord, help me tonight. I'm not sure what to say or how to act. Give me the right words.* After another minute of quiet prayer, she raised her head and turned the key in the ignition, smiling at the smooth purr of Ladybug's engine. It wouldn't do for Chloe to see her like this since her tender-hearted child might think something was wrong. Hopefully, her daughter was still sitting next to Dottie, engrossed in storybook adventures. Looking first one way then the other, Winnie pulled out of the parking space. *Be with Josh, too, Father. May he keep You close. We're both going to need You.*

Heading off the highway exit twenty minutes later, her pulse raced and she deep-breathed in and out a few times as she squirmed in the seat. Shantung silk wasn't exactly made for car trips, and she frowned when she noticed a few light wrinkles in the skirt. Drumming her fingers on the steering wheel at the light before the turn-in to the restaurant, she spotted a sleek, dark blue BMW turning the corner and into the parking lot. Although she couldn't get a good look at the license plate, it was the same model as the one parked at Sam and Lexa's house. She leaned closer, staring. *It's him.* Squinting into the early evening sunlight, Winnie frowned, making a snap judgment. As soon as the light turned green, she raced through it and zoomed past the parking lot.

~

Josh glanced at his watch for the third time in less than a minute. In his office, time flew by, but now, each second dragged while he waited for Winnie. She was twenty minutes late. Had she changed her mind? The waitress stopped to refill his water glass and shot him an empathetic look. "Do you want to go ahead and order, sir?" Her voice was low, and she blinked her big brown eyes a few times too many.

"No." It came out more of a bark, so he softened it with the best smile he could muster. "I'll wait. She's probably just running late." The maître d'—the one he'd tipped well to give him a corner table—nodded in his direction. With his brows drawn, a vertical line visible between them, he was probably calculating lost tips if he tied up one of the best tables all evening. Little did the man know that made him all the more determined to sit there all evening, if needed. *Winnie, please come. I need to see you again.*

Josh marched his fingers on the tablecloth, grinding his teeth so hard his jaw muscles flexed. Another server stopped to ask if he needed anything; he waved him away with a grunt. He must look more pathetic than he thought. If one more person gave him one of those I'm-really-sorry-you-got-stood-up looks, he'd blow a gasket. They meant well, but it wasn't helping. Winnie was twenty-two minutes late now, not two *hours* late. Maybe she was stuck in traffic. He didn't know anything about her sense of direction, so it was possible she'd taken a wrong turn and gotten lost. But no, *she* was the one who suggested this restaurant. It was a nice one, too. Romantic, which surprised him, given her initial reaction to his suggestion of dinner.

If she couldn't come, the Winnie he knew—at least he *thought* he knew—would call and either give an explanation or apologize instead of leaving him sitting here alone. Retrieving his cell phone from his pocket, Josh stared at it, debating the merits and disadvantages of making the call. He found her number, but closed his phone instead. No matter if had to tip the guy in the penguin suit all evening, fend off the female server with the flirtatious smile, or keep ordering food to keep this table off-limits to anyone else, he wasn't leaving until they closed their doors or respectfully requested he depart the premises. He'd waited a long time for this moment and he wasn't about to be put off that easy. If Winnie didn't show up, he'd need to come up with another plan.

~

"Lord, the man wears designer suits, drives an imported car and works in a prestigious law firm with an office and a secretary and an expense account. Surrounded by sophisticated, intelligent, Ivy League-educated, career women. I'm sure he has a bachelor pad equipped with all the latest gadgets, appliances and state-of-the-art everything." Winnie resisted chewing her lip since that would definitely mess up her lipstick. "Bottom line, Lord? Josh Grant has no need for someone like me in his life. He's perfectly fine without me." She slowed the car as the light turned yellow, ignoring the honking behind her. "Yellow means slow down, people!" At the risk of angering the driver behind her, she needed the extra time to think. She'd circled the block around the restaurant five, six, how many times? She'd lost track.

Startled out of her daydreaming a minute later by another honk from behind, she frowned and pulled through the light. Darting a glance at the parking lot, she spied the BMW. "Okay, so he's still there. Should I call him? Maybe we could talk on the phone instead of face-to-face?" Guilt started to wend its way through her conscious mind. Even if she wasn't thinking for herself, she needed to think of Chloe. Whether or not she and Josh had much of a chance for a relationship of any kind in the future, Chloe needed to know her father. That would bind her with him the rest of their lives. Not that it would be a bad thing, but it meant letting go of the one thing she'd hugged close to her heart the last four years, the one thing she'd done *right* even though it came from that huge error in judgment. *Oh, again with the irony, Lord.* She released a sigh full of enough oxygen to fill a balloon. A hot air balloon. *Face it. You're afraid to tell Josh. Chloe's been* your *secret. When you tell Josh, she won't belong only to you. You'll have to share her and life as you know it will never be the same again.*

Sometimes Winnie wanted to argue with that pesky inner voice. She reasoned it was justification for talking to herself out loud while driving. Surely everyone on the planet talked to themselves at least once every day. Sitting in Ladybug was the only place—other than in her bed late at night or early morning in the shower—where she had any alone time. The concept of privacy had flown out the window once Chloe could walk. *Again, not a complaint, Lord.*

Five minutes later, she waved aside the scowling valet in the red vest as she headed into the restaurant's parking lot. Why tip some teenager when she was perfectly capable of parking Ladybug herself? Pulling into a reserved-for-compact-cars-only space, she stepped out and locked her door, then glanced at her top and skirt to assess the wrinkle damage. Not too bad. Stuffing her keys into the tiny handbag, she walked toward the entrance, concentrating on moving forward without wobbling. As soon as she stepped inside, the maître d' gave her a nod and snapped his fingers in a haughty, obnoxious way. He nodded his head in her direction and whispered something to a young man standing nearby who turned and smiled. "Miss Doyle? Good evening. Mr. Grant is waiting. I'll show you to your table."

Well, okay. Had Mr. Smooth shown them her photo? In that moment, she felt like a movie star. Lifting her chin and squaring her shoulders, Winnie followed the man, employing her best imitation of Grace Kelly and pretending she had even an ounce of Grace's sophistication. Only it was *Josh* Grant—not Cary—waiting for her somewhere in this restaurant. For a half-second, she pondered turning around and fleeing back to the comfort and security awaiting her outside. But no, she'd probably just teeter on these ridiculously high shoes and fall flat on her face. Decidedly *not* a Grace Kelly move. She swallowed her pride, ignoring the looks from other patrons as she moved through the lovely dining room, following the man and hoping he didn't expect a tip.

The atmosphere was quiet, hushed almost. She liked that, but wasn't sure how to react. She'd never been anywhere so elegant. With its dim lighting, soft music, fresh flowers and the glow of candles in the middle of each table, this place sure set the mood for romance. Great. She'd chosen a haven for love. Why hadn't she picked a loud diner with booths, crying babies, banging pans, clanging dishes, silverware and chefs engaged in verbal warfare? Definitely would have been a safer choice.

The look on Josh's face as he rose to greet her was tentativeness tinged with relief. *He looks unbelievable.* He wore another power suit, tonight's version a dark pinstripe with a crisp, white dress shirt and a deep red, patterned silk tie. To be fair, a man in his position would need an impressive wardrobe. When Josh's sleeve hiked as he raised his hand in greeting, she glimpsed shiny gold cuff links. She suppressed a sigh, remembering how she once told Lexa she considered cuff links a symbol of financial success and total sophistication. She couldn't explain her fascination with them as they were only worldly representations. Never in her life would she imagine she'd be on a date—if that's what this was—with a man who wore cuff links like most men wore a watch. By his raised brow and puzzled expression, he must be curious as to why she was staring at his hand. She forced her gaze upward, but that proved every bit as dangerous.

~

What an elegant, incredible woman. Josh rose to his feet, thanked the man for bringing her to the table and pulled out her chair. When he planted a light kiss on her warm cheek, he loved how she flushed a pretty pink. This woman could hold her own with anyone, but still seemed shy and hesitant around him. Why, he couldn't understand, but he wanted to find out. "Thanks for coming, Winnie. You look beautiful. Green's a great color on you."

She shot him an intriguing look. "Thanks. You look . . . patriotic, always a good thing. I'm sorry I'm late, Josh. It was very rude."

He felt her eyes on him as he took his seat across the table. *This is too far away.* "It's not rude unless you were late on purpose." Catching the look on her face, he narrowed his eyes. "You weren't, were you?"

She lowered her gaze. "No, not really. No."

"You're not afraid of me for some reason, are you?" *Back off. Let her explain.* He slowly sipped his water, attempting to act nonchalant while his insides churned. He wasn't used to it, not sure he understood it. *Because it's not as simple as an apology anymore.* He'd barely reconnected with her yet felt some kind of pull toward her he couldn't understand. Physical attraction, yes, but it was so much more. He'd purposely avoided female companionship for a long time, but the woman sitting across the table jumpstarted his heart with the force of a blowtorch.

At least she didn't make him wait long. "Don't be silly. I've known you long enough to know I don't need to be afraid of you. That's not the right word."

"Pick a more suitable word, then. Lady's choice."

Her eyes rose to meet his. Winnie had always been pretty, but she'd blossomed in the last few years. *Was I so lost in sin back then I didn't notice how gorgeous this woman is?* In some ways, she was more frank and outspoken now, but even that intrigued him. He could get lost in those sparkling blue eyes and that hair—shiny as spun gold—hanging in loose waves to her slender shoulders. Her skin glowed with health, a beautiful smile, and those lips . . . . Josh averted his eyes, his thoughts swimming with a memory he'd pushed to the back of his mind. He'd drown in a heartbeat if he allowed that train of thinking to continue. His mind searched for a lifeline. Rarely was he at a loss for words.

"Uncertain. Now *that's* a word," Winnie said, her words a welcome interruption. "So, there I was, riding around the block in Ladybug, talking with God. We had quite the conversation, but He let me know it was time to come inside." The way she scrunched her nose and tilted her head added *adorable* to her growing list of attributes, not the least of which was humor.

"First of all, why do you call your car Ladybug? Is there such a thing as a yellow ladybug?"

Winnie laughed. Hearty, wonderful. His pulse quickened, and Josh cleared his throat.

"I don't know, but Ladybug is such a pretty yellow. Like a buttercup." Her eyes widened, and she had that look—not quite panic, but like she'd said or admitted something wrong. Time to put her at ease, if he could.

"So, you were driving around, talking to yourself—and God—and He gave you some kind of sign?" Straightening in his chair, he waited for whatever fascinating thing she'd say next. He loved that she talked to God on a regular basis and her faith wasn't simply lip service.

"Well, I certainly look at it that way." Winnie smoothed one hand over the tablecloth. Her fingers were long and slender. She wore no polish, probably because she worked with food all the time. "I pulled up to the stoplight and this blue minivan was in the next lane over. A little boy in the middle seat had his mouth pressed against the window, blowing guppy kisses."

"Guppy kisses?" You'd think she taught kindergarten.

"Yes, you know the kind." He watched, spellbound, as she demonstrated, but again, all he could focus on were her lips.

"Gotcha." He laughed and pretended he understood what she was talking about or that he'd be able to get past the lip action. One brow quirked higher. "Guppy kisses aside—although I suppose I'm grateful for them—how *long* were you driving around, choosing *not* to come in?"

"You're the one with the law degree. I'm sure you can figure it out."

Josh frowned. "Having a law degree has nothing to do with it, but this won't do." He rose to his feet, catching her look of panic. In an odd way, it pleased him. Even more so when she put her soft hand on his forearm.

"You're not leaving, are you? I'm sorry."

"Of course not." Now she looked positively stricken. "I mean, of course I'm not leaving." To emphasize his point, he pulled out the chair next to her and sat down. Her frown eased a bit. "Winnie, any woman who tells me guppy lips convinced her to meet me for dinner has my undivided attention. All I meant was, I want to sit closer to you so our conversation isn't heard by everyone around us."

Her infectious smile made its reappearance. Much better. "Guppy *kisses*, to be perfectly clear. But, I get it. You're afraid they'll bring the straitjacket for me."

He laughed with her. "If they do, then they'll have to bring one for me, too." The server approached, putting a glass of ice water on the table for Winnie and giving them menus. Taking his menu in hand, Josh returned her smile. Guppy kisses sounded like an intriguing concept. "I hope you're hungry. I know I certainly am."

CHAPTER TWELVE

WINNIE FIDDLED WITH her cloth napkin, hoping she'd have an appetite. Coming from Josh, the most innocent statement came across as flirtatious or provocative. Out of practice or not, it must be instinctual with the man. That alone should warn her she needed to steer clear. "So, what did you do with yourself all day?" Spreading her napkin over her lap, she wondered if he'd been out and about making apologies all over Greater Houston. *Stop it. That's just mean.*

"Believe it or not, I worked. My paralegal called and warned me of an e-mail from a client, and I needed to address his questions immediately. It couldn't wait since it's a merger that's closing early next week, so I spent a good portion of the day restructuring the deal."

"Were you able to allay his concerns?" *Allay?* She'd never used that word in her life. Maybe Chloe wasn't the only one learning new words. Still, Josh's dedication to his job and attention to his client was admirable.

"I hope so. I gave it my best effort." Josh put down his menu and gave her a smile, but he looked a little tired. The faint lines around his eyes were new, but only served to make him even more attractive. "Have you decided what you want to order?"

"No, but I'm famished." That statement wasn't the entire truth. In fact, it was as close to an outright lie as she'd told and added yet another confession for tonight's discussion with the Almighty. She had a suspicion that list would grow quite long before this evening was over. Her stomach had been unsettled most of the day, but whether in anticipation or dread, she couldn't be sure. She doubted she'd taste much of her food so might as well order something inexpensive. "I might be in the mood for lobster . . . or caviar. Or both. Hope your credit card's loaded." *Oh, my goodness. Where did that come from?* She forced a smile. What was *with* her? If he didn't find her rude before, that statement should do it. Obviously, any sense of reason she possessed had evaporated.

Josh laughed. "Winnie, you can order ten lobsters if it makes you look at me like that again."

She'd let that one go. It was going to be an uphill battle to keep this man at bay and not flirt. "Tell me what you like to eat over there in Louisiana," she said, putting down her menu. "I hear gumbo's very popular, as are crawfish and other equally disgusting things. It helps to know these things in terms of the catering business. For research purposes." Now she was rambling.

"We have those things 'over there,' yes. I like seafood, boudin, fricassee, jambalaya. They all have their place, but I also have what you'd probably call more *normal* tastes in my cuisine." He took a long drink of water.

"Such as?"

"Steak, burgers, chicken. You name it. I don't have too many weird Cajun cravings, if that's what you're afraid of, although I've been known to indulge from time to time."

She shook her head. "I'm not afraid of anything like that." *What I'm afraid of is why you're looking at me like I'm a dessert on the menu.* Something to hold and focus her attention on would be good. The menu was the closest available distraction, so she opened it again and pretended to study it. Josh mirrored her as he did the same. Stealing a glance, her eyes met his, but he tore his gaze away first.

"I never did hear how long you and Lexa have been in the catering business together. How did it first come about?" he asked after they ordered—prime rib for him and lobster for her since he insisted—and waited for their salads.

"Within a few weeks after getting home from the Montana trip, Lexa approached me about forming the partnership. We'd talked about it off and on, and she was heavy into her pie-baking phase at the time. Without knowing it, Marc and Natalie added to the cause by suggesting she start her own pie business, or something along those lines. That started her thinking about it more seriously. I'd been stuck in a dead-end job and jumped at the opportunity. I had to hire some part-timers when Lexa was very pregnant at Christmas, our busiest season, but—" She stopped. "Sorry. You don't want to hear all that. So, have you tried any of her pie yet?"

Josh shook his head. "No, but I've been promised a taste in the next day or two."

"Well, put sampling it high on your to-do list because you haven't lived until you've tasted it." His hand rested on the table and she reached out to pat it.

"You're still doing it, you know." His fingers wrapped around hers.

"Doing . . . what?" She withdrew her hand and looked at her lap.

"I don't need a mother. I have one and she does a more than capable job."

"Well, then, what *do* you need?" Nothing like being direct. *Why am I sitting here flirting? This can't go anywhere.* That thought made her inexplicably sad. No doubt she'd confused him plenty with her roller coaster emotions.

Josh looked at her for a long moment and those green eyes deepened. "You know, I'm sitting here trying to figure out that very thing."

"Honesty. I like that. Couldn't ask for anything more." Winnie looked around the restaurant—anything to avoid those eyes—drumming her fingertips on the white linen tablecloth. "Now, where are those salads?" As if on cue, the waiter approached, placing their salads in front of them.

"May I?" Josh asked, lowering his head.

"Of course." She bowed as he prayed, but didn't hear much as she studied him beneath half-veiled eyelids. Why couldn't something be wrong with him? Save for that unsavory part in his past, he seemed nearly perfect. It made her heart ache. How could it all be so simple and yet so complicated at the same time? *Has he truly reformed, Lord?* From the way he was looking at her a minute ago, she couldn't know. Problem was, she liked it. Some things never change.

As they ate their salads, at Josh's prompting, Winnie told him more about the catering business. "It's going so much better than we could have hoped. One thing's for sure: the economy may fluctuate, but people always need to eat. Companies and organizations still use catered events to attract new business and entertain clients. With Lexa's cooking skills and finance degree, and my marketing and organizational skills, we make a good team."

"Did you go to college?" He took a hearty bite of his salad.

"I wanted to, but didn't have the funds. Maybe someday, but not in the foreseeable future." If this was some kind of unconscious test, Josh passed with flying colors. The man didn't bat an eyelash.

"I'm really happy the catering's going so well for you and Lexa."

"Thanks." She stabbed a small cherry tomato before plopping it whole into her mouth. Next to her, Josh dabbed at his eyes with his napkin.

"Is something wrong?" Winnie asked, bringing her napkin to the corner of her mouth. *Oh, no, what now?*

"No," he said, dabbing at his eyes some more.

"Do you have allergies? Is there something in the salad? You can't take any chances if you're having a reaction." She tossed her napkin on the table and rose to her feet. "Let me go get Ladybug and we'll get you to the nearest ER."

"Sit, please, Winnie. Trust me, it's nothing serious. No ER visit is necessary." The beginnings of a grin creased his lips as he reached for her hand, pulling her back down to her chair.

"Well, then, what is it?" *What did I do?*

"Your tomato got me, that's all. I never liked this tie much, anyway."

With a gasp, Winnie's gaze followed the stream of tomato juice that landed on his shirt, gorgeous silk tie, and then shot upward from that point. Or maybe the other way around. *I never had good aim before and now look at me.* She couldn't have done that if she'd tried.

"Oh, Josh, I'm so sorry!" Jumping to her feet again, she almost knocked over her water glass. She felt the traitorous flush creeping into her cheeks, but it was way too late for embarrassment. Taking an extra napkin from the table, she dipped it in her water and dabbed with a gentle touch, following the trail of juice on his tie, stopping when he enclosed her fingers in his. *He must think I'm a complete idiot or else a walking disaster. Take your pick. It's not good any way you look at it.*

~

"It's fine." Still holding her hand, Josh smiled. "I appreciate your efforts, but it's nothing the dry cleaners can't handle. Sit, please. This is the most exhilarating conversation I've had in ages, and I can't wait to hear what you have to say next." *That's it. Throw her off-kilter.* Still, he should cool it. He hadn't flirted with a woman in so long he thought he'd forgotten how, but that wasn't the case with Winnie. She probably thought it was strange how he used every available opportunity to hold her hand.

"Or *do* next, you mean. I guess you can't take me anywhere," she grumbled, dropping back into her chair. "Who knew one tiny cherry tomato could cause such trouble?" The slightest hint of a grin surfaced, and it completely disarmed—and charmed—him.

"You keep life interesting, that's for sure." With her cheeks flushed and her eyes bright, she was even more beautiful. *I like her flustered.*

"It's my goal in life."

Tomato incident aside, he thought the dinner was going fairly well, but they hadn't gotten to the main course yet. He kept the conversation light as their dinners were delivered. When she offered to share her lobster, he put a portion of his prime rib on her plate.

"It's delicious. Thank you, Josh. This is a rare treat." Their eyes met as they sampled each other's entrée. After a long moment, Winnie smiled. "I don't think you invited me to dinner tonight to actually discuss *food*, did you?"

He raised his hand. "The floor's open. I have no hidden agenda." That wasn't the exact truth, but he didn't want to send her running away and out of his life. It was pretty obvious she was skittish, and he needed to proceed with care. "What would *you* like to talk about?" Taking another bite, he waited. The answer to that one might be pretty interesting. Winnie's spontaneity, combined with her honesty, would keep him on his toes, but he welcomed it. He hadn't felt so energized and alive in years.

Her cheeks colored. "I'd like to hear more about what you do in that fancy office of yours at the law firm."

"How do you know it's a *fancy* office?"

"Well, for one thing, any man who wears expensive gold cuff links like you're wearing tonight has a matching office. If you worked in a bowling alley, for instance, you wouldn't be sporting those babies."

The corners of his mouth upturned. "I suppose my office is a little pretentious. Working in mergers and acquisitions sometimes requires . . . a certain wardrobe, especially on the day we close a deal." *Is that what you're doing with her? Sealing the deal?* He needed to say something quick. "I know enough to make the corporate image work to my advantage. It's just business." *It's not exactly what I'd hoped to get into after law school, but it's a good living.*

"But, do you *like* it?"

Not really. "I like it enough." *Say something sensitive before she thinks you're a total corporate phony.* "I like to balance it out by helping with hurricane relief efforts. I'm also involved with a number of corporate and civic organizations in Baton Rouge." *Now you sound like a public service announcement.*

"I've heard about the hurricane relief work you did after Mitch and Floyd. It must be very gratifying. So, what happens next?"

"Next?"

"I mean, are you going to be another Sam and travel all over the world wherever there's a natural disaster calling your name?"

Interesting question. "I honestly don't know. I'm hoping there won't *be* many disasters to chase—natural or otherwise."

She sighed. "I can't even imagine what you've seen, what you've done, what you've been able to accomplish." Her eyes met his. "It's a wonderful passion to have, helping people who've lost so much."

"Everyone should be passionate about *something.*" He wiped his mouth with his napkin. "Makes life more rewarding." When he tried to capture her gaze, she lowered her eyes. "Care to share what *you're* passionate about?" He wondered what inner struggle caused that frown to appear on her expressive face. While he wanted to see her smile again, he wanted to hear her answer to his question even more.

Josh busied himself carving his prime rib before savoring another succulent bite. Waiting for her response, he lifted his fork slowly to his mouth. *Stop it. You're making her uncomfortable.* Still, he couldn't help it. Like he told her, he could be uncommonly patient when he wanted to be, much more so now than a few years ago. He had all the time in the world. At least for tonight.

~

I'm passionate about my daughter, but I don't know how to handle this, Lord. When do I tell Josh about Chloe? Do I invite him to the apartment and introduce them? I have to prepare her to meet her father, but how? Somehow, I have to prepare him, too. Stifling a sob, Winnie buried her face in her napkin. *That ought to do it all right.* Now he'd definitely think she was a fruitcake and hightail it back to the bayou. Most men couldn't handle tears, although Josh Grant didn't fall under the "most men" category. But that's not why she was crying. No way could she sit and carry on a conversation and pretend this was a casual dinner date. Her nerves twisted inside, the rising dread so real she'd never be able to taste—let alone enjoy—the remainder of the food on her plate. She prayed she'd be able to stomach the food she'd already eaten.

Josh put his hand on her forearm. "I'm sorry. I didn't mean to make you uncomfortable. Forgive me for upsetting you again. I seem to have a talent for that." He lowered his voice. "Please don't cry." It was sweet, really, the way he was sympathetic and attentive to her needs.

"No, *I'm* sorry, Josh." It came out barely more than a whisper.

His eyes widened, and Winnie knew. He was remembering the night she'd clung to him and wept in his arms. *Even if he was only in it for his own gratification, he couldn't have forgotten the way he held me as I cried.* Her tears hadn't been because of him in any way.

Raising his hand to get the waiter's attention, Josh spoke in low tones. Retrieving his wallet, he pulled out a crisp bill and placed it across the man's palm. "Come on," he told her, "let's get out of here and get some fresh air."

He pulled out her chair and waited. She didn't shrug him away when he put his arm around her. Embarrassed, she buried her head against his solid shoulder. The waiter scurried back with a bag in less than a minute. The sight of it made her sob even harder. Putting one hand over her mouth, she hurried out of the restaurant with Josh close behind.

She gulped back her sobs and tried in vain to control her breathing. "I don't even know where or how to begin . . . what to say."

"Then don't say anything." Leading her over to a bench at the side of the restaurant, he pulled her down beside him, gathering her in his arms. He did it so effortlessly, and it seemed so natural. Leaning her back against him, he fit her in the protective curve of his arm. He nestled her close, similar to how she cuddled Chloe when they sat together on the sofa.

Lord, why does it have to feel so right? Winnie gave into her sobs, but kept them as quiet as she could as they wracked her shoulders. He didn't say anything, but kept his arm around her shoulders and leaned his head against hers a few times. Smoothing her hair away from her cheeks a few minutes later, she raised her tear-streaked face to his.

With gentle fingers, Josh dried the moisture from her tears. His eyes scanned her features in a leisurely path from her hairline and across her cheeks before traveling down to linger on her lips. One thumb brushed across her lower lip, his fingers skimmed her jaw in a light caress. Even though he must have intended it to be comforting, it was so much more. Everything Josh did was seductive. *Dangerous.* Cupping her face between his two strong hands, his expression was indecipherable.

When he rested his cheek against hers, Winnie breathed in, absorbing his masculine scent, loving the slight roughness of his beard. The memories it brought threatened to overwhelm her as they crashed like waves in her mind. Lifting her chin, she grazed his cheek with her lips. Maybe she shouldn't have done it, but she was powerless.

Josh startled at the touch of her lips. The amber flecks danced in his eyes, a reflection of the moonlight and soft illumination from the streetlamp overhead. He leaned forward, his face a mere heartbeat away. His lips hovered above hers, his lids heavy. Most likely, he was trying to decide whether to kiss her or turn away and resist the strong temptation.

Winnie knew what her heart wanted, but her mind fought it, just as his must. They sat frozen in the same position for what seemed like an eternity, neither one daring to move. Her pulse was out of control and she wondered if his was the same. They were teetering on a precipice. A kiss from this man wasn't just a kiss. She should tell him about Chloe, but right now she wanted something entirely different.

After what seemed like an eternity, he finally lowered his head and kissed her on the side of her mouth, not fully in the middle. His lips lingered, the warmth of his mouth on hers, and she felt his sigh.

Turning her head, she repositioned her lips to welcome his, this time directly on-target.

Josh whispered against her mouth, "*Winnie.*" It was an achingly sweet, barely-there kiss, and soon enough, it was over. "It's been a long time since I've felt a woman's kiss. And it was *yours*."

"I'm *glad* it was mine." Feeling bold, she moved her hand near his heart, its strong rhythm her anchor.

He moved his arm around her shoulders, pulling her close again. "Me, too."

They sat for a long time on the park bench, not speaking, but it wasn't awkward. He stroked her hair, holding up strands to catch the moon's rays sifting through them.

I need to get home to Chloe. "What time is it?" Josh dropped his arm as she sat up straighter on the bench, darting a glance at her watch. *Almost ten.* She ran a hand over her skirt, but it was a lost cause. "I didn't know it was that late." She disengaged from his arms and jumped to her feet. "I have to be getting home."

"Why? Will Ladybug turn into a pumpkin?"

Her tears had long dried and she raised one hand to her face, self-conscious. "I must look like such a mess."

"You've never looked lovelier. Early start tomorrow?" He walked beside her as she headed to the car.

"Something like that."

"Here, you take the food," he said, handing her the bag.

She looked at it, regret settling in her heart. "I'm so sorry."

"I'm not."

"I'm talking about running out of the restaurant, the food, everything." She stared at the pavement, feeling silly and more than awkward. She was pathetic and really needed to get out more.

"I'm not," he said again, stepping closer.

Turning, she led him to stand beside Ladybug. "I . . . I have a confession."

"What's that?" His eyes canvassed her face.

How did Josh expect her to think—much less form a coherent sentence—when he looked at her like this? Winnie swallowed hard, reaching deep inside to try and find the words. *Tell him.* "You were the last man I ever kissed." The words came out in a rush. "Guess that makes us even. Not that it matters." She attempted to sound halfhearted, but failed in spectacular fashion. *Coward.*

"I disagree. I think it *does* mean something." He waited as she unlocked the car. "Are you coming over to the house to meet with Lexa tomorrow? We could have lunch together. Or dinner. Something. *Anything.*"

Oh, his voice did such things to her, too. "I think so. I can't remember," she said, shaking her head, her thoughts concentrated on anything but business as she lost herself in those impossible eyes. "Do you want me to?"

"Yes." His gaze held hers without wavering.

"Well," she said before being cut off as he drew her into his arms and lowered his mouth to hers again. This time, his kiss was firm and convincing. Josh Grant was making up for lost time but good, the years melting away. She moved her hands around his neck and leaned into him as he drew her closer, tightening his hold. Along with his kiss came memories that stirred a yearning deep within her. *Go away. Now is not the time.*

"Yes, I do," Josh said, his voice quiet as he pulled back.

She'd already forgotten the question. Winnie bit her trembling lower lip as he withdrew his arms from around her waist with obvious reluctance and graced her with that dazzling smile. What a time of prayer she faced tonight. She shouldn't have kissed him. Not only once, but *twice.* That second one she'd certainly never forget. Confessions would be made, forgiveness asked for the thoughts running rampant through her mind. Oh, she'd be up all night long.

Sometime during their embrace, the bag of leftovers slipped to the ground. She stared at him, not moving.

Retrieving the bag, Josh took her hand and curled her fingers around it. "Don't forget this." A slow smile upturned the corners of his mouth. "So, lunch tomorrow?"

Her lips still swollen from his kiss, Winnie nodded, dazed. "I'm, uh, sure it can be arranged." Whirling around and climbing into her car, she started the engine and pulled away before Josh had a chance to say—or do—anything else. *Safer that way.*

As it was, they were in deep enough trouble.

CHAPTER THIRTEEN

Thursday Morning

WINNIE DROVE TO Sam and Lexa's after dropping Chloe off at daycare. Lexa had an appointment with the pediatrician for Joe's checkup early in the afternoon, so she'd left a message on Winnie's cell phone asking if they could get an earlier start. On the agenda was reviewing the menu for their event the following Saturday night and making the list of items and ingredients they'd need.

Lexa stretched her arms wide, not bothering to hide her yawn as she opened the kitchen door and ushered her inside, still dressed in her nightgown and robe. "What has you smiling so bright this early in the morning?"

"Someone lose a little sleep last night?" Winnie asked, ignoring Lexa's question. Better to keep her secrets a little longer. "Baby Joe keep you up?"

"No, but his daddy did."

Winnie groaned, pulling out a breakfast bar stool and parking herself in it. "You know, Lexa, I really don't want to hear intimate details about your love life with Sam."

"No, no," Lexa said, sitting down across from her. "Actually, it was the sweetest thing in the world. I finished nursing Joe and was half-asleep in the bed. Then I started thinking about things and sort of woke up again. I looked across the room and there's my husband in the rocker, singing to our son. He was looking down at him and singing 'In the Garden.' I love hearing Sam sing, and that was my mom's favorite hymn. He pours all his emotion into it." She sniffled. "Just when I think I can't love him more than I already do, he does something that takes my breath away."

Winnie teared up and waved her hand. "All right, woman, give me a tissue. You can't say something like that and not have one handy. Tell me something—doesn't Sam know any regular baby songs—you know, lullabies? It must be hard living with such a pillar of faith all the time."

Lexa shook her head. "Would you prefer he'd sing to our impressionable child about a cradle falling out of a tree? Some of those nursery songs have questionable meanings and dark undertones. Trust me, Sam has his moments. Besides, perfection is highly overrated, not to mention boring." She retrieved the box of tissues from the small desk in the corner of the kitchen, handing one to Winnie and taking one for herself. "Sorry for getting all sappy on you since I know how much you hate it."

That comment made Winnie smirk; she dabbed at her eyes. "If I didn't like sap, I certainly wouldn't hang around with the TeamWork crew. Marc always says we're tailor-made for a Hallmark ad. By the way, I hear Marc's pushing for

Sam to write down those seven rules of marriage. My two cents says he should seriously consider it."

Lexa's eyes widened. "Winnie, how do you know about Sam's rules?"

"I thought everyone knew about them. Why? What did I say?"

Her friend shook her head. "Wait until Sam hears about this. I guess Marc couldn't keep them to himself, could he?"

She looked irritated and Winnie hoped she hadn't gotten him into trouble. "Let's get over the fact that others know about the rules of marriage, shall we?"

Lexa snorted. "You've been talking with Amy again, haven't you? You're starting to sound like her. It's a little scary sometimes, I have to say."

She bypassed that one. "Come on, Lexa. It sounds like an awesome plan for marriage and it works for both men *and* women. Marc's a genius when it comes to things like this. Any man who owns an advertising agency in the Prudential Tower in Boston—hugely successful, but that goes without saying—is definitely worthy of paying attention to. He recognized a great idea as soon as he heard those rules and told Sam as much."

Lexa chewed on her bottom lip, silent, but nodded for her to continue.

"Sam's certainly got the qualifications," Winnie said. "He's a leader in his professional life and in the church. Think of the possibilities! He could use the royalties for all things TeamWork—camps for kids, new ministries, whatever. People eat this kind of stuff up. Besides, there's a whole lot of good that can come from a godly man sharing his personal plan for loving his spouse. He could expound on the rules and make it a premarital marriage guide or something, or maybe take a couple from the premarital stage to after-the-vows. Now, *that's* an idea."

Lexa held up one hand. "Been talking to Natalie and Marc, too, have you? Are you their secret weapon to try and convince me?"

"It's a great idea and you know it. Honestly, I don't see what the problem is. Just promise to think about it, okay?"

"No promises, but I suppose it *would* bring positive attention to TeamWork, and that angle would definitely appeal to Sam," Lexa said. "But you make it sound like writing a book is easy. It takes a major time commitment. He's already so busy at the office and church, I don't know how he'd find the time even if he wanted." Sliding down from the stool, Lexa headed for the coffee pot. "Want a cup?"

"Thanks. Thought you'd never ask. I need to wake up a little more before we start working."

"Late night?" The question was deceptively casual as Lexa measured out coffee.

"I was home by ten-thirty." This could be fun, letting her guess.

"Oh."

"I have a child, Lexa. I can't stay out as late as I used to. I'm sure you know a little something about that yourself."

Lexa opened the refrigerator and pulled out the hazelnut creamer. She brought it over to the counter with napkins and spoons. The aroma of fresh-brewed coffee filled the kitchen soon enough. "Have you had a chance to look over the menu for next Saturday yet?"

She shook her head. "I was going to when I got home last night, but I was tired and fell asleep early." That one was like dangling a carrot in front of a hungry rabbit.

"Oh." Lexa sat down, watching her. She started to ask something else a couple of times before stopping, closing her mouth.

Winnie laughed. "Just ask, Miss 'Oh.' It was one date. I haven't seen Josh in more than four years. I have to be realistic. I'm not some lovestruck teen with stars in her eyes. Once he goes back to Louisiana, I don't know when I'll ever see him again."

Lexa's grin was coy. "Who said anything about love?" She slid off her stool again and pulled two coffee mugs from the overhead cabinet, standing on her tiptoes. Winnie hid her smile. Sam sure must come in handy around the kitchen, although she knew a stepstool was stored in the pantry. "We're talking Baton Rouge not San Francisco, Winnie. All I'm saying is, there've been enough sparks around here the last few days to power a car. A really *big* car. Or maybe a small jet."

"I wouldn't go that far," she said, grabbing a couple of artificial sweetener packets. "But, okay, I'll admit there are sparks." More like a small inferno.

Lexa poured their coffee. "You know you want to talk about it and I'm the logical person. Your partner, your *confidante*," she said, carrying their mugs and lowering them to the counter, being careful not to spill the contents.

The aroma of hazelnut made her smile. "Josh wants to have lunch today, but that's all I'm saying."

"Fair enough," Lexa said. "I'm going to fix pancakes for the guys before we get started. Would you like some?"

"No, thanks. I ate a quick breakfast with Chloe before I left the house." She glanced at the menu for the event on the counter in front of her and gave it a quick rundown.

Lexa busied herself at the stove, pulling out the griddle and a pitcher of premade batter from the refrigerator. "Joe's been fed and I had some instant oatmeal right before you got here. Let me whip up these pancakes and then we should be good for a couple of hours."

Winnie jumped as the swinging door flew open and Sam walked in with Josh right behind him. Sam was fully dressed, but Josh was still in his sleep pants—and wrapping a robe over his bare chest. *Have mercy.* Lexa kissed her husband good morning, ignoring them, and didn't see the view she'd just enjoyed. Obviously, Josh didn't expect her to be there so early, but had the grace to look embarrassed. Sipping her coffee, Winnie averted her gaze, doing her best to ignore the chest—the man—seated less than a foot away.

"Forgive me," he said, leaning close, his voice deep and a bit husky. *Very nice.* "I didn't know you'd be here quite this early."

"No need to apologize. It's nothing I haven't seen before. Just not with any frequency, or any time in the last four plus years." She heard his chuckle low in his throat. Sam and Lexa talked together by the stove and Sam pulled out plates, stacking them on the counter as she flipped the pancakes. Observing them, Winnie suppressed a sigh that sounded suspiciously like longing.

"You look very pretty this morning," Josh said as he accepted a mug of steaming coffee from Sam with a grateful smile.

His compliment made her thankful she'd taken the time to dress in nice khaki shorts and a new trendy, white cotton top. It was feminine and fitted, but not in an I-want-attention-from-men way. She'd pulled her hair back in a smooth, high ponytail and wispy tendrils framed her face. Coral nails winked at her from beneath the straps of her sandals and contrasted well against her lightly-tanned skin. She hadn't bothered to paint her nails in a long time—until Josh came to Houston. Of course, Chloe noticed right away and was fascinated. Next, she'd be begging for *her* nails to be painted, too, so they could be "twins." Ever since she heard about Josh, she'd asked all sorts of questions about how two babies could be born at the same time. That was only the beginning, she feared.

Sam engaged Josh in a conversation about some political event in a foreign country, but Winnie tuned them out, choosing to steal glances at Josh, praying they wouldn't ask her opinion and thereby prove her ignorance and inattentiveness. He hadn't taken the time to shave yet either, and that morning stubble on his face was nothing short of incredibly sexy. She blushed at the thought.

Within a couple of minutes, Sam brought over two plates stacked high with pancakes. They smelled out-of-this-world delicious. Given his preference for all things peach, it must be the special, not-so-secret ingredient. Pulling out the counter stool next to his wife, Sam bowed his head and asked the blessing. "I understand you ladies have a lot to discuss this morning," he said. "I thought I'd take Josh to the TeamWork office and catch him up to speed on what he's been missing, maybe convince him to join us again on one of our missions." He winked at Lexa.

Josh grinned. "Nothing like being direct."

"As you can see, subtlety isn't their strong suit," Winnie said.

"Lexa, should we be insulted?" Sam asked.

"Never," she said with a smile. "I think it's a great plan. Winnie and I probably only need a few hours and then she's all yours, Josh. At least until about two this afternoon." Intentional or not, the statement sounded provocative.

Winnie snorted and coffee almost spouted from her nose. Grabbing a napkin, she hid her smile.

"Where do you recommend we go for lunch?" Josh asked, directing the question to her.

Nice of him to help cover her obvious embarrassment. "I'm sure I'll think of something." She hoped she could come up with a place where she wouldn't burst into tears, not that geography had anything to do with it.

As she sipped her coffee, Winnie felt those mesmerizing green eyes on her. She couldn't complain since she was doing the same thing and checking him out when he talked with Sam. *I'm certifiable.* The man was back in her life forty-eight hours and she was falling hard for him all over again. Had she learned *nothing* in the past few years? The tension in the air between them was palpable, but it was the best possible kind.

"Sam, you must dream about peaches." Josh took another hearty bite and made a big show of savoring it. "I'm surprised they don't ooze from your pores. Seriously," he said when Sam laughed. Picking up a daintier bite of pancake with his fork, Josh offered it to Winnie, but she shook her head.

Now he wants to feed me.

"What do *you* love, Josh?" Sam asked.

Winnie shot him a chastising glance. She dared not look at Lexa.

Josh didn't hesitate. "Are we talking metaphorically, figuratively or simply fruit?"

They all laughed. "Fruit," Sam said. "Name your favorite."

"Hands down, strawberries."

"Winnie?" That from Lexa.

"Mango." That probably sounded ridiculous since most men wouldn't know a mango from a papaya, if even that.

"Is that a fruit?" Sam asked.

"Yes. Of course," Winnie said, and Lexa concurred.

"Well," he said, rising from his seat, "if you're finished, Josh, what do you say we get ready to head downtown?" With a quick kiss of thanks for the pancakes and a promise to meet Lexa at the pediatrician's office, Sam carried his dish to the sink.

Josh finished his last bite, and followed him. "Thanks, Lexa." He planted a quick kiss on her cheek. "Those were the best pancakes I've ever had in my life even if they weren't strawberry." He ignored Sam's grunt as he gave her one of his trademark smiles. "I'll see you back here in a few hours, Winnie."

Watching him go, Winnie swallowed her sigh. Seeing Lexa's knowing grin, she grunted. "Not a word. Time to work, partner."

CHAPTER FOURTEEN

Thursday, Early Afternoon

SHORTLY AFTER ONE o'clock, Winnie and Josh sat across from each other in a park close to Sam and Lexa's neighborhood, sharing a foot-long hotdog. "Now, isn't this better than a fancy restaurant?" she asked, laughing as she used her pinky to wipe off a dab of mustard at the corner of her mouth. She needed to get it before Josh could try and wipe it off . . . or kiss it off. Not that it would be such a bad thing, but they were toeing a very fine line.

"Without a doubt," Josh said. He had on khakis and a short-sleeved blue shirt—effortlessly casual chic.

"Not to discount the lobster last night . . . or the prime rib . . . or the cuff links," she said. A giggle escaped and again, it worked its charm on the man. *Why, he's a pushover in so many wonderful ways. This could be fun.*

"Were you and Lexa able to get your plans made?" he asked, surveying the hotdog, holding tight onto his end as she took another bite. "Bad timing. Sorry. Please chew," he said and took another bite.

"Yes, I'm happy to say we got everything accomplished this morning. It's a private party at one of the museums. I always love museum galas. They're so . . . sophisticated and elegant." Realizing what she'd said, she laughed. "Spoken by the woman eating the foot-long hotdog."

"More people should try this. The hotdog's quite good, actually, and this open air ambience *is* much better than a stuffy restaurant, especially at lunch." Josh's gaze fell on a young couple with their toddler son and puppy playing nearby.

Winnie's heart quickened at the reminder. She needed to tell Josh—and tell him soon. Just the way he looked at the cozy scene spoke volumes. *It's time. He's ready. Work up the nerve to tell him. Now. Soon. Sometime in* this *lifetime.*

"How about another hotdog?" she asked, dusting her hands together. "My treat."

He sat up straighter on the bench and took the last bite. "I have an idea. Surely there's an ice cream vendor somewhere nearby?"

"There's a great little family-owned ice cream shop not far from here. We're regulars there." She paused, hoping he wouldn't wonder what she meant by the use of that pronoun. *Don't be paranoid.* "We could go there."

Wiping his hands on his napkin, Josh nodded. "Sounds like a plan. Let's go get the car and you can be my navigator."

"Do you own your house?" she asked as they drove along the backstreets.

"Yes. It's fairly small, but it's in a nice, quiet area of Baton Rouge."

"Tell me about it." She leaned her head against the seat.

Glancing over at her, Josh smiled. "What specifically would you like to know?"

"There's no underlying reason. I'd just like to know."

"It's a two-story, three bedroom with two full baths upstairs and a half-bath downstairs. I bought it new, and although it's only two years old, it's made to *look* old. It has hardwood floors, a fireplace in the living room, a sunken dining room with a small but gorgeous chandelier, wall mural, and window seats in one of the two guest bedrooms. But the best feature of all is the kitchen." He darted a quick look at her. "It's completely modern with stainless steel, state-of-the-art appliances."

Winnie sighed. She knew he must have a state-of-the-art something. "Sounds like heaven. Do you cook much?"

"That's the irony. I'm working so much, I don't have time to cook. The few things I make aren't bad—broiled fish or chicken, and I usually toss in a little pasta or shrimp for variety." He shot her a grin. "Spices add to the flavor, too. Maybe sometime you can come visit and I'll cook for you?"

"Cajun spices, I presume? I'm learning all sorts of interesting things about you today." She didn't know how to respond to that last comment about visiting him in Baton Rouge, so ignoring it was the easiest thing. "Tell me more about your law firm."

"We have offices in four Louisiana cities, and ours is the biggest in terms of attorneys and staff. There are twenty-eight partners, twelve associates and about thirty staff."

She paused a moment. "Where do you see yourself in ten years?"

He looked her way. "That's a very thought-provoking question."

"And do you have a thought-provoking answer?"

"Are you speaking in terms of my career or personally?"

"Depends."

"On what?" he asked.

"On how you choose to answer, I suppose," she said. "I don't know how *I'd* answer that one, so don't worry about it. Forget I asked. I respectfully withdraw the question."

"Oh, but you *did* ask, so it's on the table. Let me think about it. When we get to the ice cream place, I'll do my best to answer whatever questions you have for me. On one condition."

She avoided looking at him. "What condition is that?"

"You agree to do the same. I'll ask questions and you agree to answer them as openly and honestly as possible."

"Hmm." Maybe if she didn't offer her definitive agreement, he wouldn't hold her to an answer. *Oh Lord, this is not a good thing. This could definitely lead to big trouble. Huge trouble.* Funny how she'd talked with Chloe about conditions a day or two ago. With the man beside her, it seemed like a lifetime and yet only a minute ago. Glancing at her watch, she smiled, thinking of Chloe. Dottie would pick her up and be at the apartment when she got home around five-thirty.

"Looks like you just enjoyed a sweet thought. Care to share?"

The man missed nothing. "A girl has to have *some* secrets, Josh. Turn left at the next side street."

He followed her direction. "It's over here on the right," she said, pointing out Richardson's Ice Cream Shoppe. "They've got the best homemade ice cream in the Houston area. Sam loves their peach, but I guess that goes without saying. I highly recommend their strawberry, too." He found a spot further down the street. After he pulled the car to a smooth stop, Winnie put her hand on the door handle and started to climb out of the car.

"Would you please sit still and let a gentleman open the door for you? You've got to get used to being treated like a lady."

The irony of that statement hit home, and again she hovered on the edge of fresh tears. Coming around the car, he opened the passenger door and helped her from the car. Such a chivalrous gesture only highlighted his words.

"Winnie," he said, "come sit over here with me." Taking her by the hand, he led her to a park bench in a shaded area to the side of Richardson's and lowered himself beside her, his hand still firmly clasped over hers. "I think we need to forget about that night and start fresh. In many important ways, we're different people now." His voice softened. "And yet the same in all the *best* possible ways."

She shook her head. "We can't push it aside, forget it ever happened, Josh."

He blew out a sigh. "I know. I wouldn't be honest if I didn't tell you it's hard not to think about it sometimes when I look at you. You were beautiful then, but you're even more so now. And yes, I mean physically beautiful as well as in every other way. When we kissed last night, it brought back memories. A *lot* of memories—all of them spectacular. But you're right. They're incredible memories and I can't push them aside. Because I, for one, don't *want* to."

"Then maybe we shouldn't kiss anymore." She held his gaze.

He looked at her for a long moment. "Is that honestly what you want?"

"No. Not really. Honestly. No."

"Was it the same for you?"

"What?"

"You can be obtuse when you want, can't you? Did kissing me last night bring back memories for you, too?"

"I'm not blind, or stupid or totally numb," she snapped. "Of course it did."

Those green eyes settled on her again, the gaze intense. "Winnie, you have always been a lady, you are a lady now, and you will be a lady as long as you live. Please don't tell me I made you feel cheap that night."

"That's the thing. You didn't make me feel like I was doing anything sinful. You made me feel special, cherished, and *loved.* You held me, you listened to me, you let me cry. Believe it or not, I rarely cry, but you'd never know it judging by my behavior when I'm with you—then *or* now."

"You're incredibly sweet and vulnerable, and always have been. Sure, you sometimes put up this tough exterior for the rest of the world to see, but it doesn't fool me for a second."

"I do not," she said, resisting the urge to cross her arms.

"Oh, yes you *do*." The words were low and firm. "Do you think you can get past that night? I guess that's the bottom line here. Look," he said, "you might find this hard to believe, but that night we spent together in San Antonio probably meant more to me than you."

Winnie stared straight ahead, her heart pounding. "Why do you say that?" *How is that even possible?*

"Because I really cared for you. You touched something deep inside no woman ever has, and I do believe it was my heart."

She swallowed hard. "Really?"

He tipped her chin and her eyes met his. "Really. It took me a few months to understand it, but by that time I was too ashamed of my behavior and figured you hated my guts. You might spend the rest of your life regretting it, but that night was a turning point for me." He rubbed a hand over his brow and a sadness passed over his features.

Part of her wished she'd known. *Even so, would I have done anything differently?* It took her a moment before she could speak. "Josh, I need to ask you something else, and please answer as honestly as you can."

He nodded, waiting.

"If Sam hadn't thrown you out of the TeamWork camp, do you think anything . . . might have . . . developed between us?" Articulation was hard when the potential for further heartache came calling. Maybe it wasn't a fair question, but one she needed to ask.

He looked at her for a long moment. "I don't know that I can answer that question. In some ways, we have to look at it from the perspective that the Lord allowed that night to happen for a reason. Just as we've made our way back to one another now. There's a reason, a purpose, for it." He sighed. "You want to know the thing I struggle with most of all?"

"What?" She could barely breathe.

He touched the side of her face, those green eyes deepening. "Even though I know we violated God's law, that night with you didn't feel wrong in my heart. If anything, it felt completely *right.* I've made my peace with the Lord about it, but I hope *you* can forgive me for feeling that way."

She sniffled. *I feel the same way, but can't tell you.* "There's really nothing to forgive." Shaking her head, she put her hands on her knees. "I can't believe we've managed to get through this entire conversation without me bursting into tears. Now, how about that ice cream?"

"I've never minded your tears, Winnie. It shows how caring and compassionate you are. And now," he said, helping her up from the park bench, "I'm going to buy you whatever ice cream cone, sundae, banana split or anything you want. Buy one of everything. Your choice. Although they might not have *mango* ice cream." His smile was warm and teasing.

"I love strawberry, too."

"Good. We can share."

A few minutes later, cones in hand—strawberry for Josh and mint chocolate chip for her—he looked around the small shop. "What do you say we go back outside to our park bench?" He held the door as they walked together, the bell on the door jingling as they left.

"Bye, Winnie," Bea Richardson called with a wave as they departed.

"Thanks. See you again soon." She knew Bea looked at her with renewed interest. After all, she'd never come into the shop with any man other than Sam. Even when the church singles group had come to Richardson's, she always sat with the other ladies. Bea had done her share of sizing up Josh as they'd ordered their ice cream. Judging from the wink and thumbs up, she approved.

"What other questions do you have for me?" Josh asked as he settled beside her on the bench again. He stopped eating and watched as she licked around the base of her cone so it wouldn't drip on her blouse.

"What?" She grinned.

"Nothing." He shook his head. "Question number one, please."

"I don't know if I'm really up for twenty questions. Let's just enjoy sitting here together." Their conversation up to this point had been heavy enough.

"All right, but feel free to ask anything. I don't mind answering your questions."

"Same here." Maybe that offer wasn't wise, but too late now. "Here, have a bite of my cone."

"No, thanks. Not my favorite." He held up his cone. "Strawberry?" He watched, wide-eyed, as she sampled and pronounced it delicious. "Okay, here's a question," he said. "What was the dead-end job you mentioned, the one before you started the catering business with Lexa?"

That one was easy. Winnie spent the better part of the next five minutes telling him how she worked as a marketing assistant at a medium-sized advertising firm. It was good experience, but paid poorly and offered no advancement, especially since she didn't have a degree. She told him about some of her favorite projects, being careful to gloss over the part where she didn't work for a few months after having Chloe. "So, you see, the catering really *is* my niche. At least I think so." She giggled, feeling much more relaxed. "The hours and the schedule work well for me and Chloe." *Oh no. Did I just say her name? Oh no. Oh no. Oh no.*

"Who's Chloe?" From the way he asked, she could tell he had no clue as to the existence of her daughter.

"A very dear friend," she mumbled, purposely allowing a dribble of ice cream to fall on her khaki shorts so she could busy her hands. *Please, Lord, let him drop it.* "I'd, um, better go get a wet paper towel or something. I'll be right back." She jumped up from the bench and hurried back into the shop. The bell jingled as the door opened.

"You okay?" Bea called to her from behind the counter.

Winnie nodded, but knew her cheeks were flushed and her eyes must look a little wild. "I spilled ice cream on my shorts. Do you have a damp paper towel or a napkin?"

Bea handed over the cone she was scooping to a teenage employee. "Come with me," she said, stepping to the end of the long counter. "You're with a very handsome young man today." She smiled. "Boyfriend?"

Winnie sighed. "Maybe. Sort of. Could be. I'm not sure." *He's already turning me into an even bigger rambling fool.* "He's been a friend for ages, one of the TeamWork guys, but he lives in Baton Rouge. Until this week, I haven't seen him for a few years."

After running a paper towel under the faucet, Bea squeezed out the excess water and handed it to her. "Well, if you don't mind my two cents, it's nice to see you with a man for a change. I've been praying for a couple of years a good one would come along. You've got so much to offer, honey. He sure looks smitten with you—as well he should be—and he's got nice manners, I can tell that much. My advice, not that you asked, is to hang on to him."

Thanking Bea for the paper towel, Winnie set about removing the spot of ice cream. It was a half-hearted effort as she tried to self-calm. It wasn't working. In the recesses of her mind, she heard the bell on the door, but paid it no heed. With a start, she realized what Bea was asking her. "Where's Chloe today?"

Winnie didn't need to look to know it was Josh who'd come into the shop. Why should the Lord waste a good opportunity? She chewed her lip and tapped her foot. Her cheeks must match the retro-looking milk shake machine behind the counter. "She's with Dottie," she whispered. It came out more a hiss. He must be standing right behind her. If Bea's expression didn't tell her, his warmth and presence did.

Turning around, Winnie forced a bright smile. "All taken care of now."

As they headed back to Sam and Lexa's house, Josh was quiet, no doubt biding his time. Turning into the driveway, he pulled the key from the ignition and shifted in his seat to face her. Not a man of idle purpose, this one. Those little lines surfaced around his eyes as did the vertical one between his brows. She wanted to smooth them, but left her hands where they were.

"Okay, Miss Doyle, I have a question for you. Remember, you promised to answer."

Here it comes. "Did I agree to that?" Her voice cracked with a nervous giggle.

"You did."

"Are you sure?" *Stop being coy and act like a responsible adult. Like a mother.*

"Positive. Maybe I should have made you sign a binding contract, but you agreed."

"Okay, then. Go right ahead." She sank down a little further in the leather seat, praying she didn't faint. Her pulse was out of control as it was.

"Who's Chloe?"

"You already asked that question. Do-overs aren't fair."

He stared at her again; it was unnerving. "I also told you I'm a very patient man. I can sit here all day if you want, but I'd like a straight answer." His voice was quiet, but earnest.

Winnie crossed her arms and frowned. "This isn't the way I wanted you to find out."

"Find out what?"

"Chloe . . ." She heaved a shuddering sigh. "Chloe . . ."

"Yes, Winnie . . . Winnie . . .?"

"Chloe is a darling little girl." *That's open and honest.*

"And do you take care of her?"

Is he talking childcare? She nodded. "Yes."

"Do you feed her?"

"Yes."

"Do you also clothe her?"

"Yes."

"And do you give her shelter?"

Winnie nodded. "Yes. Yes to all those things, Josh."

"Then you love her."

More than life itself. "Of course, I do. You're asking an awful lot of questions."

"Did you give birth to her . . . Winnie?"

"Well, now, that's a really big question, isn't it?" Flippancy wasn't becoming. She lowered her eyes.

"One I hope you'll trust me enough to answer."

Winnie nodded, still unable to look him in the eye. "Yes."

Josh shifted in his seat. "Okay, then, one more question, and I'm done. Promise."

She steeled herself for this one. *Just ask and get it over with, Josh.* Her emotions were raw and ragged as it was. If he showed disappointment or, worse yet, repugnance or revulsion, how could she bear it?

He tipped her chin with two fingers, waiting. "Can I meet her?"

Not what I expected. Dragging air into her lungs, she dared to lift her gaze to his. What met her was compassion that surprised her with its intensity. No condemnation, no judgment. Relief flooded her heart, her mind, but she needed time to think and plan her next step.

"I'm sure . . ."

The corners of his mouth upturned. "Sure it can be arranged?"

She nodded, unable to return his smile, knowing she had to escape. "Thanks for the hotdog, the ice cream . . . everything." Leaving the car door open, she sprinted to Ladybug. As much as running from Josh, she was running away from the truth, afraid her past would catch up with her.

Why wouldn't her fingers cooperate? She fumbled with her keys, dropping them to the pavement as she attempted to insert them in the lock.

He retrieved her keys, and his warm hand covered hers as he unlocked the door. Stepping aside, he waited as she climbed into the car.

Turning on the engine, Winnie lowered the automatic window. "Give me a little time, Josh."

"I meant what I said. When you're ready, I'd really like to meet Chloe." He closed the door and leaned close, elbows crossed. "If she's anything like her mother, she's gorgeous as anything, with pretty blonde hair." Speaking slowly, his voice low, his eyes roamed from the top of her head to her lips, lingering there. "Beautiful blue eyes, funny and smart as a whip, and blesses everyone she meets."

You've got it except for the eye color.

Even if she hadn't heard the words, this man had a way of making her feel cherished with those expressive eyes alone. He *really* needed to stop looking at her like that. Then again, she never wanted him to stop. Josh raised his hand, and she thought he might touch her hair, her face, but he pushed away from the door instead. She melted a little more inside, like her ice cream in the warm sunshine. When Josh's lips curved in a devastating smile, Winnie bit her lip to keep from crying out. When he met Chloe—an inevitability sooner than later—he'd *know*. Yes, her daughter inherited certain physical qualities from her, but she belonged equally to Josh Grant. He deserved to know, and his family deserved to know. Deserved the blessing of getting to know the sweetness, the *joy* of loving his daughter. As much as the Lord blessed her with Chloe, it was now time to *share* that blessing.

"Chloe's the best thing that ever happened to me." She stared out the front window. "I'll talk to you later, Josh." *Does he not remember I told him he was the last man I kissed?*

"Call me if you want to talk, Winnie. About anything." He tapped the door with his hand as he moved away from the car.

She nodded and pulled away from the curb, managing to keep her foot steady although she wanted to floor the accelerator.

Turn around, go back there and tell that man he's the father of your child.

Sometimes the Holy Spirit worked overtime.

Winnie looked in the rearview mirror. Josh stood in the driveway, watching, and was still there when she turned left at the corner and faded from view.

"One thing at a time, Lord."

CHAPTER FIFTEEN

Late Thursday Afternoon

ALL IT TOOK was a quick look at Lexa's Rolodex on the small desk in the kitchen to find Winnie's address. A check on the laptop computer showed it was about ten minutes away. After a short perusal of his e-mail and listening to voicemail messages, Josh stretched out on the bed made by Sam's father and propped his arms beneath his head. Every time he closed his eyes, all he could see were Winnie's big, sad eyes. They tugged at his heart. Why was she so afraid to admit she had a child? Was she ashamed or embarrassed?

Some of the comments she'd made—offhand or not—gave him the impression she hadn't dated much. She'd also told him he was the last man she'd kissed. *Did she lie?* The thought brought him upright on the bed. How old was Chloe? Did the other TeamWork members know? If they did, it was a very closely-guarded secret. That made no sense either since their lives were pretty much an open book. Surely Beck would know, but she'd never said a word. Nothing made any sense.

At the risk of angering Winnie, powerless to understand it, he needed to know more. Being around her brought unexpected emotions to the surface. She'd been his friend, certainly, but the tug on his heart was way more than the deep friendship he felt for the other TeamWork ladies. He sensed a newfound peace in her. She was more self-assured and settled. The catering partnership probably had a lot to do with it, but Winnie would accept the job of motherhood as the most important one of her life. No wonder she acted so nervous when he made that comment about how she'd make a wonderful mother.

Two hours later, he stood on the doorstep of Winnie's apartment. An attractive, white-haired woman opened the door the second time he rang the doorbell. She gave him a tentative smile, probably hoping he wasn't selling anything. Maybe he *was*, but not to this woman.

"May I help you?"

"Hi. I'm Josh Grant, a friend of Winnie's. I was wondering if she's home? I'd like to speak with her." Based on what he knew about Winnie's background, this couldn't be her mother or a stepmother. Must be Chloe's nanny or a babysitter.

"Your last name is Grant?" She looked vaguely amused, and something akin to recognition flickered in her light eyes.

"Last time I checked."

She tilted her head to one side. "You're the young man who took Winnie to dinner last night."

"Guilty."

"The twin."

He raised his brows. "Again, guilty." This conversation was going nowhere fast. "Do you expect her soon, Mrs.—"

"It's nice to meet you, Josh. I'm Dottie Cooper. Winnie's not home right now, but I'm expecting her around five-thirty."

He glanced at his watch, surprised she'd volunteered that much information to a virtual stranger. It was well over an hour away, but he had all the time in the world when it came to Winnie and her daughter.

"Chloe's fascinated by the whole concept of twins," Dottie said. "She's a very bright child, just like her mother. I need to pick her up from a play date in a few minutes, as a matter of fact." Her eyes were kind and the palest blue imaginable. "Maybe you could call Winnie and she can meet you somewhere? I could stay with Chloe if you want to . . . maybe take her to dinner?"

At least he'd met with the approval of this woman. "Perhaps another time."

She nodded. "I'll be sure and tell her you stopped by."

"Thanks, Dottie. If you could, please tell her I'd like to speak with her. It's important."

"I'll do that. It's nice to meet you, Josh." She started to close the door, but paused halfway. "I hope I'll see you again sometime."

"Same here. Thanks."

Lost in thought, he walked to his car parked in the adjacent lot while still in full view of the apartment. If Winnie returned home to find him parked in front of her door, she'd probably flee in the opposite direction. She seemed prone to flight, as it was. He climbed into his car and then drummed his fingers on the steering wheel. Saying a quick prayer, he kept his eyes trained on the apartment, sliding down further in the leather seat.

A couple of boys played catch nearby and they cast wary glances in his direction. Turning his head, Josh ignored them, hoping they'd return the favor. He didn't have long to wait before Dottie left the apartment on foot. Walking with a determined air, she headed toward a nearby street. For a split second, Josh considered following her. Better not. It wouldn't bode well for his reputation to be charged with a stalking accusation.

"What are you doing here?"

Josh jumped. One of the boys stood beside his open window. His adolescent voice cracked with righteous anger—a zealous kid protecting his neighborhood, a thing to be admired. A scowl downturned the corners of his mouth.

"I'm waiting for someone," he said to the little vigilante. He countered the kid's dark eyes with a matching stare. "Don't worry about it."

"Oh, he ain't worried," a lanky, mop-headed boy said, coming alongside the first boy and propping an arm on his shorter friend's shoulder. "We thought maybe you was FBI, CIA, CSI or one of those guys, what with your fancy car and all." Stepping back, he eyed the dark BMW with an approving nod.

Josh's grin slipped out. "Sorry to disappoint you, but I'm not FBI or anything else with three initials." He almost chuckled at the expressions on their faces but played it straight. "I'm just your routine, average, run-of-the-mill lawyer."

"My mom hates lawyers," the first kid said. "Says all they do is take her money and don't do nothin' to earn it."

"Then she should get another one," Josh said. "Some of us try to do the right thing by our clients."

"Maybe he's spying on your mom?" the second kid said. "She's coming home soon, right?"

The first kid nodded and his eyes narrowed with suspicion. "My dad send you to spy on us?"

"That's enough, guys," Josh said, starting to open the car door. "No one sent me here. I'm here on my own time."

"Okay, okay," the lanky one said. "We was just leaving, anyway."

"Hey, kid," Josh called after them. Both turned back. "Tell your mom to call the Houston Bar Association. I'm sure they could recommend someone who'd do right by her." *And make sure you get to English class more often.*

The kid look confused. "Say what?"

"The H-B-A. Tell her to look for a lawyer at the HBA."

The initial thing must have computed. "You with this HBA thing?"

"Afraid not."

The second kid slapped his friend's shoulder. "Didn't you see his plate? He ain't from here. He's from Louisiana." He shot Josh a half-grin. "Thanks, man. Carry on." They disappeared together into a nearby apartment.

"Don't mention it." Josh settled back in his seat. He was rewarded when Dottie came around the corner and into view ten minutes later. Holding onto her hand and skipping was a little girl with shoulder-length, blonde curly hair and a pink bow on one side. This had to be Chloe. *Adorable.* She wore a pretty outfit the same color as her hair bow and held a book in her other hand. For some unknown reason, that pleased him. His eyes trailed to her pink and white sandals. Josh hunched forward, leaning both elbows on the steering wheel as he stared out the front window. *She looks just like her mother.* Same color hair, same nose and—as they came closer into his range—even the perfect shape of her lips looked like Winnie's. *Incredible.*

Dottie laughed at something Chloe said, and the girl wrinkled her nose. Through the open window, he heard her giggle, making his heart skip a few beats. She looked two, maybe three years old? It was hard to tell with kids, and he hadn't been around enough of them to know. He glanced at his watch as Dottie and Chloe disappeared into the apartment. Ten after five. Hopefully, Dottie was right and Winnie would return home soon. An unexpected sense of urgency seized him as something he couldn't define nagged the back of his brain. *Help me be patient, Lord.*

Winnie pulled Ladybug into a reserved parking space a couple of minutes before five-thirty. Right on time. He watched as she climbed out and reached into the back of the small car, pulling out a plastic box. She'd changed into a pretty blue dress, and her hair was pulled back in its usual ponytail like earlier. He wondered where she'd been. *None of your business, man.*

A long, flowered scarf was tied around her waist like a belt and trailed behind her. When she leaned against the car door, closing it with her hip, the scarf caught in the door. Josh pushed his fist against his mouth to stop from hollering out the window to warn her. If he revealed his presence now, it would not endear her to him. He wasn't overly fond of himself as it was. He winced when the scarf ripped as she started toward the apartment. Winnie turned back around and let out a small cry. Her sigh was palpable as she put the plastic box on the ground and opened the car door again. Pulling out the shredded remains of the scarf, she examined the damage.

Why did he feel the irrational urge to run to the nearest department store and buy her a handful of pretty scarves? He shook his head. *You're around her a few days and you're already falling over the edge.* Maybe he'd been without a woman in his life for too long, but there were valid reasons for that self-imposed exile. Reasons that had everything to do with self-respect and leading a life honoring to the Lord. But before he made any confessions, Josh had to know about Winnie's mini-me. Waiting until he saw Dottie depart a short time later, he stepped out of his car and walked with slow, purposeful steps toward her apartment.

He stood there a full minute, staring at the door, as different thoughts battled for supremacy in his cluttered mind. What if she refused to let him in, wouldn't allow him to meet her daughter? Now that he'd seen the child, he was more determined than ever. It was a burning need he couldn't understand. *Enough. Get on with it.*

CHAPTER SIXTEEN

FISTING HIS FINGERS, Josh rapped on the door, loud enough to get her attention, but not so loud as to be obnoxious.

"Just a minute!" A few seconds passed. "Who is it?" He imagined Winnie standing on the other side of the door, peering at him through the peephole.

"It's Josh."

"Josh!" Unless he was mistaken, that was more than surprise in her voice.

Splaying the fingers of his right hand against the door, he leaned close. How to explain? "I'd like to"—he hesitated for a split second—"Winnie, can we talk?" He prayed she'd let him in.

"Um, sure. Okay. Can we meet somewhere in a little bit? I'm . . . not dressed." From the muffled sound of her voice, she probably had one hand halfway over her mouth. A few seconds passed before he heard the security chain being removed. Winnie opened the door, wearing a white, plush bathrobe and an expression of something he couldn't define. "I didn't expect to see you again so soon."

"Sorry to show up unannounced, but we need to talk."

She leaned against the door, crossing her arms. "So you said. What do you—oh!" Her eyes widened and she flailed her arms, losing her balance as the door swung back and hit the wall.

Instincts kicked in. He hadn't made a catch so fast since he played Tigers baseball at LSU. He crushed her against his chest as he swept her in his arms. Planting a foot on the carpet to steady his balance, he wrapped his hands around her waist—that tiny, trim waist.

She laughed a little, but it came out more of a snort. "If we were in one of those romantic comedies, this would be the point where I'd have some cute, witty thing to say." She pushed away from him, gently disengaging his hands. "But I've got nothing, except to say thank you to the big, strong man for coming to my rescue," she breathed. "Again." A pretty pink flush spread upward from the V in the neck of her robe to her cheeks. "Makes me sound like a real liberated woman, huh?" She crossed her arms then uncrossed them before dropping them to her sides.

"I like rescuing you, and I prefer to think of you as an independent woman. And you are definitely that, Miss Doyle." Oh, but she was fetching, although now was not the time to tell her as much. Better to get on with it and spare her further embarrassment. Standing in front of a bunch of stuffed suits was nothing compared to this. Most of the work was done behind the scenes from the comfort of his office. By the time they sat down in the boardroom it was to sign the contracts. But, in this moment, he was rendered speechless. This woman standing in front of him now—in her bathrobe and barefoot—could hold her own with anyone, friend or foe. Maybe she was tougher than he thought?

"You might as well have a seat, then. Let's talk." Winnie pulled the belt on her robe—her symbolic chastity belt perhaps—tightening it before waving him over to the sofa. Based on his thoughts at the moment, he couldn't blame her.

Keep me focused, Lord. Josh tore his gaze away with great effort and encompassed the small apartment in one sweeping glance. Neat and tidy, basic layout with no distinguishing characteristics other than personal touches to make it welcoming—throw pillows, flowers, photos, afghans. Chloe was nowhere in sight. She'd probably been sent to her room when Winnie realized it was him knocking at her door.

Closing the door, Winnie walked across the room. "I need to change. I'll be right back."

"You look fine. Stay."

Her pretty mouth settled in a firm line and she raised her chin. "I'd feel a whole lot less vulnerable if I'm fully dressed. It'll only take a couple of minutes."

"Which shows you don't trust me."

Her ponytail swung behind her, swishing back and forth, as she shook her head. It was enough to drive him to distraction. Every movement, every word, captivated him. Not that he didn't trust himself, but perhaps it would be better for them *both* if she was fully dressed.

"That's where you're wrong. Trust has nothing to do with it." The honest emotion in those big blue eyes had the potential to bring him to his knees.

Man, get hold of yourself. "Then why should you feel vulnerable?" He raked his fingers through his hair. Two minutes into the conversation, and he was already blowing it. Forcing a deep breath, he stepped closer. Time to state his case. "You're not a very good liar, Winnie." Based on her stunned expression, he needed to clarify. "Why didn't you want to tell me?"

"I *did* tell you about her." Now he'd disgruntled her. At least she no longer looked like she was on the verge of tears. Tears from Winnie had proved his weakness in the past, but he never wanted to be the *cause* of her angst. He'd much rather see that effervescent, slow-moving smile.

"Not until I practically forced it out of you."

She raised her chin. "That's hardly lying, Josh."

"Same difference. Call it the sin of omission then."

"Don't talk to me about sin, if you please."

Better not answer that one if he didn't want to be thrown out of the apartment. As it was, he teetered on the edge. Crossing the room, he dropped onto the sofa. "Please come sit down and let's talk about this like two rational adults without trying to hurt each other with verbal arrows."

She stared at him for a prolonged moment. Watching her facial expressions was like following a revolving carousel of emotions. Winnie was nothing short of fascinating and as difficult to read as any woman he'd ever met. Without a word, she seated herself beside him, apparently wanting to be careful and keep a safe distance. Her nerves betrayed her as she pulled at the collar of the robe. Crossing her legs, she tugged at the hem when it gaped open in the front, revealing more of those gorgeous, long legs. He averted his eyes, but caught her furtive glance in his direction as she pushed herself upright on the sofa and tucked her legs beneath her. Admirable though it was, her attempt at modesty only highlighted the fact that—wrapped any tighter in that robe—she'd be preserved like a mummy.

"I don't think any less of you because you have a child, and it has no bearing on wanting to spend time with you. If that's the case—"

"What would be the point?" Her eyes narrowed, her voice much stronger.

"The point of what?"

"Spending time together."

His lips pressed together in a firm, hard line. "You can't tell me I was the only one enjoying those kisses last night." *Wanting more but knowing we needed to stop.*

Her frown grew deeper. "We've already discussed that. I can't believe I'm saying this, but we're getting off topic here."

"Okay, fine. You told me you hadn't kissed anyone since that night we were together in San Antonio, and there's no way Chloe's adopted. She's a carbon copy of you."

Her eyes moved to his in a heartbeat, blazing. "How . . . how do you know that?" She untangled her legs and jumped to her feet, hands on her hips. "Have you been spying on me?" Her voice had risen to a dangerous level. Starting to pace, she crossed her arms.

He shouldn't have surprised her in her home like this. What a foolish move. A bullheaded mentality was an asset in business, but not in dealing with the fragile emotions of a woman like Winnie. No doubt, she viewed it as nothing short of a violation of her privacy. Still, she'd let him inside her apartment. "Not really. Okay, look, here's the deal. I came over earlier and talked with Dottie. She told me she was going to pick up Chloe and that you'd be home around five-thirty." She scowled at that; he hoped he hadn't caused trouble for the kind-hearted woman. "Look, fault me if you want, but I've been sitting in my car, waiting for you to come home. This is a conversation we need to have in-person."

Spying a photo of Winnie and Chloe on the end table, Josh reached for it, staring as he held it in his hands. Winnie was silent, watching him. "She looks just like you. Beautiful. Happy." He gave her a pointed look which she ignored as she stared at something on the wall behind him. Her foot was wearing out the carpet and she bunched the sleeves of her robe with her fingers. "Does she share any characteristics with her father?"

Winnie blanched and put her hand up to her throat. Her reaction filled him with immediate regret. That question was way too personal and he had no right to ask. "Forgive me. That question wasn't fair. I respectfully withdraw—"

"Mommy?" Both Josh and Winnie startled, and he turned. Chloe stood in the doorway of a bedroom, a kitten nestled in her arms. As she came into the living room, he heard Winnie's sharp intake of breath. It passed through his mind she might demand her daughter go back to her room, but she still looked too stunned to speak. *What's wrong with this picture? Why does she act petrified that I'm meeting her child?*

Chloe—all bouncy blonde curls—marched straight to the sofa, stopping in front of him. She was so sweet, she stole his breath. "What's *your* name? Are you my mommy's friend?" She kept her attention focused on the kitten since it was a bit squirmy.

"Yes, I'm a friend of your mother's. My name's Joshua Grant, and I understand your name is Chloe. That's a very pretty name. What's your kitten's name?"

"Butterfinger." She stroked the kitten. "You can pet her if you want. She's a friendly kitty."

Josh laughed. "That's a creative name." Appropriate too, with its dark brown and orange-red markings. She stepped closer and he ran his hand over the kitten. He'd always preferred dogs, but a cat was the wiser choice for the daughter of a single, working mother. The small creature purred and he felt the rumble beneath his fingers.

"What's creative mean?"

He darted a glance at Winnie.

She gave him the first semblance of a smile he'd seen since he arrived. "She likes to learn new words."

Chloe nodded. "I learn ten every day."

"Well," he said, "that's quite admirable. Creative is like when an artist paints a picture, or when an author writes a book . . ."

"Like when Jesus made the world?"

That stopped him cold and his words stuck in his throat. He managed a nod. "Yes, exactly." His voice was raspy, clogged with emotion. "And admirable is what your mommy is, Chloe. She's very brave and smart, and a great mommy for you. Just the way God made her."

Winnie's eyes were wet and one hand rested over her heart.

Chloe nodded. "God made *you* a twin."

Even Dottie knew that—had they shared a round table discussion about it?

"That's right. I have a twin sister named Rebekah." Maybe that's what she found fascinating, that his twin was a girl.

"Uh huh. She's beautiful, like Mommy." Her eyes met his for the briefest of seconds and something he couldn't define passed between them. Soon enough, Chloe returned her attention to the kitten. He looked away, his mind racing.

Winnie cleared her throat. "Chloe saw the wedding photos from Natalie and Marc's wedding. Beck and I were bridesmaids together."

"Right." *She's telling me Beck doesn't know about Chloe.*

Chloe looked at him again, still holding Butterfinger. "Mommy and me are twins, and you look like a prince. Mr. Josh, will you be my mommy's—"

"O . . . kay then, Buttercup," Winnie interrupted. He'd never seen her move so fast. Clamping a hand on her daughter's shoulder, she turned her around. "Why don't you go in the kitchen and give your kitten some food?"

"I already fed her."

"Then feed her again."

Chloe frowned. "The cat doctor said—"

"You know what?" Winnie corralled and steered her in the direction of the small kitchen. "Cat doctors don't know everything. Why don't you go play with Butterfinger while I talk with" —she stole a quick glance his way— "Mr. Grant, and I'll come and make you some hot chocolate in a few minutes."

"It's not time for hot chocolate yet. Are you making supper tonight?"

Josh fought the urge to grin. From all appearances, Chloe also inherited her mother's stubbornness.

"Of course. Whatever you want, sweetie. Anything. Go. Play. With. Butterfinger."

"'Kay. Bye, Mr. Josh!" Even a child as young as Chloe had pretty good instincts and knew not to push her mother further. She disappeared into the kitchen. It was crazy, but he missed her the moment she left. This small child single-handedly managed something no one else had ever done—she'd wiggled her way into his heart in a matter of minutes. With her inherent sweetness, her trusting innocence, Chloe pulled on his heartstrings. *Yanked* was more like it. Just like her mother. What kind of man wouldn't marry Winnie in a heartbeat and claim Chloe as his own? His thoughts threatened to go in a hundred different directions, but he refocused his eyes on her. *Lord, help her understand how much I care about her.*

She kept her back turned. Her shoulders rose and fell a few times, but whether from deep sighs, silent sobs or quiet laughter, he couldn't be sure. This was Winnie so anything was possible. Perhaps it was best to hold his tongue and wait it out. When she turned around to face him, at least she wasn't gasping for air or clutching at her throat. But her shoulders slumped and she *did* look like she might dissolve into tears at any moment.

Why does she look like she lost her best friend? Why she cried so much in his presence was another point worthy of consideration. His only motive in coming to see her was to find out about her child. He also wanted to find out if what he felt was reciprocated and warranted making the trip between Baton Rouge and Houston every other weekend. And certain holidays and birthdays. His gut instinct told him something was going on, but he wasn't privy to it. If he couldn't grasp the significance of whatever it was, no way could he understand its ramifications.

Winnie's blue eyes lifted to meet his and she looked not unlike a martyr. "Ask, Josh. Just ask."

CHAPTER SEVENTEEN

WHEN HE STARTED to rise from the sofa, she waved him back. Coming slowly across the room, Winnie seated herself beside him again. After opening her mouth a couple of times, she closed it, her eyes watery. A lone tear streaked down her cheek and she wiped it away.

Josh breathed out a deep sigh. "Look, it's pretty obvious you had a relationship you're reluctant to tell me about for some reason. Either that or you were artificially inseminated and—"

Winnie gasped and her hand flew to her mouth. "*What?*" She managed to keep her voice low, but her glare was intense enough to shoot down that idea. "I can't believe you'd even suggest such a thing."

"Okay, maybe not. Sorry."

That defiant chin raised and she lowered her voice. "Maybe that's the thing to do in *your* inner circle, but not in mine."

Say something quick. "I understand. Chloe wasn't planned." Her incredulous look told him he'd pushed too far. Again. "Trust me, I'm the last person in the world to presume anything, and I'd never judge you. I've made far too many mistakes in my life to point fingers at anyone else. Look, all I wanted was to meet her. The one thing I *don't* understand is why you were so obviously against me meeting her."

Shaking her head, Winnie brushed the back of one hand over her damp cheek. "Ask me how old she is." She fussed with her robe again; he reached for her, stilling her hands. She lowered her eyes to her lap.

What does that have to do with anything? "Okay. How old is Chloe?"

"Almost four."

A little older than I thought.

Winnie swallowed hard and looked up at him. "Chloe was born in mid-May, a week after Mother's Day. Nineteen ninety-eight." A shuddering breath escaped.

Josh sat, elbows on his knees, running a hand over his jaw, focusing his gaze on the pattern of the carpet. Quiet beside him, Winnie waited for him to do the math since she couldn't seem to tell him the straight-out truth. The tears flowed freely down her cheeks and she made no pretense of wiping them away.

"San Antonio." It came out strangled. "And . . ." he began, his voice trailing. *Is this really happening, Lord?* If nothing else, it would explain that inner nudging to find out the truth, that insatiable need to know more about her little girl.

"I didn't lie to you, Josh. I never have and I never will. You were the first and *only* man I've ever . . ." She hesitated before drawing in another shuddering breath. "As I told you before, you're the last man I ever kissed."

His chest tightened, as if an iron fist pummeled him. Never in his life would he have expected something like this. "Chloe is mine? She's *our* child, Winnie?"

He prayed Chloe wouldn't overhear and come back into the living room. If she did, he wasn't sure how he might react. It would certainly be a good test of his emotional fortitude. What a shocking revelation, and nothing like what he'd imagined. *I'm Chloe's father.*

"Yes, Josh. Did you see her eyes? They're yours, right down to those flecks of amber. She might have gotten a lot from me, but she got those incredible green eyes and her smile from you."

"How? Why?" Josh croaked, swallowing the huge lump lodged in his throat.

"Because we didn't do anything to prevent it from happening," she said. Her voice sounded much stronger now. "That's the answer to the *how*. As to the why, oh, I don't know." She waved her hand in the air. "Maybe God knew I needed someone, a reminder of you to keep with me when I couldn't have you in my heart otherwise." She stopped, her eyes widening, as if she'd said too much. Another tear slipped out and fell to the carpet. "I pray you don't hate me for not telling you," she said. "I should have and I'm so *very* sorry. I wasn't sure what to do. You had enough problems of your own without being saddled with a pregnant woman. I was an emotional wreck. When I didn't see you, didn't speak with you, it seemed easier all the way around. Safer. So, I didn't say anything, and the longer I kept silent, the easier it was *not* to say anything. The passage of time was both a curse and a blessing."

Josh stared into space for a long time, not speaking. For one thing, he couldn't believe he hadn't taken the steps to ensure this very thing *didn't* happen. It was something he'd always taken care of first or he might have other offspring running around he didn't know about. That thought made him cringe and pierced him to his core.

"I know it's a lot to absorb."

Unless he was mistaken, that was relief he heard in her tone. Probably thankful her secret was finally out in the open. He shot her a look, and she lowered her eyes. She might have interpreted it as anger, but he was powerless to define it. Maybe Chloe had a word for it, but he sure didn't. He rubbed his hand over his forehead, staring blindly at a painting on the opposite wall. "How could you not tell me, Winnie?"

"How *could* I?"

She was right. He wouldn't have been ready. Wouldn't have been ready until the last year or so, truth be told. Still, he had a right to know.

"The Josh Grant I knew in the San Antonio work camp was reckless and immature, but you were so handsome and charming, I couldn't resist you. You were my friend. You made me laugh. And, that night," she said, "I felt truly *loved* and cherished for the very first time in my life." She reached for his hands, held them tight, and waited until he moved his eyes to hers once more. "The man you've become—the man sitting here with me now and the man I've seen since you've been here in Houston—is strong, solid, loves the Lord, and is capable of so *much*." She touched the side of his face, her touch featherlight as her fingertips grazed his cheek. "*This* man is ready for the truth."

He swallowed. "Do Sam and Lexa know I'm Chloe's father?"

Something flitted through her eyes and she withdrew her hands. "They've never asked, but I'm sure it's because they already know. To my knowledge, only Lexa, Sam and Amy know I have a daughter. No one else from TeamWork knows. You can rest easy on that point. The only times I've been away from Chloe involved Marc and Natalie—first to be in their wedding and then at the TeamWork mission Sam cooked up last year when Natalie had amnesia. I hated to leave her, but when Sam told me they were in trouble and needed our help, I didn't hesitate. You know how it is with Teamwork, the all for One, and One for all mentality kicks into high gear when Sam calls."

Josh shook his head, running a hand through his hair. "I'm not worried about any of that." It was just the first thing he could think to ask, no matter how pointless. "I can see what an excellent mother you are. You don't need to sell me on that point."

She visibly stiffened. "I'm not trying to *sell* you on anything or anyone, Josh."

"Does Chloe know?"

"No, of course not. She's too young."

"I've seen how bright she is. She's going to start asking questions."

Winnie twisted her fingers and looked suspiciously close to wringing them. "Don't you think I've thought of that? When she found out you're a twin, that's as close as she's ever come to asking how babies are born. I realize it's only a matter of time."

They stared at one another for a few seconds. How a child Chloe's age stayed still long enough not to interrupt them was a miracle in itself. Even he knew enough about kids to know how stir-crazy they got after a few minutes.

Winnie rubbed her hands up and down her robe-covered arms. "Maybe now you understand why I was so nervous around you. I didn't know how to act, but I knew I had to tell you. I *did* intend on telling you before you went back home to Louisiana. I don't know how much you remember from that night in San Antonio—"

He remembered everything about that night, but he was still trying to slow his breathing.

Winnie rose from the sofa and walked to the front window. "You've got parents and a sister who love you and would do anything for you. I never had that." She lowered her head. "All I had was a mom who left when I was ten, lived her life like there was no tomorrow and had a one-night stand with a stranger who killed her." She wrapped her arms around her middle. "If nothing else, she taught me how important life is. How valuable a gift my daughter is. I'm going to be the mother for my child the way my mom never was for me."

How she managed all that without breaking down was admirable, her inner strength indomitable. When she looked over at him, the pain in her eyes tore at his heart and ripped right through him like a physical blow. She looked so sad, and every instinct within him urged him to hold her tight and protect them forever—*both* Winnie and Chloe.

In a heartbeat, Josh hauled himself off the sofa and moved behind her in a matter of seconds. Planting his hands on her shoulders, being as gentle as he could, he turned her to him. "Oh, Winnie." Not knowing what else to say, what to do, he opened his arms.

Thankfully, she didn't protest and came willingly to him, laying her head on his chest. He stroked her hair and pressed his lips to the top of her warm head, inhaling the scent of her hair. *She still uses the same shampoo.* His hold on her tightened, and his heart raced.

"Then my dad and stepmom . . ." She couldn't finish and pressed her cheek against his shirt. Although she hadn't revealed too many details on that fateful night, she'd said enough. He knew she'd been emotionally abused, but as bad as that was, Josh prayed it didn't go any further. If it had, were physical wounds easier or more difficult to heal than emotional ones? He knew Winnie left home at eighteen, never looking back. Somewhere along the way, Beck told him Winnie's dad and stepmom died in a single-car crash, and drugs and alcohol were involved. His heart hurt for her when he first heard it, as it did now. So much tragedy in her life. It wasn't fair, but the Lord never promised fair. Only that He'd be there.

She raised her chin, still encircled in his arms. His hands moved across her back, brushing against the softness of the robe. Talking about her family in San Antonio started all this between them in the first place, and even though he was older and wiser in some respects—forgiven, redeemed and everything else—he would always be a flesh-and-blood man, still wanting this woman. He closed his eyes and loosened his hold, inhaling a deep breath. *Lord, keep me strong.*

"I meant it when I told you Chloe's the best thing that ever happened to me." Winnie leaned her forehead against his chest before raising her head again, looking him in the eye. "God gave her to me, Josh. She's given me the love I never had growing up. That unconditional love that doesn't expect anything in return. Chloe's filled all the holes in my heart so much it's overflowing with a love I never knew even existed."

Tears slipped down her cheeks again and a few slipped down his. "Shh," he whispered, kissing her temple. She sniffled and moved her arms around his waist.

His sigh was one of relief, of wonder, of something more.

"I know what we did was wrong," she said, "but I wouldn't have that beautiful little girl otherwise. At only three years old, she knows Jesus better than I do." She sobbed a little and pressed shaking fingers to her lips. "You can't know how much that thrills my heart."

He smoothed his hand over her hair. "I have a pretty good idea. You might not believe this, but I've prayed for you so many times the past four years. Prayed you wouldn't hate me. Prayed He'd someday lead me back to you—lead us back to *each other*—although I had no idea when or how. I'd like to move forward from here."

She pulled out of his embrace and stared out the front window. "When are you leaving Houston?"

"Sunday. I'll stay for church and then head home. I have some major acquisitions coming up in the next couple of months that'll involve a lot of late nights and weekends." He stepped closer. "None of that matters right now. I'm not sure what all this means just yet, but do me a favor and answer your phone when I call. Once I get back to Baton Rouge, we'll be talking. *A lot.*"

He scratched his head. "I want to come back and see you and Chloe, even if it's only for a night or two at a time." He tipped her chin. "There's so much we need to discuss. Especially now. Now that I have *two* beautiful reasons for coming to Houston, I'll be back as often as I can." He stopped, almost overcome with the overwhelming desire to see his child. How surreal that sounded, and yet how incredible. "It's probably best if I leave for now, but I need to see Chloe again before I go."

Winnie turned away from the window and nodded. "Give me a second and I'll bring her out." She disappeared into the kitchen. Within a minute, she returned and Chloe—minus Butterfinger—skipped over to where he stood by the window. "Mr. Grant has to leave now, Buttercup, but he'd like to say goodbye."

Crouching down, he opened his arms. Winnie must have somehow prepared her or else she was a very trusting child. It might be a combination. At least she didn't seem scared of him, and didn't protest. With a shy smile, the little girl walked into his embrace and straight into his heart, leaning against his chest, laying her head on his shoulder. Putting his arms around her small frame, Josh closed his eyes and pulled her close, holding her like the precious jewel, the *treasure,* she was. Planting a gentle kiss on her cheek, he whispered, "I'm going to come see you and your mommy again soon, Chloe. I hope that's okay with you."

"Yup," she said, smiling as she disengaged from his arms and skipped into her room.

Wiping away a tear, he rose to his feet and blew out a breath. God help him, this little girl turned him inside out, flipped his heart in ways he didn't think possible. "Chloe's the best thing I ever did, Winnie, and I have you to thank." When he looked at her, the tears in his eyes spilled over. He rarely cried, but he wasn't ashamed or embarrassed. The Lord knew Winnie must have shed enough tears over him, over Chloe and everything else in the past four years, but she wouldn't be alone again, not as long as he could help it. He prayed she'd want him in her life as well as Chloe's.

"No, Josh," she said, her voice soft as she cradled his face between her hands. "She's the best thing *we* ever did."

CHAPTER EIGHTEEN

DEEP IN THOUGHT, Josh pulled out the house key Sam had given him and opened the side door. Sam sat on one of the kitchen stools, an open newspaper and a cup of water on the counter. His reading glasses were perched on the end of his nose and he lowered his head, looking at him over the rims. "Hey, Josh. How was your afternoon?"

"Enlightening." That was an understatement. "Yours?"

"Joe's healthy and thriving according to the pediatrician." He folded the newspaper and pushed it aside. "I took him back to the office with me so Lexa and Winnie could go to a meeting downtown. By the way, your number one fan says hello."

Josh looked up, surprised. "Who would that be?"

"Bennie, of course. Especially after you were there with me this morning, she's even more determined to set you up with her daughter, the single one in Baton Rouge." He sipped his water. "Pull up a stool and let's talk. Grab some water, or I can make some coffee."

"I'm fine, thanks." Josh settled across from him, leaning his chin on one hand.

"Have you met Chloe?"

The man got right to the point. Heaven help little Joe. *The kid doesn't have a prayer.*

"Yes, this afternoon. She's an incredible child and looks so much like Winnie she takes my breath away." He took a deep breath. "And she's mine."

Sam didn't even blink.

"You've known all along, haven't you?"

"One look in those green eyes of Chloe's pretty much gives away any secrets Winnie might try to hide. For whatever reason, she's never confided in us about Chloe's paternity. Based on when she was born, we figured out the basic timeframe when she was conceived."

Both Sam and Lexa had been financial planners. Of course they'd know. Josh hung his head. "And obviously I was the logical choice as the father even before you knew Chloe had the green eyes." He chewed his lip, unable to look his friend in the eye. "What must you have thought of me? To think—" Deep shame engulfed him. Even after spending that night with Winnie, he'd made insinuations about Lexa. How lost he'd been. The saving grace was how far he'd come since then.

"The only thing I *did* was pray for you to get yourself straight with the Lord. Once you did that, I knew you'd be fine." Sam paused. "So much for my insistence on being the only one driving in and out of that work camp." He shifted on the counter stool. "Just goes to show, no matter how hard you try to protect others—and free will and sin nature being what it is—people still do what they want, anyway."

He knew Sam didn't mean it as a personal condemnation, but he grimaced. "I have no excuses. It only happened once." He blew out a breath. "That's all it takes."

"I don't need details, Josh."

"I know you don't, but if I feel the need to share, congratulations, you're it. And, for the record, I didn't have an interlude with Sheila or anyone else in that TeamWork camp. Only Winnie."

Sam nodded. "Here's something you might find surprising. I've got a confession of my own. Lexa and I came close to giving into physical temptation that summer ourselves."

That was a shock and Josh didn't try to disguise his surprise. "You're right. I find that incredibly difficult to believe." Almost impossible, in fact.

"I'm sure Beck filled you in about the night Lexa and I went searching for Sheila. There was a gun, a mission, ropes, Howard taking Lexa with him to get the little girl . . ." He waved his hand. "My wife was the brave heroine in that whole crazy scenario. She could have been killed. When she put her life on the line, I prayed like I'd never done before in my life. And then when she came back and I knew she was safe, we got caught up in the passion of it all."

"What stopped you?" Personal question, but Sam seemed to be putting it all on the table.

"Lexa. It didn't go very far in the physical sense, but I'm sure I don't need to explain my thought process. In my heart, I was there. As strong as I always tried to be in guarding myself against physical temptation, I wanted her that night. She thinks I would have put the brakes on eventually, but I guess we'll never know. For the first time, I fully understood how you and Shelby were so tempted. My point being it was possible another child could have been conceived in the TeamWork camp that summer . . . if it hadn't been for Lexa thinking straight for both of us."

"Thanks for telling me, Sam. It actually makes me feel better. You have quite the reputation to live up to, you know."

He shrugged. "In a lot of ways, that year-long TeamWork mission overseas was a good thing." He drained his water, putting his cup on the counter. "The Lord has blessed the fact that we waited. You're the only person I've told and I'd like it to stay that way, but I don't want it to sound like a personal indictment against Winnie by any stretch of the imagination."

"Of course not."

"I realize her situation was different from Lexa's," Sam said, "but both of these women are orphans in terms of family. I can't say I fully understand what it was like for her growing up without the support and encouragement I've always had, and like you've had from your mom, dad and Rebekah."

"Right." Looking up, Josh met his good friend's sympathetic gaze. "No one should suffer like that from people who are supposed to love and protect them. Do you know if what Winnie suffered from her family went beyond emotional abuse? Was she hurt physically in any way?" If anyone knew the answer other than Winnie, it would be Sam and Lexa. As it was with Chloe, he felt a burning need to know.

Sam shook his head. "To my knowledge, it was neglect as much as anything else. I think the only one who really cared for her was a grandmother, but she died when Winnie was in her early teens." Sam put one hand on the top of the counter, appearing to weigh his words. "We all need that touch from someone else to let us know we're cared for, that we're valued. *Loved.* It was sin, yes, but you gave that kind of love to Winnie."

"But then I went and blew everything by my unbelievable stupidity." Josh looked away and ran his hand through his hair.

"Don't even go there." Sam's eyes were bright. "That's in the past. You're the same faithful, loving, God-honoring man I've always known."

Josh's eyes filled with tears. "I hate that I missed out on the first word with Chloe, the first steps, all those things."

Sam leaned closer. "I understand, but can you honestly look me in the eye and tell me you would have been ready for parenthood four years ago?" He sat back, crossing his arms. "Look, I understand it's a lot to swallow, knowing Winnie's kept this from you. In your shoes, I'm not sure how *I'd* react."

"As I told Winnie, I'm the last person to point the finger of blame. I've made so many mistakes in my life that I have no business criticizing anyone else. The way I look at it, we move forward from here. It'll be an interesting journey, but we'll make it work . . . however it's meant to play out."

"Enjoy the ride, brother. Winnie's a great mother and one of the strongest women I know. When some of the ladies in her church found out she was pregnant, they basically told her she wasn't welcome, including the woman who'd taken her under her wing and counseled her. It broke her heart, but instead of turning bitter toward God or anyone else, she started co-teaching a Sunday school class in our church for single moms with the full blessing of the leadership, me included. She carried her child to full term and brought her into the world, knowing they'd both have an uphill battle. Winnie has one of the most tender souls I've ever known, which is all the more surprising considering her background." The corners of Sam's mouth upturned. "Chloe's a dead ringer for her mother, and I'm not just talking physically. She's an incredible child."

"She inherited some of Winnie's best qualities from what I can tell." Josh blew out a breath. "And now I have to go back home to Louisiana soon and try to figure out what to do."

"You can't expect to rearrange your life overnight." How he appreciated the concern in Sam's voice, the compassion in his expression. "You need time to adjust, and so does Winnie. Because of her past, she's fiercely protective of

Chloe, and she's not going to let anyone—not even you—into her daughter's life without a lot of prayer and careful consideration. My advice, if you want it, is not to make any rash decisions and pray about it. Trust me, if there's one thing I've learned from being married, it's to leave the line of communication open. You know our door is always open. Come as often as you need, stay as long as you'd like. Hang onto that door key. You're going to need it."

Josh nodded. "Next thing I know, Winnie and Lexa will be running a bed-and-breakfast."

Sam laughed. "Don't even suggest it, my friend." He put the glass in the sink and walked the newspaper to the recycling bin in the corner of the kitchen. "Lexa and I are taking Joe for a spin around the neighborhood and then heading out to get a bite to eat. Care to join us?"

"No, thanks. I'll probably just stay here. Maybe do some work, maybe just . . . absorb."

Sam nodded. "I understand. For what it's worth, I'm glad you finally know. Lexa picked up the phone a couple of times to call you, especially when she knew Winnie was feeling a little overwhelmed by it all. We both knew she would tell you eventually, and it was *her* place to tell you, not ours." He came back to stand by the counter. "I'm glad you've been able to stay most of the week, knowing how busy you are and dedicated to your work."

Josh's eyes narrowed. "This is what you were talking about in your office, isn't it?" Sam watched, but said nothing. "About having faith that God can take my sin and turn it into my greatest blessing." His eyes misted again. "You told me that's where I'd find my redemption."

When a tear rolled down his face, Sam retrieved the tissue box.

"Thanks." He plucked out a few and pressed them against his eyes. Finished a moment later, he half-laughed. "You tell any of the TeamWork guys I've cried in your presence, I might just be forced to silence you."

"No worries. It stays right here, between us."

Josh wiped his eyes again and looked up at Sam. Next to his dad, he was the strongest man he'd ever known. "Who could have guessed I'd find my redemption in a little girl named Chloe?"

CHAPTER NINETEEN

Friday, Early Evening

SLIPPING INTO THE Friday night teen worship time, Rebekah saw a couple of the girls waving her over to sit with them. The musicians were already playing at the front of the gym and she heard Kevin's distinctive tenor voice. She exchanged a few whispered words with the girls and settled into her seat. He was in his element on stage, and she recognized the song as one he'd written a few months ago. She closed her eyes, listening, humming the catchy chorus under her breath. *Your eyes reflect the sunshine, your lips the wonder, your heart the spirit of His love . . . how many times and how many ways can He reveal Himself in you . . .*

One of the girls nudged her arm. "Did Kevin write that one for you?"

Rebekah was saved from answering when her friend shushed her. "Of course, he did."

At the end of the song, amid the applause, Kevin moved to the front, speaking into the floor microphone. He strummed his guitar as he said, "The praise songs are great, but there's nothing like the old, familiar hymns to get my heart pumping. There's a reason they've been around so long and I want you to really listen to the words of the next few we're going to sing. Join in if you know them, and meditate on His word. Let's raise it up!"

Rebekah looked around the gym as a lot of the kids joined hands and sang along with the band. The girls on either side of her grasped her hands as they all sang along to "Amazing Grace," "I Stand Amazed" and "The Old Rugged Cross." She caught their smiles and it warmed her heart. She'd always preferred the hymns, but knew how much these kids liked the blended styles.

At the end of the time of worship, Kevin pulled the strap over his head, leaving his guitar on the makeshift stage. He walked to stand on the side of the gym with some of the other musicians, leaning close to listen to what Mandy, one of the girls from the band, whispered in his ear. No matter how innocent, Rebekah didn't like it. Kevin was smiling, but his eyes were trained on the speaker. It was the look on Mandy's face—combined with the big eyes, beaming smile and especially the hand on his arm—that disturbed her. Shifting in her chair, she tore her gaze away. She had no claims on Kevin. If some other girl wanted to flirt with him, that shouldn't bother her. But it did. Turning her head his way again, she didn't see him. The whisperer was nowhere to be found, either. Disgruntled, Rebekah looked around the room before slumping lower in her chair.

"Looking for someone?"

Her eyes widened as Kevin slid into the chair to her left. The girl who'd occupied the seat until a minute ago now sat on the row behind them. "Hi there."

"It's my turn to say this is a nice surprise. First time here?" He kept his voice low.

"Yes, as a matter of fact. Thought I'd see what all the fuss was about. Heard the band was pretty good."

He laughed under his breath and focused again on the speaker at the front while she did the same. Forty minutes later, Kevin excused himself to go pack up his guitar after first asking her to wait for him. Rebekah talked with a group of the girls, laughing at their funny stories about everything from parents to boyfriends. A couple of them asked for her advice. She liked that they asked and seemed to value what she told them.

"Want to go grab some dessert?" Kevin asked, rejoining her a few minutes later, guitar case in hand. From the corner of her eye, she noticed some of the teen girls eyeing him with giggles and smiles.

"If you have time. I know you didn't expect me, and if you have to be at the lumberyard early—"

"I'm working in the store tomorrow and don't have to be there until nine. That means I can sleep in until at least seven. You're worth lost sleep." He frowned. "Not sure that came out the way I intended."

Bless his heart, he looked genuinely concerned. "It's okay, I know what you meant. Let's go get that dessert."

They agreed to drive separately and meet at a local restaurant known for their homemade praline cheesecake. As they headed out of the church, Rebekah listened as Kevin exchanged smiles, waves and a few words with a number of the other guys. Mandy waved to him and gave her a slight nod. Kevin held the door and she inhaled the sweet scent of the flowers planted along the front entrance. She reached for his hand and her heart skipped a beat as—for an odd, fleeting moment—she worried he might reject it. Wrapping his hand around hers, Kevin squeezed. That squeeze gave her more reassurance than he could know.

After ordering a slice of cheesecake with two forks and hot tea for her and coffee for him, Kevin asked about her mom and dad. So thoughtful, this man. Adam asked about her parents often, but he'd only met them once over dinner. Considering they didn't say much afterwards, it wasn't a stretch to say they weren't too impressed. She could practically feel the squall of relief floating her way when she turned down Adam's marriage proposal. Josh told her their dad was irritated because he hadn't asked his permission to marry her. That and the fact they'd only dated for two months at the time.

Noticing Kevin watched her closely, Rebekah focused on their conversation.

When the server brought their dessert, he moved to the chair beside her. *He didn't ask me if it's okay like he usually does.* That made her smile. Taking her hand, he said a prayer and motioned for her to try the first bite. They talked as they ate, taking turns. He didn't try to feed her, and although comfortable, tonight didn't *feel* like a date. None of the quiet flirting or loopy grins were in place. She didn't understand how much she missed it all—until now. As he finished the last bite, Kevin's smile sobered. *Oh, oh.* Her heart started beating faster and she stared at her lap for a long moment, wondering what he'd say. She sensed he wanted to talk with her about something.

"I have a question for you," he said.

"Okay." She tried to keep her voice calm. "I'm listening."

"I want your straight answer."

She nodded, her heart sinking. *He knows.*

"Are you going to London with Adam Martin?"

Her eyes widened. "What makes you ask *that*?"

"Straight answer, Rebekah."

"No. I'm not going to London with Adam."

The relief on his face made her feel horrible. It was the direct answer to his question, but she couldn't keep up with her juggling act any longer. Josh was right. It wasn't fair to Adam, wasn't fair to Kevin.

"Confession time. When I came to the school, I saw the entry on your calendar. It was on your desk. The one with the big red circle around it."

When she stared at him, not speaking, he continued. "It said something about a trip to London Bridge and had the initials A.M. beside it."

"Oh, you dear, sweet, silly man. Give me your hand. Come on," Rebekah said when he looked at her with a raised brow. "Please, Kevin." Reluctance was written all over his face, but he did as she asked. "I'm so glad you told me." She rubbed her thumb over his knuckles. "Yes, I'm going to London Bridge, but remember, it was moved to Arizona a number of years ago. I'm going to *Arizona*, not London. A.M. stands for *Anne Morgan*, another teacher at my school. We're planning a trip sometime next fall. I'm sorry I didn't mention it to you before, but there was really no need."

It surprised her when he still looked pensive, his brows knitted together. "Is Adam still in your life?"

She swallowed hard, the words caught in her throat. "Define—"

"Just answer the question, please. It's pretty much a yes or no kind of thing."

Her eyes welled and she looked away.

Kevin withdrew his hand. "Well, then, I guess that's my answer." He threw his napkin on the table, but stayed in his seat.

"Yes." It was barely more than a whisper. The look on his face sent an arrow through her heart. He clearly felt betrayed. But why should he? It wasn't like he'd made a commitment to her.

"So, you're seeing both of us." To his credit, he kept his voice low, controlled. "Adam asked you to marry him before the trip to Montana, and when you came back home, you turned him down."

Crossing his arms, he waited until she gave him a silent nod. "Which tells me he's either back in your life or else you never stopped seeing him. Which is it?"

"When I turned down his marriage proposal, Adam agreed to continue dating, but on my terms. I liked him, but I hadn't known him long enough when he asked me. I started seeing him long before you and I started dating." She sounded as miserable as she felt. *Although I've known you a lot longer. You just didn't ask.*

"You're telling me *I'm* the other man in this scenario?" Kevin's inner turmoil was obvious. "I never would have started this relationship with you if I thought you still had ties to another man. That breaks an entire moral code—not to mention ethical boundary—I wouldn't cross."

She nodded slowly. "I know." The words were barely audible.

"Then why? Why did you lead him on? Lead *me* on?" His eyes shot fire as he glared at her.

She wouldn't have believed him capable of such a steely look. "I certainly deserve that question," she said, wanting to sink into the floor.

"And do you have an answer?"

"Kevin, it took you a long time to finally work up the nerve to tell me how you felt and ask me out. I love spending time with you. You're one of the most honest and humble people I've ever known. The *best.* I didn't intend to lead anyone on, and I hate the thought that I've hurt you." She paused, taking a deep breath. "The truth is, I haven't made any kind of commitment to either you *or* Adam."

"So you didn't want to disappoint me by telling me he's still in your life? Tell me this," Kevin said, waving away the waiter, "where do things stand now in your relationship with him?"

"He . . ." she said, not sure how to answer. She winced. *Might as well get it all out now. Confess.* "He wants me to meet his family."

Kevin's eyes widened. "So he *has* asked you to go to London with him? As in England—just so we're clear it's not any other London."

Rebekah cringed. "Yes."

"Okay, then, I have to ask this next question."

"Go ahead." She could barely look him in the eye.

"If I asked you not to go to London with Adam, what would you do?"

"Are you asking me or are you telling me not to go?" Her evasion tactic was annoying enough to herself, so it had to grate on his nerves. Even Kevin only had so much patience. Still, it was a valid question and an important distinction.

"Don't. Go. It's a request from the deepest part of my heart."

Rebekah hesitated for a moment and that was all the impetus Kevin needed as he stood to leave. "Kevin, sit down. *Please.*" She didn't care he heard the desperation in her voice. "I'm not going to London with Adam. I didn't need you—or anyone else—to tell me it wasn't the right thing. I discovered that all on my own."

Kevin swallowed hard. "If you went to London with him, Rebekah, I fear my heart would never be the same."

She felt as if a little part of her heart was separating as she looked at him, eyes wide. "That's what you meant by telling me not to go, isn't it?"

He nodded. "I misunderstood the situation, but as it turns out, maybe it was the same thing all along."

"What am I doing?" She didn't expect an answer. Wiping aside tears, she bit her lip to keep from erupting into a full-blown sob.

He shook his head and gave her the sweetest, most loving look imaginable, as if his anger subsided and faded away, along with her tears. "I won't allow you to break my heart, Rebekah."

She dabbed at her eyes with a tissue and snapped her head up, surprised. "Are we okay, then?"

"We're fine. But here's the thing."

Rebekah nodded, not sure she wanted to hear what was coming. Kevin had his own terms, it seemed.

"Until you resolve things with Adam one way or the other, it's best if we don't see one another . . . romantically. It's not what I want, but it's the honorable thing to do. I'm going to step aside until you make your decision. Pull myself out of the running."

When he looked into her soul with that blue-eyed gaze, she felt loved beyond measure. "It's not a competition."

"Isn't it?" He didn't flinch, but she did.

"Kevin, if you asked me to go to London, asked me to go pretty much anywhere with you, I wouldn't hesitate." She didn't know it until that moment, but it was the truth.

"Like I said, let me know when you make your decision." His eyes bore straight through her. "One way or the other."

CHAPTER TWENTY

Friday, Late Evening

"KEVIN KNOWS."

Josh fished his keys and wallet out of his pocket and tossed them on the bed. It had been a long day—without Winnie. He was emotionally spent and not up to this conversation, but he couldn't disappoint Beck. She'd always been there for him. "I'm listening."

Rebekah sighed. "Thanks for not being all big-brotherish and saying *I told you so.*"

The catch in her throat got to him like it always did. Closing his eyes, he sat on the edge of the bed and kicked off his shoes. "Anytime. Tell me more." He listened as she talked, sobbed a little, talked some more, then sobbed again. When he could get a word in edgewise, he sympathized and murmured appropriate words of encouragement.

"To make matters worse, there's a pretty blonde who plays in the praise and worship band with him, and it was more than obvious she's got designs on Kevin."

"Designs?" Josh stifled his chuckle. "No offense, but have you been reading Mom's old Christian romances again?"

"No. You know what I mean. As soon as that girl finds out about this, she'll probably swoop in and—"

"Hang on a minute. First of all, Kevin doesn't strike me as the type of man to go around telling people you're broken up or whatever. And, trust me, no woman is going to swoop in and steal his heart without knowing him, oh, at least three years or more."

"Not now, Josh." He might have pushed the limit with that one. The exhaustion in her voice made him frown.

"I'm not making fun of him, honey. I'm trying to make a point here. Look, the biggest part of your problem with the guy is that it takes him a long time to make a move of any kind, much less a commitment. But I'm telling you if Kevin can't make one to *you*, he's not going to make one to some girl in his band until things are resolved with you, one way or the other." She wouldn't like that last part, but it was the truth.

Long pause. "I know. That's pretty much what he told me." She sounded defeated. "I feel awful. It's my own fault for leading him on when I was still seeing Adam, but I was afraid if I didn't go out with Kevin, he *would* turn to someone else." Another small sob escaped. "Now, I've gone and made things an even bigger mess. Tell me the truth. Am I a terrible, selfish person?"

"Not by any stretch of the imagination. You're just young and confused." She didn't make a comeback at his lame attempt to make her smile. Propping the pillows, he reclined against the headboard. "If you think about it, Kevin didn't say goodbye. Look at it this way: he's biding his time."

"Wh . . . what do you mean?" she asked, in between more sniffles. He wished he could give her a hug. He could use one himself.

"He's waiting to see what happens." Waiting for the Brit to mess up was more like it, but he couldn't say that to Beck. Maybe that was unfair since he'd never met the guy, but it seemed inevitable. Kevin was smart and intuitive and had to know sooner or later Adam would either do something ill-advised to blow it with Beck, or else she'd wake up and see Kevin for what he was—the love of her life. Call it gut instinct, but he was usually right where his twin sister was concerned.

Rebekah asked him how things were going with Winnie and whether they'd shared any more special moments. He gave her the basics but played it off like everything was fine and his world hadn't been shaken to its core in the last twenty-four hours. News like this needed to wait until he could see her in person. Although he itched to tell her, he still had to get used to the idea himself. He also needed to tell his parents. This would shock them, and they thought they'd heard it all.

"Beck, let's meet for dinner one night this week."

"Sure. Name the when and where." He smiled when he heard the lift in her voice. No matter how hectic things were at the office—huge merger or not—he always made time for family. More and more, he questioned whether the corporate world was where he belonged. He was good at it, but his heart wasn't in it.

"Thursday night. Olive Garden. Seven sound okay?"

"I'll look forward to it. Thanks for listening as always. Love you and see you soon."

This time, he let her have the last word. He doubted she even noticed.

~

"Tell me more about Chloe." Josh reclined on the bed, fully stretched out with one arm crossed behind his head. After resting for a couple of hours, he called Winnie, the need to hear her voice overpowering. "I want to know everything."

"That's a pretty tall order," Winnie said. "Maybe it's a good thing she's only three."

The amusement in her voice made him smile. "Four in less than two months," he said. "Wait. Back up a minute. Tell me about your pregnancy and Chloe's birth." His voice lowered. "Was it hard for you?" He hated to think she'd been alone, wished he could have been with her.

"I had a little morning sickness, but it wasn't bad. The delivery was long and arduous, but no complications, thank the Lord. She was born here in Houston."

"Who was with you? Did you have one of those birthing coaches?"

"Amy and Lexa were with me, standing on either side, holding my hands as Chloe kicked and screamed her way into the world." One of her trademark giggles escaped. It did his heart good. At least she sounded much more even keel and like herself again. "I'm glad I didn't scare Lexa from having a child, and Amy's tough enough to handle anything."

The Amy he'd known wasn't so tough, but Beck told him the same thing. Working in the cut-throat world of New York publishing probably had a lot to do with Amy's burgeoning confidence. "Chloe really screamed?" He found it difficult to believe that sweet little girl was capable of such a thing. *My little girl.*

"You'd better believe it. I'll admit, I was a little worried at first when I heard all the power in those tiny lungs, but I knew she was healthy and that was the most important thing."

"We'll just have to channel it into voice lessons. I'm thankful you weren't alone."

Winnie's sigh was audible. "Are you sure you want to do this, Josh?"

That question made him sit up on the bed. "What do you mean?" He tried to keep the irritation from his voice. Now that he knew about Chloe—now that he'd seen her, talked with her and fallen head-over-heels for her—did Winnie believe he'd shirk his parental responsibilities? It was about rights, too. She knew him well enough to know he'd want to be a big part of Chloe's life. If anything, he was more determined to find out everything he could about his daughter.

"It's a big step. I've been fine on my own and I don't want you to feel obligated. I'll forever be grateful and indebted to you."

Grateful? Indebted? Not words he wanted to hear. He pinched his fingers on the bridge of his nose. Anger with Winnie never entered the equation . . . until now. She might not have any expectations, but he sure did. Counting to five under his breath, he prayed for the right words. "I didn't plan on this, but I need to see you. Tonight. This is not a conversation we should be having on the phone."

"Why don't we just go back to the questions and answers."

Don't let her change the subject. "I'm coming over. I'll be there in twenty minutes. You'd better answer your door, or I might just have to break it down."

"When you put it like that, do I have a choice?" She sounded irritated now.

That makes two of us. It might be best to wait and have this conversation in the morning, but he wouldn't get much sleep as it was. "Not really. It's too important."

She sighed. "We don't have to make any life-changing decisions tonight. Like you said, you need time to absorb all this. So do I. It's too soon and I don't want us jumping into anything we'll regret."

Josh's jaw muscles flexed. Now she'd done it. Didn't she know it was torture going the entire day without talking to her? *Did she think about me at all today? Want to see me?* Shoving his feet in his shoes, he tucked his shirt in his jeans. "I, for one, am not going to regret anything. You might not have thought about *me* today, Winnie, but you and Chloe were all I could think about." He tried to work several times, but couldn't concentrate. Started e-mails he couldn't finish. Went to meet Sam for lunch and fended off Bennie when she handed him her daughter's phone number. At least he'd taken care of that one and told her he was taken. It wasn't just an excuse. It was the truth. *Now, I need to convince Winnie.* "I'm coming over. Be ready." He closed his phone before she had the opportunity to tell him not to come.

Darting into the bathroom, Josh finger-combed his hair and brushed his teeth. As he drove the short distance to her apartment a few minutes later, his mind raced. Without question, he'd need to tread carefully. It's not like he could invade Winnie's world and rearrange her life according to his terms. She didn't work that way. She was fiercely independent and protective of her child, as well she should be. It was one of her best qualities. No doubt they'd butt heads over certain things down the road, but they'd take it one step at a time.

While he agreed they shouldn't make any big decisions tonight, he didn't like how she sounded almost resigned to being a single mother. That wasn't the way his thinking was headed.

Pulling into the parking spot next to Ladybug a short time later, he whispered a prayer. *Lord, give me the right words and curb my tongue. I don't want to push her further away.*

~

Josh sat in his car without getting out for a couple of minutes, his head bowed. In her heart, Winnie knew he was praying. Just as she'd been doing ever since his call. She opened her door before he could knock, giving him a small smile as he stepped through the doorway, ducking his head. He wore faded jeans that fit him to perfection and a green polo. *No fair with the secret weapons.*

Closing the door, she caught him staring at her. Before she knew he was coming over, she'd changed into a pair of her most well-worn jeans and a faded TeamWork T-shirt. If he wanted to talk to her, he could talk to her "as is." Not that she didn't want to look nice, but he might as well get used to the "real" Winnie, the way she normally dressed at home. Judging by the look in his eye, maybe she should rethink it. He didn't say anything for a few seconds. She'd taken a shower after dinner and hadn't bothered smoothing her hair. Josh appeared fascinated by her natural waves. *Maybe I should wear it this way more often.*

"Thanks."

"For what?"

"Watching for me by the door." His lips curled. "If that's what you were doing."

"Well, I was afraid you'd break down the door otherwise. I didn't want to frighten Chloe."

"Idle threat. Sorry for sounding so abrupt on the phone. May I please sit down?"

"Of course. It's the least you can do after barging over here." She ignored his smirk. "Let's go into the kitchen. Did you have anything for supper?"

"Actually, no," he said, shaking his head. "To be honest, I didn't even think about it. Sam, Lexa and the little guy went out somewhere, but I . . . wasn't hungry." He followed her into the kitchen and sat at the table.

"Chloe and I had broiled chicken and vegetables. Let me get you a plate."

"Thanks. That would be great," he said with a grateful glance. "Can I help?"

"No, just stay where you are."

He looked around, tapping his fingers on the tabletop. "Chloe in her bedroom?"

Winnie gave him a look. The man was clueless, something she found rather endearing. He must not know anything about a child's bedtime, or else he'd forgotten it was almost ten at night. "Poor kid. She played hard today and practically fell asleep with her head on her plate during dinner." Pulling a few plastic food containers from the refrigerator, she put them on the counter. "You know, the Lord never ceases to amaze me the way He works sometimes."

"Yeah, I thought the whole guppy kiss thing was pretty cool."

A giggle slipped out before she could stop it. In a way, it was good he could be calm enough and lighthearted for both of them. It put a more normal spin on this whole scenario since it was decidedly surreal. She portioned the chicken and broccoli onto a plate. "Care to guess what one of her recent words was?"

"I have no idea. Tenacious?" His smile flipped her insides around. Better to look away. She'd already caught the way he watched her, and how he seemed to like the way she was dressed and her hair in its natural state. Maybe she should go change into her robe.

"Something tells me she'll learn that word soon enough, especially if . . ." She let that one dangle in the air between them. "Believe it or not, one of her words was 'grant.' As in a scholastic grant. But still," she said, feeling that dreaded flush invading her cheeks, "it was a grant all the same." *Why did I even bring it up?* She sounded like a bumbling fool again.

"Care to share what your definition was for that one?"

Okay, Lord, way to be subtle. "I told her it was something given to someone. Like a gift." She scooped mashed potatoes from one of the containers and plopped them on his plate. Using more force than she intended, a little landed on the kitchen floor near her feet.

"Allow me." Grabbing a napkin from the table, Josh stooped down beside her and wiped it off the floor. Rising to his feet, he tossed it in the can under the sink when she opened the cabinet. "Do you mind if I go look in on her?"

She considered it while she covered the plate with plastic wrap and put it in the microwave. Maybe allowing Josh into Chloe's room wasn't the best idea, but seeing the look on his face, she couldn't deny him the privilege. "Go ahead. Just don't wake her or you'll answer to me. A word of warning: Mama Bear gets cranky if you wake up Baby Bear. Chloe likes you, but I don't want her scared to death if she wakes up and finds you in her room. Leave the door open and come back out at the first sign of movement."

"Thanks, Mama Bear. I promise to follow the rules." A hint of a grin creased his lips.

"Be sure that you do." Their gazes held and locked.

~

Turning the knob, Josh peeked inside Chloe's bedroom. Enough moonlight filtered through the slanted blinds for him to make his way over to the side of her bed without stumbling over the scattered toys on the carpet. Kneeling beside the bed, he gazed at his sleeping daughter. *Lord, what did I do to deserve her?* Blonde ringlets hung over her eyes and trailed onto her cheek. Josh lifted the loose curls and brushed them aside. Her skin was warm, her cheeks rosy as a cherub's. Her pouty, full lips curved in a smile, even in her sleep. So beautiful . . . this girl would break many a boy's heart in the future. She'd already brought him to his knees. Chloe's chest rose with the swell of her quiet breathing. She took in a deep, shuddering breath and shifted onto her side, facing him.

Josh muffled the sound of his involuntary cry with one hand. *She turns me into a quivering mass of jelly, Lord. I'd do anything for her or her mother. She already has my heart. Help me do right by her and Winnie.* Putting his hand lightly over hers where it rested above the sheet, he bowed his head and prayed. Lost in his prayer, he didn't know Winnie stood behind him until she squeezed his shoulder. Wiping his eyes, he followed her out of the bedroom.

~

The sight of such a strong man on his knees touched her in places she didn't know she possessed. "I know I'm a proud mama, but she looks like an angel to me when she's sleeping."

"Yeah. She does." Josh watched as she pulled the steaming plate from the microwave.

She carried his plate to the table, along with the silverware. "Iced tea okay?" Casual conversation might be best, at least until she caught her breath.

"That's great. Is it sweet tea? You know that's the only way we drink it in Louisiana."

Winnie shot him a grin. "I'll give you some sweetener in case it's not sweet enough." Half expecting a flirtatious response, she opened a cabinet and pulled out her sugar bowl and some artificial sweetener and put them on the table.

"What's up with Beck these days? Is the numbness in her fingers easing up any?" Getting an extra spoon from the drawer, she grabbed a napkin and handed them to him. As she opened the refrigerator, she welcomed the rush of cool air. She was heated, and it wasn't from lack of air conditioning.

"A little. She doesn't mention it except to say Kevin can always tell, and he massages them for her." He thanked her after she poured a glass of tea and handed it to him. After tasting it, he added an extra spoonful of sugar. "Just the way I like it." He winked and took a long drink.

Sitting across from him, a rush of emotion enveloped her as Josh covered her hand with his and bowed for a short prayer. "Lord, thank you for this new day. Thank you for the unexpected discoveries and blessings you've brought to my life. May I be a worthy servant as Winnie and I seek to honor Your will in all things, especially in what's best for Chloe." His breath hitched and he hesitated for a long moment. "Thank you for this food and bless our conversation tonight that it might be pleasing to you. In Jesus's matchless name we pray." When he raised his head, his eyes were shining. "Amen."

She echoed with her own quiet "Amen." Leaning her chin on one hand, she studied him with all-too-obvious admiration. She needed to stop staring. Drop-dead gorgeous looks notwithstanding, Josh's inner strength and self-confidence made him so attractive. Maybe even more so because he'd been able to triumph over the demons of his past. From all appearances, he'd emerged much stronger. Either that or the man was an uncommonly skilled actor. Still, Josh Grant must collect female admirers every time he left the house.

"Care to share your thoughts?" He paused between bites.

She straightened and cleared her throat. "Not on your life. So, everything's going okay with Beck and Kevin? Are they getting more serious?" A grin curved her lips at the same time his downturned. "Did I say something wrong?"

"No, not at all," he said. "Let's just say their status is debatable at the moment. Beck called earlier."

"It must be wonderful having a sister who's always there for you, always has your back." Winnie knew her expression must look wistful, but didn't care. Because she'd been an only child, she hoped to someday give Chloe a little brother or sister. That was another thing—ever since Joe Lewis came into the picture, she'd dropped hints she'd like to have "one of those" come to live with them.

"You're right. It can be pretty great although we annoy the tar out of each other sometimes." He shrugged his powerful shoulders. "Guess that's normal with most siblings." He took another bite. "I'm sure Beck and Kevin will be fine, but they could use prayer. As much as anything, pray my indecisive sister will wake up and see what's right under her nose." Winnie couldn't miss the way he looked at her as he said the words, couldn't help wondering at any underlying meaning. "Let's just say . . . Beck's a little confused right now. She thinks she's been waiting on Kevin all this time, but if you ask me, he's waiting on her."

That was an interesting insight. "Of course, I'll pray. I'll never forget Kevin's devotion to her in Montana." An involuntary sigh escaped. "Do you mind if I mention it to Lexa?"

"Already done. You know how Sam's always had a soft spot for my sister." Josh's grin returned. "If Beck doesn't come to her senses soon, I might have to send in reinforcements in the form of a six-foot-five TeamWork director to shake some sense into her." Cutting a piece of the chicken and putting it in his mouth, he made a comical face as he chewed. All over again, his smile reminded her of Chloe. Or maybe it was the other way around. "This is delicious. My kudos to the beautiful blonde chef."

The telltale warmth invaded her cheeks as he drained the glass of iced tea in one long gulp. She'd forgotten how much a man could eat and drink. At least she had more of everything if he wanted seconds. "Thanks. I leave the fancy stuff for the catering and keep it pretty simple here at home. Chloe's like most kids and prefers the plain, basic stuff, anyway."

"Nothing wrong with that. Especially when it's this good." He sampled the mashed potatoes and gave her a thumbs-up.

"Next time you talk to Beck, please give her my love. We exchanged Christmas cards, but I haven't talked with her in a few months and haven't seen her since we all got back from Montana." She shook her head. "It's been too long. Maybe we should plan a mini-TeamWork reunion sometime soon?"

"At the very least, I should bring you and Chloe to Baton Rouge and you can visit Beck. I know she'd love it."

Winnie stiffened at that comment and busied herself refilling his iced tea glass. He'd already started making plans. What she felt for Josh was tender and special, but oh-so-fragile. No way could she uproot Chloe's life without good reason or playing the groundwork first. Above all, her daughter's well-being was the most important consideration. "Do you want more chicken or vegetables?" She handed him the iced tea and leaned against the kitchen counter, arms crossed.

"Can't eat another thing. Thank you."

"Welcome." She started for his plate as he drained the second glass of tea.

"Here let me," Josh said, taking the plate over to the sink, setting it inside and running water over it. He had a lovely habit of at least trying to be helpful in the kitchen, and he'd been a huge help to her and Lexa at the Red Hat Society dinner.

Pulling him by the hand, Winnie caught his look of surprise. "I'll clean them up later. It's time to go have that talk."

CHAPTER TWENTY-ONE

"I BELIEVE YOU have some questions. Fire away," Josh said, settling himself on the sofa. Seating herself a good distance away from him, Winnie tucked her legs beneath her. He had his work cut out for him. "I get the distinct impression you still don't completely trust me, Winnie. We need to talk about whatever it is you're struggling with as far as I'm concerned." Might as well state his case. "I'm sure it's pretty obvious I'd like to pursue a relationship with you. A relationship that has nothing to do with indebtedness or gratitude."

Under his direct gaze, she lowered her lids and, along with it, denied him the pleasure of looking into those gorgeous eyes. He remembered those eyes—bright, shining, trusting. "Please talk to me." *Is she afraid of what I'll see?* He waited until she lifted her chin. Her bottom lip trembled, making him want to pull her in his arms. Instinct told him he needed to keep those feelings in check.

Winnie cleared her throat. "How do you deal with temptation, Josh?"

Fair enough. He'd been expecting that question and she had every right to ask. "I know firsthand what sin does to a man. It took total brokenness to see what I'd become. I won't lie and say I haven't looked at another woman. I wouldn't be human if I didn't, but it's a healthy interest and I haven't acted on it." He stopped. "Until this week." The slight smile curving her lips tugged on him deep inside. "I've been focused on getting my law degree and securing a place in the firm. More importantly, I needed that time to get my priorities straight and reconnect with the Lord." He paused and blew out a deep breath, overcome with emotion. "Sam woke me up by loving me enough to throw me out of the TeamWork camp. It forced me to understand how much I was hurting myself and others. 'In Him we have redemption through His blood, the forgiveness of our trespasses, according to the riches of His grace.' That's the verse I keep going back to, the one that reminds me where I've been and where I stand now."

"I know it well. Did you feel guilty about that night?"

"Not until I started counseling with my pastor and realized how much I'd hurt you, how much my selfishness might have negatively impacted you. As much as anything else, I *missed* being with you, Winnie." He allowed his gaze to roam over her face. She was so lovely, it was difficult to concentrate. "I love your sense of humor, that incredible giggle, and how you always rally everyone together." He turned and leaned his elbow on the back of the sofa, watching as she brushed strands of long, blonde hair away from her face. He'd always loved her hair, and knew the color was natural. It looked so soft, but he resisted the sudden urge to run his fingers through it.

"You were also the most beautiful woman in the TeamWork camp." He touched the tip of her nose. "Still are." He stopped, not sure how to explain. The look on her face was skeptical. *She has no clue how gorgeous she is, inside and out.*

"I was hardly the prettiest girl there, Josh."

"You were to me."

He wanted to kiss her to reinforce his point, and it took everything in him to resist. *Keep talking.* "I didn't feel like I deserved you and I knew I wasn't worthy of your affection. And now," he hesitated, "I'm not sure what I ever did to deserve you or Chloe."

She shook her head. "Maybe that's not something you need to worry about."

One brow raised. *What does she mean by that?*

"I wish you'd contacted me after you left the camp." She fiddled with her hands, looking away for a few seconds before returning her gaze to him. "Then again, I gave birth to your child and didn't have the common courtesy or decency to let you know I was pregnant. We're quite the pair."

"We can make up for lost time, and I need to prove I'm a changed man. I only pray you'll allow me the privilege and honor of being in your life, and especially in Chloe's life." She didn't look like she wanted to run away, so he might as well keep going. *Tell her what's on your mind.* "I'll take whatever you want to offer, but I'd be lying if I didn't say I think we should do the honorable thing." It was a mistake the moment the words left his lips, but there were no do-overs for something like this.

It started with her sharp intake of breath. Those blue eyes grew wide, a fire sparking in them. Winnie pulled away—a withdrawal of mind as well as body. *Way to go. Scare her off.* "You have to agree the Lord brought us together for a reason. I'm talking about both the TeamWork camp, and now here in Houston." He paused. "Sitting here on this sofa, with our daughter in the next room."

A deep frown tugged at the corners of her mouth. "Let me get this straight. You're saying because we spent one night together—no matter how incredible it was," she muttered, under her breath, "we should eventually get married because that's what God must want for our lives?"

Josh nodded. "Yes. Don't you? Especially since we have a child together. You don't want her subjected to ridicule from other kids because—"

"It's a sad commentary that a large majority of kids these days come from single-parent households, Josh. Of course I want the best for her, but—"

"I understand that." He swallowed his frustration.

"Do I even get a say in this? Does Chloe?"

"I'm certainly not going to force you," he said, attempting to slow his breathing and keep his voice calm and even. He wasn't doing a very good job of it. *Why is she so upset?* "At this point, I'm just asking for a glimmer of hope.

Don't you think that might be a possibility one day? Is the idea of marrying me really so repugnant to you?"

Jumping off the sofa, she started to pace. "I don't want you—or any other man, for that matter—to marry me out of some misguided sense of duty or obligation." Her face grew more flushed by the moment as she glared at him, crossing her arms. "You don't owe me anything, and vice versa." She paced some more. "And don't you even *think* about giving me the speech about the consequences of sin or . . . or I might have to throw something at you! Need I remind you, I've been living with the consequences of sin for almost four years?" Her arms dropped. "And it's been the best four years of my life."

"Look," Josh said, standing and moving over to her, "it was a mistake for me to come over here tonight. We've had an emotional week and we're both tired. But I missed you today, Winnie. Missed Chloe. There wasn't an hour that went by that I didn't look at the clock and wonder what you were doing, what you were thinking. I wondered what new words Chloe was learning and wished I could be the one reading a book to her." He stepped closer. "You know as well as I do we have a deep connection. Call it shared history, call it romance, call it sparks, call it chemistry, call it whatever you want." Taking hold of her arms—enough to keep her still but not hard enough to hurt—he forced her to look at him. At least she didn't fight him, and he prayed she knew he'd never hurt her. "Call it *Chloe*."

Staring at the carpet, he gathered his thoughts. His hands slid down her arms, releasing his hold. "You know where to find me if you want to talk," he said. "I'll try my best not to call you or see you, although that's not what I want. Selfishly, I want to spend every waking moment here in Houston with you and Chloe before I go back to Louisiana and I don't have much time left. To be honest, I should have gone back several days ago, but it's like somehow I *knew* I needed to stay. Something kept me here. It's difficult to find out something like this and then stay away. But, like I said, I'll take whatever you have to offer. No more, no less."

Her eyes were wet. "I'm not asking you to love me, Josh." Winnie looked more vulnerable than he'd ever seen her. Her voice was quiet, her lips taut.

"And all I'm asking is the opportunity to *let* me love you." He tweaked her chin. "Like it or not, you and I are tied together the rest of our lives. Now that I know about Chloe, I'm not about to let her go. I'm not going anywhere, and I'm not walking away from my responsibility as a father. You can push me out of *your* life if you want, but there's no way I'll ever let *her* go. That's not a threat. It's a promise." Turning and heading to the front door, he paused to see if she followed.

"I just need time to think," she said, coming to stand beside him. He hated the thought of leaving her and Chloe behind when he went home to Baton Rouge. The whole concept of home didn't make much sense any more. At least getting back into the routine at the firm would restore normalcy and help him regain some perspective. Problem was, he dreaded it all.

"This is all too overwhelming. My quiet, simple life has been turned upside down in a matter of days," Winnie said. When her eyes met his, they softened.

"Tell me about it." Josh moved in before she had a chance to protest and captured her lips, trying to convey with his kiss what his words hadn't accomplished. She didn't push him away, didn't deny the simmering passion beneath the surface as his hands moved around her waist, pulling her to him. Winnie slowly crawled her hands up his chest—a move he knew was uncalculated but did things to him she couldn't begin to comprehend—and moved them to the back of his neck, fingering the curls at the base of his collar. He loved it before, he loved it now. She'd been an innocent in San Antonio, and she was still an innocent in all the ways that counted most.

"Josh." He'd heard about women whimpering and thought it was some silly term coined for drugstore romance novels, but the sound escaping Winnie's lips—still on his—could only be described as a whimper. It was one of the most incredible sounds he'd ever heard, but this needed to stop before his thoughts got carried away any further than they already were.

Trying not to be abrupt, he pulled her hands away from his neck, being as gentle as he could. He stepped back, kissing one open palm and then the other. Based on her reaction, that gesture did something to her. He wasn't sure which of the two of them trembled more, and it wasn't from fear. Desire in human form had a name, a face. For his sanity, he needed to leave now and pray he stayed strong. In that moment, he understood more than ever what Sam meant about geographical distance sometimes being the best thing. Didn't make it any easier, but it was best.

"I've never forced my affections on a woman and I'm not about to start now, but your kiss just now didn't lie." He planted another soft kiss on her cheek. "That one's for Chloe. Goodnight, Winnie."

Although he didn't look back as he opened the front door and walked to his car, Josh knew she watched, hopefully wishing that—one of these days—he wouldn't have to walk away ever again.

CHAPTER TWENTY-TWO

Saturday, Early Morning

LEXA PACED THE kitchen floor and chewed her lower lip. "What do you suggest we do?"

Glancing at the clock on the wall, Winnie noted it was almost seven. They had a full day ahead of them, especially since getting the phone call late the night before imploring them to take this last-minute catering assignment. A huge one that would normally take days—if not a couple of weeks—to plan and execute. The payoff? If they could pull off this event for the large Houston corporation with any degree of success, it had the potential to generate a steady stream of sizable and profitable contracts.

Winnie sighed. "Have a little faith in your partner." Somehow, she managed to sound more confident than she felt. "You know, you've adopted Sam's habit of chewing his lip." Inside, she was quaking, too, but she wasn't about to cave into the pressure. At least one of them needed to stay strong, and it would help take her mind off the whole situation with Josh and refocus her energies. "It's just another job, sweetie. Repeat after me: we can do this."

"But it's so last minute and such a large reception," Lexa said, looking at her as though she'd lost valuable brain cells. "It's official. I've lost my mind. Tell me why in the world did I ever say yes? I've got a baby and a husband and I can't just drop everything in my life to chase some catering job that may or may not be the end of our business."

Winnie smiled and nudged Lexa's mug across the counter. "Do me a favor. Sit down and take a long, slow sip of this coffee. Then take a bite of one of these peach tarts." She took one from the tray and put it on a napkin between them. "They're to die for, if I don't say so myself, and this is the reason we do it." She watched as Lexa took a sip of the coffee and nibbled the tart. "Besides, it'll help pay our bills for a couple of months and bring us more potential clients than we'll know what to do with. That's a good problem to have."

She sipped her coffee, enjoying the last few quiet minutes before they'd start to work with furious ambition. "I feel sorry for the poor caterer who backed out or lost this job. This fiasco is certainly not going to be a coup for their business, but they've called on us, and we need to take the opportunity and run with it. Fly with it and not look back. Think about it," she said, draining her coffee and taking the mug to the sink, running water over it. "The way I see it, it's the best thing that could have happened to get our name out there." Leaning back against the counter, she crossed her arms.

Lexa finished her coffee and the eyes she turned on Winnie were wide, almost frightened. "Promise me one thing."

Winnie nodded. "Sure. Anything."

"We need to hire more help as soon as possible."

They'd talked about it, but the need hadn't been pressing until now. She'd mentioned it to a few of the young mothers at church as a part-time opportunity, but hadn't yet made any firm commitments. Neither one of them had any way of knowing this job would drop into their laps like manna from Heaven.

Lexa's words brought her back to the present. "For now, what do you suggest we do about the party tonight?" she asked. "Should we make some calls to the ladies at church? Promise them anything they want, short of my firstborn?" Her smile looked nervous.

"I'll call Marta and Gayle," Winnie said, forcing a calm into her tone. "I'm sure they'll help out if they can. Cassie might be able to help, too."

"Good idea." The lines of tension on her friend's forehead relaxed. "I know where we can probably find two handsome servers. We just have to treat them real nice and give them lots of loving or whatever they need." She ignored Winnie's withering look. Standing and carrying her mug to the sink, she turned to face her. "Desperate times and all that."

"I don't think so," Winnie said. "Josh and I need some time. I refuse to ask him to help. No way could I pass off something like this without making me sound like a clingy, needy woman desperate for his attention. It's the worst kind of ploy. Do what you want with Sam, but I couldn't respect myself in the morning."

"Oh, get over it. What's to think about?" Pushing her long, blonde braid behind one shoulder, Lexa's hands traveled to her hips. Winnie had seen this stance more than a few times, the stubborn defiance etched into her friend's pretty features. Lexa stared her down, those aquamarine eyes sparking with deep emotion. No wonder Sam could never resist the little fireball. "The way I see it, we don't have a choice today. This is our livelihood." She dropped her hands and turned. "Fine. If needed, I'll beg Sam and *he'll* ask Josh."

Enough talk. It was time to focus on the daunting task staring them in the face. Grabbing her clipboard, Winnie pulled out the notes she'd made after answering Lexa's frantic call the night before. She hoped her scribbles were decipherable since she'd been reeling from Josh's kiss at the time. It was amazing what the man could do with the sheer power of one kiss. Her cheeks grew warm. It wasn't the time to think about that now.

"Please don't tell me you're pushing Josh away," Lexa said, pulling out baking trays. *So, she's not going to give up.* Under normal circumstances, it was one of her partner's best traits. "You can't allow pride to stand in your way, Winnie. Besides, Josh is a peach." She paused, one hand on the refrigerator door. "Everything around here is always about peaches, huh? It's that ridiculous obsession of Sam's. It even has me consumed with thinking about them."

Winnie stared through blind eyes at the list. "There's an awful lot to . . . admire about Josh." She stopped short of uttering the word *love*. "This—whatever it is with him—is still so raw and fresh. I'm not sure at this point how we can even think about a future together."

"Now you're talking complete nonsense. Why not? Give me one good, valid reason."

"Spoken by the woman who could write the book on falling in love in eight weeks or less." Regretting the sarcasm in her tone, Winnie took a deep breath and lowered her voice. "One big consideration is that Josh lives in Baton Rouge. He has a flourishing career as a very successful attorney, not to mention all the good work he does for the community. Plus, his family lives nearby and he likes to fly off for hurricane relief efforts as often as possible."

"Those are just details and you know it." Lexa waved her hand in dismissal. "Mere excuses. You know what I think?"

"Not really, but I don't think I have a choice in the matter." She lowered the clipboard to the counter, pulled out a counter stool and sat down again. "I'm listening. Get it out." She waved her hand. "You won't rest until you do."

Lexa's brows knit together. "I think you want to explore a relationship with Josh, but you're scared to let anyone into your life. You've had to raise Chloe on your own with very little help and certainly no help from a man. You're scared to let him get too close because you're reluctant to relinquish any control over your life, and especially Chloe's. You're doing a spectacular job with her, but you can't be everything to that child. All I'm saying is, don't be afraid to open yourself up to love."

"Well, thank you for that psychological analysis," Winnie snapped. "You of all people know how important it is I don't mess up with Chloe. My childhood wasn't normal by any stretch of the imagination and my primary concern has to be on giving my child what I didn't have."

Lexa stared her down. "Seems to me that should include giving Chloe a stable father figure. After all, Josh *is*—"

Winnie let out an exasperated sigh. "Don't you think I've thought about all that, Lexa? Think about if you had Joe on your own and were raising him without Sam beside you, holding your hand, singing him to sleep in the rocker while you rest." She ignored Lexa's frown at that pointed barb. "Put yourself in my shoes for one little minute and I think you might have a whole different perspective. It's a lot to consider and—"

"No, that's where you're wrong."

"About which part, exactly?" They stared at one another for a long moment.

"Whoa! Do you two need a referee?" Sam pushed open the swinging door, yawning, still in his sleep shorts and T-shirt. "I could hear you from the living room." His newspaper was rolled in one hand, his glasses perched on the end of his nose, his hair disheveled. He kissed his wife's cheek. "Morning, beautiful girl."

Winnie turned away, averting her eyes. It was all good and well they felt so comfortable around her to be affectionate and playful, but it stung her heart even more since Josh came to town. "Oh, we're not really fighting, handsome cowboy," she said, sliding off the counter stool and retrieving her purse. Sam looked amused at her use of Lexa's pet nickname for him, but Lexa frowned. *Great, the woman still isn't done.*

"Sam, this is nuts," Lexa said. "Maybe I missed my calling, misread the signs from God or something." She started opening cabinets, pulling out pans and baking utensils. When she got stressed, she went to work, busying herself to keep her mind occupied.

"You didn't miss your calling, but, my earlier psychology comment aside, you'd make my psychologist-of-the-year list any old day," Winnie said, musing aloud more than anything else. "You're actually uncanny at figuring people out, what makes them tick, how their parents warped their lives, that kind of thing. Not that I don't appreciate it." Winnie raised her head as both Sam and Lexa turned to look at her. She gulped. "Did I say that out loud? Sorry." She ducked her head, sat back down and put her purse beside her as she started to work on the list of supplies and ingredients.

Lexa blew out a sigh. "At least in financial planning, I had time to prepare for client meetings and presentations. Things were orderly, planned, and rarely were there unexpected surprises or last-minute panics, but now I get a call at ten o'clock one night, and then we're expected to serve a buffet-style dinner for *two hundred people* the following night?" She threw her hands in the air. "It's madness!"

Sam's smile lines deepened and Winnie shot him a look. Humor would be ill-advised, but somehow the man always knew how to calm his wife. "Lexa. Baby." Putting both hands on her shoulders, he tilted her chin. "This is a job like all the others. You take it one step at a time, and skip a few steps if you can. Call in your helpers early, if they can come. I'll offer my services, and if he's not working, I'm sure Josh will help, too." He darted a glance at the clock on the kitchen wall. "I'm going to grab a quick shower and then come back down, so have your list ready." His look encompassed them both. "Hopefully, you'll have your differences settled by then. Keep in mind I'll probably have Josh with me and I don't think you want *him* to hear your discussion." He paused on his way out the door. "Are those peach tarts I see?"

Winnie waved her hand with a small smile. "Help yourself. I made them especially for you, Captain TeamWork."

"And that's why I love you so much." He winked at his wife as he took one from the tray. "Hang onto her, Lexa. She's a keeper." Murmuring his thanks, Sam popped the tart in his mouth with a sigh of satisfaction before disappearing into the living room.

"Listen, we've only got a few minutes so here's the thing," Lexa said, planting herself beside her at the counter. "I could better understand your reluctance at giving up control if it was anyone other than one of our TeamWork guys, but we're talking about Josh Grant."

Winnie fumbled in her purse for her new tube of lip gloss. Her lips were dry, but more than that, she needed something to do to avoid Lexa's penetrating look. Mrs. Lewis had perfected it. Must have something to do with living with Sam. Not much got past these two.

Lexa stepped closer to where she sat at the counter. "Does this have anything to do with Josh's past?"

Winnie paused in the middle of slicking on the gloss. She rubbed her lips together and shook her head. "You know, you'd think it would, but it really doesn't." She rolled the tube of gloss in her hand before looking back at Lexa. "Josh has been nothing but honest with me and I believe him. He's done his time, paid his penance, all that." Her flippancy quotient was set at high today and the day had barely begun. Turning her head, she blew out a breath.

"Josh is falling in love with you, Winnie. Actually, I think he's already there, and he fell in love with Chloe at first sight, even before knowing—" She stopped and her eyes grew wide.

Winnie's heart skipped a few beats. "You know?" It wasn't really a surprise and, in reality, a great relief to get it out in the open. The last few days had certainly been full of revelations. Definitely a "Dear Diary" week in the annals of her life.

After a long moment, Lexa nodded. "That's why I never had to ask."

"Are you shocked? Disappointed in me?" She released a light groan.

"Banish the thought. How could I ever be disappointed in you?"

"Because—"

Chloe's voice came through the monitor from Joseph's nursery. She'd carried her upstairs thirty minutes ago, still asleep, after arriving at the house, nestling her in the toddler bed Sam recently assembled and set up in the corner of the nursery. Although they didn't say anything, Winnie suspected it was for Chloe. "Joey," her daughter said, "my mommy has a new friend named Mr. Josh. He's sleeping here in your house right now. He's handsome like a prince and he loves my mommy. Then I'll have a family, just like you."

Winnie clamped a hand over her mouth, willing the tears not to fall. "I don't know if I can deal with this today."

Lexa took hold of her hand, squeezing tight. "Sure you can. You're one of the most level-headed, together women I've ever known. I wouldn't ask anyone else to go into partnership with me, you know. Watching you with Chloe the last few years has only made me love you all the more. You're independent and strong and you look to the Lord to help you." Her eyes softened. "I know it can't be easy being a single parent, but you make it look easy. I only hope I'm half the mother to Joe you've been to Chloe."

Winnie leaned into her hug, choked with emotion. How she loved this woman. Lexa was the sister she'd never had, a woman who sometimes seemed her conscience personified. She and Amy were her dearest friends, and she thanked the Lord for them every single day. Together with Chloe, she was so blessed. "Thanks. That means more to me than you'll ever know. But now, it's time to get started." Inhaling a deep breath, she tried to regain her equilibrium.

"One last question."

"What's that?" Winnie poised her pen above the list of ingredients.

That familiar, slow grin creased her friend's lips. "Since when did you start using *strawberry*-flavored lip gloss?"

Busted.

CHAPTER TWENTY-THREE

Saturday, Early Afternoon

TRUE TO HIS word, Adam pulled in front of the house at the precise moment he'd promised. How he must hate airline flight delays where he'd have no control over the schedule. Watching as he got out of the car and strolled up the front walkway, Rebekah smiled. He was wearing khakis with a maroon striped, button-down shirt and navy blue sport coat. Her eyes trailed to his feet. Shiny leather loafers. The only concession to informality was his shirt unbuttoned at the collar. British to the core, at least he wasn't wearing one of those little scarves—an ascot or whatever—tied at his neck. With his dark hair and strong, masculine features, he looked exactly what he was—a dashing British aristocrat.

Adam always dressed to kill, but—except for church—Kevin almost always wore jeans and a workshirt or polo, depending on the season. But the man worked in a lumberyard. She couldn't imagine Adam going to a picnic. He wouldn't be comfortable with the informality or know how to make casual conversation, preferring to skip a picnic altogether and drive to the coast for dinner. Maybe she should invite him to one of her church events. That would be interesting, but she shouldn't have to "test" him. That wouldn't be fair. Maybe it was the discussion with Trina, but she couldn't seem to stop the comparisons between Adam and Kevin. She startled, hearing the rap on her front door.

She opened the door with her best smile, stepping aside for him to enter her living room. "Hi, Adam."

"Oh good. I was afraid you were going to stand there peering at me from behind your curtains all day." Adam chuckled and swept her into his arms after planting a quick peck on her cheek. "My, don't you look absolutely spectacular today, Becks." He was the only person who called her that, along with his lovely endearment, his personal variation on the standard British "love." Lowering her, he took a step back and appraised her pastel pink designer dress and heels with an appreciative eye.

"Thanks." She gathered her things and after locking the front door, Rebekah accepted his hand as they walked down the front walkway. "Hello, Mrs. Michelson," she called with a small wave. Her elderly neighbor watched, holding weeds in her hand. She nodded her head before turning back toward her house, mumbling something unintelligible. As many times as she'd tried to be friendly, the woman seemed to have a permanent scowl of disapproval etched on her face.

As he opened the car door for her, Rebekah gasped in surprise when she spied a bouquet of a dozen yellow roses on the passenger seat. "They're beautiful. Thank you." Leaning into the pungent blooms, she inhaled their sweet scent and smiled. One of the most romantic stories she'd ever heard was how Sam proposed to Lexa at the Alamo with an armload of the yellow blooms in-tow. Snapping out of her trance, Rebekah forced herself back to the present as he climbed into his seat.

"They remind me of the sunshine in your smile," Adam said, caressing her cheek with one hand before leaning back against the driver's seat, watching her. "I'll give you a quid for the thoughts in that beautiful head of yours."

"A quid, eh?" she said, giving him a sidelong grin. "I'm remembering something I heard once about yellow roses. It's a very romantic story, so I'm sure you'd rather not hear about it." She loved yellow roses, although red were her favorite—something Kevin always remembered. Still, the sentiment was there, and Adam's thoughtfulness pleased her.

"Just because I'm a bloke doesn't mean I don't like romance. Remember that," he told her with a meaningful glance as he fastened his seatbelt and made sure hers was secure before pulling away from the curb. It was always disconcerting, yet rather fun, riding in the left seat since the steering wheel was on the right side in his British import. As they drove toward the highway, Rebekah noted how slow the man drove, like an old man instead of a young one with a fancy, high-priced sports car wired for speed. He even planted both hands on the wheel in the ten-and-two o'clock position like in the driver's manual. *People actually do that?*

Adam asked about her week and what was new in her life, never taking his eyes from the road as he listened. Her eyes widened in surprise when he told her about a new London-based project he helped organize to rebuild homes destroyed by recent storms in Wales. "It's somewhat like your TeamWork organization," he said. "Most of the workers are from the local churches in London—a number of them Americans. It's an opportunity to put their Christian faith in action wherever it's needed."

"How wonderful!" She loved that he was part of such a worthy project, and admired his confidence, business acumen and leadership abilities. It was also one of the few times he'd ever mentioned anything about putting faith in action. But *his* faith or the faith of others? She shook her head. Maybe she wasn't playing fair.

He smiled, still not taking his eyes from the road. "I thought you might like it."

Something about that comment didn't sit right, but she chose not to dwell on it. When she asked him a question about his work, he launched into another familiar how-fascinating-it-is-to-be-an-international-investment-banker story. She'd learned from experience to nod and murmur a "that's nice" or "really?" every now and again. As he drove them down the highway, her thoughts strayed again to Kevin. He was a very normal driver in that big truck of his, safe but not overly cautious. He usually had both hands on the wheel, but positioned lower, and he sometimes reached for her hand when they were on a straight stretch of road. His truck was a necessity in the lumber business since he was always hauling wood around somewhere.

She wondered what Kevin would think about Adam's car. No doubt he'd think it pretentious when the money could be better spent on the investment of a home or some type of ministry. Settling back against the soft, supple leather of the seat, Rebekah sighed. It felt luxurious to be in Adam's car, but she loved climbing into Kevin's truck just as much. She'd never thought much about it until now.

"Where are you taking me for lunch today?" she asked, breaking into his rundown of the top stocks on the Dow the past week. She could tell he was surprised by her lack of manners and rude interruption. "Sorry," she mumbled, sticking her nose in the roses and giving him her best humble pie smile.

"Not a problem. I suppose all my talk of stocks and bonds can get boring for you. We're going to a new restaurant called Limoge. It's French, and I hear it's quite wonderful. I hope that's fine with you, lovely."

The "lovely" nickname was starting to outwear its charm. The first hundred times she'd heard it, it was unique and special. Adam also seemed to have a predilection for all things French, even though she'd heard how some French reprobate cheated him out of something or other when he was in Swiss boarding school. Probably something to do with chess or some other highbrow thing. How the man stayed so fit stymied her since he always turned down her offer to go jogging, cycling or hiking. Maybe she should suggest eating gourmet food while running? When she first started dating him, he'd take her to museum galas and charity events, but their outings in recent months were more infrequent and revolved around lunches in expensive restaurants. If it were anyone else, she'd think Adam was preparing to break off their relationship, but when he was with her, he was more attentive than ever.

Blocking her thoughts, Rebekah closed her eyes, enjoying the smooth hum of the car as Adam wound his way down the freeway, toward Baton Rouge. She felt his eyes on her, but pretended to be a bit tired. Why was it every time she closed her eyes, all she could see were deep blue eyes and a loopy grin? Shaking her head, she attempted to rid her mind of visions of the lumber man. This was her special time with Adam, but she was inordinately distracted.

Pulling up to the entrance, he stopped at the valet station. He stepped out of the car, straightening his jacket while a valet waited. Another valet opened her door, but Adam hurried around the car. "I'll assist the lady," he said, his voice firm. Grasping her fingers in his, he helped her from the car. As he steered her toward the front door, his arm slipped around her back and his hand rested on her waist. She didn't mind although it seemed a bit territorial.

A hostess held the door open, nodding with a smile as the maître d' waited with an ingratiating expression. "Ah, Mr. Martin and the lovely Miss Grant." Rebekah cringed. Was there no other word in the English language people could use? At least they should say it in French in this restaurant. Maybe Adam tipped the man and requested he use it. *Now you're being ridiculous.*

Following behind the maître d', Rebekah stopped in the middle of the restaurant, making a slow turn. It was dimly lit and romantic. The tables were covered with pale linen cloths, arrangements of fresh flowers and a shimmering candle in the middle—in the early afternoon on Saturday. *Where are all the other patrons?* Did he rent out the entire restaurant? "Adam, why are we the only ones here?" Heart pounding, she forced her feet to keep moving. *Surely he's not going to ask me to marry him today.*

The maître d' ushered them to a table for two in the middle of the room. "I trust this is suitable, Mr. Martin."

"Perfection. Thanks, Andre."

Rebekah's eyes widened. *Suitable?* That was one of the more ridiculous statements she'd heard considering the restaurant was otherwise empty. She glimpsed folded currency passing hands before Adam assisted her as she took her seat.

With the candlelight reflected in his eyes, he leaned over and kissed her. "You taste good."

Kevin always said lipstick tasted like soap, and she rarely wore it when she was with him. *Enough with the comparisons.* She busied herself studying the menu even though Adam usually ordered for them both. Her mind swirled with thoughts, not the least of which was how she'd answer *the question* should he ask before the afternoon ended. *Please, Lord, don't let him ask.*

"The wine must match the style of the food," he said after a short consultation with the waiter. She didn't drink alcohol, but he liked to order wine with his meal. She didn't mind since he never overindulged and was always in total control of his faculties. It certainly didn't make him drive any faster. Although she nodded, her thoughts were far away. Seemed to be a recurring thing, this daydreaming. Amy Jacobsen was the daydreamer in the TeamWork bunch, but she'd been doing enough of it herself to warrant the title, based on current behavior.

"Why the frown, lovely?" Adam looked up from his perusal of the menu.

"I missed something at church this morning," she said. "I was tired and couldn't seem to pull myself out of bed."

"I'm sure God understands if you want to skip out on services every now and again." He squeezed her hand before returning his attention to his menu. Clearly, he'd already dismissed the topic.

"It wasn't a service, but it was something special for some of the preteen and teenage girls. I should have been there." Rebekah struggled to maintain her calm since she was irritated with herself, not the man across the table. Still, the words "skip out" rankled her with the implication she'd purposely disregarded the event. She'd signed on for a fun "spa" event at Kevin's church based on I Samuel 16:7 about how man looks at the outward appearance, but the Lord looks at the heart. It had been an important verse her mom taught her the first time she'd been dumped by Jake Mahoney, the high school quarterback who only liked her because she'd been voted Homecoming Queen.

The purpose of the morning's session was to encourage the girls to focus on feeding the soul, helping them understand good nutrition and developing a healthy body image. As much as anything else, Rebekah wanted them to gain confidence in themselves and their relationship with their Heavenly Father instead of trying to achieve what the rest of the world perceived as physical perfection. Kevin knew about her plans and she hoped he wouldn't ask about it. If he did, she'd feel awful telling him she'd "skipped out." As much as she hated the terminology, that's pretty much what she'd done. Even worse, she'd told some of the girls at the youth service she planned on being there. It was a commitment and she'd blown it. She'd tossed and turned half the night, the whole thing with Kevin giving her a whopping headache to the point where she couldn't get out of bed in time. Then again, she had no one to blame but herself.

She lifted her chin and pasted a smile on her face, determined to engage her handsome date in conversation. "So, what delicious dish are you ordering for us today?" Based on his ready smile, that's all it took to capture his interest. How he did love his French cuisine.

"I'm getting to that," Adam said with a wink. "First of all, we'll have an aperitif, of course."

"Of course," she mumbled under her breath.

"I was thinking perhaps leg of lamb with *pommes de terre*—potatoes—*or haricot verts*—French beans would be good. Then we'll have *le fromage*—the cheese platter—Brie, Roquefort and Camembert, followed by a nice *tarte aux fraises*—a fruit-filled tart."

His tone reminded her of the way some adults spoke to children, and that annoyed her. When he ordered for them a few minutes later—in fluent French—she turned her head and blew out a prolonged sigh. Today, his self-confident air came across as pretentious and boorish, although she'd always liked that he took charge. Had he changed? Had she?

As he handed the menu back to the waiter, Adam frowned. "What's bothering the lovely Becks?" He ran his finger around the top rim of his water glass. "Tell me what I've done to irritate you." He looked so earnest that she didn't withdraw her hand when he covered it with his.

"You're wonderful." She forced a small smile. "I'm just out of sorts today. I'm sorry."

He raised his water glass in a toast, locking eyes with her. "Here's hoping this delicious feast will appease that temper of yours."

Temper? Taking a long, slow drink—to quell her temper and all—Rebekah listened as he prattled on about his latest business coup. The little mole to the left of his upper lip garnered her attention, moving up and down every time he spoke. Had it always been there? It was more than distracting. A few days ago, she'd shared a kabob and a potato sack with Kevin. Now she sat in a posh, upscale French restaurant with another man, wearing goop on her face and ridiculous shoes that had already rubbed blisters on her heels.

Adam dropped money for his fancy clothes, meals and trips like he had a limitless supply. Maybe he did. He'd mentioned a trust fund from his grandfather so anything was possible. She'd never seen his home, but she could just imagine what a showplace it was. Why was it—more and more—she had the distinct impression he wanted a token trophy wife even if he had to buy one? Ashamed of her negative thoughts, Rebekah lowered her gaze. "Adam, please tell me you didn't rent this entire restaurant for the two of us. If you did, it wasn't necessary."

Raising his wine glass, he rotated his hand, swirling the wine and taking a sniff before tasting it. Adam the wine connoisseur made an annoying clicking sound with his tongue for a few seconds. With a smile, he nodded to the waiter. "Very good, François. *Merci.*"

The waiter darted a glance in her direction before heading to the kitchen. *François indeed.* She could be mistaken, but he sure looked like Frank from the Albertsons deli where her mother shopped.

"Limoge doesn't open until six on Saturdays," Adam said. "The owner is a client of mine and I made him quite a fair sum of money this week." His gray eyes met hers above the wine glass. "This private lunch for us today is a little bonus—a reward, if you will."

Rebekah wondered if her relief was visible. "Well, that's quite a nice perk, isn't it?" She gave him her best smile and relaxed. She'd been using the words "quite" and "actually" in her daily conversation a lot more lately, the influence of being around him, she imagined. Of course, Josh was the one to point it out. *Has Kevin noticed, too?* As they ate, Adam filled her in on the whereabouts and doings of his family in England. She took another bite of . . . something, but couldn't remember what it was. Experience taught her it might be rather disgusting so perhaps it was better not to know, although today's selections sounded rather benign.

As they finished their meal, she looked up in surprise when he reached across the table. Grabbing her hand, he squeezed hard, a grip of possession. "I know you told me you couldn't go to London with me, lovely, but I want to urge you to reconsider. I'm actually going back in a month or so and I was hoping," he said, catching her eye, "to take you along. Mum's been begging me for ages to bring you round and introduce you. She knows how much I adore you."

Rebekah withdrew her hand and flexed her fingers. Moving them to her lap, she massaged them under the table away from his line of vision. He'd squeezed so hard, her fingers felt numb. "Do you need an answer now?"

"No," he said, shaking his head and giving her an exaggerated wink, "but don't take *too* long. Seriously, I'd very much like you to meet them—and the other way around—and give you the grand tour of London. I know you'd love it."

"I'm sure I would," she said. An all-expenses paid trip to London with a handsome Brit beside her as a tour guide? *Maybe it'll help me make my decision between these two men, but if Kevin found out—especially after I told him I wasn't going to London with Adam—that would kill him.* Even if she dumped Adam after the fact, that would be it for Kevin. The frown returned. *I can't take that chance.*

"Perhaps selfishly, I was rather hoping my new project might entice you to take the leap across the pond, so to speak." He tilted his head, a smile hovering at the corners of his mouth.

That statement brought his earlier comment to mind. "Adam, tell me something."

"Anything, lovely. Name it." He sat up straighter in his chair, his eyes trained on her.

She hesitated, momentarily distracted by how handsome he was. *Focus.* "Tell me why you started this new project. I mean, it's terrific, but I know you already have a number of other worthwhile causes to keep you busy in addition to your investment work."

The slightest frown creased his brow, and he didn't answer right away. Interesting for a man who usually had all the right answers with no hesitation whatsoever. "I want to help others less fortunate, of course, and be able to utilize the resources I've been given in order to benefit someone else."

She nodded. *Very practiced answer, but not the one I need to hear.* "That's very admirable."

Adam didn't speak until she looked up and met his gaze. "Let's just say the primary reason is because it's also an investment in the future, Becks." He reached for her hand again, but thankfully kept his touch light as he put his hand over hers. "A much more *personal* investment."

Not sure how to respond, Rebekah nodded and took a sip of her water, lowering her eyes. She couldn't very well mistake his meaning with that last statement.

Walking beside her, his hand on her elbow as they departed the restaurant, Adam steered her in the direction of a nearby park. They sat on a stone bench and watched several swans on the crystal clear lake. Seeing her shiver and pull her lightweight wrap around her shoulders, Adam put his arm around her, drawing her close.

"I've always loved the swans," she said, watching them glide over the water. "They're so graceful. Serene."

"You're like a swan, you know." Adam tapped her chin before giving her a light kiss. "My beautiful Becks."

"Adam, why do you call me Becks instead of Rebekah?"

Her question appeared to take him by surprise, but as usual, he recovered quickly and gave her a dazzling smile. "It's simply a form of endearment. Not that your given name isn't perfectly—"

"Lovely?" She grinned, shaking her head.

"Don't you like it?" He leaned in for another kiss, but she turned aside and his lips landed on her cheek instead.

"It's fine. I just wondered." She reached for his hand again, squeezing it, and they sat in companionable silence for a minute. "Tell me something else. Do you ever break a sweat? You know, roll up your sleeves and do manual labor?" That sounded ridiculous, but she had an overpowering urge to hear Adam's answer to that one.

He pulled back, wry amusement lighting his eyes and upturning the corners of his mouth. "Another intriguing question. If you'd like, I suppose I could demonstrate my strength by lifting weights for you on our next outing. Or pressing some benches, or whatever it is you do in that health club of yours."

Adam looked away a moment, but she caught his grin and thought he said something under his breath about better ways to work up a sweat. Patting the bench beneath them, he chuckled. "I could offer to lift this heavy chunk of stone to impress you, but I don't fancy breaking my back in the process."

Rebekah shook her head. "This new organization you're developing, the one like TeamWork . . ." She turned to face him. "Can you see yourself getting on your knees in the dirt, using tools and wearing old clothes and—"

"Becks, is this some type of test?"

Her eyes widened. The man was perceptive. "I'm sorry. I didn't mean it quite that way."

"To answer your question, it's not my favorite thing, no, but I've been known to break a sweat on occasion. I own a pair or two of denims and even a T-shirt. Power tools have never been on my Christmas wish list, but if it's something that would make you happy, I'm certainly willing to have a go at it . . . and pray I don't sever something I shouldn't." He met her eyes. "Anything for you, lovely."

When Adam drove her back home an hour later, she looked out the window, lost in thought. She sensed his disappointment when she didn't invite him inside. Her brain was muddled, and she needed private time to think.

"Come give us a kiss, Becks," Adam said, his voice low and enticing, pulling her as close as possible in the confines of the seats of the classic Austin Healey sports car. As his lips moved over hers, Rebekah opened her eyes, staring at that mole. *I must be incredibly vain.* This from the girl who rued the day God made her halfway attractive to the opposite sex. It brought undue attention and complications she didn't want. Closing her eyes, she concentrated on pouring her energies into kissing Adam with the care and attention he deserved. Laughter rumbled in her belly and made its way upward. Eyes wide, she clamped a hand over her mouth.

"I'm trying to be romantic here," he grumbled. "Perhaps you could meet me halfway?"

"I'm sorry." How many times had she already said that to him today? Smoothing her hands over her dress, she didn't dare look at him for fear the sight of that mole would prompt another fit of laughter. "I warned you I'm out of sorts today."

"Well, it's quite obvious you've got something on your mind. Let me walk you to the door." He adjusted his collar and prepared to open the car door.

"No," she said, putting a hand on his arm. "Let's just say goodbye here. I had a wonderful time. It was very special. Thank you."

His eyes met hers, more disappointment evident in the downturn of his lips. "When you're ready to share with me, I'm willing to listen."

"I know." When she put her hand on the car door, it was Adam's turn to touch her arm.

"I do love you madly, Becks. You're a great girl." The way he said it sounded like "gull." Pronunciation aside, he was sincere. At least in his own mind, Adam thought he meant it.

She kissed his cheek. "You're too good to me. I don't deserve you."

He hopped out of the car and hurried to her side of the car, waiting as she climbed out before handing her the bouquet of yellow roses. He kissed her cheek and she spied Mrs. Michelson staring from her living room window. With a sigh, she watched Adam climb back into his car and wave, blowing her a kiss.

Walking slowly into the house, Rebekah thought over the events and conversation of the afternoon. It was true, what she'd told him. Adam deserved someone who loved him. She loved him, but she wasn't *in* love. Big difference. They were talking about two different types of love, and the love she felt for Adam wasn't the marrying kind. At least not now. But could it one day grow into that kind of love? He seemed devoted to her, enough to start an organization like TeamWork overseas. Was it egotistical to think he'd done such a thing with the express purpose of enticing her into marrying him and 'making the leap over the pond' as he put it? It was a wonderful gesture, but whether she should be flattered or pressured was the question. Adam was the type to organize and lead a project; Kevin the type of man to roll his sleeves and do the physical labor. And while she couldn't deny she enjoyed Adam's kisses, they didn't send shivers from her head to her toes like Kevin's kisses always did. *Again with the comparisons.*

Closing her front door, it didn't groan in protest, but *she* did. "Lord, what am I going to do?" She dropped into a chair in the living room, her mind swirling with thoughts as she pulled off her shoes and removed her sweater. Slumping against the back of the chair, Rebekah raised her face to the ceiling and closed her eyes. Saying a prayer comforted her in most cases, but she was so agitated at the moment, she couldn't concentrate. Adam was getting ready to propose again soon; it was as inevitable as their next date being a quiet lunch in another expensive French restaurant. *What about Kevin?* In his case, it might not matter because she'd probably be middle-aged before he'd ever try to . . .

This was pointless. Slapping her hand on the arm of the chair, she rose to her feet with new resolve and padded down the hallway to her bedroom. First, she'd change into her comfiest pair of jeans and her favorite Saints T-shirt. Then she'd do some serious multi-tasking. She could call a few of the girls and apologize for missing the "spa" event, ask how it went and schedule a special brunch. Or, if they were free, they could come over to the house tonight for popcorn and a movie. One thing was certain: she needed to do something to get her mind off the two men in her life. Fat chance of that happening. Still, staying home tonight sounded more promising by the minute.

CHAPTER TWENTY-FOUR

WINNIE HELD THE kitchen door as Cassie Thorenson, Gayle Ferrari and Marta Holcomb piled out of Cassie's Saab early in the afternoon and breezed past her.

"The TeamWork crew to the rescue again. Thanks, ladies. You're an answer to prayer," Lexa told them, grabbing a quick hug from each of the girls. It was amazing she stopped long enough. The woman was an octopus-armed marvel and they'd both been a whirlwind of activity. At times, Winnie paused in her work, watching the braided wonder in action.

Winnie winked at Cassie. "When you signed up for TeamWork, you didn't know you'd be signing up for *this* kind of mission, did you?" The auburn-haired girl with the sweet Alabama drawl had first joined them in Montana, saying Marc and Natalie's was the most romantic story she'd ever heard. Next to Lexa and Sam's, Winnie couldn't agree more.

"A fancy gig at one of the swankiest hotels in Houston? We wouldn't miss it," Marta said. "We've got our server uniforms in the car—black pants, vests and white blouses, just like you ordered—um, requested." She giggled and shot a look at Gayle.

"We've got Doyle-Clarke Catering smocks for each of you, too," Lexa said, already back at work, garnishing appetizers. "Don't let me forget to give them to you before we leave the house later."

Marta swiped a bacon-wrapped sausage and frowned when Winnie slapped her hand with a chastising glance. "What, we don't get to sample? And I thought Mother Hen patted hands, not slapped."

Would she never break free from that nickname? Not that she minded. Winnie gave Marta's cheek a light pinch, feeling a slight twinge of jealousy. She'd always wanted blonde curls like this and the newest TeamWork volunteer's unbelievable, violet-colored eyes complemented her fair complexion and short, tousled curls to perfection. "It's also a Mother Hen's job to keep her impertinent kids in line."

"Okay, ladies, you get five samples each, but that's it," Lexa said. "You can eat later tonight in shifts once all the guests have been served. Otherwise, help yourself to whatever you want from the fridge. Anytime you need anything or have a question, just ask."

"You can't blame us for wanting to nibble," Cassie said with a grin. "Everything smells soooo good in here. It would be torture. We want to be able to rave about your cooking and sampling is the best way." She burst out laughing at Lexa's expression.

"Cassie's right," Gayle said. "Besides, we might be asked the ingredients and need to know what to tell people." Popping something in her mouth, the green-eyed redhead shot Winnie a closed-mouth grin.

Lexa shook her head, but the corners of her mouth twitched as she finished the last appetizer and started on a second tray. "Any excuse will do, I suppose. Knock yourself out, kids."

"Were you able to get some more last-minute help from the agency?" Marta asked as she bit into a stuffed mushroom. "Now, this right here is my new favorite." She licked her lips. "Absolutely delicious."

"The agency promised four servers and we're blessed to get them on a busy Saturday night," Winnie said. "If we can pull this off, it'll be great for our business." Not wanting to consider the alternative, she finished counting slices of caramel cheesecake on a nearby tray. "Let's do everything we can to make this work. Not to mention you'll have our undying devotion the rest of our natural lives for helping us out."

"Always the cheerleader," Marta said, giving her a wink. She headed to the sink to wash her hands, followed by the other two girls. "You'd better give us something to do before Lexa gets after us. She's got that look in her eye."

Lexa laughed and gestured for them to join her in the breakfast nook. "First, we pray, and then you wash your hands. Come on." They gathered in a small circle and bowed their heads. Winnie prayed first and they each said a short prayer, ending with Lexa. "Amen," she said. "Thank you from the bottom of my heart, ladies."

"What happened with the original caterer?" Cassie asked, taking the apron Winnie handed to her, tying it in back and then helping Gayle do the same.

"They had some kind of unexpected disaster with their ovens," Lexa said, setting bowls and whisks in front of Gayle and Cassie. "Here, whisk away." She nodded to Winnie. "Why don't you give them their assignments for this afternoon?" Handing Marta an apron, she led her over to the stove to chop vegetables.

After a quick rundown of instructions and what they could expect throughout the course of the day, Winnie put the clipboard on the counter. "Any questions?"

"I have one," Marta said, pausing her work and looking over her shoulder. "I'd like to meet that tall, blond drink of water I saw out in the living room with Sam. I saw him through the front window when we pulled into the driveway. He's the most gorgeous guy I've seen in ages. Who is he, Lexa?"

Winnie stiffened, and Lexa darted her a look that said I'll-handle-this-one.

"Sorry. Did I say something wrong?" Marta looked from one to the other.

"Of course not," Lexa said. "He's one of our TeamWork volunteers visiting from Louisiana, but we haven't seen him in a few years. He's been busy getting his law degree and building his practice."

Cassie stopped whisking. "Oh, is that Josh Grant? I love Rebekah and was hoping to meet him sometime."

"None other," Winnie murmured, half under her breath.

"The twin, eh? The plot thickens." Marta caught Winnie's glance. "So, I take it he's off-limits?" A coy smile hovered at the corners of her mouth.

"Yes." No one was more surprised than Winnie by the firmness of her response.

She avoided her catering partner's knowing smile as Lexa brought over a tray of empty tarts ready to be filled. "Busy yourself, ladies."

~

Even if Winnie wanted to talk earlier in the day, she couldn't since the ladies were so busy. Josh lost track of how many times he'd thanked the Lord for that other poor caterer's unfortunate circumstances. Although he'd told Winnie he'd stay away, it seemed the Lord had His own agenda. He'd made himself as indispensable and helpful as possible, going with Sam to the wholesale grocer and otherwise staying out of the kitchen. It thrilled him beyond measure when he learned Chloe was in the house.

Together with Sam, he spent a majority of the day taking the two kids to the park, then to lunch, and finally for ice cream at Richardson's where Bea treated him like royalty—especially when she saw him with Chloe. Joe slept through most of it, but Josh took mental notes by watching Sam, asking lots of questions. True to form, Sam answered them all and he caught his smile more than once. The first time Chloe slipped her hand into his, he thought his heart would burst. He couldn't remember anything in his life giving him such a sense of pride. Not the college degree, not the law degree, not his most successful merger or acquisition. By the time they returned to the house midafternoon—mentally and emotionally exhausted—he was ready to take a nap with them until Sam told him it was time to get ready to help the ladies since they'd been drafted into service again.

"You don't mind, do you?" Sam asked.

"Don't even need to ask. This day just keeps getting better." Josh finished buttoning his shirt and darted a glance at his friend, mirror images of one another. He tugged on the waistband of the slacks. "Something about wearing your pants suddenly makes me feel much more powerful, Mr. Lewis."

Sam shot him the kind of wry grin he'd missed the last few years. "Try not to drag them in the mud, will you?"

He laughed. "I'll try my best. How does the bowtie look? Is it straight?"

"I'm not touching it." Sam raised both hands in the air. "Go ask Winnie. Nothing like a woman with her hands around your neck to get the sparks going."

Don't I know it. That was the very image he hadn't been able to shake when he tried to sleep the night before. "It really doesn't take much for you, does it? I hope you and the Mrs. will be able to control yourselves tonight."

"You'll see what I mean," Sam told him with a wink. "Take my advice and go see Winnie."

"I accept that challenge." The worst that could happen was she'd say no and avoid him all night.

Sam clamped a hand on his shoulder. "Let me know how it works out. But first," he said, retrieving a vest, handing it to him, "the last piece of the official waiter wardrobe."

"Aw, man," Josh said. "Why do we have to dress like penguins?"

"Trust me on this one, too," Sam said. "The vest works its own unique charm. Women like to see their men dressed up. They seem to find it sexy for some reason." Catching his look, he shrugged. "I heard it straight from Lexa."

"Lexa would think you're sexy in a brown paper bag." He fastened the cuff link on one wrist. "Winnie has a thing about cuff links. Go figure."

Sam shot him a grin as he slipped into his vest while Josh did the same, standing behind him in front of the full-length mirror.

"You're blocking my view." Josh stepped to the right.

"Only because you're too short."

"Only an inch shorter than you, but you're an Amazon."

Sam chuckled. "I thought Amazons were women."

"I have no idea," Josh said. "Okay, then you're a freak of nature."

"Hardly tall enough to qualify as the runt on most NBA teams."

"But just the right height to fit your gorgeous wife in the crook of your arm."

Josh caught a glimpse of the smile lines.

"That's all I need," Sam said.

"How does this look?" Josh fiddled with the tie, but still couldn't get it right. "Will I pass muster with the caterers?"

"I think you'll pass inspection except for the tie. Take my advice on that one. This should be fun tonight, but be forewarned, they'll keep us hopping. Thanks for being such a good sport. Not many guys would jump in to help once let alone twice."

"Anything to help the ladies. My visit with Winnie last night was a little on the contentious side, so anything I can do to get in her better graces is to my advantage."

"Understood, but don't read too much into it if either Lexa or Winnie bark at you. In fact, they might both bark. Trust me, they don't mean anything by it. You put two highly emotional women in a tense situation after being in the kitchen all day long and anything can happen."

"I don't mind if they bark," Josh said. "If anything, I'll use it to my advantage."

"Come again?" Sam's expression was curious, tinged with amusement.

"I'm sure if you use that active imagination of yours, you can figure out what I'm talking about," he said. "I'm not referring to the whole bark-being-worse-than-the-bite thing. It's simply called leverage, and a little leverage in a relationship never hurt."

Sam nodded. "Right you are, my friend. Ready to go?"

Josh squared his shoulders. "As ready as I'll ever be. Lead the way."

CHAPTER TWENTY-FIVE

LEXA'S DEEP SIGH said it all as she stood by the kitchen window, peering at the sky with a frown. Sam walked behind her, kissing the top of her head and wrapping his arms around his wife at the same time Winnie finished wrapping the last of the entrées in foil. She tuned out their words, but based on Lexa's body language and the way she visibly relaxed, she'd need to add master soother to the list of Sam's attributes.

"Got any more of those little pecks to go around, handsome?" Marta asked. They all laughed as Lexa swatted her with a dishtowel. Sam headed outside with the first load and the other girls followed to the waiting Volvos—Sam's late-model station wagon and Lexa's SUV. Josh came through the doorway and swooped one of the largest trays off the butcher block before heading outside.

"Cassie, keep an eye on the sky and let Sam know if you see the first drop of rain," Lexa said, meeting her husband at the door with another tray.

"Will do," Cassie said with a salute.

"Marta, can you get that tray of appetizers on the counter?" Winnie asked, pulling out the trays of refrigerated desserts. Sam came back in the kitchen to help with the heavier items and the larger trays. She barely glanced at Josh as they passed each other coming and going, but felt his eyes on her. Like it or not, the sight of him was enough to keep her heart singing a good long while. If she stopped and took a good long look, she might not get much accomplished. But . . . too much to do and it couldn't happen.

"Winnie, Josh needs help with his bowtie." Sam nodded toward the hallway as he hurried past with yet another tray.

She frowned. "I just saw him go outside—"

"He did, but I sent him back in here to get his bow tied right," Lexa said, shaking her head. "We can't have sloppy servers no matter how handsome. It wouldn't be good for our image."

Any excuse would do with these two, it seemed. Might as well humor them. Passing by with another wrapped dish, Gayle bit her lip as it trying not to laugh. Great. Now they had the hired servers—TeamWork friends or not—involved in their little matchmaking scheme.

"I don't know the first thing about tying a bowtie." Winnie tossed Sam a glare. "Being of the male persuasion, I'm sure you're much better at it than me." From the corner of her eye, she caught Lexa's smile, but her excuse didn't deter him.

"Okay, then," he said, digging out his wallet. "How about you give him this card?"

Taking the card, she glanced at it. Doyle-Clarke Catering. "He can get one of these—"

"Winnie, just get out there already!" Lexa's patience limit had apparently expired.

She had no words. The Lewis Love Agency was in full-speed-ahead mode tonight. With a sigh, she pushed through the swinging door. Josh stood in front of the mirror, making an attempt to tie the bow. At least it wasn't entirely a ruse. He turned as she walked toward him and gave her one of his signature smiles.

"Josh, have you ever thought of going into politics?"

"Never say never." He raised a brow. "That's an intriguing question. What makes you ask?"

"Not sure. It's just the first thing that popped into my head. I guess it's because you have a . . . well, a certain quality."

He chuckled. "That's what makes life so interesting with you. If I did decide to run for public office, it would be with specific goals in mind." He fumbled with the tie before loosening it and dropping his hands to his sides with an exasperated sigh. "And this is why the clip-on bowtie was invented."

"Tell me about these goals. And no flirting allowed. Turn around, please, and let me see what damage I can do." Straightening the tie, Winnie frowned as she made a first attempt.

"Increased funding for special education programs, social and economic reforms, environmental incentives . . . need I go on?" His smile changed from incredibly charming to nothing short of devastating in the span of a couple of seconds.

She could barely concentrate, but she made another attempt at tying the bow. "I think I get the picture. Just something to think about." Fair or not, this man could get a large percentage of the female vote based on looks alone. She stood back and turned him toward the wall mirror. "There. That should do it. What do you think?"

Looking at their mirrored reflection, Josh smiled. "We look good together, don't you think? Tell me, where did you learn how to do that?"

Thankfully, he ignored her momentary inability to breathe. Good grief, she probably looked like she was in a stupor. Recovering her senses, Winnie giggled. "Is that a compliment?"

"No." He ducked as she swatted him.

"I told them I didn't know how to tie a bowtie," she said with a mock frown. "Sorry. You're going to have to get Lexa to do it, if she can stand still long enough. No man in my family ever had a reason to wear one of these things."

"I was only teasing," he said, taking another look in the mirror. "It's actually not bad at all, but if you think I should get it redone, maybe one of the other girls can do it."

"Not on your life."

"Oh?" He raised his brows.

"Turn around, Josh." Without hesitation, he did as she asked.

Winnie's breath caught. "You look—"

"Like a penguin? It's okay, you can tell me the truth. I've never been overly fond of wearing a tux, anyway."

"You look . . ." She broke out in a big smile.

He tilted his head. "Really good? Or maybe patriotic?"

"Right. All of it." Those words didn't begin to cover it, but she wasn't sure what the word was. Maybe she should ask Chloe. She'd probably just take one look at him and call him a prince again. If Amy was here, she'd be having a field day.

With a slow smile, Josh slipped his arms around her waist. Scary how effortless it was for him, how easy for her to allow it. Knowing she should push him away, she had no willpower whatsoever. "Gorgeous. Now *that's* a word." Borrowed from Marta, perhaps, but true nonetheless.

"I'd prefer irresistible," he said, leaning in for a kiss.

Winnie pushed him back. "Thanks for taking such good care of Chloe today. I've heard all about the park, the lunch, the ice cream." She met his eyes. "I'm glad you were able to spend time with each other."

"She's the best, Winnie." His hold on her tightened. "My compliments to her incredible mother, but Lexa's going to send a search party—or worse yet, Sam—if we don't get back out to the kitchen soon. Not that I want to leave, especially standing here like this with you."

Planting her hands on his chest, she ran her finger over the pattern of the vest. Even though borrowed from Sam, it fit him well. "Did our talk the other night have any impact at all on that dense brain of yours?"

His lips curled. "You tell me. You're the one in my arms with your hands on me." He captured her hands when she attempted to remove them. "Listen, I want you to feel free to boss me around as much as you want tonight. Let me be your servant." His lips were a heartbeat away. "I'm waging my own *personal* campaign here, you know."

"Oh, what are you doing to me?" Playfully turning him around, Winnie marched him toward the kitchen. "Your first command is to help us finish loading everything into the cars." That conversation in her apartment must have been a figment of her imagination. When it came to a man like Josh, even the most steadfast resolutions were meant to be broken.

"What a taskmaster," he said, clearly in jest, "but since you're so beautiful, I suppose I can tolerate it."

"About time," Lexa said under her breath as they moved back into the kitchen, but her expression belied her words. "Good thing Sam's watching your backs or I'd have hauled you both out here a long time ago."

"Easy now, Mrs. Matchmaker," Winnie said as Josh helped Sam with the last of the trays and they headed out to the cars.

Lexa leaned in for a quick hug. "You okay, sweetie?"

Winnie nodded. "Yes. Fine, thanks."

"I have the feeling tonight is a turning point."

"I've thought the same thing all day, in more ways than one."

After another quick hug, Lexa took off to give Joe's babysitter some last-minute instructions as Winnie checked off items on her list. With one last glance around the kitchen, satisfied they had everything, she walked outside. Cassie's Saab was loaded with supplies and she pulled out of the driveway first. Marta was driving Lexa's SUV and had Gayle with her. They waved to Winnie as she met Josh and Sam at the station wagon.

"Guess you're stuck with me," Josh said as Lexa scooted into the passenger seat and Sam lowered his lengthy frame behind the wheel.

This arrangement is a little too convenient. Winnie raised a skeptical brow when she glimpsed the boxes, trays and other supplies in the back. No way could she and Josh both fit without her practically sitting on his lap. She bit her lip and looked the other way. *What am I thinking?* She climbed in first, but then thought better of it. "Since I don't want to be knocked out by a flying hors d'oeuvre, I'll just hop in the SUV and keep Marta and Gayle company," she said, starting to scoot back out again.

"Get *in* already!" Lexa said, but Winnie caught the amused glance between the two in the front seat. "Cassie's already gone and Marta and Gayle just left. You two will have to make do back there."

Somehow, they managed to squeeze in together, but it was a tight fit. Winnie thought she'd go out of her mind with Josh sitting so close. She didn't look at him, but sensed his amusement with this whole scene.

"So, how long do we have to 'make do' together?" he asked, his voice low for her ears only as Sam pulled out of the driveway.

"Depending on traffic, it should take about twenty-five minutes," Winnie said, settling on the seat, trying to ignore the way his thigh lined up beside hers. The most innocuous touch from this man sent her reeling. Oh, yes, she was pathetic in the worst way when Josh was anywhere in close proximity.

"So, Sam tells me you ran Chloe home after her nap," he said, his breath warm on her cheek. "Is Dottie watching her tonight?"

"No, she wasn't available. One of the teenage girls from the church is at the apartment with her."

He frowned, looking none too pleased. "How old is this girl?"

That question surprised her. "Jessica's about fifteen."

"You're not sure? She might only be thirteen and too young to be watching a child Chloe's age. Has she had lifesaving training? Know CPR?"

She stifled her giggle. "Relax, Papa. They'll be fine." *Papa? Well, it's true, after all.*

"Children put things in their mouths," he said.

"Chloe's almost four years old, Josh. Besides, I've never had to worry about her in that way. Trust me, she's fine."

"But she could eat something and choke while Jessica's yakking on the phone with her girlfriends. It might have been better to take Chloe to Jessica's house if her parents are there to supervise."

"Jessica's watched Chloe several times before. She's a mature, level-headed, extremely responsible young lady. I know her parents and her mom is one of my closest friends at the church. We don't have to worry." She shook her head, realizing what she'd just said. *We.* For so long, the sole responsibility for Chloe's well-being and safety rested on her shoulders. This was all happening so fast.

Relief etched itself into Josh's expression. "If you're okay with it then I suppose it's all right. No offense to Jessica, but you can't be too careful. Teenagers are highly . . . distractible."

Speak for yourself. Reaching for his hand, she laced her fingers through his. "You're a very sweet man. And very protective." She yawned and noticed the ever-darkening skies, praying they'd reach the hotel before the rain began. At least the back entrance to the small ballroom had a covered loading area. Her eyes felt heavy, and even though the man beside her stirred all her senses, she was already tired and the event hadn't even begun. Closing her eyes, she said a silent prayer.

~

"Winnie? We're almost there." Groggy, she opened her eyes when she felt a slight nudge on her arm. A loud clap of thunder made her jump. She lifted her head, her eyes widening as she realized she'd been resting on Josh's shoulder. His very broad, solid shoulder. *I hope I didn't drool on him.* Yawning again, she struggled to sit up. "I'm sorry. Did I fall asleep?"

"No, your head just needed a resting spot and your eyes decided to go on holiday for fifteen minutes."

"Sorry. Hope I didn't snore." Her cheeks felt warm and she smoothed her fingers over the top of her head.

"No." Josh chuckled. "You've already put in a full day and obviously needed the short break." He nodded toward the front seat. "Lexa took a catnap and Sam and I talked. She just woke up, too. Must be internal caterer radar that we're getting close or else the thunder woke you both up." He looked at her through heavy lids.

"Josh?"

"Yes?" His warm breath tickled her ear and she shivered.

"You'd better not do that." Lexa and Sam were engaged in an animated discussion—something about Joe, from the sound of it. Thankfully, neither one paid them any attention. On the other hand, it was possible she and Josh might need a chaperone. "You can't help yourself, can you?"

"It's been almost five *years*, Winnie, and it's only because it's you. If you had any idea how much I want to kiss you, you'd understand. You blocked my pass in the hallway, you know."

"Okay, I'll grant you one kiss." Realizing her pun, she giggled.

He cocked his head with an enticing grin. "An appetizer, you might say." His brows drew together. "Okay, that was corny, even for me. I have no excuses, woman. You make me crazy."

"Stop it, already," she snipped in mock irritation. "By the time I'm done with you tonight, you'll run all the way back to Baton Rouge on your own speed."

"Oh, I beg to differ. By the time I'm done with you tonight, you'll beg me to stay." Josh's voice was low, those lips impossibly close.

"So arrogant," Winnie whispered as she raised her face to his, meeting those irresistible lips. Warmth—not the slow-burning kind, but an all-out burst of fire—shot through her. So much so she had to suppress an out-and-out moan. *Oh, my.* It was the most remarkable kiss—tender but passionate, caring yet hovering on the edge of inappropriate. Although it only lasted a few seconds, it left her satisfied but wanting more. Leaning her head on his shoulder, she suspected Josh Grant knew exactly what he was doing.

CHAPTER TWENTY-SIX

Saturday Evening

SAM OPENED THE back door to the hotel kitchen and ducked his head outside. "At least the rain held off." He closed the door and came back inside. "An hour into the party and so far, so good. Enjoy the breather while you can. It's going to get pretty crazy in the next half hour. Our girls have done a remarkable job on such short notice."

Josh smiled at the inference. "Bring it on." A server came through the door, bringing with her the sounds of muffled laughter and music from the jazz quartet in one corner of the room. He caught a glimpse of Winnie near the door. The flash of golden blonde hair and the split-second sight of how great she looked in her uniform with that cute little Doyle-Clarke Catering apron got his heart pumping. The sound of her voice as she instructed one of the servers to take more coffee to table fifteen made him want to rush to do her bidding. Her ability to direct the staff and coordinate such a big event was nothing short of amazing. He'd rather handle five back-to-back mergers or acquisitions than tackle something like this.

Leaning against the counter, Josh returned Sam's smile. "Seeing them in action, I have all the admiration in the world for Lexa and Winnie. They must crash after one of these shindigs."

"They do." Sam glanced at his watch. "But right about now, the adrenaline should be kicking in. At least they've got a few days before the next event, but if business picks up much more, they'll need to hire a few permanent part-time helpers."

"Looks like they're born to it," Josh said. "A lot of people never find their niche, but looks to me like 'our girls' have found it."

"Not to change the subject," Sam said, waiting until the server left the kitchen, "but I have a question for you."

"Ask away."

"You're already head-over-heels for her, aren't you?"

"You could say that. I never stopped caring for her." Leaning forward with clasped hands over the stainless steel counter, he stretched his muscles to ease the tension in back and his shoulders. A moment later, he straightened up and met Sam's eyes. "I've always loved her, even back in the TeamWork camp. I understand Winnie's skittish, and I don't want to scare her away by coming on too strong." He grinned a little. "It might be too late for that, anyway. I'm not exactly known for reticence."

"Speaking from the front seat perspective, it looked like the action was pretty heated between you two," Sam said. "Winnie didn't look inclined to run in the opposite direction, but a word of caution: be careful. She's gone a long time without a man in her life and you're reawakening needs, if you understand my meaning."

"We're fine," Josh said, "but it's probably a good thing I'm going back to Baton Rouge tomorrow. Chloe brings an entirely new dynamic into the situation. I want to do what's best for both her and Winnie, but above all, I want to honor the Lord in this relationship. I also want my heart's desire, and I pray it's all the same thing." He met his friend's gaze. "I won't hurt her, Sam."

Sam held his gaze. "I know."

He ran a hand over his jaw. "I still can't believe I have a daughter. Now I need to figure out the best way to tell Mom, Dad and Beck. That's a big step, but I'll do it this week."

"You know I'm praying for you, brother. Always have and always will."

"Thanks," Josh said with a small grin. "Keep at it. I'm sure I'll need it."

The swinging door flew open and Winnie rushed in followed by a string of servers. She didn't stop moving as she tossed an incredulous glance their way. "What are you two doing just standing around? We need some more mushroom caps, bacon wraps and quiche tarts out there right now!"

"Aye aye," Josh said as both men sprang into action.

~

Late Saturday Night

At Josh's insistence, before they left the hotel, Winnie called Jessica to make sure Chloe was tucked in bed and fast asleep. She'd put him off the first five times he'd asked, and he could tell his concern for Chloe's well-being had transitioned from sweet to annoying. Exhausted from the day-long event, both ladies rested and it was a quiet ride as Sam drove them back to the house. The rain came down in torrents and Sam focused his energies on the road. He finally pulled the station wagon into the garage at quarter past eleven.

"I'll take care of all this stuff," Sam said, his glance encompassing the supplies stacked around them before settling on him. Lexa had already said goodnight and gone to check on Joe. The leftover food had been sent to a homeless shelter, but they still had a load to take back into the house. Sam's gaze fell on Winnie. "You take care of getting her home."

"Right. I don't want her driving in this rain. It's too dangerous, especially since she's so tired. I'll leave Ladybug here," he said, catching Sam's wide grin at his use of the car's nickname, "and I'll go back in the morning to get Winnie and Chloe for church." He darted a glance at Winnie still dozing beside him.

Sam climbed out of the car as he did the same. "Wait a second and I'll grab an umbrella for you."

"Never mind. I'll just pull the car up close to the garage and carry her."

Sam nodded. "Church starts at eleven, Sunday school at nine-thirty, if you're so inclined."

"Does Winnie usually go to Sunday school?"

"She does, but she co-teaches the single mom's class." Sam chuckled under his breath. "I'm sure you'd be a big hit."

"Oh, right. In that case, guess I'll tag along with you and Lexa."

"Lexa's teaching Chloe's class. I know you'd be welcome there." Those smile lines just kept getting deeper.

Josh laughed. "Sounds even better. I'll see you in the morning, buddy. Thanks for a great day all the way around. Wouldn't have missed it for anything."

Running to his car in front of the house, he pulled it behind Sam's car. Reaching into the backseat of the station wagon, he tucked Winnie in his arms and sheltered her from the blinding rain as he lowered her into his passenger seat. She stirred a few minutes later, but he didn't dare take his eyes away from the road. "Josh, I'm so tired my bones ache."

"Then rest."

"Where are we?"

He blew out a sigh as he made a left turn. "Right where we need to be."

"I'm glad."

"Me, too."

Winnie murmured something unintelligible and shifted, snuggling further into the seat. Josh cranked up the heat in case she was cold, and she was still asleep when he stopped in front of her apartment a few minutes later. Debating his options, he watched the driving sheets of rain under the streetlights. She mumbled something again. He leaned close enough to feel her warm breath. "Did you say something? Sweetheart?"

She tugged at her sweater, not opening her eyes. "Must tell Josh . . ."

Sitting back against the seat, he sighed. He'd give his annual bonus to know what was going through her imaginative mind. It didn't look like the rain was going to let up anytime soon, and short of sitting in the car half the night, he'd have to get her to the front door. Besides, a babysitter waited inside and she needed to go home.

Running around to the passenger side, he lifted Winnie from the seat and pushed the door closed. It was amazing how light she was. Looking down at her cradled in his arms as he reached the overhang outside her front door, he marveled she was still asleep. She'd worked so hard and he was proud of her, not sure he had the right. Josh allowed his gaze to travel over her face—the damp hair, the perfectly sculpted nose, those pouty, incredibly kissable lips . . .

Winnie was so beautiful in every way, nurturing and kind. Funny. Witty. What an incredible mother. Still holding her, he brought her closer and brushed his lips over hers. Raindrops dribbled from his hair and dropped onto her cheeks. He kissed her again as a gentle nudge to awaken, moving his lips to her cheek to absorb some of the moisture. He chuckled low in his throat when she shifted and—half-asleep—swatted at him as if he was an annoying insect buzzing around her face. Not able to resist, he finished the task by nibbling on her bottom lip. Winnie's eyes fluttered open and she stared at him a long moment, dazed, blinking hard a few times.

"Good evening." Her voice was hazy with sleep, deeper than usual. Sexy as anything. The corners of her mouth upturned. "I keep falling asleep on you tonight. Forgive me."

"Not a problem. I enjoy watching you sleep." That pretty but tell-tale pink flush invaded her cheeks.

"Well, um, do you mind putting me down now, please?" Her legs dangled and she shifted in the circle of his arms. There were definite advantages to holding her like this.

"I'd rather not. I like holding you."

Her smile made him so dizzy *he* was the one who needed to be steadied.

"It's best if you put me down now. Besides, I need to call Jessica's dad."

"Oh, right. Sorry." He lowered her to the step.

She paused while digging the keys from her purse and looked at him over her shoulder. "Did you kiss me when I was unaware?"

"Would you be mad if I did?"

"Yes." She didn't seem mad, but the look on her face drove him to extreme distraction. "Mad I wasn't awake to enjoy it."

"In that case, I also called you sweetheart and you begged me not to go back to Baton Rouge tomorrow."

Her lips downturned. Wrong thing to say, but gratifying all the same.

~

Winnie closed the door after watching Jessica drive away with her dad. She resisted the urge to move her hands to her hips. "Josh, how much did you give Jessica for babysitting?"

"Not getting it out of me." The look on his face told the story. Considerate though it was, he should have let her take care of paying Jessica.

"You realize you've set another dangerous precedent tonight. Now all the girls at church are going to clamor for the opportunity to babysit Chloe and expect to be exorbitantly overpaid."

"Then I'll set up a babysitting fund. No price is too high."

She frowned. "I can't take money from you, but I'm too tired to fight about it. I'm falling asleep on my feet here." She ran a quick hand through her damp hair and grimaced. "Great. I must look like a raccoon."

"Oh, but a gorgeous one." He shot her a grin. "Let me check on Chloe and then I'm on my way. Those catering ladies really worked me hard tonight." He headed to Chloe's room while she made a beeline to repair the damage.

Hearing a soft thud and a muffled groan, Winnie turned around and hurried to the Chloe's bedroom. All six-foot-four of Josh Grant lay sprawled on the carpet, flat on his bottom. "Sweetheart, you've *got* to teach Chloe to put her toys away before she goes to bed." He moaned again. "Yep, that's a bruise I won't forget anytime soon." Hearing Chloe mutter something in her sleep, Josh looked over at Winnie. "Sorry," he mouthed. Scrambling to his feet, he went over to the bed, kneeling beside it. He kissed Chloe's cheek before taking her hand so she could guide him through the maze of toys back to the living room.

"Who knew a three-year-old's bedroom could be such a road hazard?" he said, rubbing the back of his neck. "I haven't fallen like that since an unfortunate slide into third base at an LSU baseball game. Go Tigers."

"I'm sorry, Josh. I'll work with her." She couldn't hide her grin.

"Something funny?"

"You called me sweetheart."

He raised his brows. "I guess I did. You don't look like it bothered you."

"It didn't. I'm thankful I was fully awake to appreciate it."

"Me, too," he said. "I wasn't trying to tell you what to do back there, and sorry about questioning your choice of babysitter. You've done a great job raising her so far and I have absolutely no reason to question your judgment."

"Thank you, but you're right about the toys."

He grinned. "Seems Baby Bear also inherited her mother's tendency to talk in her sleep."

Her heart rate picked up again. "Why? Did I say something I shouldn't?" Whatever it was, it could have been highly embarrassing.

"Nothing I could understand, but you said my name once or twice. Sounded pretty hot, whatever it was." He took a step closer. "It's going to be very difficult leaving you and Chloe tomorrow." He had that look she was beginning to recognize and like very much. *Too* much.

She raised her hand. "Hold that thought."

"Where are you going?" he called after her.

"Help yourself to the sweet tea or water, if you're thirsty. I'll be right back." She hurried through her bedroom and into the bathroom. Looking at her reflection in the mirror, she muffled a groan. The way she looked, it was a miracle Josh even wanted to kiss her. What a train wreck. Pulling out a makeup remover pad, she scrubbed it over her face and removed all traces of leftover mascara before putting a couple of soothing drops in her tired eyes. Grabbing her toothbrush, she did the one-minute version before tugging a comb through her tangled, damp hair, fluffing it on the ends. Smiling at her reflection, she pinched her cheeks. Not much better, but it would have to do.

Josh stood by the sofa, holding the photo of her and Chloe as she walked back into the living room. He probably thought sitting together on the sofa might be too tempting. *He's right.* It wouldn't be advisable tonight with all the sparks flying between them. Not sure what to do with her hands, Winnie clasped them in front of her. "All spit-shined now." Her silly giggle escaped and he got that look on his face again. Who knew a giggle could be so powerful? She couldn't deny the hold this man had over her emotions, but it also seemed to work just as well the other way around.

He touched her hair and nuzzled her cheek. "In case I didn't tell you earlier, you're incredible. All you do with the catering business . . . you're nothing short of amazing." When it seemed those lips were headed for her neck, she stepped back.

"Josh," she said, swallowing hard, planting both hands on his chest. He had her tongue-tied to the point she wasn't sure what she wanted to say. All rational thought and reason flew straight out of her mind. She wanted him to kiss the daylights out of her, but once he went back home to his "normal" life, he might come to his senses and that would be the end of it. He'd always take care of Chloe's needs, but . . .

"You have that look again."

Winnie cleared her throat. When she started to remove her hands, he put his hands over hers. "What look would that be?"

"The look of a woman who needs to be kissed. Thoroughly."

She didn't protest when he covered her mouth with his. *Now who's the pushover?* Goodness, the man was perfecting the kiss from earlier in Sam's car, and then some.

"Winnie, I feel like I've known you my whole life," he said at length. His lips brushed her temple as his hold on her tightened. "At least my lips have always known yours."

"Okay, that's it," she said, taking his hand and leading him to the front door. "When you start spouting things like that, I *know* it's time to say goodnight. Not that I don't appreciate the kisses."

Josh released a reluctant groan and gave her a look guaranteed to send her to bed with a smile. "I'll pick you up a little before nine to take you and Buttercup to church." He tweaked her chin. "Sweet dreams, sweetheart."

Closing the door behind him, Winnie leaned against it, needing the support.

~

Driving back to Sam and Lexa's, Josh prayed the entire way. At least the rain had finally let up some. He prayed for Chloe. Prayed about his growing relationship with Winnie. It might be too soon, but he knew what he wanted. Prayed for wisdom to know what was right in God's eyes. Prayed to keep his physical yearnings for Winnie in check. Prayed for direction in his professional life and his position in the law firm.

"Lord, you've given me two precious gifts. Help me be worthy."

CHAPTER TWENTY-SEVEN

Three Days Later

REBEKAH SHARED LUNCH with Adam in a private corner of one of Baton Rouge's finest restaurants. *French* again. He'd rejected her idea of Mexican, Thai, Vietnamese and Chinese. She had the rare day off from school, and he seized the opportunity to take her to lunch. When she suggested a trip to the Museum of Art on the LSU campus, he seemed pleased with the suggestion. She always loved going back to the campus, and looked forward to showing him some of her old haunts.

Wiping her mouth and placing her napkin beside her plate, Rebekah hadn't a clue what she was eating except that it tasted sort of like chicken. Her stomach felt uneasy, but whether from the food or the conversation, she couldn't be sure. Adam was acting particularly territorial today, putting his arm around her waist like a vise when escorting her into the restaurant and putting his hand over hers at every available opportunity. His increasingly broad hints about their future together squeezed her chest so tight she couldn't breathe. She gulped a big swig of water, but that didn't help. A short break—even if only a trip to the ladies room—would be a welcome relief so she could catch her breath and gather her thoughts. "If you'll excuse me, I'll be back in a few minutes."

"I'll miss you," Adam said, standing as she departed. That seemed overkill, even for him. She felt his eyes on her as she moved among the tables. At least he hadn't rented out the entire restaurant.

Heading back out of the ladies room a few minutes later, Rebekah stopped short as she spied Kevin sitting at a table with an attractive brunette. From the lines around her eyes, she appeared a few years older. Mature was an apt description. She bristled when the woman leaned across the table toward Kevin with an I'd-like-to-get-to-know-you-better expression. No way could it be a date. For one thing, she wore too much blush and dark lipstick, and he looked like he'd rather be anywhere but sitting at that table. Small comfort. Josh had warned her tarrying with the feelings of two men would one day lead to the disaster of her lifetime.

Kevin's hand rested on the table and when the woman laughed and put one hand on his forearm and squeezed, Rebekah's breath stuck in her throat. Clamping a hand over her mouth, she choked and then coughed. Too late. Hearing the sound, Kevin looked her way, his eyes growing large. Maybe he wouldn't recognize her beneath the foundation, blush, lipstick, eyeliner and mascara. She hardly recognized herself, all painted and gussied up like she was trying to purposely lure a man. Deep shame washed over her, but she couldn't move. Removing his arm from the woman's grasp, Kevin rose to his feet so fast he almost knocked over his water glass. Rebekah started to walk away; she'd seen more than enough.

"Rebekah?"

She turned, but slanted her gaze to the floor, unable to look him in the eye.

"I didn't expect to see you here." He moved over beside her, appearing a little nervous.

"That's pretty obvious," she said. "If you'll excuse me, I need to get back to my table now." Looking past his shoulder, she saw the woman giving her the once-over before pulling out her compact to check her lipstick. *Save it. Kevin hates it.* She turned to walk away again.

Reaching for her hand, he pulled her around to face him. "You are Rebekah Grant, are you not?"

Her eyes narrowed as she yanked her hand away. That was a low blow even though she'd wondered the same thing. "I'm not going to dignify that with a response considering the Kevin Moore I know wouldn't be caught in an intimate French restaurant dining with . . . Mrs. Robinson over there."

"Who?" He shook his head, confused.

She tapped her foot. "*The Graduate.* Ring any bells?"

He frowned and blew out a deep sigh. "That's not fair."

Darting a glance at their table, Rebekah felt Kevin's eyes on her as Adam nodded and waved. More than anything else, she wanted to wipe the smug grin from his face. He obviously didn't think he had reason to worry. She lowered her voice. "I saw that woman with her hands all over you." *Okay, it was just a hand, but I didn't like it. I don't care if I sound jealous.*

"Well, if the circumstances were different, I might introduce you." It was clear he was attempting to calm himself and keep his voice steady. "From my perspective, it's a business lunch, nothing more. But your friend over there certainly looks like the cat that swallowed the canary." Just the way he said it, with an edge in his voice she'd never heard before, made her cringe. He nodded his head in the direction of their table. "I suppose that's him."

She crossed her arms. "Yes, that's Adam." A devilish grin crossed his face and Rebekah watched, wide-eyed, as he spun on his heel and headed straight toward the table. She needed to stop him. "Kevin!" she called, hurrying to catch up with him. *What is he doing?*

"Hello. I'm Kevin Moore," he said, head held high, extending his hand in greeting as he reached the table. "I understand you have a date with our lovely Rebekah."

Her heart falling to her feet, she couldn't miss the sarcasm in his voice at the use of the word *our.* Great. He'd suddenly adopted Adam's annoying habit of using plural pronouns.

"Hullo there. Adam Martin," he said, employing his most pompous—proper—English accent as he rose to his feet—equal height with Kevin—and pumped his hand. "I'd invite you to join us, but we're having a bit of a romantic date here, you know? Right, Becks?" He gave Kevin his most winning smile. His best I-want-you-as-my-client smile.

She'd seen the effects of that charm before and it made her heart sink to even lower depths. *Oh, Lord, just come back now and take me with you. I can't believe this is happening. I should have known it would come down to something like this.*

"I wouldn't dream of interrupting your date," Kevin told him, turning to glare at her. Rebekah loved it when Kevin gave her chills, but not like this. He had a fire, a passion in his eyes she'd never seen before. In a weird way, she liked it. "Becks and I are old friends." Oh, that did it. He'd used the name "Becks." The normal, sane, rational Kevin would never use that name. If he wanted to get her angry, he was doing a mighty fine job. *What's gotten into him?*

"Do you mind if I borrow her for a moment?" Not bothering to wait for a response, he took Rebekah's elbow and steered her away.

Rebekah didn't dare look back at Adam, not wanting to be the cause of a fistfight in the middle of one of Baton Rouge's best French restaurants. Still, she was surprised when he didn't call after her, much less try to stop them. *Does he even care?* She had to wonder.

Kevin headed toward a door leading to an outdoor deck and pulled her out the door behind him, releasing his hold only after he closed the door. Thankfully, the deck wasn't being used and was vacant and empty of patrons. She could almost see the steam curling from the man's ears, and his cheeks were flushed with barely-contained anger. "What are you doing, Rebekah? I know I said I'd step aside, but I can't believe what I'm seeing."

She felt the heat creep into her cheeks as Kevin took a slow appraisal from the loose curls piled on top of her head down to her four-inch strappy sandals. *Add humiliation to my list of growing shame.* The length of her dress was higher than normal, but respectable, and no more revealing than when she wore shorts. This being Louisiana, Kevin had seen her wear those enough times. The top of the dress dipped a little in the front if she moved a certain way, but she'd made a conscious effort to appear modest. Uncomfortable, she squirmed under his scrutiny. "Are you actually jealous?"

Kevin's gaze was unrelenting. "I'm angry you're allowing this man to turn you into someone you're not. Do his charming looks and British accent have you so bewitched you can't see what's happening to you?"

That was a shocker. She pulled her wrap around her, feeling a sudden chill. "What . . . what do you mean?"

"I wish I had a mirror so you could look at yourself. This," he said, gesturing the length of her, "is not the Rebekah Grant I know, the sweet, simple, unassuming school teacher. The woman I see standing before me now is not you."

Her ire rose and she tried to tamp it down. Didn't work. "Making it worse, Kevin. Now you're calling me simple?" That one hurt, although she knew he couldn't mean it the way it sounded.

The muscles in his cheeks got quite the workout. "There's nothing simple about you and you know it."

To his credit, he kept his voice low and controlled, but she suspected that might change soon enough. Business lunch or not, she couldn't miss he was dressed in a nice sports jacket, shirt and tie. He rarely wore those with her except when they were in church, and even then, he usually had the jacket draped either on his chair . . . or around her shoulders. She sighed. She'd never fought with him before and couldn't believe this was happening.

"It's called makeup. Most women of a certain age wear it, and what's wrong with my dress?" She couldn't help taunting him. Defensiveness had taken over and that was never a good thing. Swallowing the huge lump lodged in her throat, Rebekah fought to control the threatening tears. By staying angry, perhaps she could keep them at bay.

"Don't even go there," he said, "except to say it's too revealing."

"Oh, so now you're being puritanical? Kevin, you've seen more leg when I wear shorts." She resisted the urge to tug down on the hem.

He had the grace to flush. "I'm not talking about your legs."

"Well, then what are we talking about here, exactly?" Her eyes bore into his.

"I'm talking about points north."

She could tell he kept his gaze trained on her face while she looked. Rebekah gasped. The décolletage of her dress had slipped down, revealing more of her cleavage than Kevin—or any man—had ever seen. He probably thought she wasn't even wearing anything beneath the dress. Guess that's what she deserved for allowing some saleswoman at the lingerie shop talk her into buying this ridiculously overpriced nothing of an undergarment. A single woman shouldn't even need such a thing. *Oh, the shame.* Her level of humiliation reached a new low as she moved both hands to her cheeks. Of course, humiliation being what it was, the lightweight wrap draped around her shoulders slid off and puddled to the deck in a silky, colorful heap.

"You'd better let me pick that up unless you intend to give me a cheap thrill," Kevin said. That devilish glint surfaced in his eye again as he bent low and retrieved it. Holding the wrap between his hands, he reached over her head and brought it around her shoulders. Being Kevin, he was careful not to allow his hands to brush against her bare skin in the process.

Rebekah couldn't dig deep enough to find the words to defend herself. Finally, she managed to find her voice. A small one, but it was there. "I am *not* cheap, Kevin."

"My point exactly. But Adam's got you dressing like someone you're not, all painted up like a china doll. You don't need any of it." His eyes softened. How she loved that he cared, but her heart—or her words—might betray her if she dared to speak.

"Don't you know your beauty is what's inside you as much as what the outside world sees? You don't need to cover it up with the pretense of being someone you're not. Your beauty is breathtaking, and you're special the way you are. You don't need to put on airs, wear fancy clothes and doll yourself up to impress anyone. That's not the real Rebekah. I miss *that* woman." When she still didn't speak, he moved in closer. His hands dropped from his hips.

Probably gathering more ammunition. She swallowed hard. "You pretty much gave me your permission to continue seeing Adam and to see this thing through. It's lunch. That's all."

He shot her a look of disbelief. "I'm quite sure Mr. Smooth also has after lunch plans with you."

"What are you implying? I've never seen this side of you before. You're acting so jealous you can't even think straight. Furthermore, it doesn't sound like you trust me very much."

"I trust you, but I certainly don't trust *him*. I've seen his type before. He's got you so swayed by his money, his looks, and his . . . his car, his accent, his clothes or whatever that you aren't thinking clearly. Unless you're not the girl I think you are, and unless I'm giving you more credit than you deserve, I'm sure you can see straight through that and focus on the heart."

She'd never seen Kevin so animated and his eyes sparked with unbridled passion. "I don't believe this! Now you're accusing me of being shallow?" That stung—all his words did. Rebekah crossed her arms and her gaze dropped to the ground, staring at the shoes an hour ago she'd thought the height of sophistication. Ditto the dress. She forced her voice lower. "Where's the sweet, gentle Kevin I know? Is he in there somewhere?"

"Do you like this side of me?" Kevin took another step toward her. He was so close she felt his warmth. If he moved any closer, he'd knock them both over.

She crossed her arms over her chest, feeling exposed and vulnerable. "Well, at least you're not making me wait three *years* to see this side of you." The way his eyes flashed told her she'd pushed too far.

"I can be as forceful and demanding as the next guy when pushed to the limit, and I think I've reached that limit now."

"Oh, so now you're being forceful and demanding, are you?" She took an involuntary step back. Kevin's cheeks were flushed, and he crossed his arms over his chest.

"Bottom line, Rebekah? If you want some hotshot guy to parade you around on his arm like a pretty ornament, then Adam Martin's the guy for you. If you can tell me right now that's what you honestly want, then I'll march right back in there," he said, nodding over his shoulder, "shake the man's hand and say, 'Congratulations. You won the girl. Have a wonderful life.'"

She cringed. "You knew when we went to Montana that Adam had proposed to me and I was trying to make my decision."

"I know that now, yes, but you never said one word—at least to me—about it while we were in Montana. I had to find out from someone else after the fact.

Even when I sat by your side after you'd fallen in the creek, feeding you, reading to you, playing my guitar, watching you sleep . . ." His voice trailed and he shook his head. "I suppose it conveniently slipped your mind to tell me you had a guy back home who wanted to marry you? How do you think that made me feel?" He shook his head. "I'm not buying it."

"Give me a break," Rebekah groaned, her voice breaking. "I'd only known the man a couple of months and he wanted me to marry him and move to England. You and I worked a few of the TeamWork missions together, but you never once let on you were interested in me as anything other than a friend. It came as a huge shock to me when you finally let me know you liked me. It confused me a little . . . a lot, actually. And sure, you let me know you liked me when we were in Montana, but then you didn't ask me out for months after we got back home."

Kevin shoved his hands in the pockets of his dress pants. "I thought when you came back from Montana and told Adam you wouldn't marry him, he'd go find someone else. I've always been too shy for my own good. I've been concentrated on the lumberyard and the store, but I should have staked my claim earlier."

She scoffed at that one. "Now you make me sound like territorial land rights—"

"The biggest shock," he said, cutting her off, "was discovering you're still seeing him. I suppose that also slipped your mind? Until I saw that notation on your calendar about London Bridge, I never considered the possibility you were seeing anyone else. That, and the fact that one of your students thought my name was Adam. Wonder where he might have gotten that idea?" Kevin's hands moved out of the pockets and settled on his hips.

She didn't know that, and wasn't sure how one of her students would know unless they'd overheard her speaking with Hannah. Adam had certainly never come to the school. "I'm sorry if you're hurt by that. I really am." *Fight for me, Kevin.* Deep shame engulfed her like a physical blow. The man shouldn't need to fight, but he stood in front of her now, doing that very thing.

"For whatever reason, you haven't told him to fly back to London Town." He raked his fingers through his hair. "Look, I thought if I stepped aside, you'd see for yourself he's not the man for you. Sure, he might take you fancy places, buy you nice things," he said, his eyes resting on the bracelet Adam gave her earlier in the day. His eyes traveled back to her face. "Does he share his heart with you? Does he take care of you when you're sick, care about your family, take the time to find out who you really are?" Kevin sure was heaping on the guilt now, but it only served to up the ante.

Rebekah stared. Not knowing what to do with her restless hands, she wrapped her arms across her middle, forcing her fingers still. "Are you more upset by the fact that I'm dating someone else or that it's Adam? A girl's got to keep her options open. Besides, I'd like to start a family sometime before menopause."

"So I've waited too long? Is that what you're telling me?" His eyes narrowed and he crossed his arms again. How she hated this tension between them, but oh were his eyes more intense, more incredible, when he was all fired up.

"I'm not telling you that, no. You don't know," she said, "how happy I am you finally worked up the nerve to tell me you like me. You encouraged me to make my decision and that's what I'm trying to do. But now I'm so confused, I honestly don't know what I want." She fought the tears again, not willing to let him see her cave into the overwhelming emotion. If she allowed the tears to fall, she'd be hard pressed to stop them.

Kevin dropped his arms to his sides. "It's pretty clear relationships aren't my strong suit. Maybe I've been too shy, but you're either a better actress than I thought or else you feel the same way about us, but you're too proud or stubborn to admit it."

She didn't bother covering her gasp. "Are you saying I've lied to you in some way?"

"No, I'm not. Look," he said, his tone calmer, "I'm sorry for charging at you like an angry lion, but you have to know how much I care about you."

A tear slipped down her cheek, and she didn't bother wiping it away. Raising watery eyes to his, she willed herself not to crumple at the man's feet. "And what way would that be? Tell me."

"I might not have said the words, but I thought you knew by the way I look at you, the way I speak to you, the way I hold you and kiss you. I can barely get enough of you. If I could, I'd spend every waking moment with you. When you're not with me, I think about you and—call me crazy—but sometimes I hear your voice in my head. I wonder what you're eating for breakfast, what you're teaching your students, what you think about before you go to sleep, what you're reading in your Bible . . ."

Putting one hand on the side of her face, Kevin leaned close. "If all that doesn't tell you how I feel, then I'll spell it out for you so we're perfectly clear." He cradled her face between his big, callused hands. "I *love* you, Rebekah." He kissed her hard before stepping away, his eyes never leaving hers.

It all happened so quickly, she didn't have the opportunity to react. Her lips felt bereft as she stared at him, stunned into silence. Her hand traveled to her mouth, her fingers over her lips.

"I'd better leave some of that soap on your lips for the Brit to kiss off you. Tell me," he said, "does Adam give you what you need? Does he give you something I can't? Do you like it when he touches you, kisses you? Does he fulfill some need I don't satisfy?"

"Stop it, Kevin. Please."

"I think it's best if I leave. If I don't, I'll say something we'll both regret. I've already said enough. Enjoy your *cuisses de grenouille*." He turned to leave.

"What in the world does that mean?"

Kevin turned. "Frog legs. Whether you realize it or not, you're eating frog legs and seem to be enjoying them." Surprising her, he planted a feather-soft brush of a kiss on her cheek. "*Bonsoir*, Rebekah. *Je t'aime pour toujours*." Without another look back, his head held high, Kevin opened the door leading back into the restaurant and disappeared from view.

In that moment, she wished she'd taken three years of high school French instead of German. Everything in French sounded romantic, but the sinking feeling in the pit of her stomach told her whatever Kevin said hadn't been complimentary. In her shock, the words had already escaped her confused mind.

Dragging fresh air into her lungs, she put one hand on her stomach and tried to catch her breath. She couldn't remember anyone in her life speaking to her the way Kevin just did.

Movement inside the restaurant caught her attention. He'd left the door to the patio open and she moved forward in time to see the back of Kevin's head as he left the restaurant with the woman. Part of her—the part that didn't care what anyone else thought—wanted to run after him, fall to her knees in this elegant, upscale restaurant and beg him to tell her again that he loved her. Another part wanted to run home, throw herself on the bed and cry until she had no more tears. Then she'd figure out what to do next.

Rebekah lifted her chin and headed back to where Adam waited at their table. Anger surged inside her he hadn't bothered to come looking for her. He looked perplexed, but worrying about her obviously hadn't dampened his appetite, judging by his empty plate. The thought of frog legs made her ill and she slumped down into her chair. She must have tuned him out when he told her the choice for their meal.

Adam put his hand on her arm. "Why the long face, lovely? You were gone quite a fair bit of time. I was about to take a stroll about the place, looking for you." He watched as she pulled her wrap closer about her shoulders, shivering, wondering if she'd ever be warm again. "Care to share what that was all about?"

"You know, I really don't." Thankful he asked, she had no desire to elaborate.

He raised his hands. "Fair enough. Seems like a nice enough bloke, but something's stuck in his hat, that's for sure."

Rebekah sank further into her chair, avoiding his gaze and swallowing her tears. *Oh yes, he's a nice bloke all right. One who finally told me he loved me . . . right before he kissed me goodbye.*

CHAPTER TWENTY-EIGHT

Wednesday Afternoon

AS REBEKAH ARRIVED at the church at four o'clock the next afternoon, she breathed a sigh of relief. Kevin's truck wasn't in the parking lot. While she hoped to see him, she was nervous at the thought of working alongside him to the point she feared she'd break out in hives. *Did we have a really bad fight or are we completely over?* They'd signed up to work at the soup kitchen together and Kevin was a man of his word—and rarely late. The debacle at the French restaurant was still raw in her heart and less than twenty-four-hours old, but if she sulked and hid in a hole, she might not ever emerge. *Time to be a grownup.*

Walking into the fellowship hall, she smiled at a few of the volunteers and headed toward the spacious kitchen with the jello salad she'd made. It was Kevin's home church, and fairly large, but she'd been coming with him long enough to get to know a good number of the members. He kept inviting her to events with their singles group and she'd never missed. They'd also been together at a number of worship services, enough for the pastor and his wife to accept them as a couple.

"Hi, Rebekah," Paula called, giving her a sweet smile as she waved her over to where she prepared a tossed salad. "Nice to see you. You look very pretty today. The colors in that blouse really bring out the green in those gorgeous eyes of yours." She winked. "I'm sure Kevin will agree."

"Thanks," she said, knowing her cheeks must match the shade of pink in the blouse. "How's your sister doing?"

A grateful smile creased Paula's face. "Noela's much better now, and aren't you a doll to ask. As a matter of fact, she specifically wanted me to thank you for the card of encouragement you sent. Your kind words and prayers have meant a lot to her. The doctors have regulated her medicine, so she's got her energy back and is finally starting her normal activities again."

"Oh, that's so wonderful!" she said. "Please give her my best. My mom's always been a part of the card ministry at our church, and I've always wanted to carry on the tradition." Rebekah handed her jello salad to one of the other ladies and eyed the various prepared dishes already lined up on the serving counter. "So, put me to work. What can I do to help?"

"Well, if you can start on the potatoes, that might be the biggest help right now." Paula handed her a peeler and some paper towels. "The bags of potatoes are over there on the far counter."

"Will do. Thanks." As she set about her task, Rebekah listened as some of the other volunteers joked and teased one another. There was a mainstay group who took charge of the weekly soup kitchen and always provided the main course and dessert, but it was up to the rotating list of volunteers to make and serve the salads and vegetables, set the tables and clean up afterwards.

She sensed Kevin's presence before she saw him. Pausing in her work, she glanced up to see him walk in with his quiet charm and irresistible smile. It was impossible to miss how they all loved him. She wiped the back of her hand over her brow. It hadn't even occurred to her perhaps she should go back to her home church with her mom and dad.

Maybe she'd looked at their relationship from the wrong perspective. If worshipping together didn't smack of commitment, what did? While she hadn't considered them dates, and they often went with other couples or singles, it *was* spending time together. He'd pick her up in his truck and then take her home afterwards. Just because he didn't kiss her, hold her hand or flirt with her every single time, it didn't make their time together any less valid, any less special.

One of the well-meaning ladies handed a peeler to Kevin and nudged him in her direction. From the corner of her eye, Rebekah saw him glance her way with a slight frown. At least he didn't outright refuse. Oh no, he was too polite. Besides, he'd do anything to help with the soup kitchen.

"Rebekah." He nodded and took the place next to her.

"Here," she said, handing him some paper towels and a couple of potatoes. "Race you." *That's right. Break the ice. The man's always up for a competition.* That struck her as highly ironic, but her challenge seemed to work. In Kevin's quick grin, she glimpsed the fun-loving man she adored.

Picking up the potato peeler, he started to work in earnest. They worked in silence for a few minutes. When she thought she couldn't take the awkwardness any longer, Kevin finally spoke. "How's Josh doing these days?" At least he'd asked a question, generated a bit of conversation.

She hesitated, holding a potato in one hand. "We're meeting for dinner tomorrow night. Something's up with him, but I have no idea what. I told you he was in Houston and reconnected with Sam. They had a good visit, from what I can tell." They worked another minute in silence. "Kevin," she said, turning to look at him.

"Hmm?" he asked, peeling, still thinking it was a competition.

"You win. Please stop for a minute."

Halting in his task, he looked at her, and his eyes softened. They looked bluer than ever.

"When Josh didn't go to Montana, I started to wonder if he'd ever come around. You and I both know Sam forgives unconditionally, but Josh needed to go and talk to Sam for *himself*." She blew out a breath and looked away a moment. "Does that even make any sense?"

"Yes, it does." His voice was quiet, thoughtful.

She put another potato on the counter in front of him. Her hand was starting to cramp and tire; she flexed her fingers. "There's something else I find interesting." Maybe she shouldn't bring it up, but curiosity pushed hesitancy to the wall.

"What's that?"

She massaged her fingers for a few seconds, aware he watched, but he resumed peeling again. "Before he went to Houston, Josh called to ask me for Winnie Doyle's phone number. Turns out he got it from Amy, but that's not my point."

Kevin stopped, but didn't look her way. "Oh?"

"Do you know something?" She tried to catch his eye.

"No, of course not," he mumbled, carving out the eye of the potato.

Hand on her hip, Rebekah faced him. "Spill it, Kevin."

He appeared to measure his words. "Maybe Josh needs to ask her forgiveness, too."

"For what?" she asked. "Why in the world would Josh need to ask forgiveness from Winnie?"

Kevin shrugged. "I don't know. It's just a theory. Think about it. Did he ask you for the phone number of any of the other TeamWork members?"

She shook her head. "No, he didn't." Wrapping the small stack of potato peels in the paper towels, she deposited them in the trash.

"I'm sure after your dinner with your brother, you'll know more."

"You're right. Are you staying for prayer meeting tonight?" That was a silly question. Kevin rarely missed them.

"Yes. You?"

"Do you want me to?" She looked at him with what she hoped was a neutral expression. He could read her so well.

"I'm not playing games, Rebekah," he said in a low voice, leaning close so as not to be overheard. He nodded at Ken Anderson who poured lemonade and iced tea into Styrofoam cups at a nearby table.

She tried to catch his eye, but he wouldn't give in. "Look," she said, retrieving the last potato, "I can't stand the thought of you not being in my life. You mean too much to me. I don't want to lose you."

"I said we shouldn't see each other romantically. If we're in church together, that's one thing, but private lunches, dinners, picnics or anything else, are out." Kevin's glance encompassed the others in the large kitchen, busy with their tasks.

"It's hard to be around you and not want more." It came out before she could think it through. But it was honest.

He shook his head. "I don't know what to say." When he finally moved his gaze to her, she saw the raw pain in his eyes. "The only thing I know right now is I don't want to lose you, either. So I guess that means we're in a holding pattern." His mouth was set in a grim line.

As she helped with the final preparations for the salad and Kevin helped set up more tables and chairs, Rebekah chatted with the ladies—a good mix of singles, young and older marrieds and senior citizens. A number of husband and wife teams always helped with the soup kitchen, too. Try as she might, her thoughts always returned to the tall, dark-haired, handsome man across the room. She caught him watching her a few times, but looked away when their eyes met.

Once again, Josh was right. She didn't like the idea of a holding pattern, but it would have to do. At least for now.

~

As he talked with one of the men sitting beside him, Kevin kept a watchful eye on Rebekah. Sitting a few tables away, she chatted with one of the women who'd been coming to the soup kitchen since last spring—not homeless, but financially unstable and wanting a home-cooked meal for herself and her three young children. She tilted her head and leaned close to her table companions, concentrating on what was being said. He loved the sound of her laughter as she talked with the kids, and it was equally gratifying to hear their giggles and see them moving their hands in animated conversation. No wonder she was such a terrific teacher. And at least with adults, once they got past how gorgeous she was and understood she was sincere, humble and unassuming, they usually opened up and embraced her efforts to get to know them.

A stab of regret ripped through him and squeezed his heart. He'd been harsh with her, and he shouldn't have lashed out at her at the French restaurant. Seeing her with Adam made him angry, and putting a face to the name hadn't helped. Even Kevin could admit the guy had class. In the material sense, he could offer Rebekah things he never could.

She didn't have to show up tonight. To her credit, she'd jumped right in to help. A woman with less dedication or conscience might have skipped the soup kitchen commitment altogether based on the current state of their relationship. He'd always found her deep faith and eagerness to serve the Lord one of her most appealing qualities, and made her even more beautiful, if such a thing was possible.

The man beside him nudged his elbow and resumed his painfully detailed explanation of replacing the engine in his truck. As much as he hated to do it, Kevin turned his back to the blonde, green-eyed beauty a few tables over, blocking his view of her as he focused on his tablemate. It was the only way he'd be able to listen with any semblance of attention.

~

The topic of the Bible study focused on the virtue of patience. It was a frequent topic since so many struggled with it. The pastor's words hit home when he said, "Second Timothy 2:24 tells us, '*The Lord's bond-servant must not be quarrelsome, but be kind to all, able to teach, patient when wronged . . .*'"

As she listened to the pastor's short devotional, Rebekah's thoughts wandered. *I'm listening, Lord. Help me to be open to Your leading. I need you, but I haven't fully surrendered my will. Take me, mold me and fill my heart anew.* An almost unbelievable calm settled in her heart, soothing her with the peace she'd needed for so long. Kevin was right. Adam could fulfill tangible needs, but he didn't invest himself in her emotionally. He was a wonderful man, and he treated her well, but he wasn't the right man for her heart.

With Adam, she'd never shared the same type of challenging, deep exchanges she did with her lumber man. Perhaps most telling? She almost hyperventilated whenever Adam hinted at proposing marriage again. Her mind reeled whenever she thought of the downside of London high society. She'd need a different gown for every occasion and a checkbook ready for whatever charity called their name. She probably wouldn't be able to wear her jeans and T-shirts outside the house, and maybe not even inside the house. She'd put her foot down on the expectation of shipping their offspring to boarding school, no matter that it was expected and all-important tradition.

While he shared her faith, Adam didn't exhibit a tangible, personal relationship with the Lord. Her faith was too important not to share that part of her life. But it wasn't her place to judge, only to pray for him. Bottom line? It wasn't a competition between these two men; it was a choice. *Her* choice, and she'd made it. Finally. If she had to wait years for Kevin, then . . . well, so be it.

She pondered the words of the verse Pastor Jim read. Kevin wasn't quarrelsome—save for that incident on the patio of the French restaurant—but even she could admit he had his reasons. He was kind to all, patient when wronged. *Dear, sweet Kevin.* She was wrong when she told Adam she didn't deserve him. *I don't deserve* Kevin. *Lord, please help me be worthy of this man.*

Rebekah startled when his fingers, gentle but firm, pushed their way through hers as they bowed their heads for prayer. He laced them together as they listened to the heartfelt prayers of those gathered in the meeting room. His hand was warm and comforting, strong and masculine. Running her thumb across the side of his hand, she felt a small, rough callus. She wanted to raise it to her lips and kiss the spot, but dared not. Opening her eyes, she looked into the eyes that knew her soul and owned her heart. When he brushed his thumb against hers, it made her shudder. Closing her eyes again, she tried to concentrate on the prayer being offered. It was impossible.

Soon after, Kevin began his own prayer. "Heavenly Father, it's hard to make decisions sometimes. We want to rush ahead and follow our hearts instead of our heads. Help us to keep our focus on You in all things. Help us to stop long enough to listen to what You're trying to tell us through Your word and Your guidance in our lives. And help us to love one another, Father, with the kind of patience and abiding love You show us every day."

Rebekah leaned on Kevin's shoulder. Her eyes welled with tears when he rested his head against hers. When the time of prayer ended, they both sat upright, breaking apart. Chatting with the others as they said goodbye, she admired the way he interacted with everyone. Although quiet, he had a calming presence, a man worthy of respect and admiration. She wanted to tell him she'd made the decision to break it off with Adam, but she needed to actually do it before she said anything to him. She needed to come to him freely—without any ties binding her. That's the way Kevin would want it, and the way it needed to happen.

Walking together to her car in the church parking lot a short time later, Rebekah opened the door and put her Bible and purse on the backseat. Hands behind her back, she leaned against her Camry, not sure what to do or say. "Where do we go from here?"

"I don't know," Kevin told her. "I know what I'd like to do, but it's not the time."

"What do you want to do?" Her heart raced.

His eyes mesmerized her as they fell on her lips. Kevin might not say it, but those eyes couldn't lie. More than anything, she wanted to feel the touch of his lips on hers. She was staring at his lips, too.

"Don't tempt me, Miss Grant." His tone was teasing, but there was a seriousness underlying his words.

"I don't mean to tempt you. I just want to kiss you." Although she couldn't believe she'd admitted it, he'd started it with all the staring.

He shook his head and ran his fingers through his hair. "Then you know what you need to do, don't you?" With that, he spun on his heel and strode over to his truck. He didn't look back—not once—as he started the engine and pulled out of the parking lot.

Rebekah stared, open-mouthed, watching as his truck moved down the street and out-of-sight. Didn't even stay to make sure her car started. That was so unlike him. Still, she couldn't blame him. Climbing into her car, she crossed her arms, berating herself.

Well, I certainly deserved that.

CHAPTER TWENTY-NINE

Thursday Night

"BECK, OVER HERE!" Rebekah smiled as she spied Josh waving from a corner booth at Olive Garden the next night. Ever the proper gentleman, he stood as she approached and kissed her cheek. "You look great. Glad you could make it."

"Thanks. Right back at you, but I don't feel so great, to tell you the truth." She slipped into the seat across from him.

"Oh, no. Don't tell me something's wrong in the romance department?"

"Why do you always think something's wrong with my love life if I happen to be a little down? My whole life doesn't revolve around a man, you know."

Josh chuckled as he dropped into the chair opposite her. "That's right. Your life revolves around two men."

"Don't push it."

He held up his hands in mock surrender. "You know how I feel about this whole Adam versus Kevin situation—or maybe I should say it the other way around—so I won't bore you by imposing my opinion against your will. I'll try to be good."

"Josh, you know how much I love you and value your opinion. Other than Mom and Dad, misguided though I may be, I trust you more than anyone else. Rest assured, I'm going to take care of this situation."

"Anything I can do to help speed up this process?"

She resisted the urge to grin. "I'll let you know, but we're not here to talk about me."

"Sure we are. I've got all night, and I'm all ears. Tell me what's going on in the fabulous world of Rebekah."

She considered her options. Time to get back at her brother for his teasing. She'd tell him everything, but not the best part—that she was dumping Adam—until he'd heard the rest of the story first. "I told you to please stop calling it that, but let's see," she said, not giving him the opportunity to speak, "I told you Kevin knows about Adam, but I'm not sure the reverse is true. He seemed pretty clueless at lunch the other day although I thought it was painfully obvious." Her frown deepened. "Even if he did suspect anything, I honestly don't think the man either cares or feels threatened by Kevin."

"Back up. Start at the beginning and tell me more about what happened at the restaurant."

As she proceeded to tell him the whole sad story, Rebekah could tell he was inordinately amused by her trauma. When she got to the part about the frog legs, he laughed. "Before you give me the I-told-you-so spiel, please know I feel absolutely horrid about this whole thing. Completely wretched." Maybe that was laying it on a bit thick. "I'm glad my life is so amusing to you." She couldn't help it as the corners of her mouth upturned.

"I do feel your pain, but even you have to admit it's entertaining," Josh said, patting her hand on the table. Might be Mother's Hen's influence since he must have spent some time with Winnie in Houston.

The server came to their table to take their order. When the girl left the table with a flirtatious glance at Josh, Rebekah shook her head. "What must it be like to contend with that all the time, women throwing themselves at you right and left?"

"Do they? I hadn't noticed. To use your phrase, looked in a mirror lately?"

"It's a curse, Josh. I hate it."

"I'm sure Kevin's not complaining."

"That's another thing," she said, shifting her position in the booth as their drinks were delivered. "Kevin accepts me as I am and likes me best *au naturel*."

Josh spit out iced tea and it landed on the tablecloth between them. "Sorry. You took me off guard with that one." He sputtered and swiped his napkin over his mouth. "What are you saying? Kevin likes you in the buff?" As soon as the words were out, he darted a look of apology her way. "Sorry. You're too easy to tease. I can't help myself."

Rebekah threw her napkin across the table. "Focus, Josh." She crossed her arms and added a muffled, "Sex maniac."

"You know, to prove I'm redeemed and forgiven, I'm going to pretend you didn't just say that."

"My apologies." She leaned across the table, lowering her voice. "I'd be mortified if Kevin . . . or Sam . . . or pretty much anyone heard me say such a thing," she said, taking her napkin as he handed it across the table. "You've come a long way. In case I haven't told you lately, I'm proud of you."

"Thanks, but please continue. This is just too good."

She laughed. "What I meant by that statement is that Kevin likes me pure and simple."

Josh roared at that one.

"Oh, my word," she groaned. "Get your mind out of the gutter. Pervert." So much for regret at the name-calling.

"Two-timer," he shot back. They shared a grin.

"Let me say it for you. What I think you're trying to say is that Kevin likes you *sans* makeup or something to that effect?"

She nodded. "Exactly. He hates makeup. He calls it goop, especially lip gloss. He thinks it tastes like soap."

"Then I suggest you wear it as often as possible so he'll be tempted to kiss it off you."

She tilted her head. "You've got a point. On the other hand, he might be so repulsed he doesn't even want to kiss me. Do *you* think it tastes like soap?"

He shrugged. "I wouldn't say it's such a bad thing. Especially that fruity stuff. Strawberry's definitely the best flavor. So, tell me," he said as the salad and breadsticks were delivered, "have you seen Kevin since the whole frog legs incident?"

"At his church last night. We'd both signed up to work the soup kitchen. Neither one of us got anyone to take our place so we were stuck with each other." Not that they really had any time to find anyone else.

Josh eyed her closely. "Admit it, Beck. You wanted to see if he'd show up."

"I'll admit no such thing. When Kevin makes a commitment, he sticks to it no matter what."

"Bingo." He sat back with a look that bordered on smug.

She shrugged and frowned. "Must you always be right? It's a very annoying trait. All I know is, it's been quite a week. At least it sounds like your week went better than mine." The look on his face was more than intriguing. Something was different about him, but far be it from her to figure it out. Her brain was mush as it was. "Let me pray for our food and then you can tell me more." He bowed as she gave thanks.

"Go on," Josh said, offering her a breadstick and biting into one. "You're not done yet."

She blew out a breath. *How does he always know these things?* "It went pretty well until we walked out to the parking lot afterwards. We talked a couple of minutes and then he took off. Just tore out of there in his big blue truck without another glance. Gone." She attacked her salad, more hungry than she'd realized.

"Why?" He was going at that breadstick like he hadn't eaten in a week.

"Probably because I basically let him know I wanted to kiss him." Her eyes widened. "Did I say that out loud?"

He nodded. "You did. Were you wearing lip gloss at the time?"

"Shut up." She thought about it. "Actually, I don't think I was." She cringed at the "actually." It was a hard habit to break. "It was written all over Kevin's face that's what he wanted, too. To kiss me, I mean." She looked away and blew out a breath. "Forgive my inarticulateness tonight, if that's even a word. My brain is gone."

"Maybe frog legs kill brain cells." How he managed that one with a straight face she'd never know.

"Will you never stop? What Kevin *said* was, 'You know what you need to do,' in that deep voice of his." She sighed.

Josh gave her an infuriating grin and—even more annoying—snapped his fingers in front of her face. "Lost you for a minute there. What'd he do next? I need the rest of the play-by-play."

She shrugged. "That's pretty much it. That's when he climbed in his truck and hightailed it out of the parking lot. Left me in his proverbial dust and didn't even stick around to make sure my car started." She took another bite of her salad, pushing aside the jalapeño pepper, delighted to find the black olive hiding beneath it. "That's so unlike the man."

Josh feigned surprise. "Really? How dare he?"

She paused the fork halfway to her mouth. "Don't even tell me you're taking his side."

"All I'm saying is good for him. The man's got a spine, bless his heart."

"*What?*" She put her fork beside her salad plate, surprised by the rush of anger that made her heart pound. "Kevin is not timid. He may be shy, but he's a strong man. You should have seen the way he stomped over to our table, introduced himself and spoke to Adam at the restaurant. I was proud of him. As a matter of fact, in that moment, he reminded me of you. He was confident and proud . . . and downright fearless." Her shoulders slumped and her eyes welled with unshed tears. "Please don't tell me you think he's spineless."

"No, honey. If anything, it's the opposite. I just meant it took guts for the guy to walk away from you. Let's think about it. The easy way out would have been to kiss you, but no, the fearless wonder took the hardline approach." Josh ignored her smirk. "There you were," he said, waving his hand in the air, "offering your lips freely to the man, to the point of even telling him you wanted his kiss, and yet he had the strength—the backbone—to resist. A lesser man would have laid a big one on you and taken full advantage." He took another bite of his breadstick, motioning for her to keep eating. "Beck, you know I think the world of Kevin, and I've seen him be as strong as the next guy out there."

At least his words appeased her somewhat. "So, you're telling me he did the right thing by walking away from me last night." It wasn't a question.

"Yeah, I guess I am. One thing I find interesting." He finished his salad.

"Okay, I'll bite. Tell me." She nibbled on the end of her breadstick.

"You seem so concerned about Kevin's reactions and feelings, but you've said almost nothing about the Brit."

Rebekah stopped chewing. "Oh. Well, I guess other than irritation he didn't try to come find me in the restaurant, I haven't thought much about Adam." *And won't be much in the future, either.*

"A suggestion? When you're doing all your multi-tasking tonight, you might ponder why that is. And another thing?" He shook a breadstick at her. It was very annoying.

She pulled it from his hand, tossed it on his plate, then sat back and crossed her arms. "Yes?" She gave him a sappy-sweet smile.

Josh picked up the breadstick and waved it at her again. "Moving right on. Did Kevin happen to tell you why he was at the restaurant?"

"He was there with some older, fawning woman. Don't even get me started."

Josh shook his head. Considering he stopped chewing on his hundredth breadstick, he must have another important point to make. She had to give the man credit: he made a lot of sense.

"I repeat, did he say why he was there?"

She waved her hand. "Said it was a business lunch."

"Any reason to doubt it?"

"Kevin would never lie."

"Bingo. Okay, now, let's think about the Brit for a moment." He was getting fired up now. Although she'd never seen him in action in a boardroom conducting one of his big mergers, she could just imagine. His calm sense of reason and ability to think under pressure were two of the many reasons he made such a great lawyer. "Any theory on why Adam took you for lunch instead of dinner?"

She shook her head, puzzled. "I have no idea. What does that have to do with anything?"

"Did he tell you what he was doing later that evening? From what I know, most of his dates with you are for lunch, no?" His brow quirked.

"True, but you're making no sense other than to plant a big seed of doubt in my mind. Are you suggesting Adam might be seeing someone else on the side?" When he didn't answer, Rebekah sat up straighter and captured his eye contact. "Josh? Is that what you think? Tell me."

"Okay, here's the deal." He took a long drink of his iced tea. "Lord forgive me if I'm wrong, but I don't think I am. When a guy has designs," he said, with a pointed look, "on a woman, he takes her out on Saturday night. I'm not talking about Kevin or an upstanding kind guy like him. I'm talking more about the sophisticated—debonair, if you will—smarmy type. For the sake of illustration, let's say he's, I don't know, British perhaps." He winked when she scowled. "Sorry. I hate to break it to you, but the girl a man like that takes to lunch is the girl he'll marry, but she isn't the girl he *wants*."

"Leaving his evenings free." Rebekah swallowed her gasp. "I think he's getting ready to ask me to marry him again. I mean, the signs are there. At least you're saying I'm the marrying type. Thank you for that. I think." Disgruntled, she sank further down into the booth, not sure she had much of an appetite left. "So, you think he's got another woman on the side." Again, it wasn't a question. When he nodded, she groaned. "Oh, I'm such a fool." She planted her hands on the table. "I deserve it without a doubt. I've played with the affections of two men and this is my comeuppance or whatever they call it." She caught his chuckle. "I really haven't been reading Mom's old Christian romances," she said before he could suggest it again. For the briefest of moments, she considered the idea Josh might be wrong, but her heart told her otherwise. Not that she had any proof, but it didn't matter now, anyway.

"Beck, bottom line here. Does Adam know the Lord like you know the Lord?"

Her brother always had a way of drawing out the truth even when she couldn't admit it to herself. At least he'd finished the last breadstick. "No. And before you can say it, Kevin does. You know that." She raised a hand. "Don't start on me about being unequally yoked. Adam says he's a Christian, but . . ."

"The proof's in the pudding, sis. You know I'm the last person who wants to upset you, but I hope you appreciate I love you enough to tell it like it is. Doesn't seem to me like there's much to figure out." He leaned closer. "You can't tell me your heart's not talking to you in the case of these two men."

"No, it's talking to me all right, but I'm tired of thinking about it." She mustered a small smile. "Believe it or not, I decided last night—during prayer meeting with Kevin, of all places—to dump Adam."

"Then why—"

Her smile grew wider. "Because you're so much fun. And it did help to talk about it. It confirms I'm doing the right thing." She tilted her head, watching him. "Why do I get the feeling if our lives were fictionalized, you'd come across as the sympathetic one?" He shot her a grin as the server brought their entrées and sprinkled grated cheese on their food. "So, your turn. Time to tell me what's going on in your life."

"It's rather difficult to know where to begin."

"I'm sure you'll figure it out."

Josh took another gulp of tea. "Brace yourself, Beck."

"Okay. This sounds pretty serious. Are you all right?" His expression was interesting, but he didn't look sad, upset or angry. If anything, it was the opposite. Whatever it was, it hadn't affected her brother's appetite.

"Honestly? I'm better than I've been in years. I need to come clean about some things and it starts right here and now."

CHAPTER THIRTY

Three Weeks Later—Mid-April

"*MISS GRANT? PHONE call on line six.*" The school secretary's voice on the intercom sounded loud in the otherwise empty teacher's lounge. She should have known her morning break would be interrupted. This day wasn't off to the best start. Danny punched Trevor in the stomach, sending him crying to the nurse, followed not long after by Jenny stepping on a thumbtack and screeching like she'd been shot. The assistant principal, in the classroom next door, had flown around the corner, demanding to know what happened. Maybe it wasn't fair to leave Hannah alone to handle her rambunctious class, but it would be good experience for her plus she'd get a much needed break.

"*Rebekah Grant. Phone call on line six.*" She snapped out of her reverie. It was rare to get a phone call during school hours on the main line, but her cell phone was in her purse, locked away in the bottom drawer of her desk.

Getting up from the table, she picked up the receiver on the phone mounted on the wall and leaned against the counter. "This is Rebekah Grant." The banter between two television talk show hosts droned in the background as she stared absently at the screen.

"Hi, honey."

"Hi, Mom. Everything okay?" Her Aunt Janice hadn't been well, and she hoped nothing had happened. A couple of her fingers tingled with numbness. Balancing the phone on her shoulder, she anchored it with her head while she massaged the affected fingers.

"I just got word on the church prayer chain that Elizabeth Moore was taken to the hospital this morning with severe chest pains. That's all I've heard so far, but I thought you'd want to know."

Kevin's mother. "Of course. I appreciate the call, Mom." She'd had a heart attack three years before, a mild one that was a wake-up call. As far as Rebekah knew, she'd altered her diet and exercised a bit more, but Kevin told her heart disease ran in his mom's family. She hadn't confided in her mother about the awful confrontation with Kevin at the restaurant. It was too complicated, but it had been a long three weeks. Even though she never said anything, Rebekah knew her mother was irritated with her indecisiveness. She really needed to tell Adam and get this over with, but he'd been preoccupied with business or out-of-town a lot.

Glancing at her watch, she frowned. It was still so early, and a long time to go in the school day before the students were dismissed. As she canvassed the distance from the lounge to her classroom, Rebekah prayed for Elizabeth, for her husband, Richard, as well as Kevin and his two brothers. *Please, Lord, let her be okay.*

"What's wrong, Beck?" Hannah whispered when she returned to the classroom. At least the kids were quiet and trauma-free for the moment.

"Kevin's mom is in the hospital with severe chest pains. She's had one heart attack before and I'm worried."

"Then go. I can take care of things the rest of the day."

Rebekah hoped her glance conveyed her gratitude. "Let me check with Betty and explain the situation since I'm not sure what's protocol. Are you sure you want to tackle this crew? They're acting a little wild today."

"I think the other incidents scared them a little and they've been pretty quiet," Hannah told her. "You won't be able to concentrate so you should go. Talk to Betty, but rest assured someone will cover for you. The kids will be just fine."

"Thanks, Hannah. This is why you'll make such a great teacher. I'll have my cell so please call if you need anything."

~

Arriving at the county hospital a short time later, Rebekah learned Elizabeth was transported by ambulance earlier in the day to a Baton Rouge hospital another twenty minutes away. Not hesitating, she hopped back in her Camry and took off again. A half-hour later, she walked into the main lobby of the hospital. No one sat behind the information desk. As if drawn to him, she spied Kevin in one corner of the lobby, his dark head bowed, deep in conversation with another man. *Sam.*

Rebekah began the slow walk in their direction. Sam saw her first, and the look on his face humbled her. Kevin's expression was hard to read.

"Hey, Beck." Sam wrapped her in one of his characteristic bear hugs.

She disengaged from his hug and turned to face Kevin. "Hi, Kevin."

"Rebekah."

Oh, how she wanted to enfold him in her arms, hold this precious man close. "I came as soon as I heard. How's your mom?"

"She's holding her own. The cardiac care unit here is superior to ours, but she almost didn't survive the trip. They're running more tests." He looked tired, his hair disheveled, and he must have come straight from the lumberyard as evidenced by the sawdust shavings still clinging to his shirt. He'd never looked better.

She nodded. "What can I do?"

"I suggest we go to the chapel for a time of prayer," Sam said. "It's the best thing we can do for Elizabeth while we wait."

When Kevin looked at Sam, a tear dropped from one eye. He wiped it away and nodded. "That would be great. I'll get my dad and brothers and join you in a few minutes." He pointed out the general direction of the chapel.

Dipping her head, Rebekah felt Sam's hand on her arm and walked beside him down the quiet hallway.

"Looks like we need to do some catching up," he said. Opening the door, she saw a few bowed heads; two women whispered with another woman in one corner. He closed the door and ushered her to a row of chairs on the opposite wall. "Let's sit over here and talk until the others join us."

"Is Lexa here?"

"She's home with Joe, but she's here in spirit." He nudged her shoulder. "For you, too."

A lock of Sam's thick, wavy hair had fallen across his forehead, and he looked as tired as Kevin. Whenever one of his TeamWork crew was hurting, Sam hurt. His presence must mean so much to Kevin. She smoothed hair away from his forehead. "You're looking a bit weary, my friend." Those piercing blue eyes weren't as bright as usual. "Is Joe keeping you and Lexa up at night?"

"Some. He's going to be a pistol, that one. By the way, Natalie and Lexa have arranged a courtship—if not a marriage covenant—between Joe and Gracie."

"Sounds appropriate." A grin curled her lips, a welcome release. Talking with Sam was always so comfortable. "I can see it now: the cowboy scientist and the Wellesley grad. It has all the makings of a grand love story, kind of like someone else I know."

Sam's smile lines deepened. "Toss in some yellow roses and the Alamo and I think you're onto something. God love those two kids."

"When did you get here?"

He cleared his throat and stretched his legs. "I started out early this morning as soon as Kevin called me."

"Are you going to spend the night?"

"Depends. I'll play it by ear. Kevin's offered to put me up for the night at his apartment."

Rebekah's eyes welled with tears; she nodded. She felt his eyes on her, knew he waited for her to speak. Staring at her lap, she ran her fingers along the top of her handbag to keep them busy. Anything to avoid that soul-searching gaze. "Don't ask, Sam."

"Okay. I won't." He chuckled when he caught her stare. "I know better than to probe when I'm told not to ask."

She leaned her head against the wall behind the chair. "Even if you don't know the circumstances, I'm sure you have some pithy wisdom to impart."

"As one of my closest friends, you know me well enough to know the type of thing I'd say. You know how highly I think of both you and Kevin. It might have taken him a long time to speak up for your heart, but he loves you."

"I know. He told me. Finally."

"Here he is with his brothers. If you need to talk, you know where to find me. Or Lexa," he added with a gentle smile, squeezing her hand and pulling her to her feet. "Call or visit any time. Our door's always open."

"Thanks." She blinked away more tears. *Lord, help me get through this. More importantly, help Kevin and his dad and brothers.*

Kevin's oldest brother, Tommy, enveloped her in a bear hug followed by a quick kiss on the cheek. Chris, the middle brother—more reserved than Tommy—nodded and gave her a small smile. She overheard Tommy tell Sam their father, Richard, was upstairs with Elizabeth. The brother Rebekah wished would pull her into his arms stood in silence to one side, watching. At least Kevin knew she cared and she hoped her presence meant something to him.

"The chapel's free now," Sam said, holding the door to usher them inside. As Rebekah ducked under his arm, he gave her an encouraging nod. Kevin and his brothers took seats in the front row of chairs. Sensing her indecision, Sam nodded toward the row behind them and lowered his lengthy frame into the chair next to hers.

Bowing his head, Sam prayed first. Rebekah felt Kevin's eyes on her when she prayed and wished she sat beside him so she could hold his hand. Her prayer ended, then Tommy joined in, followed by Chris. She couldn't shake the image of their mother in a hospital bed somewhere on a floor above them. *Please, Lord, don't let her die.* Kevin prayed next. His brow creased as he leaned forward, elbows on his knees, pouring out his heart into the prayer for his mom. Rebekah's heart swelled as she closed her eyes and listened. His inner calm and strength of spirit were apparent in the way he kept his voice steady. This man was so solid and grounded, so good. No matter the outcome, he would accept God's will for his mother.

A few weeks ago, she'd have rushed to his side without hesitation, knowing he'd want her beside him. Her thoughts strayed to the heated conversation on that back patio of the French restaurant and then in the church parking lot. How many times had she replayed them in her mind? In light of what was happening now, those events paled in comparison. It wasn't right to think about them. At least, not here, not now.

A quiet sigh escaped her lips as Kevin ended his prayer by singing the first verse of "Great Is Thy Faithfulness," and they joined in. His voice broke as he finished. "Your will be done, Lord."

Rebekah clamped a hand over her mouth as a small cry escaped. This time she didn't hesitate and hurried to the row in front, sat beside Kevin and captured his hand in hers. She leaned her head against his, saying another quiet prayer. Finishing her prayer, she opened her eyes, touched by how he clung to her hand. This time she didn't hesitate as she raised his hand to her lips and planted a soft kiss, leaning her cheek against it. A few tears escaped and dropped from his lashes and she felt his shudder, heard his staggered breathing. She'd never seen him cry before. From the corner of her eye, she was vaguely aware when the others filed out of the chapel.

They sat together a few more minutes before Kevin squeezed her hand and then brushed his fingers under his eyes. "Thanks. I guess I'd better go back out there."

"Of course." She followed him out of the chapel.

Sam talked quietly in the hallway with Tommy and Chris. Tommy suggested they get something to eat in the cafeteria, taking turns to go upstairs with their mom and dad. Chris volunteered to go first, but as he started toward the elevator, the doors opened and Richard emerged. He looked more tired and haggard than his youngest son. With a nod toward where she stood beside Sam, Richard told them Elizabeth was resting comfortably and being constantly monitored.

"They're talking about doing a bypass in the morning, if she's strong enough," Richard said, his voice thick with emotion.

"Mr. Moore," Rebekah said, swallowing her tears and moving forward. When Richard opened his arms, she walked into them, hugging him tight. She loved Kevin's parents. Sensing Kevin's gaze on them, she closed her eyes. "I'm so sorry," she whispered. "We have to pray the Lord will see her through this. She's so special and I love both of you so much."

"I know, honey," Richard said, pulling back and cupping the side of her face with one hand. His face was lined, his eyes weary. "She loves you, too. We all do." He returned her hug and swallowed hard.

Rebekah's pulse escalated when Kevin walked toward her as his brothers and dad started down the hallway in the opposite direction. "Thanks for being here." He hesitated. "Do you want to come get something to eat with us?"

She avoided looking at Sam. Time to prove she was a big girl and could make decisions on her own. Whether or not it was his intention, Kevin forced her to see that truth during their heated exchange on the restaurant patio. Not that things had been handed to her—and she'd worked hard—but life as she'd known it had been uncomplicated. Everything within her screamed, *Yes, I'll go with you, Kevin.* If he hadn't hesitated before asking, she might agree. At least he'd asked. Clearing her throat, she raised her head. "I'd better not, but thanks for asking. I need to be getting home." All she'd think about was him and wonder how his mom was doing, but she'd deal with it. "My mom sends her love and prayers, and your mom's on the church prayer chain."

He nodded. "Tell your mom thanks. I appreciate it." Kevin started to turn away, but paused. His eyes bore into hers. "I realize you came to lend your support for my family and that means a lot, Rebekah. More than you know." With one last glance, he walked away, down the hallway to where his brothers and dad waited.

Even though they might be the same words he'd say to another close friend or church member, she'd treasure them because they came from *him.* Sincere and heartfelt. Then again, maybe she was reading too much into it, second-guessing everything.

Sam lingered behind, and when he moved in her direction, the tears threatened to spill again.

"Sam Lewis, don't you make me shed these tears until I walk out of this hospital with my head held high and my dignity intact."

"I'll call you later." Sam dropped into step beside her as she walked toward the front entrance. "I'd like to talk with you about Josh, but now isn't the time."

A small smile escaped. "If you mean about Winnie and Chloe, I know. Josh told me he'd finally come to see you. You don't know how happy I am about that."

"I think I do." The lines on Sam's brow eased a bit. "He came back to Houston again last weekend, but I didn't see much of him. It's good to see him with Winnie and Chloe. Your brother's a good man, Beck, and his focus is where it needs to be. With God's help, it'll all work out in time. Sooner rather than later as far as Josh is concerned, but Winnie needs a little more time. After a long drought of almost five years, this has all happened pretty fast." The deep smile lines surfaced on either side of his mouth, those blue eyes rested on her. "If Chloe had her way, they'd get married tomorrow. Lexa says she talks about Mr. Josh all the time when Winnie brings her to the house."

Rebekah wiped away a tear. "Kids are so resilient and accepting, and that's another reason I love teaching. Sometimes I think they teach me more than I can possibly ever give to them. Josh seems centered and happier than I've ever seen him. I pray it works out for the two of them. I think the world of Winnie and always have. When he showed me a photo of Chloe, I could see she has my brother's smile. From what I've heard, she's already got him wrapped her little finger and is quite the charmer."

"That she is," Sam said, his smile tender. "And she also got her father's green eyes."

Another tear escaped and she sniffled. "One of the most fascinating things in this journey is seeing how the Lord works miracles in the lives of those I love. I'll keep praying for Elizabeth. Please call me if there are any new developments."

"You've got it. I'll talk to you again soon."

"I hope so. I love you, Sam. Give Lexa my love and kiss that baby for me."

"Will do. We love you, too." He gave her another quick hug and an encouraging smile. "Everything will work out, Beck. Keep looking for *your* miracle. Sometimes they're right under your nose."

Driving back to her house, she couldn't shake the images of Kevin playing in her mind—the way he looked at her and thanked her for being there; the way he prayed; the way he cried. If anything, his tears made him more of a man. His family meant the world to her—so good, God-honoring and loving.

I came to the hospital for you, Kevin. Surely he knew that. At least, she hoped he did.

CHAPTER THIRTY-ONE

One Week Later

JOSH FORCED HIMSELF to concentrate on what the fourteen-year-old boy said as the teenager scarfed down the promised steak on Saturday afternoon. Trey was his right-hand man with the inner city New Orleans neighborhood project, one of TeamWork's outreach ministries.

Try as he might, today his thoughts fought him at every turn. He was a moony-eyed romantic fool these days. He was itching to see Winnie and Chloe again; they'd burned up the phone lines and traded tons of e-mail messages. Chloe had even started to type short messages, telling him the new words she'd learned. As far as she knew, he was her mommy's new friend—one who took her to dinner and kissed her on the lips—nothing more at this point. *One thing at a time.* He was letting Winnie call the shots.

"Answer something for me, Trey," Josh said, chewing a slow bite of steak.

"What's that, Mr. Grant?"

"Do you know what you want from life?"

The teen's eyes widened and he grinned. "You mean what I want to do?"

Josh nodded. "Right. What are your hopes, your dreams?"

Trey thought about it for a moment, his handsome features drawn into a puzzled frown. "I wanna shoot hoops in the NBA a little while and then have my own business, get a wife, something like that." He shrugged.

Josh suppressed his grin. "So, being in the NBA will be a stepping stone to other things?"

"Yeah, once I get old—like thirty-five—I want to have a business. You know, something I can do until I retire."

"And how old will you be then?"

Trey shrugged again. "I dunno. Fifty?"

"What kind of business would you like to own?"

"My uncle owns a pizza shop over in Slidell. I help out sometimes. It's pretty cool. That would be okay, I guess."

"If you play for the NBA and do pretty well, you could afford your own chain of pizza places," Josh said. "I have one piece of advice for you, my friend." When he saw Trey nod, he leaned closer, pushing his half-empty plate aside. "Whatever you decide to do—at whatever point in your life—give it your all. Don't do it half-heartedly. God expects us to give our best." He looked up at Trey. "Do you understand what I'm trying to tell you?"

Trey looked at him and nodded. "Yeah. I think so."

"I'll tell you something else. Sometimes life throws us a curve ball, something we don't expect. Kind of like a slam dunk that comes out of nowhere, or a line drive that ends up sailing out of the park. When that happens, accept it, embrace it." He leaned against the back of the booth. "Run with it, man."

Trey finished his food and shot him a curious look as he drained his glass of milk. "You mean like a pass in football?"

Josh nodded. "Like the quarterback's just thrown you the best pass of his life and it's up to you to run it into the end zone. Run for all you're worth, man. Fly as fast as your legs will carry you and don't look back. Concentrate on the goal, on what's ahead. Don't believe all the New Age hooey they shove down your throat in some of these shops here in the Quarter. You only get one chance in life and I want you to run it into the end zone. Take it in for the touchdown." Enough sermonizing. Josh wasn't sure whether it was more for his own benefit or Trey's. He hoped the teenager would remember that advice as he followed his own life's path. "Want any dessert?"

"No, I'm done," Trey said, swiping his napkin across his mouth and tossing it on the table next to his empty plate.

Josh checked his watch. "What do you say we go check on Dean Phelps and then Harry Darden? I think Dean needs a refrigerator moved and Harry needs me to look at a leak in his roof. Depending on time, we might stop over to see Cheryl Hixon and see if she needs anything, and then I'll take you back to meet your brother. Sound okay?"

Trey nodded. "You got it." Together they walked out of the restaurant. "Thanks for the steak. It was really good."

Josh patted his shoulder. "You're welcome. You earned it."

~

Four hours later, Josh wiped his brow and guzzled most of his water bottle. His eyes fell on four-year-old Denny sitting on the front porch, watching him. *The same age as Chloe.* Cross-legged, elbows on his thighs, he leaned his cheek against one balled fist. Wavy, dark hair fell across half his face.

Climbing up the stairs to the porch, he squatted on square eye level with the boy. "How are you today, Denny?" Small and slight for his age, Denny remained silent. Those large, dark eyes tugged with an unflagging relentlessness on Josh's heart. They looked so trusting, but lonely.

It broke his heart when Trey told him Denny's father was killed a couple of months before in a random act of violence—shot in cold blood in crossfire—the next street over from their small home. His son wouldn't remember much about his father, wouldn't know the strong, kind man he'd been. Seeing the devastation after natural disasters firsthand, and the broken lives left behind after a senseless death like David Hixon's, brought home the fragility of each passing moment. The importance of holding those you love close.

Cheryl Hixon, a proud, quiet woman with sad eyes, stepped out on the porch, the flimsy screen door protesting with a loud creak as it slammed behind her. She'd been busy in the kitchen while Josh and Trey worked to repair broken slats on the outside front steps. It had taken longer than he anticipated, but they were still okay on time.

Josh stood up and smiled. "We're almost done. I'm sure you'll be glad to be rid of us and all this racket."

Cheryl shook her head. "Here. I made you something." She thrust a paper plate of homemade chocolate chip cookies into his hands, covered with plastic wrap. "Thanks for what you're doing for me and Denny."

Josh nodded, swallowing hard. This woman barely had enough money for food and yet she'd made him cookies. Unwrapping a corner of the plate, he took a bite and offered one to Denny. With a quick look at his mom, the boy rose to his feet and grabbed one, stuffing it in his mouth. Trey took one, too, and thanked her.

"These are delicious. Thank you," Josh said. Cheryl nodded, a look of pleased satisfaction creasing her lips. "We'll be another twenty minutes or so and then we're done. I'll send someone over in the next week to fix that porch door."

As he dropped off Trey at his brother's house thirty minutes later, Josh pulled out his wallet and handed over three twenty-dollar bills. "Trey, do me a big favor in the next couple of days. Go to the grocery and get eggs, milk, bread, cheese, some ground beef—basic stuff—whatever you can get with this money. Keep a little for you, but make sure you get as much as you can for Denny and Mrs. Hixon, okay? Will you do that for me, buddy?"

"Yeah. You can count on me. Do you want me to call and let you know when I've done it?"

"Not necessary. I trust you. Thanks a lot and I'll see you next time."

Trey saluted. As he got out of the car, he shot him a grin. "You know what you were talking about earlier? All the sports stuff?"

Josh chuckled under his breath, shaking his head. "Yeah. Sorry about that."

"Nah. You're cool. I know you got a woman, Mr. Grant." He shot him a grin. "Run it in for the touchdown, man."

~

Josh rubbed his hand over his brow after a short stop to gas up the car and buy a bottled water. It had been a long day, but he'd sleep well tonight. Nothing sounded better than a long, hot shower to clean off the accumulated dirt and sweat. He couldn't remember the last time he'd felt this kind of satisfaction from a day's efforts. Something about the physicality of working with his hands and putting his faith in action thrilled him more than his corporate deals. If only he could find some type of job that combined his two passions. *Yeah, that's definitely something to pray about.* He took a long swig of the cold water as he headed down the highway.

Thoughts of 'his girls' occupied his mind, just as they had all day. Winnie and Chloe filled the most tender spot in his heart—that place which had remained hollow and meaningless far too long in his life. *Man, I really need to call her.* He needed to tell her he loved her. That wasn't something he wanted to confess over the phone lines or via an e-mail message, but he felt the overwhelming urge to tell her now. He wanted to tell her so much more—things like how he wanted to cherish and protect them always. He'd love to take her on romantic outings, help her at catering events, hold her hand when she was sad, massage her tired feet at the end of a long day. How he longed to walk Chloe to school, help her learn new words, teach her to ride a two-wheeler bike, and fend off the inevitable when boys came calling a few years down the road. But, until Winnie was ready to make that kind of lasting commitment, he'd have to take it slower than he wanted.

Seized by a sudden urge to hear her voice, he pulled over at a rest stop twenty minutes from home. Grabbing his cell phone on the passenger seat, he punched in Winnie's number. "Hey, sweetheart."

"Hi, Josh. You sound tired. Everything go okay today?"

The sound of her voice brought an immediate smile, but he liked how she could sense his mood in only two spoken words. "Everything's fine. We got a lot done today, but I needed to hear your voice."

"It's great to hear yours, too. Where are you?"

"Not far from home, yet not close enough."

She giggled. "That's an intriguing line. Am I supposed to guess what it means?"

He blew out a breath. "I hadn't planned on saying this over the phone, and please forgive me, but it's way past time."

"I'm listening."

He detected a tinge of hesitancy. Not wanting to alarm her, he plunged right in. "I love you, Winnie. Both you and Chloe. So much it hurts."

"Aw, *cher*." That brought a smile, hearing how she'd adopted his Cajun manner of speaking. "We love you, too, Josh."

Leaning against the headrest, he closed his eyes. "Picture me there with you, wherever you are, my arms around you, hugging you close. You're not someplace where that would be highly embarrassing, are you?"

She laughed, the sound touching him deep inside, as it always did. "No, I'm home. Chloe's taking a longer than usual afternoon nap and I'm fixing a light supper. Care to join us?"

"If only I could."

"Tell me about your day, if you want." Usually they talked every evening and reserved that topic for those times.

He told her about the project and his lunch with Trey, but not the part with the sports analogy. No need, but he was running in for that touchdown now. "How was your day with Chloe?"

Winnie hesitated, and he could hear her sigh. "Something hurtful happened, but then it turned into something pretty amazing."

His smile sobered and he sat up straighter in his seat. "Tell me."

"We ran into a lady at the grocery who knew me from my former marketing job. Let's just say this woman let it be known her thoughts about me being a single, unwed mother. She made my life pretty miserable at times. She always called me a goody two shoes and seemed to take pleasure in my . . . circumstances, for lack of a better term."

"I'm sorry, sweetheart. What happened?"

He heard the catch in her throat. "She pushed her cart alongside me and made small talk, but I knew she was leading up to one of her zingers. She's known for them and I learned to stay away when I worked with her. She was talking about something inconsequential and then she nodded at Chloe and made some offhand comment about a mistake and used the Lord's name in vain somewhere in the mix. The reference to a mistake was thinly-veiled, but her barb hit its mark."

That was enough to get him riled. "Okay, this is when being a Christian is difficult. Give me her address and I'll make sure to have a word with her next time I'm in Houston. She won't bother you or Chloe again." As it was, he wanted to jump in his car and head on autopilot straight to Houston.

"Thanks, Josh, but you don't need to worry about it."

"Oh? Why is that?" He heard a muffled sound and wondered if Chloe had come into the kitchen. A moment later, he knew Winnie was crying although she tried to be quiet—whether to hide it from him or Chloe, he couldn't be sure. "Sorry. I didn't mean to make you cry." The worst thing was to hear her tears and not be beside her. "Is Chloe there with you now? I can call back later, if you want."

"She's still asleep." She hesitated a moment. "Josh, Chloe heard what she said and it concerns me."

His heart pumped overtime. "Oh, no. Do you think she understood what that woman—and I use that term loosely—meant?" *How can someone be so callous?* When it came to an innocent, impressionable child, that type of offensive comment was inexcusable.

"She can't possibly understand what it meant, no. But mistake was one of her words not long ago. Chloe used the example of me writing down a wrong number on an accounting ledger and then erasing it. So, in that regard, she equates it with something wrong that needs to be corrected."

Josh ran his hand through his hair. "Where does the pretty amazing part come into play?"

He heard Winnie sniffle and envisioned her straightening her shoulders and lifting her chin. "This is how the Lord works. Chloe put her hands on her hips, marched over to her and said, 'God doesn't make mistakes. He makes miracles.'"

Josh couldn't answer for a long moment, so long Winnie asked, "Are you still there?"

"Yeah, I'm here. Always." His voice came out hoarse.

"Chloe was pretty cranky after that and I thought she might cause a scene. Maybe it affected her more than I know since she's never acted up like that before, but I didn't have the heart to punish her."

"Of course not," he said, recovering his voice after a few seconds. "She's the perfect child. A little crusader, from the sound of it." Pride swelled his chest. *Can it be my child inherited that bold, fearless gene from me?* From what he'd seen, Winnie was every bit as strong and independent in spirit. It was one of the many things he loved about her.

"There's no such thing as the perfect child, Josh, and believe me, she has her moments. I'd worry about her if she didn't, but I'll claim her any old day of the week. Sounds to me like Chloe might make a great lawyer herself one day if she's so inclined."

That statement thrilled him. "Kiss our little miracle for me and tell her I'm coming soon to give her the biggest hug of her life. You, too. I love you, Winnie."

"We'll be waiting, Josh."

CHAPTER THIRTY-TWO

Late April

"WHERE ARE WE, Kevin?"

With a cute grin, he turned his head, looking around. "Well, I'd say we're in the health club." They were both out of breath from working out, he in a pick-up game of basketball, she from working out on the rowing machine and then running on the treadmill. They hadn't planned to meet, but happened to be there at the same time—he with an A&M friend, Justin, and she with Hannah. He looked more rested than she'd seen him in weeks.

"Your mom doing better?"

The lines on his forehead relaxed even more. "Much better, thanks. Even more than the doctors hoped, so that's an answer to prayer."

"And how are *you*?" They'd seen each other in church and sometimes sat together, but he didn't hold her hand, they didn't go to lunch, and he didn't offer to drive her anywhere. Rebekah shot him a glance full of meaning, brushing loose strands away from her face that escaped her ponytail elastic. She attempted to slow her breathing, but it was pretty much a lost cause.

"I'm not sure the gym is the best place for this conversation." Unzipping his duffel bag, Kevin retrieved a towel and wiped his brow before wrapping it around the back of his neck. Soaked through to the skin, he looked good in his shorts and tank. The man played hard, like he did everything else. She hadn't missed his glances in her direction when he thought she wasn't watching and knew he appreciated her new workout clothes. Rather, how she *looked* in them.

"Where would be a better place then? Tell me and maybe we can arrange something."

He paused and his eyes fell on hers. "Are you asking me for a date?"

"Depends. If I did, would you accept?"

He gave her a sharp look. "No, I wouldn't."

"What does that mean?"

He looked away. "If it makes you feel any better, I'm not mad at you. I'm mad at me. It's my fault for confusing you. You obviously have feelings for the man."

"I'm going to end it with Adam." He looked up in surprise, but didn't speak. "I decided that night in the prayer meeting when Pastor Jim spoke about patience. I wasn't going to say anything until I'd broken it off with him, knowing that's what you'd want, but Adam hasn't been around much. I haven't seen him or even talked with him for some unknown reason, and breaking up by telephone isn't the way I want to end it." The more she thought about Josh's suspicions, the more she suspected her brother was right. But how could she fault Adam when she'd been seeing two men at the same time?

"Don't do anything rash on my account." Kevin turned aside.

"Rash?" She scoffed at that one. "It's been weeks since that prayer meeting, Kevin. Trust me, I know it's something I've needed to do for a long time. Forgive my assumption, but I thought you might be happy about it. My mistake, apparently."

He tossed the towel back in his bag and zipped it closed. "Maybe you should spend some time single for a while, Rebekah."

That was enough to send her heart plummeting. "What does *that* mean?" She couldn't believe what she was hearing. Once he knew she'd dumped Adam—or planned to break it off with him—she expected . . . . Her mouth gaped when Kevin grabbed his bag and started to walk away, leaving her sitting alone on the bench.

"Kevin?" She prayed she didn't sound desperate, but really didn't care. She'd pretty much left her pride in the dirt that night he'd taken off from the church after the prayer meeting.

The muscles in his cheeks flexed as he walked back to stand in front of her. "I didn't agree to sit by and watch that man steal you from right under my nose. One thing I'm not is stupid. I knew you'd either come to your senses or Adam would mess it up with you. Or both." He stepped closer, all flushed, hot, sweaty male and surging testosterone. "I've loved you enough to wait this long and I can wait longer, but jumping from his arms straight into mine isn't the answer. Figure out for yourself who—or what—you want first. *That's* your answer. Before the next Adam comes along and turns your head. I can't compete with that, and I shouldn't have to." He turned to walk away again.

Rebekah swallowed hard, her heart somewhere down around her ankles. *I know what I want. You.* She bit her lip. Oh, she'd blown this one royally. "And what do you want, Kevin?"

He turned halfway, giving her such a look of love she thought she'd melt right on the spot. Even without him telling her—and oh, how she wanted to hear those words again from this man's lips—she knew he loved her.

"The same thing I've always wanted for you."

She waited.

"The Lord's best."

For once, that answer didn't satisfy. It wasn't enough. "Kevin," she said, rising to her feet and planting herself in front of him. "That horrible day at the French restaurant, what did you say to me? Please tell me."

A slow grin upturned those tempting lips. It gave her incredible hope. "That will have to wait."

~

Early May

Kevin blinked twice. Hard. Adam Martin was in the store portion of his family's lumberyard. From the tilt of his head, the set of his shoulders, the man looked like he belonged in a smoking jacket in the drawing room of an English castle. *What could he possibly want? Did Rebekah tell him about me?* Determined no one else would wait on him, he waved aside the store manager and strode in Adam's direction. "May I help you, sir?"

Adam turned and looked at him. It was obvious from his expression he didn't recognize him as the man who'd manhandled Rebekah in that French restaurant. Of course, he wouldn't suspect another suitor for the lovely Rebekah's heart would work in a lowly lumberyard in jeans and a work shirt. He brushed the sawdust from his shirt.

"Ah, yes, my good man."

Kevin swallowed his laugh. *People actually talk like that?* This guy was more than impressed with himself and wanted to play the British card. "What are you looking for today?" His dad always said, "Kill 'em with kindness." That advice never rang more true especially now that Adam was in his store and a potentially well-paying customer.

"Why, I'm looking for some lumber, of course. I wouldn't be here otherwise." Adam looked around the large warehouse as though an immigrant landing on the shore of a newly-adopted country.

"Well, then, you've certainly come to the right place. Are you planning on building something?" Kevin bit his lip not to call him by name.

"I want a gazebo."

That was a surprise. By the wildest stretch of his imagination, he couldn't envision this man building anything. "You want to build a gazebo?" As soon as the words were out, he realized how ridiculous they were. He wouldn't have a callus anywhere on his body and his hands were probably softer than Rebekah's. *Down, boy.*

Adam laughed. "No, of course, *I* don't want to build it. Don't be daft. I'd like someone here to build it and have it delivered." Focusing on him, really seeing him for the first time, he tilted his head.

Better say something quick to circumvent any questions. Being called "daft" by a Brit twit wasn't sitting well with him as it was. *What does Rebekah see in this guy?* Kevin grunted. "Do you have any specifications in terms of size, color?"

"I'm thinking of something on the smallish side, but very private. Elegant."

"Why don't you come with me and I can show you some diagrams for prefabricated gazebos?"

As they walked, Adam said, "I'm planning on presenting a very special woman with the gazebo." The man almost swaggered like a Texan. He was dressed in gray slacks and a light blue sweater, most likely cashmere that cost more than his entire wardrobe. He oozed old money and sophistication, and he *was* smooth.

Now the situation didn't seem so amusing. While Kevin didn't want to believe Rebekah lied to him, at the very least she apparently hadn't cut Adam loose. *What's the holdup?* And she thought *he* was taking it slow in terms of their relationship?

"I'm one of the owners of this store," Kevin said, uncertain why he felt the need to throw that out there especially since he'd only assumed part-ownership the week before. "I'd be more than happy to personally assemble a gazebo for you. She must be a very special lady." *Oh, that was wicked.*

Adam smiled and slapped him on the back. It wasn't a real man's man slap, but one of those you're-an-agreeable-chap pats. "She's the prettiest girl this side of the Atlantic. Much more beautiful than those supermodels. Curvier. Softer. I'm quite the lucky man."

Kevin averted his eyes and turned his head. *Curvier? Softer?* True enough, but he felt like punching the guy for saying it. Maybe the men in Adam's social circle talked like that, but he sure didn't. He cleared his throat. "May I ask the special occasion?" Retrieving a notepad, he made random calculations, needing something to do with his hands.

"I'm planning on asking the fair maiden to marry me for a second time. She didn't know me well enough the first time around, but this time, she won't disappoint me."

Don't be so sure. Kevin stiffened, wanting to give this man a piece of his mind. Before or after he punched him out was the bigger question. *Focus would be good. Be a professional.* "So, you're planning on asking her to marry you in the gazebo?"

Judging by the look Adam tossed his way, he was being daft again. "No, mate. I'm planning to *marry* her in the gazebo so make certain it's big enough for at least four to six people, if you would. Although, perhaps you're onto something there." His brow furrowed. "I *should* also propose to her in the gazebo. She's a fairly simple girl, in spite of her beauty, and doesn't like a lot of fuss."

At least that much was true. Kevin nodded. "Uh huh." Walking to a nearby book, he opened it and flipped through the pages. He pointed to a photo of a white, medium-sized gazebo. "What do you think of this one?"

Adam leaned closer. "It's adequate, yes, but looks a tad bit on the anemic side. Anything larger or nicer?"

"Sure." Kevin flipped a few more pages, looking for something really obnoxious and ostentatious. Thinking better of it, he backtracked, pointing to another photo. "How about this one?"

Adam's smile was broad. "I think that one looks perfect, actually. Be a good man and write us an estimate, please."

"Yes, sir," he said through gritted teeth. Thinking better of it, he hesitated. *I can't believe I'm about to say this.* "Tell you what. Since it's for such a special girl and such a happy occasion, let me build you a one-of-a-kind gazebo using select materials from our lumberyard."

Adam eyed him up and down. "You?"

He nodded, the muscles in his cheeks flexing. "Yes, me. I've built a lot of things, including playhouses for kids, tree houses—" *Why do I feel the need to sell myself to this guy?*

"Gazebos?" A look of skepticism was etched on his otherwise smooth brow.

"No, but I assure you, you won't be disappointed. I'm thinking I can add hearts around the top of the gazebo, commemorating this special occasion." *Now who's being ridiculous?* His brain was apparently functioning independently from the rest of his body.

That did the trick. Adam's smile returned. "Why, that sounds splendid!"

"I can even add a name or a message and carve it into the gazebo. Adam and Hortense forever." He shrugged. "Something like that." He'd gotten a little carried away there and offered more than enough.

"How did you know my name was Adam?" Crossing cashmere-covered arms, he stared. "I don't believe we traded names."

Think quick. Kevin's pulse raced and he closed his mouth. "I felt sure we did." The Lord would have to forgive him that one. "Sorry, but you look like someone I know whose name is Adam."

The other man's hard gaze relaxed. "Tell me, mate, do I look like the sort of chap to be out and about with a Hortense?" He shook his head, chuckling under his breath. "Unfortunately, it happens to be the name of my dear second cousin." Gray eyes focused on him again. "Tell you what. I do like your idea. All the way around. It's quite spectacular." Adam broke into a smile, looking more than pleased. "I say let's have a go at it then, shall we?"

Yes, let's. "Why don't you give me her name and I'll make sure it's added to the gazebo."

"Very well. Her name is Rebekah." With his accent, it sounded like a rolled R at the end of her name. "Rebekah Grant."

"And how do you spell that?" Kevin held the notepad a little higher, thankful he had it to hold onto, praying his shaking hands didn't betray him. Why should this man intimidate him?

"R-e-b-e-k-a-h," Adam said slowly. "You look rather familiar. Have we—"

"I'll call it Rebekah's Heart." Kevin settled his gaze on him, hoping he wouldn't finish that thought.

Adam nodded slowly, watching him all the while, a thoughtful look on his face. "Perfect."

He finished making his calculations. "I can't give you an exact amount until it's built, but this is the amount I'd need for a deposit." He'd written down an outrageous, exorbitant dollar amount, but, thinking better of it, scratched it out. With a sigh, he jotted a more reasonable number and showed it to Adam, careful not to shove it under his nose.

The man didn't flinch. "Fine. Does that also include the price for assembly?"

"Yes, but there would be an extra surcharge for delivery."

"Fine. Thank you." Now he sounded both bored and annoyed as he pulled out his wallet.

Kevin mustered his most polite tone. *Kill him with kindness. Thanks, Dad.* "While I process the payment, I'll ask you to write down her address so we'll have it for our records. For the delivery."

"So, are we all set then?" Adam asked, pocketing his credit card and the receipt a couple of minutes later after he completed the sale.

"Just one more question. Do you have a date when you need the gazebo completed?"

Adam held his gaze. "I don't want to keep my lovely Rebekah's heart waiting too long, after all." Gray eyes fell on him. "Tell me, mate, is two weeks too soon?"

"No," Kevin croaked, swallowing hard. "Not at all, sir."

CHAPTER THIRTY-THREE

The Next Day

"ADAM, WE NEED to talk." Rebekah hated leaving that message on his voice mail, but she knew the quicker he got it, the sooner they could speak. It had been long enough. No more postponing the inevitable, especially since she'd told Kevin that was her plan. *Then I guess I'll be single for a while.* It was a surprise when Adam called her back within a half-hour and she was shocked to hear he was in England. She couldn't be so insensitive as to break up with the man over the telephone when he was a continent away. That wouldn't be fair.

"Something unexpectedly came up, Becks, and I had some family business. Forgive me, lovely. I miss you, and I'm terribly sorry I've been out of touch. I'll be back around on Thursday night and we can talk then."

"Come around and see me then, please." Goodness, now *she* was beginning to sound like a Brit.

"As soon as I step off the plane, I'll be there with lots of kisses. Shall we say sevenish or thereabouts?"

"I'll see you then. Thanks. I'll be praying for a safe trip." Hanging up the phone, Rebekah slumped down onto her sofa cushions. It was only four days away, but seemed like forever.

~

True to his word, Adam showed up on her doorstep on Thursday night. As soon as he entered the house with a perfunctory kiss on the cheek, Rebekah knew he had a purpose in mind. He smelled great and looked debonair, as always. She steeled herself not to let either his accent or his powerful presence sway her in her resolve. It had to be done.

Life without Adam was possible, but life without Kevin was unfathomable.

"You look beautiful as ever, Becks. Come give us a real kiss."

Adam seated himself on the sofa, patting the spot beside him. Sitting next to him, Rebekah allowed a small kiss on the cheek. Just a light peck, nothing more. Not the best way to start a breakup conversation, perhaps.

"I missed you so much while I've been gone, but this can wait no longer."

He missed her? *He hasn't been around in weeks.* Her breath caught in her throat as he slid to one knee on the floor beside her.

Reaching into his inside coat pocket, Adam pulled out a dark blue velvet-covered box.

"Wait!" Rebekah said, holding up one hand. *This can't be happening.*

"Marry me, my beautiful Becks." He opened the box.

Nestled inside was the biggest, emerald-cut diamond she'd ever seen. Momentarily dazed, she touched it, then snatched away her hand as if she'd been burned.

"I love you madly and want you by my side. Always. I want to give you everything—parties with royalty, fine dining, a lovely home—" He prattled off a number of enticements, none of them what she wanted to hear. None of them what she *needed* to hear.

She stared at him for a long moment. Something was conspicuously absent from his speech. "Tell me something, Adam. Where do children fit into your life?" She was careful not to say *our* lives.

His eyes widened. "Well, if you must . . ."

She rose from the sofa, clenching her fists. "If I *must*? I'm a teacher, Adam. I love children. They're precious gifts and I want as many as the Lord will give me."

"We've never discussed this before, but I'm quite sure we can come to a suitable compromise—"

She crossed her arms and tried to steady her voice. "There is no compromise when it comes to children. You don't fit children into your life, around all the things, the parties, the travel and the fancy home. You bring children into the world and build your life around *them*. They're more important than anything else. At least to me." Rebekah shook her head. Her head pounded and it saddened her to think she'd wasted so much valuable time on a man who didn't share one of the most important values in her life. Even though she'd never discussed it with Kevin either, she had no doubt he'd be all for it. Probably want to procreate like crazy and have a dozen. Her cheeks colored and she lowered her gaze from Adam's.

"Our lives will be quite full, I assure you, what with all the expectations to attend functions, some even at Buckingham Palace. You'll have the finest couture gowns, an unlimited charge account at Harrod's, fabulous trips to exotic locations every year, anything you could ever want—"

"Stop." The word barely came out. She held up one hand. "Just stop right there. Adam, I'm sorry, but I can't marry you." She would have stopped him sooner but was momentarily distracted by the Buckingham Palace part. "Please stand up."

His eyes widened and he rose to his feet. "May I ask why not?" He cleared his throat as he closed the lid of the box and returned it to his pocket.

It pierced her heart when she glimpsed the tears shining in his eyes. "Lovely as they are, I don't want any of those things . . . because that's all they are. *Things*. I was momentarily distracted and thought I did, but I don't." She shook her head. "I do love you, Adam. You must know that, but it's not the marrying kind of love."

Shoving his hands into the pockets of his slacks, Adam faced her again. "What is your definition of a marrying kind of love, Becks?"

She blew out a long breath. "I need a man who cares about my family. A man who loves the Lord like I do. A man who knows when my fingers are numb and massages them. A man who loves and accepts me the way I am and doesn't make me pretend to be someone or something I'm not." Her eyes clouded and she turned away, facing the window but not seeing anything. "A man who listens to my opinion and values it. Who writes songs for me and plays them on his guitar. And smells like . . . sawdust and sweat and has the best, loopiest grin in the world when he looks at me like I'm the *only* woman in the world." Rebekah wiped her eyes and turned back to face him. She'd said enough, but wasn't done yet.

"Answer one question for me, Adam."

"Anything." He stepped closer.

Maybe it wasn't fair, but her brother had the best instincts of anyone she'd ever known, male or female. She had to know. Her eyes met his. "When you were taking me to lunches at fancy French restaurants, were you taking someone else to dinner?"

The stricken look crossing his face told the true story.

"Don't bother answering," she said, wiping her eyes. What she didn't expect was the overwhelming sense of relief that invaded every pore of her body. *Thank you, Josh.* For the first time she could remember, little beads of sweat dotted his brow, and he looked slightly disheveled . . . and sad, but it was for the best, and they both knew it.

"Beautiful Becks," Adam said and faltered, his gaze sliding to the floor as he gathered his thoughts. Taking her hand, he led her to the door. "I'll never regret the wonderful times we've shared together." When she opened the door, he stepped outside, pausing on the top step.

"Neither will I."

"It has indeed been my greatest honor knowing you. I'm not such a bad guy, really." His eyes met hers. "Just not the one for you, eh, lovely?"

A tear slipped down her cheek. She opened her mouth to speak, but was at a momentary loss for words.

"I wanted it to be you, Becks." He stared at their hands clasped together. "I suppose it's something you might not understand, but tradition is everything in my family. If nothing else, I am my father's son."

What does that even mean? At this point, it was moot, anyway. Time to move on. "You're a very special man, Adam, with so many wonderful qualities. I wish you the Lord's best always." Not very original, but Kevin would approve.

He planted a quick, soft kiss on her temple and released her hands. "I hope the Yank deserves you." With a final lingering glance, he departed, taking his lovely accent, expensive clothes and cologne-scented masculinity through her front door and out of her life.

Rebekah's eyes widened. The Yank? *Does he know about Kevin?* She suspected she might never know. Stepping onto the front walkway as he climbed into his car, she smiled and put one hand over her heart as he blew her a kiss. Turning to go back inside, she spied her elderly neighbor by the side of her house. She held her garden hose in her hand, watering her prized blooms.

"Hi, Mrs. Michelson."

"Rebekah." A hint of a smile creased her lips. "Lovely evening, isn't it?"

"Yes," she said, "it is." Feeling a sudden chill even though it was a very warm evening, she rubbed her hands up and down her arms.

Mrs. Michelson turned off the water and dropped the hose onto the ground. "Would you like to come join me inside for a cup of tea?"

She blinked back the tears. "Yes." She walked across the short expanse of yard. "I'd like that very much."

CHAPTER THIRTY-FOUR

Early June

REBEKAH SAT AT her kitchen table, enjoying a leisurely Saturday morning breakfast when her phone rang. She didn't bother checking the display for once.

"Rebekah Grant." Sitting back down at the table, she moved her spoon around her almost empty cereal bowl.

"Beck, it's Josh." Something in his voice sounded strange and she sat up straighter. An unmistakable chill washed over her.

"What's wrong?"

"It's Dad. He had a heart attack this morning."

The news sent a jolt straight through her. "Is he . . . all right?"

"I'm headed over to your house now. I'll be there soon."

"Josh," she said, her voice rising. "Tell me now."

"Dad's gone, honey." He choked on the words. "About an hour ago. I just talked with Mom. It happened quickly and he wasn't in pain."

"Oh, no." It came out a strangled moan. Rebekah almost dropped the phone, but somehow managed to keep one hand on it. "I can't believe this."

"I'll be there in twenty minutes and we can go see Mom together. There will be some . . . decisions that need to be made."

Rebekah nodded, but her brain was numb. "Dad's always been so healthy. I just saw him yesterday. What happened? Where was he?"

"He was reaching up into the cabinet to get that awful, cardboard-tasting stuff he calls healthy cereal. Mom said he winced a little and grabbed at his chest." Josh hesitated. "Then he fell to the kitchen floor. She couldn't move him and called 9-1-1. They came within minutes, but it was already too late."

Rebekah bit her lip, trying her best to hold back the sobs. "Was he able to say anything to Mom?"

"Yeah." Josh's voice cracked and he cleared his throat. "He told her to watch over us."

"And also that he loved her, no doubt."

"No. That much was a given. Beck, Dad's last thought was of *us*." She heard the deep emotion in her brother's voice.

It was so typical of the way Lucas Grant lived his life. He was the most giving, generous, kind-hearted man she'd ever known. Unbidden, Kevin's face popped into her mind. She squeezed her eyes closed and pressed her fist against her lips. Of all the men she'd ever known, Kevin was most like her father.

Shoving her chair away from the table, Rebekah took her bowl to the sink. *Lord, keep us strong.* Right now she had to go with Josh and take care of their mother. Her dad might have asked their mother to watch over them, but it was their responsibility to watch over *her*. Again, time to be a grownup.

~

The next few days were a whirlwind of decisions, planning, preparations and family and friends coming to visit before the service early on Wednesday afternoon. Both Rebekah and Josh moved back into their childhood bedrooms upstairs. The women from their home church stopped by with quiet words, condolences and casseroles. Pastor Scott from their church came by at least once each day to share scripture and words of encouragement. Some of the members of Kevin's church, including Pastor Jim, stopped by with words of comfort and brought pies and baked goods as well as a ton of sympathy cards.

Rebekah escaped upstairs to her bedroom for a few precious minutes of privacy late Tuesday, seeking refuge from the constant coming-and-going. It had been a long day at the funeral home. She stared through blind eyes at the pink and green floral wallpaper she'd begged her mom for when they redecorated her room. She'd been in eighth grade, maybe ninth. Her white canopy bed fit for a princess was the same one she'd slept in growing up in this wonderful house designed by her father as a wedding gift for her mom. He'd always been so involved in their lives, taking Josh to his ballgames, attending her cheerleading competitions, and never failing to go to the many recitals, concerts and school programs. He'd taught her to ride the two-wheeler she got for her seventh birthday—all blue sparkles, banana seat and a little white basket with blue-and-white streamers. So many wonderful memories . . . so many things she'd tell him if only she could see him again.

Josh knocked and ducked his head in the open doorway. "Beck, the Moores are downstairs."

"Is Kevin with them?" She wiped her eyes and gave him a feeble smile. She'd attended church with her mom and Josh on Sunday morning, but hadn't talked with Kevin although he'd left her a message on her home phone, maybe more than one. She'd been existing in a fog. For whatever reason, she couldn't call him back. His family had been at the funeral home; he'd given her mom a hug and kiss and talked with Josh. He'd said a few words to her, but kept his distance. That hurt, but she couldn't blame him.

"Yes, of course. I hope that's a good thing?"

Rebekah focused on him with a hint of a smile. "Yes. He just doesn't know it yet."

Josh grinned and it eased the lines on his face. From the looks of him, he'd gotten no more sleep than she had the last couple of days. Smoothing a wrinkle in her navy dress, she paused, gathering her thoughts and whispering a quiet prayer for strength. It didn't take much these days to bring her to tears. One look from Kevin might send her over the edge.

"Is Winnie coming?" she asked.

"Later tonight with the rest of the TeamWork crew and she's bringing Chloe. Her nanny, Dottie, is coming and she's agreed to watch the kids. Everyone's congregated at Sam and Lexa's and they're bringing a caravan over." He tweaked her chin. "Your hero's even flown in from Boston."

"Marc?" Rebekah's heart swelled. "With Natalie and Gracie, too?" Josh nodded and her eyes strayed to a photo of the two of them on the wall back when they were both gawky, long-legged teenagers with big dreams and mouths full of metal. *Were we ever that young?*

Josh pulled her close. "You okay, squirt?"

She loved the hug from her eight-minutes-older brother. Refusing to cry, she swallowed fresh tears. "I'm fine. It's just hard to be a grownup sometimes, you know?"

He kissed her temple. "You're one of the most grownup people I know. You and Kevin will be just fine, and right now, he's waiting to see you."

She nodded and squared her shoulders. "Thanks. Let's go."

Josh waited and came down the stairs behind her as she descended the staircase. She zeroed in on Kevin as soon as she reached the living room. She'd recognize that head of wavy, dark hair anywhere. He talked with a couple who'd worked the soup kitchen with them the last time they were there together.

As she reached the bottom stair, Rebekah greeted Elizabeth and Richard with hugs. Tommy swooped her into one of his characteristic bear hugs and planted a kiss on her cheek.

"I'm so sorry," he said. "When you came to see Mom in the hospital, we had no idea we'd be here like this today."

"Thanks, Tommy." She drew in a deep, shuddering breath. "I'm thankful to see your mom's doing so well."

He smiled. "Yeah, she's doing great, eating healthy stuff, and Dad's got her walking around the neighborhood every night now. Even bought her one of those Exercycle things so she can pedal while she watches those game shows she likes so much." He squeezed her hand and turned to greet Josh.

From the corner of her eye, Rebekah saw Kevin talking with her mom, her Aunt Selena and cousin Ben. Her eyes misted when she saw him give her mom a gentle hug and kiss on the cheek. How her family adored him.

The doorbell rang and she opened it to more friends from their home church. They came bearing a fresh floral arrangement and a peach pie. Her mother took the flowers and greeted them. Mumbling her thanks, Rebekah hurried to the kitchen with the pie. Putting it on the kitchen counter, she gulped deep breaths. *Must breathe.* Putting a hand over her stomach, she moved her other hand over her mouth.

Two strong hands touched her shoulders and turned her around, drawing her into the warmth of his embrace. *Kevin.* She'd held the tears back until now, but as he held her, she sobbed freely, tears crawling down her cheeks. Not knowing what to do with her arms, she let them fall to her sides.

"Put your arms around me, Rebekah," he whispered against her hair. "Let me hold you." When she wrapped them around him, he pulled her close.

"They brought *peach* pie, Kevin," she said, wiping her nose, embarrassed. "I suppose that doesn't even make any sense. Sam's the one with the peach fixation, not Dad."

He pulled her along with him and retrieved a tissue box on the counter. Moving her back to the sink, leaning against it while not releasing his gentle hold on her, he handed her a few tissues.

She cried a little more, snuggling against his chest, loving the steady sound of his heartbeat. He stroked her hair and she was thankful he didn't say anything. Words weren't necessary. He was there. That's all that mattered.

"Thanks," she mumbled against the soft tissue, turning her head and blowing. She tossed the tissues in the direction of the sink, not caring where they landed. "I got mascara on your shirt."

"I don't care. I have others." He pulled her close again. Somehow she knew he needed it as much as she did.

"I hope the stain comes out. It should."

"Doesn't matter. I can throw it away." Pulling back, he stroked the back of his hand over her cheek in a light, sweet caress.

"Kevin, my daddy's gone. He's always been here for me and I'm not sure what I'll do now. I feel so lost."

"I know." He cleared his throat. "But he left you a wonderful gift to help you carry on when he can't be here."

She looked up at him, puzzled. "I'm not sure what you mean."

"Josh. Your dad gave you *Josh* to watch over you and your mom."

And you, too, Kevin. You just don't know it yet. Even though it's because of the saddest circumstances, his death brought you here today, into this kitchen. Thank you, Daddy.

Kevin's lips grazed her forehead and she leaned into it, closing her eyes. His hold tightened even more and they held each other. For how long, she had no idea. It was a miracle no one came into the kitchen—usually a hub of activity in situations like this—but she suspected Josh had something to do with it. When they finally returned to the living room, her eyes sought her brother. Seeing him standing in a corner talking with their neighbors, she nodded and mouthed her thanks. He raised a salute.

Rebekah prayed she made some kind of sense as she went through the motions. Names, faces, conversations blurred together. Josh checked in with her every now and again, making sure she was okay, asking if she needed anything and being incredibly attentive. Kevin stayed nearby, too, and his presence was comforting. Leaving an hour later with his family, he paused in the doorway as she called to him. "Thank you for being here."

He nodded, stepping closer. "I'll see you in the morning. Sam, Lexa and some of the TeamWork crew are coming."

She welled up again as he told his parents to go to the car and he'd join them shortly. He tipped her chin, meeting her eyes. "'But we do not want you to be uninformed, brethren, about those who are asleep, so that you will not grieve as do the rest who have no hope. For if we believe that Jesus died and rose again, even so God will bring with Him those who have fallen asleep in Jesus.' Cling to those verses, Rebekah. Let them comfort you."

She nodded as he started to walk away. "Kevin?" Her voice sounded small, carried away on the soft breeze. But he heard and turned back toward her.

I love you. Not able to speak the words—not like this—she put her hand over her heart and hoped her eyes and expression told him.

Kevin mirrored her when he raised his hand, and placed it over *his* heart.

CHAPTER THIRTY-FIVE

The Next Day

"ARE YOU READY for this?" Josh asked early Wednesday afternoon as they prepared to enter the church.

Rebekah helped him straighten his tie, so proud of the man he'd become. "Not sure," she said, taking a deep breath to steady her nerves. "You?"

"Same." He grabbed her hand and she held on tight, drawing comfort from it. Putting his other hand in his mother's, the three of them walked together to the front of the church, nodding to friends and family along the way. Dad wouldn't want them to be sad, but it was difficult to ease the constant ache in her heart.

As the service started, Rebekah felt an unbelievable calm wash over her. Glancing over her shoulder, three pews behind them were their TeamWork family—Lexa and Sam, Natalie and Marc, Winnie, Amy, Dean, Marta, Cassie, Gayle and Eliot. Kevin and his family sat one row behind. She darted a quick glance at Josh and nodded over her shoulder. Seeing him cry almost did her in as his shoulders rocked. Rebekah pulled him close, kissing his temple. On the other side, Mom squeezed his hand and—retrieving a package of tissues from her purse—she pushed one into his hand and handed one across to her. Wiping his eyes, Josh lifted his head, giving her a nod.

Several of the men in the church gave remembrances of their father, speaking of his faithfulness to the Lord and doing His work in and around the church in many different leadership roles through the years. A young man spoke about the impact Lucas Grant made in his life when he'd led the teen boys' Sunday school class. A couple of longtime coworkers from his architectural firm spoke of his expertise, strong work ethic and innovative designs.

When Josh rose to go to the podium, Rebekah was stunned, but she shouldn't really be surprised. It didn't look like he had anything prepared as he gripped the edge of the wooden podium and looked out over the capacity crowd gathered in the sanctuary.

He thanked them for being there and relayed several childhood memories. Josh was a natural orator, always had been, although speaking in public proved a stumbling block for her. In school, she'd write down everything on index cards and then memorize it. Fixating on a focal point on the opposite wall, she'd stare at it while reciting her speech. The carpet beside her bed was worn from where she'd knelt all those nights, praying the Lord would honor her desire to be a teacher and give her the courage to stand in front of a group of kids. It wasn't easy, but she loved her students and, bolstered by a confidence only the Lord could give, she couldn't imagine herself doing anything else.

Josh's words brought her back to the present. "My dad taught me about more than fly fishing. He taught me about being good and strong, and how to be a man of unwavering faith. When I faltered in my own path," he said, lowering his head, "Dad never hesitated. He was beside me the whole way, praying for me, guiding me and waiting patiently for me to find my way back." He looked around the crowd, his eyes bright. "My dad was the kind of man I can only *hope* to be. Lucas Grant taught me one of the greatest lessons in life, and that's forgiveness." His gaze found Sam.

"Forgiveness is unconditional when you love someone." His eyes moved over to Winnie and he nodded. "Whether or not you knew Lucas Grant well, he was a man saved by the grace that covered *my* sins when I couldn't seem to help myself. I pray you all have or will one day come to know that same grace." He turned. "I love you, Dad, I'll miss you, and I'll look forward to seeing you again." With a salute at the photo of their dad poised atop the closed casket—draped with an American flag symbolizing his military service in the Army—Josh moved away from the podium.

The next few hours went by in a whirlwind of activity. At the graveside service, Rebekah jumped when rifles fired three times in her dad's honor. She put her hand over her heart, clutching her wrap around her, steeling herself to be strong. Perhaps the hardest thing was when they lowered her father's casket into the ground. Something about it was so *final.*

Placing the red rose on top of the casket along with her other family members, Rebekah whispered, "I love you, Daddy." As she backed away, a large, rough hand wrapped around hers. *Kevin.* Another hand touched her shoulder and squeezed. *Sam.* Lexa was right behind him as well as the rest of her TeamWork family. Her *other* family. They might not see each other often, but if one of them was in trouble or needed their support, they were there. That thought gave her immeasurable comfort.

Pastor Scott prayed and said a few closing words before dismissing them. Josh stood on the opposite side of the open grave as the small crowd began to disburse. Rebekah's eyes welled with tears as she saw him pull Winnie close and kiss the top of her blonde head. He leaned his head against hers, talking quietly. Seeing them together, seeing how happy he was in spite of the overwhelming sadness prompted her first genuine smile in days.

Sam hugged her and she clung to him for a long moment. "I'm so sorry, Beck. Your father was a great man and he raised two wonderful people to carry on his legacy."

She murmured her thanks, unable to speak as Lexa enveloped her in a long hug and kissed her cheek. Kevin waited until she walked toward him. Taking her hand, he didn't say anything for a long time as he helped her into the cab of the truck before sliding behind the wheel. Allowing the tears to fall, Rebekah didn't bother to stop them. He pushed another tissue into her hands. She rested her elbow on the door, staring out the window as he drove, not seeing anything, lost in memories of her father. When he reached for her hand, her breath caught in her throat. As he turned the corner nearest the house, she turned to look at him.

"You know about Josh and Winnie, don't you?"

"Yes. Do you want me to drop you off in front of the house? I'm going to have to go a little further down the street because of all the cars."

Rebekah shook her head. "Doesn't matter. I'll stay with you and we can go in together." She treasured the look on his face, and understood how her words pleased him. "And Chloe?"

He nodded and gave her a gentle smile. "I do now, but I didn't when you first asked me about it."

It didn't matter how he knew, but she was so thankful he did. "Good. I'm glad you know."

"Me, too."

CHAPTER THIRTY-SIX

REBEKAH WATCHED SAM introduce her brother to the man who'd saved her life in Montana. Josh pulled Marc into a hug and said something to him she'd never know, but appreciated all the same.

Lexa came to stand beside her, slipping an arm around her waist. "Your dad sounds like a great man, Beck. I wasn't as close with my dad as you were with yours, but I loved him and I still miss him. If you ever need to talk, call me. Know we're praying for you and Josh. Our door's always open."

"Thanks. I will." Lexa's eyes strayed over her shoulder and she nodded, stepping aside.

"Rebekah." No mistaking that sweet, gentle voice. She turned and embraced Winnie.

"Winnie, thank you for being here. Most of all, thanks for making Josh so happy." She pulled back, wiping away more tears as Winnie did the same.

"I regret your dad never—"

"I know, but somehow I like to think he *does* know. He knew about Chloe and Josh showed him the photo." Likewise, he knew she'd ditched Adam and she prayed her father knew Kevin would take good care of her.

"I should have told Josh, should have told all of you sooner. Can you ever forgive me?" Winnie's words brought her back to the present.

More tears escaped as Rebekah gathered her in her arms. "Like Josh said at the service, you don't even need to ask." She smiled through her tears. "We start fresh from here. I can't wait to meet Chloe. You don't know how excited I am to be an aunt. Winnie, you've given my brother the most incredible gift of his life, and something precious for my mom." She glanced at the other members of the TeamWork crew and lowered her voice. "Do they know?"

Winnie dabbed under her eyes with a tissue. "They've accepted everything the way you'd expect them to—no questions asked, but with open arms and hearts."

"TeamWork," Rebekah said for them both.

A few minutes later, she joined Natalie on the sofa, giving her another hug. She had to store them up to take her through the drought before she'd see them again. Hopefully, the next occasion would be a happy one. They talked for a few minutes, catching up on the latest news just as she'd done earlier with Amy. Introductions had been made for the newest TeamWork members, and Sam watched them all like a proud papa.

"Thanks for coming all this way, Natalie," Rebekah said. "I can't wait to meet Gracie and Joe and our expanding TeamWork crew."

"We wouldn't miss it, but we need to go rescue Dottie soon," she said with a soft laugh. "She's watching them in the church nursery. The poor saint will probably be flat on the floor with an infant, a toddler and a four-year-old."

Rebekah smiled. "I hear you and Lexa have a . . . little arrangement between Joe and Gracie."

Natalie laughed and her deep blue eyes sparkled. "I think it's more Marc and Sam that are pushing for that relationship. We'll see how the Lord leads."

Glancing around the crowded room, Rebekah spied Amy and Winnie talking together in one corner. They were so close, and she was thankful distance didn't deter the tight friendships they all shared. "Where's Marc?"

"Waiting to speak with you." Natalie nodded across the room.

Thanking her and giving her a quick kiss on the cheek, Rebekah walked to where Marc talked with Kevin, giving his arm a squeeze from behind. "How's my hero?" With a small smile, Kevin departed, giving them privacy.

Marc swept her in a hug, held her tight for a few seconds and kissed her cheek before releasing her. "Beck, I can't tell you how sorry we are, but in spite of the circumstances, I'm glad to see you."

She laid one hand on the side of his handsome face. "You don't know how thankful I am for the Lord's protection and watch care over you, my friend."

Marc nodded, his eyes bright. "Each day is a precious gift."

"Fatherhood certainly agrees with you. I can't wait to meet this beautiful daughter of yours I've heard so much about, especially before she marries Joe Lewis."

His laughter filled her heart. "How are your fingers?" he asked. "Do you still have the numbness?"

"Sometimes." She stole a quick glance at Kevin and saw him talking with some of the newer TeamWork ladies across the room. "The doctor tells me I might always have it, but it's a small price to pay." Her eyes met Marc's again.

"God put me where I needed to be out in Montana. Those two weeks were an awakening of sorts for all of us, you know."

She tilted her head. "How so?"

"It opened the door to Natalie's forgiveness and love for me. It also opened Kevin's eyes to what he almost lost." His eyes captured hers. "That man loves you, Beck. Sorry to be so blunt, but do you love him?"

Her eyes strayed across the room again. As if sensing her eyes on him, Kevin smiled.

"Yes."

"Then tell him. He needs to hear the words, but he needs to hear them from you."

She inhaled a deep breath. "I'm not sure he wants to hear it from me, at least not right now. Things have been a little tense, but they're getting better."

"Trust me," Marc said. "He does."

"I'll tell him, but there's too much emotion right now."

"Promise me something."

Looking back at up at him, she nodded. "Sure. Anything for you, Marc."

"Please don't wait too long."

~

"Let me help you," Kevin said as Rebekah said goodnight to the last of their friends.

"You don't need to stay."

"I know I don't need to, but I want to, if you'll allow me."

She nodded, giving him a small smile. "Thanks."

Josh swung around the corner from the family room. "Beck, let's go upstairs and talk with Mom. Make sure she's okay. She'll be back down in a bit, Kevin."

"Go with Josh," Kevin said.

"I'm not sure how long it'll be."

His smile was gentle. "I'll wait."

She nodded, her eyes welling again as she followed her brother upstairs to their mother's bedroom. They sat on either side of the bed with her, holding her hands and talking. Josh sat on Dad's side. *How difficult must it be for Mom? How many times must she reach for him in the night?* Maybe it was still too new, too fresh, and she hadn't absorbed it all into her daily reality.

"Your dad loved the two of you so much," Lorena told them, looking from Josh over to her and back. "You were his greatest pride and joy, and I hope you know how proud he was of the man and woman you've become." She squeezed their hands. They talked together for the next half-hour, laughing and sharing special memories. It was surprising how easy it was to talk about her father, how much lighter it made her spirits.

Rebekah rose from the bed. "Kevin's downstairs, Mom. Are you going to be okay? Do you want me to stay in here with you tonight? We could snuggle." She leaned down to kiss her mother's cheek.

Lorena brushed a stray strand of silver hair away from her forehead and smiled. "No, sweetie, I'll be fine. Unless *you* need to snuggle."

"I might. I'm going to go talk with him, and then I'll be back upstairs to check on you."

Her mother smiled and it eased the lines on her forehead, making her look years younger. She'd always been a beautiful woman, but she'd aged ten years alone in the last few days. When all their friends and family departed, it was Rebekah's prayer she'd settle into a familiar and comfortable routine. She'd attend church events as always and continue her charitable work in the community. Still, after being by her father's side for over thirty years, it would be a hard road to walk. As much as anything else, their parents modeled a beautiful example of a strong marriage with Christ firmly at the center. That legacy was a gift.

"When do you have to get back to work?" Rebekah whispered to Josh on the way down the stairs.

"I have a major deal closing tomorrow but then I'm taking off until next Monday." He frowned.

"What's wrong?"

He stopped at the bottom of the stairs. "I'm trying to convince Winnie to stay a few extra days. I want to show her and Chloe the house, for one thing. I think it would be a very good thing at this point in our relationship."

"And exactly where are you in this relationship?"

Josh didn't answer for a long moment. "Exactly where we need to be right now."

She laughed. "With an answer like that, I think you're destined for a career in politics."

"Hmm, you never know. You're not the first person to suggest it." Giving her a grin, he pulled her in a quick embrace. "I love you, sis. We'll get through this together. I've got your back."

"Same here. Winnie and Chloe can stay with me. It might be too overwhelming for Mom right now. On the other hand, it might be the thing she needs to help her get through this transitional time. It's got to be hard for her."

"I need to talk with Winnie more about it before we make plans. She's at a hotel right now, but that would be great if she could stay with one of you. She says she has to get back for some catering event or something, but I wasn't aware she had anything on the calendar for the next few days."

"Well, then, it sounds like you need to ask Lexa about it. She'd know."

"Right. If needed, I'll ask her as a last resort. The TeamWork crew is having breakfast at Kingston's tomorrow morning before they all caravan back to Houston."

She smiled. "That's great. I still haven't met Chloe, you realize."

"You will tomorrow, and the little betrothed couple, too."

Rebekah laughed outright at that one. Good to see his humor was intact. "I can hardly wait. What time?"

"We're meeting them at Kingston's at eight. I'm going back home tonight, but I'll come pick you and Mom up at seven fifteen. That way we can swing by the hotel first so you can have privacy with Winnie and Chloe when you meet her for the first time. Pray for me as I talk with Winnie tonight, Beck. I told her I'd fly them back to Houston in a few days. Chloe overheard me telling her. She's never been on a plane before and that's given me a big advantage." His lips curled a bit. "My little girl is very persuasive."

How she loved hearing her brother say those words. "I know this is a tough concept for you to accept, Josh, but you can't just barge into Winnie's life and expect her to fall at your feet. You might need to take this a little slower than you'd like. She's a terrific woman, but she's got a lot at risk, a lot to consider. Being a single mother is one of the hardest things in the world, and she's not going to uproot her life or Chloe's without good or just cause." She gave him a knowing look. "Being a lawyer, you should know something about that."

"But remember, I'm a lawyer who specializes in mergers and acquisitions."

"Right."

Josh's smile was blinding. "I'm working on the biggest deal of my *life*, Beck. A merger with Winnie Doyle, and the acquisition of Chloe Doyle."

She laughed. "Well, now, that's a bit impersonal yet quite profound, isn't it?"

"I thought so." He winked and they shared a grin.

As if on cue, they heard the sound of running water followed by dishes being loaded in the dishwasher. Her eyes moved to the kitchen door.

"I can't believe he's doing dishes," Josh said. "Go grab him now and never let him go. That man's a keeper. Either that or he's doing one whale of a job trying to impress you. Speaking of which, have you told Kevin yet that you cut Adam loose?"

She shook her head, bracing herself for the coming lecture. *Now he calls him Adam.* "Not yet, but I will."

Josh sighed and ran a hand through his hair. "What in the world are you waiting for? Don't you realize all that's standing between you and lasting bliss with Kevin are three little words?"

Rebekah grumbled.

"What was that? I didn't hear you." He laughed and leaned down to regain her eye contact.

"First Marc and now you. At least Sam cut me some slack today. Trust me, I will tell Kevin, but you've got to give me a little space. It's been too emotional, especially today. I don't want him to think my declaration of everlasting love has anything to do with losing Dad."

"Tell him soon."

"Goodnight, Josh."

"Night, Beck. Love you."

"Love you, too." Starting into the kitchen, she paused. He'd let her have the last word. With a smile, she pushed open the door to the kitchen. Kevin's jacket was draped over a chair and his white dress shirt was rolled to his elbows. As she watched, he plunged a pan into the water and started to scrub it. *He must really love me.* What man would do such a thing otherwise? Something about a man with his hands immersed in dishwater made him even more masculine.

"This goes above and beyond the call of duty, you know."

"It's only dishes," he said. "It's not a duty. It's an honor and a privilege. Your dad was special to me, too, Rebekah. I want to help."

Walking over to the sink, standing beside him—his hands still in the dishwater—she put both hands on either side of his face. Pulling him close, the color of his eyes deepened when he understood what was on her mind. Then he gave her another one of those glorious, loopy grins. Oh, how she loved them. How she'd *missed* them.

"Unfair advantage," he said, his voice low as he met her lips in a tender kiss.

They talked as they tackled the remaining dishes, pots and pans together. He encouraged her to talk about her dad, sharing more of her favorite memories. Listening as they worked, he asked questions every now and then. It was comfortable, it was easy, it was *right.*

"You remind me of my dad, you know," she said. They stood in the front doorway a short time later. "In all the best possible ways."

The overhead porch light illuminated his face, highlighting his pleasure from her words. "That's quite the compliment. I thought no man could ever measure up to a little girl's daddy. Your dad's shoes are mighty big to fill."

"He's a tough act to follow, but you definitely fit the bill."

"You keep saying things like that," Kevin said, taking both her hands in his, stepping closer, "I might just kiss you whether or not it's appropriate." He brushed his lips over her cheek. "Goodnight, sweet Rebekah. I'll be praying for you, Josh and your mom. Are you going to Kingston's in the morning?"

"Wouldn't miss it. You?"

He smiled. "I'll be there."

"Thanks for being here today, Kevin. It meant so much to us. To *me*."

He nodded and kissed her forehead. The man sure was making his way around her face. Rebekah leaned against the doorframe as he departed with a small wave. Watching him leave, she knew this day would always be bittersweet. Gazing at the sky, the warm night air enveloped her as she eyed the stars, picking out a few constellations. Kevin was much better at naming them. In San Antonio, he'd pointed out some of them to her, telling her some of the legends and myths. She closed her eyes, wishing he sat beside her now, strumming his guitar, singing one of his wonderful songs.

"Rebekah?"

Startled, she opened her eyes. "Hi, Mrs. Michelson."

The elderly woman stood on the front walkway, a dish in her hands. "I brought you a casserole. I heard about your dad and I'm real sorry. I'm sure he was a fine man."

Rebekah moved forward, taking it from her. "He was. Thank you."

She nodded at the dish. "That's my special chicken and rice dish. I put broccoli and water chestnuts in it. People seem to like it."

"That's very kind. I'm sure it's delicious."

"I've been picking up your papers and mail since you've been gone from the house."

She hadn't even thought about that. "I appreciate your watching out for me."

The lines around her eyes crinkled and Mrs. Michelson nodded. "That's what neighbors should do for each other."

Rebekah found her smile. "Let me treat you to lunch sometime next week."

"Oh, that's not necessary," she said, waving her hand. Still, there was no mistaking the look of pleased satisfaction creasing the weathered lines on her face.

"Yes, it is. In the meantime, is there anything I can do for you, Mrs. Michelson?"

"Take care of your mama, child. She's gonna need you. And then take care of that sweet young man I saw kiss you goodnight. He's the right one for you." With a small smile, she turned to leave.

"Yes, he sure is."

CHAPTER THIRTY-SEVEN

The Next Day

LOOKING DOWN AT her daughter, Winnie squeezed Chloe's hand as they walked toward Josh's house in the quiet Baton Rouge suburb. She had to be strong for both of them, even though inside she was quaking and her knees felt like Jell-O. As they approached the front of the house, she took a deep breath, blowing it out slowly. *Maybe this wasn't such a good idea, letting Josh talk me into staying in Baton Rouge for a couple of days.*

At least Josh's mom and Beck accepted them both with open arms and without question. Likewise the TeamWork volunteers. Even though no public proclamation of Josh's fatherhood had been made known, they had to know. Earlier in the day, after the TeamWork breakfast at Kingston's, Josh showed them his impressive office. Walking between them, holding their hands, he introduced them to everyone. Her head still reeled with all the names. It was clear how much they valued him and his work at the firm. She also felt the envious stares from some of the women boring holes in her back.

He had an afternoon deal to close, so Beck and Lorena took her and Chloe to lunch at a fun tearoom where little girls could play dress-up. They had a ball and took lots of pictures. Chloe charmed them both, but everyone was careful. She didn't want Chloe calling them Aunt or Nana until things were more solidified in her relationship with Josh.

The door swung open and Josh stood in the doorway. He'd changed from his suit into his jeans and the same green polo he'd worn on his first visit in Houston, the one that matched those incredible eyes. He'd been back several times now, each visit better than the one before.

He was barefoot which somehow made him even more appealing, a virtual impossibility. His smile made her weak, as it always did. "Please, come in, ladies. Welcome to Chez Grant."

Chloe looked up at her. "What's that mean, Mommy?"

"He's talking about his house, sweetie. Mr. Josh wants us to feel comfortable."

"'Kay." Chloe dropped her hand and walked into the living room, her eyes lighting as she saw the fireplace. "Do you use that?" she asked, pointing to it.

"Not as much as I'd like," Josh told her, closing the front door. "Like Houston, we stay pretty warm here in Louisiana most of the year. I don't really need a fireplace, but I like it. It's cozy." He bent down to her level and gave her a big grin. The look on his face when Chloe giggled warmed Winnie all over.

"Let me give you ladies the grand tour," he said. "Feel free to kick off your shoes and stay awhile." His eyes met hers before stooping down to help Chloe with the straps on her shoes as Winnie pulled off her high-heeled sandals, the same ones she'd worn on their date. It seemed so long ago although it wasn't. So much had happened in their lives and in their hearts.

Josh led them around the house. She smiled in appreciation of the moldings on the ceiling and the lovely wallpaper in the living room. The rooms downstairs were all painted a soft neutral color, and the color scheme flowing from the living room into the dining room featured complementary shades of maroon, gray and blue. Definitely a bachelor's house, but it was tastefully furnished and seemed almost too clean and tidy. *He must have a housekeeper.* The hardwood floors were highly polished with scattered floor rugs to match the same color scheme. Winnie knew enough to know they weren't just any rugs, but high-end Persian carpets. His selection of paintings and artwork showed a good eye for investment. Nothing was cluttered and everything had its place.

"What do you think?" He watched her closely as they stood in the dining room with its cherry oval table—big enough to seat eight people—and matching pieces. The modest chandelier was elegant and beautiful. Chloe walked over to the hand-painted mural of a pastoral scene on one wall and frowned when Winnie told her not to touch.

"You can touch it if you want, Chloe," Josh told her, winking at Winnie.

"You can't help yourself," she said, laughing under her breath. "Setting bad precedents, I mean." Better not let him think she meant anything else. "In answer to your question, I'm thinking you must have a housekeeper. No wonder you love it here. Lead on. I can't wait to see this state-of-the-art kitchen you've told me about."

"Your wish is my command, my lady. Please follow me." Leading the way through a small study with a wall of books and an executive desk with a computer, Josh asked her to close her eyes. Taking her by the hand, he surprised her by scooping her in his arms and carrying her over the threshold and into the kitchen at the back of the house.

"Put me down, please," she said, giggling as she opened her eyes. She wasn't about to ask why he'd done it and would never admit she secretly loved it. As he lowered her, she looked around, awed. "Wow." At first glance, it was nothing short of the kitchen of her fantasies. Her eyes widened as she took it all in—all the latest appliances a caterer could ever want: double ovens, butcher-block counters, tons of shelf and cabinet space, an expansive pantry, side-by-side refrigerator and freezer. The appliances were all stainless steel, shiny and modern—and looked barely used. What a shame.

"This is absolutely amazing. When can I move in?" She bit her lip. That one slipped out unaware. No way would Josh let that one go unanswered.

"That could be arranged," he said, never one to waste an opportunity. Circling her waist from behind, he kissed her neck and hugged her close. "It does seem a colossal waste to have a kitchen like this and not be able to put it to good use."

"I meant," she sputtered. She felt the flush invading her cheeks. *Why did I have to say anything?* She looked around for Chloe, not wanting her to see them together like this as she disengaged herself from his arms. She avoided looking at him. It was too distracting, especially with the top two buttons of his shirt undone. *Keep me strong, Lord.*

"Relax. I know what you meant. Chloe ran upstairs already."

"She did? Well, that's rather rude. I'm sorry."

"Why? No harm done. She's a typical kid, and I wouldn't expect anything less. I'm wondering if she'll find the secret hiding place."

"Oh? What's that?"

"Remember I told you how the house is new, but it's made to look old? Come on. I'll show you as part of the second floor tour." She allowed him to take her hand as he led the way up the staircase to the second floor. With each step, she wondered if he'd show her his bedroom. That seemed almost too personal. He paused as they reached the top. "You have me puzzled with all these interesting looks today."

"Don't dig too deep, Josh."

He gave her a look that said *this conversation's not over*. "This is one of the guest bedrooms," he said, opening the door to a bedroom at the front of the house. The oak, full-size, four-poster bed in the middle of the room was covered with an elegant, floral comforter in shades of sage green and soft yellow. The matching triple dresser and tables on either side of the bed were beautifully made and looked antique, and curtains matching the comforter framed the windows.

Winnie drew in a breath. "This is so pretty."

"Thanks." She could tell her approval pleased him. "This is Beck's room when she stays the night. She doesn't stay over often, but it's ready when she does. And this," he told her, moving to the back of the house again, "is the other guest bedroom. It's where Mom and Dad always stay." His voice was tinged with sadness. Winnie slipped her hand in his again as they walked into the room. It had a queen-size canopy bed made from oak and covered in an ivory silk bedspread with a running pattern woven in gold filigree. Matching pillows sat on a window seat in front of the large window. A settee, rocking chair, a high dresser and end tables completed the charming look.

"Who's your decorator?" she asked, stepping closer to run her finger along the intricate needlework design in the bedspread. It appeared to be hand-stitched. "Everything's so beautiful," she said, knowing full well how wistful she sounded.

"Would you believe me if I told you I picked out everything myself?"

"No." She laughed. "I might worry about you if you did."

He laughed with her. "Mom and Beck did it all, but a lot of this furniture came from my grandparents on Mom's side. Rebekah has a lot of the furniture from Dad's family." It was one of the first times since the funeral service she'd heard Josh mention Lucas Grant without the familiar sadness surfacing in either his eyes or his voice. "These two bedrooms share a bath, and there's a half-bath downstairs. Do you want to see them?"

She shook her head. "That's okay, thanks." She had no idea a bachelor would have such a wonderful house. Pity he wasn't home much, but at least he had a great place to call home.

"We're not done," Josh said next, taking her hand again and pulling her along behind him. He stopped in the middle of the hallway. "Do you not want to see my bedroom for some reason?"

She avoided his gaze. "It just seems so personal."

"Please?"

Why he seemed so determined, she had no idea, but humoring him seemed best. "Fine. Lead the way." Stepping inside the doorway behind him, she looked around and smiled. "Aha!" she said. "Now, this is a man's room." Even though it was a very handsome room, the bed had obviously been made in haste and a trail of clothes littered the floor. The bedroom had a plaid comforter with deep, rich jewel tones in green, blue and maroon accented by the colors in the matching rugs on the hardwood floors. The furniture was a medium wood she couldn't identify, but it offset the darker tones of the decor.

"Sorry," he mumbled, bending down to pick up socks, pants and a shirt or two. Throwing them across an armchair, he shot her a sheepish grin.

"Don't be. Now I know you're human. I was beginning to think you had some kind of neat fetish, or else you just rented this place for show."

Josh laughed and waved his hand to one corner of the master bedroom. "My bathroom's back there and you'd know without a doubt I'm human if you dared set foot in there. I wouldn't advise it. Although it does have a sunken tub which is pretty cool. I never use it, only the shower stall." He caught her look. "Sorry. Too personal?"

"Of course not," she lied. Time to change the subject. "So, where do you think we'll find Miss Chloe?"

"I'm thinking she might be in here somewhere," he said, walking back out into the hallway. Stopping midway next to what must be the upstairs bath with its door closed, he leaned down and pulled a handle on a small door. Opening it, Josh poked his head inside. "Is there a little girl named Chloe in here?"

Surprised, Winnie stepped back. She heard her daughter's giggle before she glimpsed the blonde hair.

"I'm here," Chloe said.

Sunshine from a window on the side of the house flooded into the small space, the perfect place for someone Chloe's size. It was otherwise empty, but it was easy to see why it would be a favorite hiding place.

"Ready to go back downstairs, Buttercup?" When Chloe scooted out, Winnie kissed the top of her head. "Isn't this a beautiful house?"

"Yup. Can we live here, Mommy?"

"Chloe, let me show you the backyard," Josh said, sparing her having to answer. After all, she'd asked the very same question a few minutes before. He held out his hand to his daughter. Winnie followed as they walked down the stairs together. Watching them, Josh so straight and tall with Chloe beside him, his hand wrapped tightly around hers, she glimpsed the future. A future that included this man, the father of her child. It felt completely *right.*

Grateful to have a few moments alone to compose herself, Winnie put her hand on her chest and walked to the front of the house. It was such a nice, quiet street with even a white picket fence or two. She loved Josh's house and she could understand why Chloe would prefer to live here instead of their small, cramped apartment. One of these days, she was going to give her child a nicer place to live with the pink and white bedroom she'd always wanted. Taking a deep breath, she made her way back downstairs.

Walking through the hallway, she noticed the half-bath off the side of that fabulous kitchen. Its colors coordinated with those in the living and dining rooms. *Rebekah and Mrs. Grant certainly did themselves proud.*

Following the sounds of their laughter, she walked into the kitchen and looked out the large window. Josh pushed Chloe in the swing in the neighbor's yard. The look on his face was full of joy and contentment. She was thankful Chloe could give him that peace. Crossing her arms, she walked to the door and leaned against the frame, watching them through the screen door. She heard Josh ask Chloe questions about Butterfinger, and she was doing her best to explain the ways of her funny cat. Her sweet little laugh thrilled Winnie's heart every time she heard it and now those giggles from their daughter made Josh laugh, too.

Sliding down from the swing, Chloe surprised Josh by throwing her arms around his neck and planting a sloppy, wet kiss on his cheek. Winnie's heart caught in her throat and she turned away for a moment, emotion overtaking her. It was all too perfect, too normal, too real. She never expected to see her daughter with her father like this, kissing him and falling in love with him in her own trusting way. *Just like her mother.* It was almost too much.

~

"Something wrong?" Josh asked, coming in with Chloe and closing the kitchen door behind them. "Buttercup, why don't you go take a look at that big clock on the wall over there." He pointed it out to her. "My Grandpa Grant made it a long time ago."

Chloe smiled and skipped toward the clock.

"Are you okay?" Josh touched her arm.

"I'm fine. Really. It's almost too perfect." She kept her voice quiet so Chloe wouldn't hear. Josh looked curious, but he didn't push. She couldn't expect him to understand. Perfect was an illusion, it wasn't reality, but being here in this house, with this man, seemed as close to perfection as possible.

He ran a hand over his jaw. "Chloe, do you want to go out to eat tonight or should we cook something here? I'll let you make the decision."

Her eyes lit. "I know that word! Dezission," she said, rolling it on her tongue a couple of times. "It means I get to choose."

He laughed. "It sure does. What do you think? What sounds good?"

"Do you have pizzas?" It was her current favorite.

"I don't, but there's a wonderful place down the street that has them," he said with a wink. "Why don't I call them and order some pizzas for us? They'll even bring them right to my front door."

"Yummy!" When she was excited, Chloe's eyes looked nearly identical to Josh's.

"You've made a friend for life now. There's no turning back," Winnie whispered as Chloe scampered out to the living room with a book she retrieved from her purse.

"No way on earth would I want to turn back now." Josh tipped her chin with his hand. "I'm glad you and Chloe like my house, and I think you know why I care so much about your opinion."

Winnie matched his gaze. "You don't have to sell anything, Josh. Not you. Not your house," she said, looking down at her hands.

Josh took them in his own. "I love you, Winnie." He tipped her chin and waited until she looked at him. His eyes searched hers. "I think I've always been in love with you." Cupping her face between his hands, he kissed her. "I need you."

She startled at that one. "You need me . . . in what way?"

He raised his head and blew out a sigh. "I'm not going to sweep you in my arms and carry you upstairs to my bed. Even if it's what I want, I know better." His brows knit together in frustration. "Looks like I've still got my work cut out for me in the trust department."

"No, Josh." She shook her head.

"Then what is it, sweetheart? Please tell me."

Sweetheart. Oh, that does such funny things to my heart. Kind of like little flips in my stomach and other places. Say it again, Josh.

"I'm not sure I trust myself. Trust me, it's not you. It's me. All me." Winnie sighed, but held his gaze. Those green eyes deepened. It seemed he needed to hear those words from her. When he slipped his arms around her waist again and kissed her, she never wanted to leave. For the first time, she fully understood what Lexa meant when she said she was home in Sam's arms. *This* was home. The fear slipped away, replaced by the most incredible peace.

"Are the pizzas coming?"

Winnie jumped back and looked at Josh, unsure which one of them flushed a deeper pink. Josh didn't blush often and it made him look like a little boy, especially with his hair mussed from her fingers. Chloe looked from one to the other, but she didn't look upset in any way. Winnie breathed a sigh of relief.

"I'm just calling in our order now." Josh retrieved a phonebook beneath the kitchen counter. Thumbing through it, he found a tagged page. Keeping his finger on the book, he reached for the phone with his other hand. "What kind do you like?"

"Cheese for her and veggie or pepperoni for me," Winnie answered, still flushed. He gave her a heavy-lidded smile. The rhythm of her heart increased tenfold. Yes, it was a very good thing Chloe was in the house. A rush of emotion swept through her.

Josh ordered three pizzas, one cheese, one half-pepperoni and half-sausage, and one veggie. "Coke?" Winnie shook her head. "No, thanks," he said into the phone. "Okay, see you in about twenty minutes."

"Chloe, want to help set the table?" he asked, not waiting for her answer. Opening a cabinet under one of the counters, he pulled out napkins. Reaching to an overhead cabinet, he pulled out stoneware and Winnie put them on the table. He handed forks to Chloe. "Just put them on the table by each plate." She did as he asked before skipping out of the kitchen again.

"I thought she'd never leave," Josh said, rushing over to her, bundling her in his arms, cutting her off mid-sentence.

"Josh," Winnie said, "we shouldn't—"

"Shouldn't what? I'm kissing the woman I love. That can't be wrong."

"But," she said, her lips firmly pressed against his mouth, "kissing leads to other things."

"Only if we let it, and I won't let it. Remember what I told you. I promise you, it's only kissing, Winnie. But," he added with a small laugh, "kissing can be *so* much fun. You'll see," he said, pulling away after first sealing that promise with another tantalizing kiss. "Besides, we have an adorable four-year-old chaperone. She's not going to let us get away with anything."

"You're doing such things to me," she said, swaying. She was thankful he was there and leaned into him. "Catch me or I might just fall."

"Good," he whispered. "I like you off balance."

"Oh!" Raising a hand to her face, Winnie escaped into the living room. She could get used to this kind of dizzy.

CHAPTER THIRTY-EIGHT

THIRTY MINUTES LATER, they sat around the kitchen table together, holding hands as Josh asked the blessing. Chloe asked to pray, too. Winnie peeked, watching Josh as he listened to her prayer. It was worth it to see the expression on his face. Of course, Chloe used as many of the words she'd learned that week as she could, so it came out a little nonsensical and lasted at least a full minute. Probably gave the Almighty a chuckle or two.

"Amen," Josh said, giving her a wink across the table. "You're like the Prayer Princess, Chloe." That brought another giggle that was silenced soon enough by Chloe taking a first big bite.

Her heart full, Winnie watched as her two favorite people in the world dug in like neither one of them had eaten in a week. At least mourning didn't diminish Josh's appetite. He served her a slice of the veggie pizza. It was the best pizza she'd ever had, but perhaps she didn't really taste it and was reacting to everything else going on inside this wonderful house.

"Isn't this the best pizza ever, Chloe?"

Her daughter nodded and gave her a tomato-covered grin. My, but the child managed to make a mustache out of almost anything. Now, she had a little bright red goatee, the same as when she devoured "pasghetti," her recent personal favorite. Laughing, Winnie cleaned her up. Out of the corner of her eye, she knew Josh watched their every move with a look of sweet tenderness shining in his eyes.

"I'm stuffed," he said not long after, picking up Chloe's plate with his. "Finished?" He reached across the table for her plate.

She nodded. "Thanks, I can't eat another bite."

He eyed her empty glass as he took their plates to the sink. "Want more to drink, cookies or anything else, ladies?"

"I'm fine," Winnie said. "Chloe's still got some milk. Wearing it above her upper lip, as usual." She handed her daughter the napkin and motioned for her to use it. "Do you want a cookie to go with your milk, sweetie?" Surprisingly, she shook her head.

"Is it okay if Chloe goes upstairs to watch a movie for a little while?" Josh came back to the table and sat in the chair beside hers. "So her mother and I can talk downstairs?" He raised his brows and Winnie couldn't help but laugh. "Don't worry, I'll get you back to Rebekah's in good order."

Her heart rioted in her chest. "I'm not worried, just—"

"Just . . . what?" Josh asked, giving her a devilish grin.

She smirked. "Just go get Chloe settled upstairs already and then I'll show you."

"*Show* me?" The look on his face was priceless. "Hold that thought," he said, scooting out the door into the living room. "*Wizard of Oz* okay?"

"No!" Winnie hurried out the door behind him. "Let's not tempt nightmares." He turned with a questioning look. "Flying monkeys and the Wicked Witch," she mouthed. "Do you have any Disney cartoons?" she asked, following him up the stairs. Based on the scampering she heard upstairs, Chloe was already there.

"I'll find something or we can just put on a cartoon channel. They have tons of those on cable, right?"

"Usually, but don't leave the remote nearby."

Josh paused, turning to look at her just inside his bedroom. "Why? Is your little Buttercup a channel surfer?" He crouched down on all fours, digging in the cabinet beneath the widescreen television. "How about *Veggie Tales*?" His expression was triumphant as he pulled out a DVD from the cabinet and held it in the air, waving it back and forth.

"I like Bob!" Chloe squealed.

"Of course, you do," he said, laughing. "He's the tomato, right?"

Chloe started singing the *Veggie Tales* theme song, giggling as she took a running jump and plopped in the middle of the bed. If she could stop laughing, Winnie would remind her daughter to mind her manners, but seeing how happy she was, and knowing how comfortable she was with Josh—not to mention the look on his face—she hadn't the heart to scold.

"I think we have a winner." Josh pulled the DVD from its case and inserted it into the player. "Okay, sweetheart, we have thirty minutes," he whispered, giving her a gentle nudge on the small of her back as they headed downstairs.

~

"I have a question." Sitting sideways and propping her feet beneath her, Winnie arranged the folds of her dress, its floral fabric fanning around her on the sofa.

"What's that?" Josh propped his elbow behind her and surveyed her with a look of extreme contentment.

"Why do you have a *Veggie Tales* DVD? I didn't realize talking and singing vegetables ranked high on the list for a bachelor's television viewing."

His grin emerged. "Sometimes the singles group from my church comes to the house. We have some parents in the group and that DVD has come in handy on more than one occasion. But," he said, scooting closer, "is this something you're dying to discuss in detail right now?"

"No. Not really. No." Why did she have to ramble like an idiot when he got close?

"Do you want me to start a fire?"

Well, that's a loaded question. "At this time of year?" She smiled as she caught his expression.

"I see what you mean," he said. "I just thought it would be romantic."

"Well, it would be romantic, but first, we have enough fire between us as it is, and second, it would take too much time." Stealing a glance at him, she giggled. Nothing like a giggle and blunt honesty to charm this man. *And there it is, the lazy, sexy grin.*

"That giggle of yours gets me every time," he whispered, pulling her chin toward him.

"Josh," she said, pulling back. "Isn't it a bit disrespectful, if we, you know, kiss after you just . . ." *Maybe it's his way of burying the pain.*

He sat back against the sofa cushions with a deep sigh. "This isn't a line, Winnie, but I know my dad would be all for . . . this. Trust me, he'd approve. I'm sad, yes, and I hate that he was yanked out of our lives without any warning. I hurt for Mom, but she's strong and knows he's in a much better place. I'm just thankful he didn't suffer. Dad would have hated that more than anything." He stroked her hair. "The Lord had his reasons for taking Dad when he did. For one thing, there were a lot of people at his service who might have needed to hear the message from the pastor."

She snuggled into the curve of his arm. "I was so proud of you. Your eulogy was wonderful, Josh. Short, hard-hitting, but oh-so-powerful."

He rubbed one hand over his jaw. "Thanks, but if you say I sounded like a politician, I might have to kiss you to shut you up."

"Josh?" she said, sitting up straighter.

"Yes?" That irresistible grin surfaced again. "I don't have much alone time with you, but if you want to talk because you think it's disrespectful to my dad's memory to kiss me on the couch, then let's talk. Tell me more about Chloe's nursery school. Tell me about your upcoming catering jobs." Those green eyes searched hers. "Tell me anything but why I shouldn't kiss you right now."

Winnie swallowed hard. "I really can't think of anything."

Cupping her face with one hand, he leaned close, claiming her lips. Oh, how he claimed them. The respectful suitor, the complete gentleman, he wasn't inappropriate in any way. Just sweet and gentle yet able to ignite every hormone in her and then some. His dad would be very pleased with the polite man beside her. He'd raised a mighty fine son.

Josh leaned his forehead against hers as they both fought to slow their breathing. "I hope now you understand what I meant about kissing being fun. *Just* kissing."

"I have no complaints."

He smoothed his thumb over the tender skin on her chin. "I'm afraid my beard roughed you up. One look at you and Beck will know exactly what we've been doing." He shrugged. "I just hope she'll get roughed up by Kevin sometime soon."

"Josh!" With her fingers, Winnie smoothed some of his hair back into place and reached for her purse. "I'll dart into the powder room and try to repair any damage. Do you mind getting Chloe?"

"Not at all, sweetheart. My pleasure." He headed toward the stairs.

Sensing his eyes on her, Winnie noticed he paused on the stairs, watching her. "Everything okay?" Her heart jumped when she glimpsed his expression. He looked happy, content, and completely besotted. No man other than Josh had ever looked at her this way. She could get used to it so easily. That thought would have scared her out of her mind a few months ago, but now it was the opposite.

"Everything's the way it should be," he said.

As she headed into the powder room, Winnie heard him bounding up the stairs, two at a time from the sound of it.

Ten minutes later, she glanced at her watch with a slight frown. It was quiet upstairs and it was getting really late. As much as she hated for this day to end, it was time for Josh to take them back to Rebekah's. Tiptoeing up the stairs, she halted at the threshold of his bedroom and clamped a hand over her mouth. Chloe was fast asleep on the bed with Josh curled around her, his eyes closed. From the steady rhythm of their breathing, both father and daughter were fast asleep.

It was too much. Retreating to the hallway, Winnie slumped down to the top stair, holding onto the rail, giving into the overwhelming emotion as her tears fell. They were cleansing tears, healing tears from all the hurt and pain of the past, making way in her heart for the tenderness she felt for this man. *Oh, how I love him, Lord. I always have.*

Taking a deep breath and wiping her eyes a few minutes later, she went into the bedroom. She stood at the side of the bed, watching them sleep. Josh never looked more appealing, still curled around Chloe, his chin resting on top of her small blonde, curly head. Shifting in her sleep, Chloe put one hand on his chest and he instinctively tightened his hold on her. As much as she tried to resist Josh and all the reasons why they wouldn't work—why they *couldn't* or *shouldn't* work—it came down to this moment. She'd never find a man more devoted to her or Chloe. That he happened to be the only man she'd ever loved, and Chloe's father, made it all the more wonderful.

Easing onto the bed, Winnie leaned across Chloe and kissed Josh's cheek, brushing her lips over his.

He startled and opened his eyes, blinking a few times as he focused on her. When another tear escaped, he wiped it away. "Don't cry, *chère*. Everything will be okay. I promise."

"I know," she whispered. "Don't mind me. It's just my heart overflowing."

"It's been great having you both here tonight. Sorry I didn't bring her downstairs, but I love talking with my daughter." He touched Chloe's cheek and yawned. "Ten minutes ago, she was a chatterbox, but then she fell asleep on a dime. Does she always do that?"

Winnie smiled. "A lot of times she does. I call it talking herself to sleep, which reminds me, I have some videos and photo albums I haven't shared with you yet. I found them when I was cleaning the other day."

He stretched his arms over his head with a light yawn. "Can't wait. Ready to go back to Beck's now?"

She shook her head, trailing her fingertips across his forehead and down his cheek. He leaned into it, his eyes searching hers. "Not yet. We *are* home. We'll stay a little while longer."

The look on his face in that moment filled all the remaining empty spaces in her heart. "I'm glad."

"Me, too." *Oh yes, I'm home.*

He kissed her and it was the most tender, gentle caress. Pulling away with a deep sigh of contentment, Josh dug in the pocket of his jeans and pulled out his phone. "Hey, Beck." He darted a glance at Chloe and lowered his voice. "Winnie and Chloe are going to stay here a while longer. I'll bring them back later. Don't wait up." Turning off the phone, he put it on the nightstand and slid out of the bed, careful not to disturb Chloe. "I'll be right back." He returned a minute later, a blanket in his hands. Stopping by the side of the bed, he draped it over his child. "The air's on and the vent is blowing on her. I don't want her to get cold, but I'm afraid I'll wake her up if I move her to turn down the comforter."

She hadn't even considered it, more than surprised he had. Thoughtfulness was one of Josh's best qualities, his sensitivity endearing. In so many ways since they'd reconnected again, he'd shown her how much he cared for her and Chloe, some ways more subtle than others, all wonderful.

His eyes met hers. "Should I go to the guest room? I don't want to do anything to make you uncomfortable."

She shook her head and patted the spot on the other side of Chloe. Still warm, it's where he belonged. Sinking onto the bed, he switched off the bedside lamp. With the moonlight filtering through the window, Winnie glimpsed his sleepy, contented smile. With Chloe snuggled between them, Josh reached for her. Wrapping his arm around her shoulder, he pulled her into his warmth. His *love.* The place she needed to be and where she'd always belonged. With her head on his shoulder and Chloe resting her head on his chest, he smiled as his eyes closed.

Her hand rested over his heart and he covered it with his.

Cast all your cares on Me. Closing her eyes, Winnie sent up a silent prayer, thanking the Lord for loving her and harboring her from the uncertainty of the pain of the past. *For saving me.* Now, He'd blessed her with this strong, loyal and faithful man. *For leading me home.*

Her heart swelled with tenderness. *I love you, Lord.*

It had been almost five years, but once again, she was treasured and cherished by a man. A flesh-and-blood man who'd been through the fire and emerged all the stronger for it. Settling further into the curve of Josh's arm, the space above his heart, a smile creased her lips as she allowed her eyes to close.

"I love you, Josh Grant."

He squeezed her hand and held on tight. "I love you more, Winnie Doyle."

CHAPTER THIRTY-NINE

One Week Later

KEVIN FIDGETED IN the chair in the waiting room of the Baton Rouge law firm, running his fingers over the rim of his dark brown, suede Stetson. The artwork and impressive furnishings defined posh and elegance. He still puzzled over why he'd driven into the city when he was supposed to be at the store. Of course, Tommy thought it was great and, based on his good-natured ribbing, knew his motives better than Kevin did. It's like his truck was on autopilot and brought him to Josh Grant's office of its own accord.

Spying a spot of dirt on one of his boots, he spit-shined it.

"Mr. Moore?"

He broke out of his musing and rose to his feet. "Yes?"

"Mr. Grant will see you now if you'll follow me."

"Thank you." As he followed the woman down a long hallway, Kevin smoothed his hand over his work shirt. If he'd known he'd end up in such a fancy place, he'd have dressed better. It was pretty obvious he was out of his element as he sensed many eyes following his path down the hallway. She paused beside a door at an office near the end of the hall. Thanking her again, he nodded as he entered the office, feeling somewhat like a kid facing the principal.

"Kevin. Come in." Josh came around from behind his desk, his hand outstretched. Shaking his hand, he pulled him into a quick, warm hug. That hug went a long way toward easing his anxiety. "This is a welcome surprise. Have a seat." He waved to the pair of matching chairs facing his desk.

"Sorry I didn't call first. I hadn't really planned on coming here when I started out this morning." He sat in one of the chairs and Josh dropped into the one opposite him.

Josh's face creased into a broad grin. "Then it must have been a God thing, which means it's even more important."

That one stumped him. "How do you mean?"

"Everything has its purpose. You rarely do anything without thinking it through first, am I right?"

Kevin blew out a breath. "Right, and that can be both good and bad. Where Rebekah is concerned, I'm afraid it's been to my detriment."

Josh leaned close. "You've captured her heart so I wouldn't say it's been a major obstacle. She needs a strong anchor, my friend, and you're it."

Kevin brows shot upward. "I hope you're right about that."

"Trust me on this one. I know Beck better than anyone else. Where you're concerned, I might just know her better than she knows herself. Tell me what's on your mind." He sat back in the chair, waiting.

Gathering his thoughts, Kevin put the Stetson on top of the desk. "My family's business is expanding into Texas. I've known about it for a few months, but haven't been at liberty to discuss it with anyone, not even with Rebekah, even though it killed me. The board of directors tapped me to head up the new Houston operation." He felt strange talking about it and hoped he didn't come across as boastful. "I'm leaving in two days to go oversee the project." His eyes met Josh's. "I'll be there indefinitely."

Josh whistled under his breath. "Congratulations. I'm glad to hear the business is doing so well. That's a great opportunity. So, you haven't told Beck yet?"

"No. That's why I'm here, I guess." Kevin shifted in the chair. "Things are . . . complicated with her right now."

Josh didn't look surprised so she must have told him. These two shared such a strong bond and were so close, it transcended the brother-sister relationship. Maybe it was the twin thing. He'd seen them finish each other's sentences—intimidating in a way, but it was also amazing. But where Josh seemed centered and focused, Rebekah still seemed unsure of her direction.

"Want some water?" He walked over to a cooler in the corner of his office. Not waiting for his answer, he filled a cup, then a second.

"That'd be good. Thanks." His throat was dry, but he hadn't even thought of it.

Josh put the cup in front of him on the desk and took his seat. "You have to understand something. Beck's always been a proper girl. Adam put the rush on her before she went to Montana, and he finally outstayed his welcome. He confused her. I guess someone like that would turn any girl's life upside down. Basically, he offered her the world. I'm convinced it was only the accent that kept her hooked so long." He gave him a wry grin.

Kevin's heart pumped harder. *She finally did it?* He cleared his throat. "She told me she was going to break up with him." *But never told me she did.* He drained his cup with one gulp. "I know I've gone slow in this relationship, but do you think she's ready to make a permanent commitment to me? I mean, so soon?"

"She loves you, Kevin. Forgive her. The girl can't seem to help herself. You've taken your sweet time and now it's her turn to repay the favor, but she's not doing it on purpose. "

Kevin stiffened a bit, not liking the implication. "I meant going slow in terms of . . ." He faltered, lowering his eyes. "In the physical sense as well as anything else." That didn't come out right either. "You know what I mean."

A wry grin creased Josh's lips. "You're the most proper guy I know, and I respect and appreciate that. I know Beck does, too. It's one of your special charms. Let me see if I can explain it." He drained his cup. "First of all, I'm going to tell you something Beck would have my hide for, but you need to know."

"What's that?" he leaned forward, eager for his words.

"She kicked the Brit to the curb right before Dad died. You have nothing to worry about as far as he's concerned." Josh waved his hand. "Temporary distraction, but he's out of her life for good. Let's just say Beck got a taste of her own medicine."

His mouth gaped at that one. "You mean Adam—"

"Put it this way: if you're concerned about another Adam coming along to turn her head, you needn't worry. You've won the girl, Kevin."

Kevin swallowed hard. "Thanks for telling me. I may not look like it, but the inner me is jumping up and down and yelling for joy at the top of his lungs." He broke into one of the grins Rebekah would call his loopy one. Probably meant he looked like a lovesick fool, but he didn't care.

"After Dad died, Beck was afraid to tell you, believing it was too soon. She thought she was somehow being disloyal to Dad's memory by focusing on her own happiness instead of properly grieving for him or something. She's been very emotional lately and didn't want to further complicate things. You ask me, she was waiting for the right time to tell you in her own way."

"All I want to do is love her, Josh."

His friend nodded, clearly touched by his sentiment. "Do you have a plan?" He looked like he harbored a secret, and a pretty good one.

"A plan?" Knowing Rebekah's brother, Josh would have plan.

"Do me a favor, lumber man."

Kevin quirked a brow at the nickname. Josh had called him that ever since the San Antonio work camp. He liked it since it accurately pegged him, but liked it even more when Rebekah used the term. Probably because she used it in moments of closeness. *Focus*. "Sure. What's that?"

"Take her to dinner—but not just any dinner. Dress in your best suit, leave the boots, the hat and the guitar at home . . ." He raised one hand. "Not that she doesn't love those things, but shake her up a little. Give her what she thinks she wants, and then she'll wake up to what she *needs*." He ignored Kevin's frown. "Splash on some of that musky stuff you wear sometimes. Drives her out-of-her-mind. Be romantic as anything, give her flowers like you always do, and pour on the charm."

Josh straightened in his chair and leaned closer. "This is the key—take her home at the end of the evening and kiss her like you're saying goodbye without actually telling her anything about leaving for Houston." He shot him a look. "Don't say a word if she wears goop on her lips or anywhere else on her face. Treat her like the treasure we both know she is, and then make her practically beg you to kiss her. Leave her hanging and end the evening just short of telling her you love her. In other words, make it a real memorable evening, Kevin, but leave her wanting more." He grinned. "Got all that?"

Kevin was stunned. He looked away, raking one hand through his hair. "I think so, but I can't lie to her. I can't take off for Texas and leave her without even telling her."

"I understand, but you'll be back and forth between Texas and Louisiana, right?"

"Of course, especially if she commits to this relationship, I'll be back as often as possible. It'll be hard to stay away. As it is, it's been torture these past few weeks."

"I know a little something about that myself," Josh said.

Kevin nodded. "I'm happy for you and Winnie, and pray it works out."

Josh hesitated, not speaking for a long moment. "Thanks."

Kevin's lips curled. "That little girl is a Grant through and through, and I'm not just talking about the green eyes."

Josh's eyes were wet when he looked up at him again. "She's adorable, isn't she? She got the best parts of her mother, too."

"You've got that right."

"If anyone I trust asks me about her, I won't hesitate to tell them, sure, but until Chloe's a little older and can understand it better, I really don't want to be telling everyone." He straightened his shoulders and grunted. "My daughter learns new words every day, but 'illegitimate' isn't one I want her learning anytime soon. Pray that Winnie will marry me as soon as I can get her to the altar. I might even have Sam do the honors."

"Understood. So, you don't think I should tell your sister I'm leaving for Texas?" He wasn't so sure of this plan, although it was intriguing. What exactly would be the point? "It'll be difficult, but I suppose I can do it. Why *shouldn't* I tell her?"

Josh broke out in the widest grin yet. "This is the fun part. Hear me out on this, buddy. Force Rebekah to admit how much she cares about you. She knows you're waiting, but this is the key: she doesn't think you're going anywhere so she's taking her own sweet time."

"I also told her to figure out what she wants before she comes to me. I'm sure she hasn't forgotten that part." He'd never forget the look on her face, the wide eyes and tremor in her voice after he'd confronted her in the gym. But it was true, and she needed to hear it.

Faint lines stretched across Josh's forehead, but they disappeared quickly enough. "Not a problem. If you take my advice, mark my words, she'll wake up and take action. You told her to find out what she wants, and after this date-to-beat-all-dates, she won't have a doubt in her mind she wants you. This is about you loving her enough to force her to admit how much she loves you. Then she'll come to you freely. My point being, make her come to *you*."

"You really think she'll come after me?"

"I know so. Trust me on this. Let her stake her claim on love. It'll be good for her." He paused and shifted. "And when she does, I'll be right there beside her, ready to claim Winnie and Chloe."

"There's also the matter of a gazebo."

"A what? Excuse me?"

Kevin grinned. "Imagine my surprise when Adam Martin walked into the store and commissioned a gazebo. Turns out he wanted to marry Rebekah in that gazebo. I insisted on waiting on him, and I guess I somehow gave him the brilliant suggestion he should also propose to her in it, too."

"That must have been a real interesting conversation. Didn't you meet him at the restaurant?"

"Yes, but he didn't remember me. Maybe because I was in my normal work clothes. Let's face it, a man like Adam wouldn't expect a suitor for Rebekah's heart to be dressed so plain and simple."

"There's nothing plain and simple about you, Kevin." Josh's gaze was penetrating. "You're one of the most loyal, upstanding, godly men I've ever known. Your strength is in your quiet confidence. I've seen you in action and you're a leader, even though you might not see it. For one thing, any man who can play a guitar like you and get up in front of people and sing has my utmost admiration." He shot him a sidelong grin. "She also told me about the frog legs. That was rich, my friend. Didn't know you spoke French. That's quite a surprise."

He shrugged. "I know enough to get by."

"When she saw you with that other woman, Beck was so jealous she couldn't see straight not to mention mortified you thought she looked . . . inappropriate."

It surprised him Rebekah told him that much, but maybe it shouldn't. In any case, it was gratifying to hear she'd been jealous. "I probably shouldn't tell you this, but the front of her dress had slipped down so far I wanted to throw my jacket over her. She obviously had no idea, but I had to get her out of there before Adam devoured her with his eyes."

Josh laughed. "Thanks for protecting my sister's virtue. Now, got your cell phone?"

The man was always focused so he must have a good reason for asking. "Sure."

"Good. Before you leave the parking lot, call Beck and ask her out to dinner tomorrow night, and then make sure that dinner is one she'll never forget." He thumped his hand on his desk. "Not that I'm trying to tell you what to do, of course."

Kevin's brows rose. "Done." Grabbing his Stetson from the desk, he stood to leave. "Thanks, Josh. I'll let you know how it goes."

"I'll be praying, brother."

Climbing into the truck a couple of minutes later, Kevin stared at his phone. He liked the sound of that. *Brother*. Even a guy with two of them could always use another one, especially one like Josh Grant. He punched in Rebekah's number. Time to put Operation Rebekah's Heart into action.

CHAPTER FORTY

The Next Afternoon

KEVIN'S DINNER INVITATION surprised—but thrilled—her. Maybe he knew she'd parted ways with Adam and decided to stake his claim after all but, after what he said about wanting her to figure out she wanted, Rebekah couldn't be sure. Still, he'd been so attentive during the time of Dad's funeral. Been beside her or close enough for her to sense his presence.

Am I ready to tell Kevin how I feel about him? Is it too soon after Daddy's death, disloyal to his memory?

As she surveyed her reflection in the mirror, she nodded with satisfaction. She looked entirely appropriate. The neckline of the dress was modest and didn't dip anywhere it shouldn't. It was a classic little black dress that nipped at the waist, flared at her hips and flirted around her knees. Opting for the less-is-more look, she'd applied only a little blush, a hint of mascara and the tiniest bit of lipstick. Her eyes misted as she put on the teardrop pearl earrings and fastened the matching pearl necklace, her dad's Sweet Sixteen heirloom gift to her. She'd piled her hair on top of her head in a loose chignon and prayed it would stay in place all evening. If not, she knew Kevin liked it down. He'd probably prefer it that way.

The doorbell rang at four o'clock. The man was like clockwork, but she liked that he was reliable. Why he wanted to meet so early in the afternoon, she had no idea, but no way would she complain. Now that school was out, she'd been able to take her time getting ready.

Opening her door, Rebekah stared, trying not to openly gape. It was rude, but she couldn't help it. She'd never seen Kevin so dressed up or incredibly handsome. *Wow.* Her heart pumped a bit harder as she ushered him inside. *Double wow.*

"Hello, beautiful." That didn't even sound like Kevin, and yet, it did. This was very confusing.

"Hi," she said, feeling almost shy, like this was some new guy and it was their first date. But that made her feel disloyal. She closed the front door, unable to tear her eyes away. He was wearing a dark suit with a starched, light blue shirt and silk tie with varied hues of blues, purples and greens. It was an unusual tie, and incredibly stylish. As he moved past her into the living room, she caught a whiff of that musky cologne he wore for special occasions and wanted to fall into his arms right then and there. The man plus that particular cologne were an enticing, dangerous combination. His hair was different, too. Must be what it normally looked like before she got her hands on it. It looked so silky and touchable, she ached to run her fingers through it. *Later.* She swayed, prompting Kevin to reach out and steady her, his hands on her waist.

"Forgive me," she murmured. *Oh my, I'm in trouble here. I've never seen him like this before.*

His look was tender. "Are you okay, sweetheart? It's really me. I thought I'd dress up for once." Making sure she was steady on her feet, he released her.

She shook her head. "This is great, but am I missing something here?"

He put two fingers over her lips and stepped closer. "No expectations, no promises. Tonight is about a man taking a beautiful woman he adores to dinner. Time to enjoy being together. Nothing more."

She tilted her head, her eyes wide. "That does it. What'd you do with the *real* Kevin?" Stepping closer, she gave a gentle tug on his silk tie. "Is he somewhere in there?" The man standing in her living room was sophisticated and suave. It wasn't loopy Kevin, and she missed that man.

"He's here, I assure you." His smile was slow, assured, self-confident and more sexy than loopy. *Oh my.* "You look incredible as always, Rebekah. You are grace personified."

"I don't break, you know." That's all the invitation he needed. Stepping closer, he took her hands in his. Leaning forward, he brushed her lips softly, just enough to whet her appetite and leave her longing for more. "No fair," she muttered.

"Later."

"Oh, right. Sorry. I forgot about the silly lipstick."

That spurred him into action when he stepped forward and put his arms around her, planting a long kiss guaranteed to leave her devoid of the goop on her lips.

"Okay," she said, swaying again. It was a great kiss, as always. This was going to be one interesting evening. "Where are you taking me to dinner? Nowhere French, I hope." She couldn't resist, and smiled as Kevin laughed.

"I've made special reservations for us tonight. The French part is entirely optional. Your choice." He gave her a wicked wink. It was downright provocative, but so unlike sweet, reserved Kevin.

You can't just shove shyness out the window. What's going on here?

"Do you have a lightweight coat or something? You might need one."

"Yes, my wrap's right over here. Let me get it."

"Allow me," he said, taking the lightweight, shimmery shawl from her. "This doesn't look like it's made for warmth."

"Oh, I'm sure you'll think of something to keep me warm," she said with a coy grin. Two can play at this game, if that's what it was.

"No doubt," he said. In a move reminiscent of the day at the French restaurant, Kevin pulled it over her head and, his eyes never leaving hers, brought it around her shoulders, pulling it together in front. She moved her hands so they made contact with his and gave him a look of wonder.

"Kiss me again, Kevin."

He tilted his head. "Third time's the charm? My pleasure, but then we must be going if we hope to get to dinner." He touched his lips to hers, but only a soft one. Tantalizing. That was the word for it. Enough yet not enough.

"Unfair advantage," she said as he released her, a look of amusement lighting his eyes.

"Later," he said, taking her elbow. "Shall we go to dinner?"

Rebekah didn't trust herself to speak. Finally she sputtered, "As ready as I'll ever be." Locking the door behind him, she stopped and stared at the sleek silver sports car parked at the curb.

"Your carriage awaits." Kevin bowed and waved to the car.

This made no sense. The car was so expensive she couldn't identify its make. "Kevin, where's your truck?" She looked up and down the street.

"I left it at home. I rented this one for the night; I'm thinking of trading in the truck. Upgrading."

"You *what*?" It came out an unladylike screech. She grunted and cleared her throat. "Um, why would you do that? I love your truck." Besides, renting a car like this for one night would set him back some serious money. That was so unlike his usual cost-conscious self. She couldn't fathom him even walking into a dealership to rent such a car.

He stopped on the walkway. "You do?" Now *that* sounded like the old Kevin.

"Yes, I do. It fits you." *Suits me, too.*

"At least for tonight," he said, "I didn't want you to have to climb up into the truck, especially with that fabulous dress." She appreciated how he was careful to tuck the hem of her dress inside the car before closing the passenger door. When he slid behind the wheel, he brought another wonderful whiff of that cologne into the car with him. It should be illegal. Maybe it was a good thing this car had bucket seats and a console in between.

The unmistakable scent of new car and expensive leather also enveloped her. Running a finger over the seat, she smiled. "Well, this is quite nice, too." She snuggled into the soft, leather seats. "Are you sure you're really Kevin and not some handsome, suave imposter?"

"Oh, I'm Kevin all right. I just thought it was high time I . . . expanded my horizons and tried something new. I'm too predictable and I never want to get stagnant. Especially where you're concerned." As he pulled away from the curb, she sighed with relief when he drove like Kevin: both hands planted on the bottom of the wheel. She felt a small stab of disappointment when he didn't reach for her hand. Probably afraid to take his hand off the wheel since the car was so expensive. She couldn't blame him.

"I like you just the way you are, but . . . this is rather fun, sort of like role playing, which you are in no way to take as a complaint."

His look assured her he was pleased. For the next few minutes, he let her rest. With a start, she opened her eyes a short time later. *Is he actually nibbling on my ear?* Wasn't that a kick. *Oh, that's good. He's pushing all the right buttons tonight.*

"Wake up, sweetheart. We're here," Kevin said, his warm breath tickling her ear. Sure enough, there was that little telltale rumble.

Sitting up and looking out the tinted window, her eyes widened. "Where are we?"

"The airport."

"The airport?" she said, dazed. "What for? Where are we going?"

Helping her from the car, leaving it near a small hangar, Kevin walked with her across the tarmac to a waiting private jet.

"A Learjet, Kevin?" *Is this really happening?*

"I hope your stomach's not squeamish," he said. "Probably should have thought to ask earlier, but I didn't want to spoil the surprise."

She shook her head. "I've only been in one private plane before, but I was perfectly fine."

The pilot met them at the door as they climbed onto the jet. He tipped his hat. "Miss Grant. Mr. Moore."

Kevin shook his hand and stepped closer, lowering his voice as they talked for a moment. Rebekah's heart raced and she ran her hands up and down her arms, wondering what parallel universe she'd entered by mistake.

When the two men broke apart, the pilot pulled up the steps and closed the door. After securing the overhead compartments and showing them a few features of the jet, he headed toward the cockpit. "If you'll take your seats and buckle in, we've got clearance for takeoff in ten minutes."

"Thanks, Tom."

The middle-aged man nodded and smiled. "Glad to be of service, sir."

"Do you know him?" Rebekah whispered.

Kevin smiled, taking her hand. "I do now."

Stunned speechless, she concentrated on snapping her seat belt in place. Tom left the door open and she leaned forward so she could see inside the cockpit. She'd always loved to fly and watched as Tom took his seat and began his pre-flight check. Soon, he flipped switches, turned dials, and radioed the tower. Rebekah's stomach fluttered as a thrill rushed through her when the engines started, and she gave Kevin a bright smile. Although he smiled back, he looked this side of nervous. Leaning close, he made sure her seat belt was secure before buckling his own. Taking hold of her hand again, he raised her fingers and kissed them, one by one.

"You're turning my head, Mr. Moore. I feel like Julia Roberts in *Pretty Woman.* One of my favorite parts was when he takes her by private jet to San Francisco to the opera."

"I didn't know. Score one for originality on my part."

"Oh no, I didn't mean it like that at all," she said. "This is absolutely incredible. I never thought I'd be doing something like this. I love . . ." She felt him stiffen beside her. She squeezed his arm. "I love that you've planned such a special night for us."

She sensed his smile as she leaned her head on his shoulder. Lifting her head, she stole a glance at his incredibly handsome profile. If he was disappointed, he didn't show it.

Tom's voice came over the speaker as he closed the door between them. "Looks like we'll have a smooth flight. The winds are in our favor. We'll get there in good time, maybe even ahead of schedule. Enjoy the flight, folks."

"Just where are you taking me tonight?" she asked.

"You'll see soon enough, sweetheart. It won't be too long."

She thrilled at his use of the endearment. As the plane made its ascent, Kevin bowed his head. Slipping her hand into his, she said her own silent prayer even though her inner child was tempted to gawk out the window and point out passing landmarks below.

"I always pray during take-off," he told her, finished with his prayer a minute later. Although she'd never flown with him before, Rebekah remembered him telling her once it wasn't his favorite thing to do. "Landings, too."

But he was here. *He did it for you.*

~

Kevin prayed under his breath the whole way. Trained as an engineer, he knew better than most the dangers, but then again, it was still less dangerous than driving a car. They bounced a few times and he swallowed hard, hoping he wouldn't lose his manhood and embarrass himself in front of Rebekah.

She'd tempted him before leaving her house. He shouldn't have kissed her so much, but except for that second kiss, kept it appropriate. From the looks she darted his way every other minute, he knew he'd confused her. She hinted at his exciting news about the store, obviously wanting to know more, and it was difficult not to tell her everything. *Lord, don't let this plan backfire.* With Josh's help, they'd pulled in enough favors to arrange the private plane and pretentious car. They'd even involved Sam and he pulled a few strings to make this evening a reality.

Rebekah tugged on his hand as Reunion Tower came into view in the far-off distance of the otherwise flat landscape. "Dallas, Kevin? We're in Dallas?"

Tom's voice came over the loudspeaker. "We'll be arriving at Love Field in five minutes. Make sure your seat belts are fastened and I'll make the landing as smooth as possible."

Kevin bowed his head again as the wheels of the jet connected with the tarmac. Looking out the window, he exhaled a slow sigh of relief. He waited until Tom came out of the cockpit and lowered the stairs. Taking Rebekah's hand, he led the way, standing a few steps below to assist her. She paused midway, those green eyes locking with his, thanking him without words. *So far, so good.*

Kevin spotted the waiting silver Rolls Royce. Nothing like going in style. What a phony, but he figured he might as well go all out. Considering it was probably the only time in his life when he'd live like this, he might as well relax if he could—which was debatable—and enjoy it. Just watching the expressions flitting across Rebekah's beautiful face was reward enough.

A black-coated driver tipped his cap as they walked across the tarmac. "Mr. Moore? This way, please." When he looked at Rebekah, his admiring gaze lingered a little too long for Kevin's liking. He was used to stares from other men when he was with her, but wasn't in the mood. Not tonight, of all nights. He willed the man to keep moving if he wanted a decent tip. "I'd have known you and the young lady anywhere," he said over his shoulder. "Mr. Lewis gives very accurate descriptions."

Rebekah's eyes widened in surprise. "Are Sam and Lexa meeting us tonight?"

Kevin chuckled. "No way is Sam Lewis cutting into this night. Sorry to disappoint you."

She shook her head and allowed him to seat her in the luxurious car. "I'm not disappointed. Not at all." They sat close together, and as the driver pulled away from the airport, their knees touched. "You know how much I love Sam and Lexa," Rebekah said, her voice quiet, "but this night is reserved for you. Only *you*."

~

Did Kevin plan on proposing? Rebekah had to wonder. *He doesn't know—at least I don't think he does—that Adam's no longer in the picture.* This had to be his attempt to sway her heart, to show her he was every bit as capable as Adam of looking sophisticated, taking her to elegant places, doing nice things and being more adventurous. A gentle smile curved her lips. In another way, as wonderful as it was, she'd be just as happy sitting on her back porch, sipping sweet tea, talking with him as evening slipped into twilight, stealing looks, sharing kisses and dreams, and falling more in love with each new memory—and each other.

The Rolls Royce rolled up to an old, ivy-covered hotel twenty minutes later. Leaning forward, she glimpsed a sign: THE ROSEWOOD MANSION AT TURTLE CREEK. She knew it by reputation as one of the oldest, most revered institutions for fine dining and romance in Dallas. It was in a league all by itself. As they stepped through the entrance, she looked around in awe of its elegance and beauty as they followed the maître d' to a special, private table on a back terrace. A candle glowed in the middle of the table and a bouquet of gorgeous fresh roses sat by her place setting. Red, of course. After helping her into her seat, Kevin took the chair across from her.

Rebekah smiled. "You're sitting too far away."

Pushing back his chair, he moved to the seat on her right. "Does this mean you want to share your food with me tonight?"

"I wouldn't have it any other way."

The food was excellent, but if anyone asked her what she'd eaten, she wouldn't have been able to tell them. She sat, enthralled, as Kevin told her about plans for a new TeamWork mission Sam had shared with him. His eyes were bright, and the passion he felt for the ministry thrilled her. He asked about her plans for the summer and they discussed upcoming events with the praise and worship band and his Sunday school class. She asked about his mom and he asked after her mother. It was comfortable, it was easy. It was *Kevin.*

He glanced at his watch as they finished their meal. "I'm afraid we don't have time for dessert. Sorry."

"I don't need dessert." The words left her lips and floated on a sigh. "I'm sure we need to be getting back home now." She hoped her smile conveyed her appreciation. "I can't believe you did all this, Kevin. It's been a spectacular evening and one I won't forget. Ever." She loved how he'd taken complete charge and planned this entire evening. It was spontaneous and the most romantic date of her life.

"*Laissez les bon temps rouler.*" Rising to his feet, he held out his hand, waiting.

"Let the good times roll. Lead the way." Was it the headiness of the man beside her or the fragrant roses filling her senses? She knew other women watched as they headed to the door. As well they should since she was with the most handsome man in the world. Lumber man by day and debonair gentleman by night.

As he assisted her into the waiting Rolls, he gave an address in Fort Worth to the driver. Rebekah looked at him as he slid onto the back seat beside her. "There's more?"

"That's my last name, isn't it?" Kevin chuckled at her look of dismay. "Of course there's more."

"Where are you taking me next, oh wonderful man of mystery?"

His smile grew brighter. "Someplace I never thought I'd be going, to be honest."

Kicking off her shoes, she snuggled into the curve of his arm. This night got more interesting by the moment.

CHAPTER FORTY-ONE

THE ROLLS ROYCE pulled to the front of a stately building in Fort Worth that resembled a theater. Rebekah glimpsed a poster in the marquee window advertising a performance by the Texas Ballet Theater—for tonight's date. She glanced at her watch. Starting within the half-hour.

"The ballet, Kevin? You're going to sit through a ballet? As if you haven't already done enough tonight, you'd do that?" *Goodness, if everything else didn't already tell me he loves me, this does it. I can't believe he'll watch men in tights prancing around a stage.* The thought was ludicrous. A grin curved her lips as he helped her from the car. "What are you doing to me?"

His look was so loving it stole her breath. "The same thing you're doing to me."

Kevin accepted the program from an usher as they went inside the theater and found their seats. Stealing a glance at him during the first act, Rebekah marveled all over again how he'd been willing to sit through something he probably hated with every fiber of his being because he wanted to make her happy. Her heart felt pretty close to reaching its full potential for loving this man. He had to know. She felt his eyes on her and slipped her hand in his.

They shared a glass of ginger ale during the intermission. She laughed as his eyes widened when she mentioned the next intermission.

"There's a *third* act?" He hadn't poured over the program like she had.

During the second act, she leaned close to whisper in his ear. "If you want to leave when this act is done, I won't be adverse to the idea."

His smile was broad in the darkened theater. Taking her hand, he raised it to his lips.

It was difficult to concentrate on the dancers on the stage when all she wanted to do was stare at the man beside her.

The man I love.

~

The return flight to Baton Rouge was quiet and uneventful. The lights below winked at him. Rebekah snuggled close, tucking her hand in his and resting her head on his shoulder.

"This has been the most perfect night of my life. Thank you, Kevin."

He squeezed her hand in silent agreement. Shortly after midnight, he drove her back to the house. Her eyes were closed, but he knew she wasn't asleep, just content. That's all he could have asked. All in all, the night had been a rousing success, but now . . . the final test. His defenses were gone and he needed to keep his wits about him. It didn't help when he couldn't stop staring at her long, gorgeous legs as Rebekah emerged from the sports car.

"You're staring at me," she said, tipping his chin with one finger as she walked past him on the sidewalk leading up to the front door. Her sandals dangled from one hand and he carried the roses for her as she pulled her keys out of her handbag.

"I can't help it. Those legs God gave you are much too spectacular, not to mention all the rest of you," he said under his breath, hoping she hadn't heard. But he knew she had. That comment came from his alter ego tonight, but it was true. A curtain moving next door caught his attention. "I think Mrs. Michelson is watching."

Rebekah laughed as she unlocked her front door. "She likes you so it's all good. Might as well give her a real good show."

"What do you have in mind?"

"Well, as much as I'd like to smooch you on my doorstep, it's probably best if you come inside. I do have *some* pride, after all. Get in here, Mr. Moore." She took him by the hand and hauled him over the doorway and into the living room.

"It's really late, sweetheart," Kevin said even though his heart wanted nothing more than to go inside with her . . . and never leave. *Lord, keep me strong.*

"Indulge me. *Please.*"

"Ready for your dessert now?" he asked, taking one step closer.

"Uh huh," she said, putting the roses on a side table. "Your lips will do quite nicely."

Moving his arms around her, he pulled her close. For a moment, he lost himself in her soft lips, the wonderful scent of her perfume, the warmth of her so close to him. Breaking away, he groaned. He definitely had a lot to pray about, but this night had been very rewarding.

"Oh, Rebekah," he groaned. "Keep this up, and I'm going to fly you to Reno and put a ring on your finger tomorrow." He shouldn't have said that, but he couldn't help himself. This woman was driving him crazy, had him thinking things he shouldn't.

Rebekah laughed with no clue as to the tangled emotions raging inside him. "Would you like some ice cream before you leave? Some real dessert?"

"Not really, but if it means prolonging the eventual goodnight, I suppose you could talk me into it." This was just as crazy. He had to leave for Houston first thing in the morning and he shouldn't be tired when he hit the open highway. As it was, he wouldn't get much sleep. He hated to leave without telling her the truth, but he'd followed "the plan" this far and couldn't mess up now. He trusted Josh. A sting of conscience threatened to waylay him, but he followed her into the kitchen. *Just a few more minutes, one more kiss—maybe two—and then I'm out of here.*

"Chocolate?" she asked, and he nodded. She knew his preferences just as he knew she liked vanilla. *French* vanilla, of course.

Removing his suit coat, he tried to ignore the time on the wall clock. Watching as she moved around the kitchen, pulling out the ice cream from the freezer and two spoons from the drawer, it looked like she'd gotten her second wind.

"You know what?" she said, "I'm not standing on ceremony. We've shared enough tonight. Here." She put both pints of ice cream on the table along with the spoons. "Chocolate for you and vanilla for me. We can keep them separate or blend them. Your choice."

He raised a brow. "I have a better idea." Taking one spoon and digging in, scooping up a good size bite of the vanilla, he held it up to her lips.

She took the bite and returned the favor, scooping chocolate on her spoon, offering it to him. "You realize we're hopeless," she said, her voice quiet as she scooped another bite, this time vanilla for herself.

"I know. Wouldn't have it any other way." He stopped his spoon halfway to her mouth. She never looked more adorable than with that hint of a vanilla mustache lining her upper lip. "Finish that bite," he said.

She was obedient and did as he asked, and he was thrilled the ice cream remained on her upper lip. Feeling bold, he ran his index finger around the upper rim of the chocolate container and slicked some ice cream across his lower lip. He sat back in the chair, arms crossed, waiting to see if she'd take the hint. Laughing, Rebekah leaned close. Oh yes, the woman was creative in so many ways.

"Hmm . . . delicious. You taste good, Kevin."

I need to go. The woman was seductive without even trying. She had no idea what her words, the look in her eyes—and especially those lips—did to him.

"I'd better go," he said, jumping up from the table. His resolve was melting as fast as that ice cream and he needed to put physical distance between them. Based on her expression, he'd surprised her with his abruptness. "Let me put this away."

"I don't care if it melts," Rebekah murmured, watching him.

From all appearances, he'd accomplished his purpose tonight, done his job. Maybe he'd done it *too* well. *Please, Lord, don't let her hate me when she finds out I left town.* He wasn't sure how she'd find out, but she'd know soon enough, one way or another. The gazebo sat in the warehouse. Timing being everything, he'd left strict instructions for it to be delivered after he left for Houston. Kevin pushed the lids back on the ice cream and returned the containers to the freezer. Wiping his hands on a dishtowel, he grabbed his suit coat with one hand and Rebekah by the other as he led her back into the living room.

"There's one more thing I have to do before I go tonight," he said.

"What's that?" Her eyes searched his. It was obvious she didn't know what to make of him. As it was, he wasn't sure what to make of himself.

"This." Pulling gently on the clip securing her hair, he was utterly entranced as the mass of long, silky blonde strands tumbled around her face and shoulders. He touched her hair before moving one hand behind her neck. He stopped when his lips were a heartbeat away from hers. She raised her chin and her lids lowered. She wanted his kiss, and he needed hers more than the need to breathe. It took every ounce of strength inside him to pull away, to step back.

But he did.

It was on the tip of his tongue to tell her he loved her. *Oh, Lord, I need to hear those words from this woman.* He wanted to hear them so bad he ached. After tonight, he thought it might actually be true that she loved him. "I hate saying goodnight to you, but I need to go." He shrugged his arms into his suit coat.

"Call me tomorrow?" The hint of disappointment in her voice didn't escape him.

"We'll talk soon," he said. That's the best he could offer, but it pained him like a physical blow. Stopping at the door, he knew he couldn't leave without telling her with his kiss what he couldn't with words. He'd followed the plan. He didn't *tell* her he loved her.

He opened his arms and she walked into them. Wrapping her in the cocoon of his suit coat, he held her as close as he dared, kissing her again and again. He couldn't get enough of her. He needed to stop, but found it nearly impossible. So dazed he wasn't sure his legs would hold him upright, so full of love he couldn't speak, Kevin lowered his arms. Rebekah took a small step backward. It was a beautiful sight. What started out as a hint of a smile on her lips grew into the most glorious, loopy grin he'd ever seen. One he soon hoped to see every morning for the rest of his life.

His heart in his throat, he turned to go. *I love you.*

"Kevin?" she called after him when he was halfway down the walk.

He turned. "Yes?" His heart lurched pretty good at the look on her face.

"I . . ." Heaving a deep breath, she looked away.

He waited. *Please say it, Rebekah.*

The moonlight reflected her tears as she met his gaze again. "This was the best night of my life."

He nodded and turned to go, not trusting himself to speak. If she would come after him, run to him, throw her arms around his neck and tell him she loved him, he wouldn't hold back anything. He'd confess it all—everything—but try not to implicate her brother. She'd probably figure that one out, anyway.

But Rebekah didn't come after him, didn't call to him. He started the car and pulled away, leaving his heart on her front walkway.

Give her time.

Still, it was going to be one very long, lonely ride to Houston.

CHAPTER FORTY-TWO

The Next Afternoon

REBEKAH POURED A glass of water and walked over to the kitchen window. It was a sunny, beautiful day and the humidity wasn't too oppressive. Over the top rim of her glass, her eyes grew large. Slamming the glass down with such force it nearly broke, she flung the side door wide and ran outside, circling the gazebo several times. It was beautiful. Incredible. Hers? Where in the world did it come from? Who sent it? Was it a gift, or simply a delivery to the wrong house? It was so charming, and she never expected to see one of them sitting in her backyard.

Spying a tag attached to the side, she grabbed it and spotted the familiar logo. *Moore Lumber*. She shook her head, puzzled, and turned the tag. *Why in the world would Kevin send me a gazebo?* Her eyes were drawn to the words on the back and she put a hand over her mouth. "Rebekah's Heart." What could *that* mean? Her hand shook, but she examined it again. Those two precious words were written next to *Design Name* on the back of the tag. Someone had drawn a little red heart beside it.

Rushing back in the house, she paused long enough to grab her purse. Slinging it over her shoulder, she headed to her car. She could call, but she needed to see Kevin in person. As she drove, she wondered if the gazebo was why he hadn't called her since their date. Their unbelievable, fantastic date. Maybe he knew the gazebo would be delivered and was waiting for her to call and thank him. As soon as she arrived at the lumber company, she headed straight for the customer service desk.

"Welcome to Moore Lumber. May I help you?" A thirty-something, red-haired woman wearing a name tag that read NANCY gave her a friendly smile.

"I'm looking for Kevin Moore. Does he happen to be here this afternoon?" Her quick glance encompassed the large warehouse building, observing the hub of activity. It was good to see business was good with lots of customers buying lumber and home supplies, many trying to save money with do-it-yourself projects.

"Kevin left this morning."

Rebekah snapped her attention back to Nancy. "Left? For where?"

"Why, Houston, of course."

Did he go to visit Sam and Lexa? After all, it seemed the thing to do these days. "I hadn't heard. Thanks." She started to walk away, but then turned back. "Will he be back anytime soon?" *Why didn't he tell me?*

"I'm not really sure, sweetie. Opening a new location can take some time so I imagine he's going to be there for quite a while. At least eight months or more, maybe even a year."

Her heart sank. *A year?* "Thank you. I appreciate the information." Her head reeled, her pulse pounded. Turning away from the counter, Rebekah clutched her stomach and hoped she wouldn't be sick in public. Walking outside with slow steps, not paying attention, she was almost plowed down by Tommy on his way back inside. He looked like a lumberjack in his denim overalls and plaid work shirt rolled at the elbows, and his arms were piled high with lumber as he turned the corner. Seeing her at the last second, he swerved to avoid hitting her. In her surprise, she lost her balance and—with a startled cry—found herself sprawled on the ground a moment later.

"I'm so sorry, miss," Tommy said, dropping the boards on the ground and reaching out to touch her arm. His eyes widened in recognition as they fell on her. "Why, Rebekah, honey, I didn't know that was you. Are you okay?"

She shook her head, dazed. "I'm . . . I'm not really sure how to answer that question right now."

"You don't look so good, a little green around the gills. Here," he said, putting one big hand under her arm and helping her to her feet, "you come inside to the office and let me get you a cup of water. Need an aspirin?"

"No. I'll be fine, but I'll take the water and some answers, if you don't mind."

"Answers? Well, sure thing. I'll do what I can," Tommy said, steering her by the elbow and into his office at the back.

"Mommy, look, it's *Tommy*! You know, the one on TV!" squealed a little girl. He'd become a popular local celebrity as Moore Lumber's spokesman with a string of thirty-second television commercial spots perfectly suited to his fun-loving, outgoing personality.

He lit up like a Christmas tree. If possible, that chest puffed out even more as he waved and gave the child and her mother a huge smile. "Go see Nancy at the desk and she'll give you a special surprise," he called to the girl. Coming into the office behind Rebekah, he closed the door. "The price of fame, what can I say?" He shrugged and gave her a sheepish grin. "Sorry about that."

"No, you're not." She managed a small smile. "I think you've found your true calling."

Tommy laughed under his breath. "I'm pretty shameless. If it brings in customers, I'm all for it. You should hear some of the ideas I'm planning for future commercials. Kevin thinks—" He stopped. "That's not why you're here. Tell me what's up." Crossing over to the water cooler in the corner, he gestured for her to sit in one of the chairs in front of the messy desk piled high with papers and littered with empty coffee cups. Pouring her a cup of ice cold water, he handed it to her. He watched as she drank all of it before handing the cup back to him with a grateful smile.

"Thanks. Nancy told me Kevin's gone. He's in Houston?" She tried not to crumple, but wasn't doing a very good job of it as her bottom lip trembled.

"Yeah. Left this morning." Leaning his elbows on the desk, his eyes softened. "I take it he didn't tell you, huh?" Tommy rubbed his hand over his face and leaned his chin on his fist.

Rebekah shook her head. "He's been a little . . . frustrated with me, but last night we had the best date in the history of the world. Oh, this is all my fault." That one came out a near-wail. She was past the point of being embarrassed. "I'm so stupid and I waited too long. I should have told him." Her head fell into her hands and the tears started flowing. She tried to stop them, but they streamed down her cheeks. Even her nose was running now. Any minute, she'd be wringing her hands. What a mess.

"Aw man, not the tears," he muttered, running into the bathroom off the side of the office. Coming back, he shoved a wad of paper towels in her hands. "Sorry. I'm not too good with crying women. Ask my wife. She wants to send me to sensitivity training."

She knew he was trying to lighten the mood and make her smile, but she was already too far gone. "I'm so . . . so . . . sooo . . ." She gulped. "So . . . sorry." Unable to stop, she cried as her heart broke. "Kevin can't leave. He just can't!" She buried her face in her hands, trying to stifle her sobs. She knew she was causing a scene now. "This is such a mess, and it's all my . . . my . . . fault."

Tommy flew to the office window and jerked the cord to lower the blinds—but not all the way down—before moving back to stand beside her. "Honey, listen to me." He put his big hand on her shoulder and squeezed.

"The business is doing so well that we're expanding into Texas. Being single—at least for now," he added, probably for her benefit, "Kevin's the logical choice to scout out locations and get everything all set up, meet with the contractors, laborers, stuff like that. Besides," he said with a grin, "he's the smart one of us brothers. Dad needs to stick around to take care of Mom, and it's pretty obvious my little brother's the one who's going to take over the business and run the whole show eventually. It's not forever. He'll be back."

Getting control of her emotions, Rebekah squared her shoulders, dabbed at her eyes and looked up into his kind eyes.

"What's this really all about?" He pulled over a chair and sat down beside her. "Talk to Tommy. I'm all ears."

She dabbed at her eyes again. "Did Kevin say anything to you about Adam?"

"Nah. He never said anything about any Adam. What's his last name?"

"Martin." She sniffled again and blew her nose.

He scratched his head and pushed a strand of dark hair away from his forehead. "I know someone with that name paid us a whole lot of money for some fancy gazebo."

"That's now sitting in my backyard," Rebekah said, shaking her head. "Adam ordered the gazebo?"

"Well, his American Express paid the deposit, but I saw Kevin refunded the guy's money a few days ago." His brows knit together. "You say it's in your backyard?"

She nodded. "Did someone here in the warehouse put it together?"

Tommy chuckled. "Now it's starting to make more sense. My little brother supervised that project all by his lonesome. Normally, some of the employees put those things together, but this one was all Kevin's baby. He insisted on doing all the work himself, and designed it, cut the wood and everything. He put in a lot of hours finishing it up, working late into the night and even coming in on Sunday afternoon, which is something he's never done before. You know Kevin," he said, "he always sticks to the rule about keeping the Sabbath holy. But that Martin fellow insisted it be done within a certain time, so he had to scramble."

Judging by the timing of the delivery of the gazebo, Adam probably intended to propose to her in it. But then she cut him loose. *Why didn't Adam just cancel the order after I broke up with him?* Maybe he did, and that's why Kevin refunded his money then decided he wanted to follow through with it. Kevin wasn't a man to abandon a project once he'd started. Rebekah sat up straighter in her chair. "Tommy, do you know if Kevin's already left for Houston?"

He glanced at his watch. "I'm not sure. He was scheduled to drive there sometime this morning, but I think he got a later start than planned." He shot her a grin. "Said he was out really late—or early—this morning." He reached for the phone on the desk. "Tell you what. How about we call him and find out? If he knows you're here and upset, he'll turn right around and come back here pronto."

"No!" Rebekah said. She lowered her voice. "I wouldn't want him to do that. Don't call him, but can you do me a really big favor?"

"Anything for you, honey." When he looked at her, those blue eyes sparkled. She'd never noticed before how much they resembled Kevin's.

"Please don't tell him I was here. And mention it to Nancy, too. I'll talk with Kevin, but I need to do it my own way. I hope you understand."

Tommy chuckled. "Sure sounds to me like love's involved." He tilted his head. "Just what are you planning, pretty lady?"

"I'm not sure yet, but I think a trip to Houston might be involved. Have any idea where he's staying?" As soon as the question was out, Rebekah knew the answer.

"He's staying with Sam and Lexa Lewis, at least for now."

"Of course." She couldn't expect anything else. She smiled a little as they both rose to their feet. "Okay, then, mum's the word. Thanks for being here."

"Sure thing. You know I'm always here for you." He grinned and winked. "Go get him, Tiger."

Raising her chin and squaring her shoulders, she took her leave. "I'll do my best."

CHAPTER FORTY-THREE

That Same Afternoon

"JOSH, WHERE ARE you?" Rebekah asked.

"In my office, of course. Where are you?"

"In my car headed from Moore Lumber back to my house, which now has a gazebo in the backyard, by the way. Never mind. I'll tell you later. I have a question. If you could be anywhere else in the world right now, where would it be?"

"Houston." No hesitation. "Why? Where would you want to be, Beck?"

"Same. How soon can you be ready?"

"Are we driving or flying? How soon are we talking here?"

"Well, I think a roadtrip might be in order to plan our respective strategies." Good thing school was out for the summer. Closing her eyes, Rebekah lifted a silent prayer. *Thank you, Lord.* She'd been praying for answers and things were finally falling into place. The Almighty must be amused watching their antics. No doubt about it, He had a sense of humor.

"And what might those strategies involve?"

"Well," she told him slowly, savoring each word, "it's time to finalize the biggest merger and acquisition of your life." Knowing Josh, he'd probably had a bag packed for weeks.

"And you?"

She sighed. "I have to go get my lumber man and tell him I love him."

~

Two hours later, Josh jumped out of his BMW and hurried up the front walkway. Remembering the gazebo, he walked around to the side of the house and laughed. There it was, all white and brand-spanking new and, sure enough, had hearts carved into the top, just like Kevin said. "What do you know?" Turning toward the side door to the kitchen, he spied Beck's elderly neighbor. She stood by the side of her house, watering her plants.

"Hi, Mrs. Michelson!" He waved and graced her with his best smile.

"Josh," she acknowledged with a nod. "Nice gazebo."

"Yes, isn't it?" He caught her rare smile as he headed into the kitchen. He was too jazzed about the upcoming trip to get after Beck for leaving her door unlocked. "Beck? I'm here. Your door was unlocked." He figured she didn't hear that one.

Not hearing an answer, he walked into the living room. "Beck?" he called up the stairs. He heard her muffled voice and bounded up the stairs, two at a time. He found her sitting on the end of her bed. He wasn't sure if she was crying or praying so he dropped onto the bed beside her, putting his arm around her shoulders. She leaned against him and grabbed his hand.

"I was just asking the Lord's blessing on our little roadtrip-to-end-all-roadtrips and asking Him for the right thing to say to Kevin." She gave him a little smile and her lip trembled.

He squeezed her shoulder. "I'm sure He'll give you the right words. Are you packed?"

She nodded. "As ready as I'll ever be. I assume you want to drive?"

"Don't I usually?" Standing, he smoothed his hands on his jeans. "Ready to go?"

"Sit back down first. Calm down, stop pacing, and let's pray together."

"You're right. Just pray I don't break any speed limits between here and Houston. The closer we get, the faster I'll want to go. Fair warning. Maybe you should take over at that point." Bowing their heads, holding hands, they prayed for the Lord's will to be done and asked His blessing and safety on the trip.

"Kevin's been so patient with me while I was acting like an indecisive twit. It's my turn now. I should have told him I loved him the other night when I had the chance."

"I'm not refuting anything you've just said," he told her as he loaded their bags into his car. "Now, time to tell me about this big date of yours." It was great hearing it from her perspective. Kevin had done him proud.

~

A couple of hours later, after stopping for a light supper, Rebekah looked over at her brother. "Did you call Sam and Lexa before we left the house?"

"No. Call it an unfortunate oversight," Josh said. "I take it you didn't either?"

"No. Since it's getting late, as much as I hate to admit it, why don't we find a place to stay? Then we'll call Lexa and Sam and can start out fresh again in the morning."

"As much as I hate to wait another minute, and I do have a spare key to their house, you're right." He gestured to the glove compartment. "I think there's a travel book in there if you want to pick out a place to stay."

"How do you feel about a bed-and-breakfast?" she asked a short time later. "We just passed a billboard that advertised one called THE ELLIS INN about an hour away. I love bed-and-breakfasts. It's in a little town called Wellspring." She opened the map and found it, frowning. "It might be a little off the beaten track, but not too far."

"That's fine. Whatever you want." Josh sounded distracted and looked even more so.

"Did you have trouble getting away from the firm?"

"Not really. I'm missing a couple of mergers, but one of the other associates can handle them. I brought what I could with me and have my laptop. There's no reason I can't put in a little work time tonight and the next few days, even though my heart won't be in it." He darted a glance her way. "I have the feeling my days at the firm are numbered."

"Really? Are you okay with that? I know how important the firm is to you."

"It's not so much the firm that's important," he said. "I love practicing law, but the last couple of months have shown me how much more there is to life than all-work-all-the-time. I've been praying for the Lord to show me where He wants me." His fingers tapped the steering wheel. "And I don't think it's at the firm in Baton Rouge."

Rebekah watched him closely. "Something tells me you already have an idea in mind."

"What makes you say that?"

"You're not going to tell me, are you?"

He shook his head. "Believe it or not, for once I don't have a set plan. This isn't about me anymore. I have Winnie and Chloe to consider now, and they're what's most important. When I find out what's happening, trust me, you'll be the first to know."

"That's flattering."

"After my other two girls, of course."

She laughed. "That's a given and the way it should be. Take the next exit for the bed-and-breakfast."

~

The next morning, Sam stood in the doorway of their home as Josh pulled into the driveway. The only thing brighter than the sun was the smile on their TeamWork leader's face.

Looking over at her, Josh squeezed her hand. "Ready?"

"As much as I'll ever be. Let's go." Rebekah started up the front walkway as Josh pulled their overnight cases from the car.

"You two certainly look like you're on a mission." Sam wrapped her in his arms before taking their bags and leading them into the spacious house.

"You could say that," Josh said, closing the front door behind them. "Thanks for putting up with me again. My little sister, too." He gave her a wink.

"Always good to see you," Sam told them. "Let's go in the kitchen." He waved his hand for her to lead the way.

Rebekah loved the wide-open floor plan and the welcoming touches everywhere. It was so warm and inviting. She glanced at the row of family photographs on the wall by the stairs and marveled all over again how much Sam's younger brother, Will, looked like their host. She caught a glimpse of the photograph of Lexa's mom and dad and knew how precious that was for her dear friend since both were now gone. Pushing the swinging door, she smiled as she heard Lexa singing, cradling Joseph.

Looking up, Lexa stopped singing and gave them a bright smile. "Good morning!" She looked a little tired, but prettier than ever in jeans and a pink cotton blouse, her long hair braided as usual.

Rebekah hurried across the room and gave her a hug before dropping a quick kiss on the baby's rosy cheek. "Oh, I think he's grown even since we saw him." She shot a grin in Sam's direction where he talked with Josh. "He's growing into more of a miniature version of Sam every day," she said, loud enough for both men to hear before returning her attention to Joe.

"Yeah, scary, isn't it?"

That statement came from her wayward brother. She caught the look of wry amusement Sam exchanged with Josh.

"If you line up Sam's baby pictures next to Joseph's, you'd think it was the same child. One of God's miracles," Lexa said, kissing her son.

"Seems there's plenty of those to go around," Rebekah said. "Miracles, that is. Oh, he's the most handsome little guy I've ever seen May I hold him?"

Lexa smiled and lowered Joseph into her waiting arms.

Looking at the precious child, Rebekah lifted a silent prayer that, if it was in God's will, she'd have several little miracles of her own with her lumber man. *Kevin might be upstairs right now.* Her heart pounded at the thought. She ducked her head, knowing her face was flushed, and kissed his cheek. So warm and soft. He squirmed a little and opened his eyes, blinking a few times and reaching toward her. When she put her hand near his, Joe curled his chubby fingers around hers and let out a belly laugh.

"Did you have breakfast?" Sam asked.

"We managed to eat something at the bed-and-breakfast," Josh said, moving across the kitchen in her direction. "Enough hogging the baby. My turn."

Eyes wide, Rebekah handed him over, more than a little surprised. What a natural he was. It brought out a nurturing side of him she'd never glimpsed before. She'd talked with Winnie quite a bit lately and knew Chloe adored Josh. It was hard *not* to adore her brother. He had "the touch" with children every bit as much as with adults judging by the way he handled Joe.

"Do you, um, happen to know where I might . . . be able to find a handsome lumber man from Louisiana?" she asked Sam. *Why am I so tongue-tied all of a sudden?*

"He headed out to the construction site right after an early breakfast," Sam said.

"Have they already broken ground?" Josh asked.

Sam shook his head. "No, that's still a week or two away. Kevin's got a trailer set up as an office and the construction equipment and building supplies are being brought in. He's meeting with the contractors, the architects and construction crew." His gaze moved to her. "He's the lead guy with this project and I think he's in his element."

"That's what I keep telling her," Josh said. "That man's a natural born leader, and he doesn't rely on his own decisions, but has that all-important silent Partner on his side. I predict the man will go far." He glanced her way. "Especially with Beck right beside him."

Rebekah appreciated their confidence in Kevin. "Have you been to the construction site?"

"Meaning do I know where it is and how to get there?" The smile lines she loved deepened. "I'll do you one better."

Lexa walked over to the small desk in the corner of the kitchen and retrieved a piece of paper. "Here are the mapped out directions as well as the phone number for the construction office." She smiled. "I assume you have Kevin's cell phone number, if needed."

"Yes, thanks," Rebekah said, glancing at the paper. "You two think of everything."

"Speaking of which, do you happen to know the whereabouts of a very lovely lady named Winnie Doyle this fine morning?" Josh asked. He ignored her when she rolled her eyes. Sam moved over to Josh and he transferred Joe to his father's waiting arms.

Putting his son over his shoulder with ease, Sam proved how at home he was in the role of papa. Rebekah glanced at Lexa, and the look on her face as she watched her husband and child made her breath hitch.

"Your timing is impeccable," Lexa said a few seconds later. "We've got a couple of days before the next big job. As a matter of fact, I heard Winnie say something about taking Chloe on a picnic today." She glanced at her watch and gave him a smile. "You have just enough time to drop Beck off at the construction site and then scoot on over to the park. I'm sure it's the one closest to her apartment."

Josh nodded. "I know just the place." He looked ready to bolt that second.

"Let's make sure Kevin's at the work site first," Rebekah said, giving him a look of warning. "I know how anxious you are to see Winnie and Chloe, but if you know what's good for you, you won't leave me in your dust with a bunch of construction guys if he's not there."

"Now *that's* an idea," Josh said, wincing as Rebekah swatted him on the arm. "Need to freshen up before we head out? Slick on some lip gloss?"

Time to act like a grownup and ignore her irritating brother. He couldn't get to her today. She was on the most important mission of her life, and so was he. Nothing could stop her.

"We'll be praying!" Lexa called to them as they left a few minutes later.

"Have fun, kids," Sam said. She heard his chuckle as they headed out the front door.

CHAPTER FORTY-FOUR

"OKAY, YOU NAVIGATE. How many miles are we talking?" Josh glanced over at the map Rebekah held in her hands as he strapped himself in and started the car. Thinking better of it, he cut the engine and reached for her hand. She looked at him in surprise, but left her hand in his. "I feel this overpowering need to pray. Again. Right here. Now. Indulge me, please."

"Not a problem." She didn't know which of their hands trembled more.

Ten minutes later, headed down the highway, Josh glanced her way. "Nervous?"

"Like Marie Antoinette."

He chuckled. "We're talking about your heart here, Beck, not your head. Well, maybe both. This is going to be great. I can't wait to see the look on Kevin's face when he sees you."

"Do you think he'll be happy to see me?" She'd been so focused on wanting to tell Kevin she loved him she hadn't thought about it from *his* perspective. "Pray the Lord will give me the right words and that he'll be receptive to what I have to tell him."

"You know it," Josh said. "I have no doubt he'll swoop you in his arms, plant a whopper on you and never let you go. He's been waiting for you to come around."

"But why didn't he step in and stake his claim on me a long time ago?"

"Because that's the kind of man Kevin Moore is. Whether you realize it or not, he staked his claim on your heart a long time ago. Back in Montana, from all indications. Adam was just a minor roadblock in the way, but Kevin gave you the precious time you needed to come freely to him. By being there as your friend, first and foremost, he's allowed you to see who he really is. The kind, loving, quiet, loyal suitor for my sister's heart, and what do you know?" He tapped the steering wheel and shot her a self-satisfied grin. "It worked like a charm."

"Are you saying I'm predictable?"

"I don't think you have to worry about anyone accusing you of that."

"I hope you're right. Turn right at the next main intersection," she said, glancing at the map. "We're about three minutes away now, according to the directions." Her knee pumped up and down as she massaged her fingers.

"Numb?"

She nodded. "A little, but it's more nerves than anything else."

"Kevin will know what to do."

She blew out a breath and stared out the window. "I only pray he'll want to do it." As much as she wanted to believe Josh, the wings of doubt fluttered in her heart. Straining forward in the seat, she pointed to a dirt road off the side of the highway a short distance ahead. "I think that's it."

"That has to be it," Josh said. "Good thing Sam wrote on here to watch for the tracks in the mud." The car dipped and dust swirled everywhere—making it difficult to see—as he turned off the main road. He slowed the car as the tires hit rough ground.

"Sorry about all this dirt," she said, hoping he wasn't upset. Josh loved his car.

"That's the least of my worries. Just pray there's no nails or glass out here."

Rebekah spied a long, white trailer ahead and squirmed in the seat. Her knee pumped overtime and she started to gnaw on her fingernail. "I haven't been this nervous since that play in the third grade. Turn around."

"Not on your life. And yes, you were the princess about to be rescued by the handsome prince and scared out of your mind Jason what's-his-name *would* kiss you. Somehow, I think it's a little different this time."

"Sleeping Beauty," she said, her attention focused on the trailer. "Jason had obnoxious garlic breath and I wasn't about to sacrifice my first kiss to him. I wasn't this scared when I was dumped in the swimming pool and forced to tread water in swimming class when we were six, or when I was the senior class president and gave my speech at graduation since someone else in this car couldn't be bribed to take my place." She faltered a moment. "Or even the moment I knew Daddy was never coming home again during my lifetime." She looked up at the ceiling of the car and squeezed her eyes shut. "Come back now, Lord, just come back now. Make this a whole lot easier."

Josh pulled the car to a stop, another cloud of dust swirling around them. Good thing the windows were up. He turned in the seat to face her. "Take a deep breath and focus. It's time to go get him, Sleeping Beauty."

"Don't leave me until you know Kevin's here," she said. It sounded pleading, but she didn't care.

"I don't think you have to worry." He nodded in the direction of the trailer.

Rebekah's heart caught in her throat. Kevin stepped out of the trailer, closed the door behind him and called to a couple of the workers standing nearby. He looked over in the direction of the car, but she couldn't glimpse his expression.

"Do you need a push?" Josh hopped out and came around the front of the car to open her door.

"Maybe." Her legs wobbled and her voice was even shakier. "I can't move my legs. They're stuck."

"Just take it one step at a time, one foot in front of the other." He looked over his shoulder, blocking her view. "He's coming, Beck. Kevin's coming over to the car."

"Is he? Oh, my. Hope I'm still alive in a minute to say hi to him." Her heart pounded so hard she felt dizzy. She put one hand up to her head.

"You're being dramatic. Enough of this. Come on. It's showtime." He pulled her by the hand, practically hauling her out of the passenger seat.

Quaking inside, she stepped out of the car to stand beside him. Her knees threatened to buckle beneath her. *Be strong. I can do all things through Him Who strengthens me. Remember that. Now is not the time to be afraid or timid.*

"Hey, Josh," Kevin said.

"Kevin." She'd never seen such a big grin from her brother.

Those devastating blue eyes moved over to her. "Rebekah."

There was a long pause as both men watched her. "Hi, Kevin." It came out barely more than a whisper, but he heard. He looked great in his well-worn jeans and a deep red T-shirt. She always loved red on him since it brought out the intensity of those incredible, intense blue eyes. Her gaze trailed to his feet. Construction boots.

"Thanks for bringing her out here. I'll take it from here."

Josh nodded and pulled Kevin in a quick hug. "Take good care of her, Kev."

"Always."

Rebekah's eyes grew wide. *Do they not realize I'm standing right here?*

"Meet you back at the ranch, Beck. Love ya." With a quick kiss on the cheek, Josh headed back around the car and started to climb in.

"Josh!" She pivoted, her feet spewing more dust.

Her brother lowered the window on the passenger side as she planted both hands on the open window. "Don't you dare get back in this car."

"No, no, it's not that," she said. "I just wanted to tell you that I'll be praying for you and Winnie . . . and Chloe."

"No, you won't. At least not now. You'll be otherwise occupied. We'll compare notes later."

"Bye, Josh. I love you." She blew him a kiss.

"Bye, Beck. Love you more." In a cloud of dust, he was gone, leaving her fanning her face and coughing. He'd had the last word again, but she'd deal with him later.

Waving her hands to clear the air—a lost cause—she turned around. Kevin waited, as always. When he saw her head back in his direction, he took a few slow steps to meet her. My, he looked great. All rugged and handsome. So Kevin, but better than ever.

"Hi there," she said, shoving her hands in the pockets of her now off-white shorts. They'd been white when she left Sam and Lexa's. "Sorry, I started out with the best of intentions this morning, but now I look like a ragamuffin."

"I'll take it," he said. "You're beautiful as ever and the best sight I've seen since our date a couple of nights ago. What brings you all the way out here, Rebekah? All the way to Houston to my work site in the middle of nowhere in the dirt and dust?"

The oxygen was slowly filtering back into her lungs. "It's not nowhere, Kevin," Rebekah said, looking him in the eye, taking a step closer, "if it's where *you* are."

"Well," he said, moving toward her so only a few inches separated them. "First things first. Let me take care of those numb fingers."

His eyes never leaving hers, Kevin captured both her hands in his. Gently massaging them, he worked his way carefully from one finger to the next, knowing the exact pressure needed for each finger, the right touch, to help soothe and ease the numbness. They stood there for several minutes without speaking, as he massaged her fingers. His gaze spoke volumes as he drank in the sight of her. All over again, he had her heart.

"Thank you. Can we maybe go somewhere private?" she asked. Anyone watching them must think they were completely nuts. *Not that I care.*

"I thought you'd never ask." Putting one arm around her shoulders, Kevin led her in the direction of the trailer. "This is our only option, but it's preferable to standing out here on public display. I think we've already got an audience," he said, "but I don't want all the men within shouting distance ogling my woman."

"Am I your woman?" she asked as soon as the door closed behind him.

"I think *you* should answer that question, Rebekah."

"I think you know the answer. I wouldn't be here otherwise."

"Tell me."

"What do you mean?" Confused, she shook her head.

Kevin sighed and crossed his arms. Walking to the small desk, he half-leaned, half-sat on it. "We're going in circles here. Do you realize you've never told me how you feel?"

Rebekah looked deep into the eyes of this wonderful man waiting for her to awaken and come to her senses. The man God intended for her for all along. She took a deep breath and gave him a shaky smile. "Kevin."

"Yes?"

"Please uncross your arms."

He obeyed, and she saw the beginnings of another grin flirt with the corners of his lips as she took slow, purposeful steps toward him. Stopping in front of him, she traced the lines of his mouth with a soft caress. His smile faded somewhat, replaced by something deeper she'd never before seen in his eyes. "Put your arms around my waist," she said, her voice quiet.

Kevin sighed. "Is it really that difficult for you to say three little words?" he asked. "Only three . . . little ones?"

Still, he was obedient and did as she asked, wrapping two strong arms around her. It was quite possible she'd never want to leave. "It's not difficult at all." Taking a deep breath, she planted both palms against his firm, solid chest. "I just want to make sure I do it right."

The love etched in his expression was a beautiful thing. "A word of advice?" he said, his voice husky. "Hurry. Please."

"I. Love. You. Kevin. Moore." She paused between each word for emphasis, not to tease him, but to draw out the sweetness and to prolong the pleasure of seeing his face as she told him she loved him for the first time. *And oh, how those words are so long overdue.* Rebekah moved her hands upward, clasping them behind his neck as she molded herself against him.

"Pull her closer," Kevin said, taking over. He didn't even try to move her back away from him. "Cup her face," he said, tracing the line of her cheekbone down to her jaw with the fingertips of one hand before resting them along the side of her face. "I'll love you forever, Rebekah Grant. I always have, and I always will. Kiss the girl." Kevin lowered his mouth to hers. It was reminiscent of the day on the deck of the restaurant in Baton Rouge, but this time it was perfect and went on forever. Finally pulling apart, Kevin sighed. "So, when did you come to this epiphany, sweetheart?"

She smiled and looked up at him. "You had me at frog legs. Tell me now what you said that day."

"I said I'd always love you. In French," he whispered against her lips, giving her a very real demonstration as he finally took the initiative to deepen their kiss. "We'd better stop," he said a minute or so of bliss later, putting a safe distance between them. They were both flushed, breathing hard. "I'm glad none of the guys came knocking on the door. I think they somehow knew to stay away until we leave this trailer together."

"It might start rumors," she said, still trying to catch her breath.

He shrugged. "People will talk. The only one I answer to is the Lord."

"Do you really speak French?"

"When I want to. I have some hidden talents you don't know about, sweetheart, and I plan on sharing all of them with you. Besides, I'm sure together we can find some more shared . . . talents."

"Kevin! Stop it. You're making me blush. I can't believe you said that."

"Trust me, I know my limits, but I want you to know what you have to look forward to one day soon."

"Oh!" She put her hands on either side of her face. "You're driving me crazy with all this flirting. Tell me something else."

"What's that?" From the amused look on his face, it was obvious he was enjoying her discomfort and liked getting her on edge.

Rebekah loved this side of him. "Where and when did you learn how to build a gazebo?"

"Some things just come naturally."

She stared and forced her mouth closed. "I'm not sure I even want to know what *that* means." She fanned herself with a paper she picked up from his desk. "Is there any place to sit down in this trailer?"

He nodded to the one chair behind the desk. "We could test it out." His wink was provocative.

Oh, my. "No thanks." She gave him another warning look, but was also close to bursting out with laughter.

"I have a confession," he said.

She looked at him in surprise. "What do you mean?"

"Technically, Adam ordered the gazebo and paid the deposit. I offered to make a one-of-a-kind design because I knew it was for you. I wish I could say I was the one—"

"Shh," she said, putting one finger over his lips. "I know."

He tilted his head. "You do?"

"Your brother the TV star told me you built it yourself and refunded Adam's money."

Kevin's grin was a little sheepish. "I wish I'd thought of it myself. It was extremely creative."

Rebekah laughed a little. "He's an idea man, but you're the one who followed through and finished the job. I love my gazebo. It's gorgeous, and I love the design name. But, it means so much more because you designed it and built it, knowing all along it was for me." Taking his hand, she lifted it to her lips, kissing the callus on the palm of his hand.

"Is Adam still in town, Rebekah?"

She looked up at him and shook her head. "The last I heard, he was packing up and moving back to England. I think he's had enough of the States. He's gone, Kevin. I finally woke up to what was under my nose all along, and Adam's out of our lives. Permanently."

"Good. Glad to hear it. About time." He nudged her toward the wall of the trailer, tangling her fingers with his as he moved her backward, pinning her flat against the wall.

She couldn't move if she wanted, not that she wanted to leave. Ever. A long sigh escaped her lips. Kevin's kisses were whisper soft and as gentle as a butterfly's touch as he peppered her cheeks, her jaw, her forehead, her eyelids. It was beyond romantic and anything she could have imagined. He loved her with his eyes and murmured how much he adored her and she did the same for him. He increased the intensity of his kisses with a passion that left her weak. When she started to fall, he swept her close, enfolding her in his arms as if he'd never release her.

"Kevin," she gasped, fighting to steady her breathing, "I didn't know you had it in you."

"Me either." He shrugged. "Who knew? Besides," he said, kissing her a few more times, making her beyond giddy, "you know what they say." His lips trailed a slow path to her neck.

Oh, he shouldn't do that. Putting both hands on his cheeks, she lifted his head, waiting until his eyes met hers. She loved she could make the man so crazy, and knew her expression mirrored his. Those sparkling blue eyes promised her so much. One thing she knew: life behind closed doors with this man would never be dull. That rumble in her belly was going at full-throttle now.

She gasped, trying to catch her breath. "No, what do they say?" She leaned forward and kissed the tiny scar on his forehead, loving it.

"Watch out for the quiet one."

Throwing her head back, she laughed and he joined in. "Promise me something, lumber man."

He kissed her again. "Anything, Rebekah. Name it."

"Please don't make me wait too long."

The loopy grin emerged. "Promise."

CHAPTER FORTY-FIVE

WINNIE AND CHLOE sat side-by-side on a blanket in the park nearest to the apartment. A picnic basket sat beside them and Winnie balanced a book on her lap. Chloe leaned across her leg, her finger on one of the pages, probably learning her ten new words for the day. Stepping out of the car, Josh closed the door, being as quiet as he could.

The two loves of my life.

He watched his girls a few seconds, thankful they were oblivious to his presence. When he heard Chloe's giggle, he could wait no longer. Pushing his hands in his pockets, he walked in their direction, quickening his steps the closer he came. If he gave into his impulse, he'd break into a sprint.

Chloe saw him first. "Mr. Josh!" she squealed, jumping to her feet and running toward him. Crouching down, he held his arms open wide. She threw her arms around his neck as he hugged her tight. "I missed you." She put her hand on his cheek.

"I missed you too, Buttercup. So much, you can't even know." He surprised her by scooping her into his arms and carrying her back to her mother. She giggled the whole way. He locked eyes with Winnie, drinking in the sight of her wearing the same pretty dress she'd worn the first time he saw her in Sam and Lexa's living room. Though not that long ago, it seemed like years. She rose to her feet, all grace and elegance. The best thing was she didn't look nervous. She looked like a woman in love.

Lord, I don't deserve her. Thank you.

Lowering Chloe, Josh wrapped one arm around Winnie's waist and drew her close. "Hello, Guppy." He planted an open-mouthed kiss on her cheek.

Her soft laughter was infectious. "If that's my new nickname, I certainly hope it's not a commentary on my kissing technique."

"Never. Your technique is incredible." She blushed and ducked her head as he stole a quick kiss on her neck. "That's when I first knew I was in love with you, you know. When you told that ridiculous story about guppy kisses. It was the most creative—not to mention nuttiest—thing I've ever heard. Put it this way: you had me at guppy."

"Like I said, you must not get out much."

"I need another demonstration," he said, turning her chin with one hand. Her skin was so soft. Her hair was in its usual ponytail, brushing past her shoulder. She was so beautiful it made his heart almost burst to think she belonged to him.

Winnie nodded over her shoulder where Chloe now sat on the blanket, holding the book and sounding out words. "Sweetie, close your eyes."

Impressive how fast she obeyed. Stealing a few soft, sweet kisses—some of the guppy variety, some not—Josh released her, chuckling when he spied his daughter still sitting on the blanket, her hands covering her face. Bright emerald eyes peeked at them from between her fingers. She moved her hands back and forth over her eyes, playing peek-a-boo.

"I was right," Chloe said.

"What do you mean, Buttercup?" Winnie asked.

"Mr. Josh *is* your prince."

Winnie rested her head on his chest and he put his arms around her. "Yes, he is. Get used to it. Mr. Josh is going to be around a long time." She looked up at him. "Have you eaten? I brought an extra sandwich."

What a woman—affection then food. She had her priorities straight. "I thought you'd never ask." He dropped down to the blanket beside her, leaning back on his hands, stretching out his legs.

"Turkey or ham?"

"What do you think, Chloe?"

Chloe tilted her head. "Turkey, please."

He loved the way she said please. "Turkey it is then, please." Winnie handed him the sandwich and a bottle of apple juice, and he said an abbreviated prayer. If he thanked the Lord now for all his blessings, he wouldn't be done until sometime tomorrow. They laughed and talked together, and Chloe entertained them with stories of some of the antics at her nursery school. Her imagination was lively and her enthusiasm made him smile.

"As much as I hate to break up our little party," Winnie said a short time later, "I think there's a little girl who needs her nap." She ignored Chloe's protests. "If you hush and go quietly, Mr. Josh will teach you five new words." They both laughed when she snapped her book closed and jumped to her feet.

"Do you want me to drive you back to the apartment?" Together they gathered the remains of their picnic lunch and put them in the basket.

Winnie shook her head. "It's such a beautiful day and not far so why don't we walk? If you have time."

He smiled. "For you and Chloe, I have all the time in the world, sweetheart. Let's go." Standing, he retrieved the picnic basket and held out his hand. A warm hand slipped in his. Chloe's hand. It was one of those moments he'd never forget. She skipped beside him, her hand firmly encased in his, as they headed back to the apartment. *This is exactly where I need to be.* If only Winnie agreed. When he was with Winnie and Chloe, he was home. A part of his heart ached when they were here and he was in Baton Rouge. Maybe they'd always been in his heart, stored away in that secret, cherished place, but now, it was time. He'd move to Houston. Surely the HBA wouldn't mind adding one more mergers and acquisitions attorney to its roster.

Tiptoeing out of the room after they both tucked Chloe in for her nap, Josh closed the door.

"Chloe's not the only one who's missed you," Winnie said, her lids heavy as she gazed up at him.

He planted both palms on either side of her face. "Is it too soon, sweetheart?" He prayed she'd understand his meaning.

"No," she said. "I could look in your eyes forever, you know. They change colors and go from light emerald to dark depending on your mood. They're incredible."

"Good thing," he said, "because that's why I'm here. In Houston. In your apartment. With our daughter sleeping in the next room. On a weekday. In the middle of the day."

Her smile was a wonder to behold. "You're here so I can stare in your eyes?"

"Marry me, Winnie. Then you'll have my eyes and all the rest of me. I want to marry you and Chloe. She can have that pink and white bedroom you've always wanted for her, and I can give you anything you want, in the bedroom and otherwise," he growled against her neck.

"Josh," she said with a small laugh. She looked a little stunned, but allowed him to lead as he pulled her by the hand to the sofa.

"Sit, please." She was a most obedient woman when she wanted. He pulled the ponytail elastic from her hair, thankful it slid out easily. Her hair fell to her shoulders and he moved closer, running his fingers through it. "I've been wanting to do that ever since I first saw you in the park today. Here, I have something for you." He reached for his sport jacket and retrieved the small, black velvet box from the inside pocket, smiling when he heard Winnie's sharp intake of breath. Her eyes filled with tears and one hand moved over her mouth.

"Well, if it's going to make you cry," he said, pretending to pocket it again.

"Joshua Alexander Grant, pull out that box now and get on with it." At least she'd recovered her voice.

Sliding down to one knee, he pulled open the lid. He didn't get out a word before Winnie slid down beside him, throwing her arms around his neck, covering him with kisses.

"I didn't even ask the question yet," he said, loving the feel of her so close to him, her hands clasped around his neck. "Winnie Doyle, what is your full name?"

On her knees beside him, she laughed. "It doesn't matter."

"Oh, but it does. I need to know your full name. Right now."

"I don't share it with just anyone, you know." He gave her a look and she sighed. "Winifred Justine Doyle. Sad, but true."

Josh tilted his head to one side. "I love it. But I think Winifred Justine *Grant* sounds much better. Winnie is such a whimsical, fun name. I've never known anyone else with it except . . ."

"I know, I know," she said. "No one except a chubby little bear with a red T-shirt and a honey pot."

"Oh, but you'd look real cute in a red T-shirt and a honey—"

"Josh!"

"I like you whimsical and fun," he said, helping her to her feet. "You can't always be no-nonsense and practical all the time."

"As a mother, I need a dose of both."

"As a *wife*, you'll need both."

"Josh, do me a big favor. I know we have a lot of nicknames around here, but please don't call me Pooh . . . or Guppy." She giggled.

"Then what do you prefer? Ladies choice. Pick a name."

Her smile lit up his world. "Mrs. Grant. Now *that's* a name I could live with the rest of my life."

"Winnie, is there anyone I need to ask officially for permission to marry you?"

"No." Her eyes clouded, but it was gone as soon as it surfaced. "No one except maybe—"

"Sam," he said, and she nodded.

"I know Chloe already approves, but we should probably ask her, too," Winnie said. "But, first things first. Let me see my ring, please."

"Oh, sorry. You've been incredibly patient." Josh opened the top of the box again, relishing her delighted gasp as he pulled it from its velvet nest and easily slipped the diamond on her finger. With the ring tucked close to his heart the whole trip, he prayed she'd love it. It looked like it was made for her finger as it winked at him.

"It's perfect. How did you know my ring size?" Her voice was breathy.

"Lexa helped."

Winnie raised a brow, still staring at the ring. "How did she know?"

He shrugged. "How do Lexa and Sam know anything? Beck helped me pick the cut and everything else. My twin sister's uncommonly talented and knowledgeable when it comes to diamonds. Who knew?"

"I'll be sure and thank her." Holding out her hand, she stared at it as if she couldn't believe he sat beside her and she was wearing his ring. "And wouldn't you know?"

"Hmm?" he asked, nuzzling her neck. He pulled back. "What's that?"

"The cut of the ring, Josh. Do you know what it is?"

He shook his head. "No. I'd much rather kiss you some more."

She laughed, obliging him in the best way. Between kisses, she sighed. "It's an emerald cut diamond."

"Sounds perfect," he said against her lips.

"Perfect. That's a word we should teach Chloe."

He smiled. "Somehow, I think she already knows."

~

Rebekah and Kevin sat next to each other at The Grotto later that evening. All the dust and grime had been washed off and he looked even more handsome than on their special date because this time he was dressed in his khakis and a dress shirt, his hair combed like usual. He drove his big blue truck with the guitar in the back and wore his boots.

"I think you kissed away whatever brain cells I had left today," she said. "You make me as nutty as one of those grins of yours. Not that I'm complaining. Not at all." She loved the grin that spread across his handsome face. "Tell me something."

"Go ahead." He took a long, slow sip of water. "Ask away."

"Where on earth did you learn to kiss like that?"

Kevin had to catch himself not to spit out his mouthful of water. Putting his napkin up to his mouth, he laughed. What was it about her that made guys spit their drinks on the tablecloth?

"Unfair advantage. It's because it's you, Rebekah. Trust me. I've never kissed anyone else like that. You're my one and only."

How she loved hearing those words. "I love you, Kevin." He squeezed her hand and they spent the next few minutes acting like the lovesick fools they were. By far, it was the most exhilarating feeling in the world. Love was a process, at least for her. The journey with Adam was one way the Lord revealed His truths and helped her appreciate *this* man all the more.

After their food was delivered, Kevin asked the blessing. Releasing her hand, he began telling her about the dish he'd ordered, a local specialty some of the guys at the construction site raved about all the time.

"Kevin," she said, watching as he took his first bite and pronounced it delicious.

"Yes, sweetheart?" he asked after taking another generous bite.

"If you never ever want to tell me about the food—how it's prepared, or pretty much anything about it—I'm perfectly fine not knowing."

He winked. "Not a problem. Still want to share?"

"You'd better." She scooted her chair closer to his and waited for her first sample of whatever it was he ordered. It could be anything in the world short of sawdust and it would taste like the sweetest nectar because she was sharing it with her lumber man.

As she finished her meal, Rebekah noticed he'd stopped eating and pushed his plate aside. He leaned his chin on one hand, watching her. "You are the most incredibly beautiful woman I've ever known and I'm blessed to know you much less be graced enough to love you."

"Don't say anything else for a full minute," she said, raising one hand and closing her eyes. "I just need to savor your poetic words."

Kevin nudged her arm. "You'd better stop. People are starting to talk."

She laughed. "I thought you didn't care. As long as we're in the center of God's will for our lives, let them talk. There's nowhere else I'd rather be."

"Well, as long as people are talking, anyway . . ." Her eyes widened as he slid down on one knee beside her, taking both her hands in his. "Marry me, Rebekah Nicole Grant. You're the greatest gift of my life. I thank the Lord every day for the honor and privilege of loving you, and I'll spend the rest of my life making you happy." He reached into his pocket and gave her a sweet look when he heard her gasp. "This is just a proxy ring. If you'll have me, then we'll go ring shopping tomorrow. I was going to pick one out, but decided I want you to pick out the perfect ring. Sam knows a guy downtown . . ."

She laughed. "Of course he does." Taking her finger, Kevin slipped on the ring. Costume jewelry or not, it was the most beautiful thing she'd ever seen. "We'll pick one out together." Her eyes filled with tears. "Wow, you really took my advice."

"What advice is that? I'm on my knees here."

"I told you not to wait too long and you were a most obedient man." She took his face in her hands and pulled him to her. "Decisive," she whispered, "I like that. Saves a lot of time." Knowing he would want to hear the words, she whispered, "Yes, I will marry you, Kevin Curtis Moore. Whenever you say. I'll be honored to be your wife and I will cherish you as my husband."

He kissed her, but pulled away when claps and quiet cheers erupted around them. A small group of servers and those at neighboring tables congratulated them. Kevin acknowledged the nods from other male diners and the ladies winked at her as if to say "Great catch."

Don't I know it.

~

Lexa and Sam sat next to each other, enjoying a private, romantic dinner by candlelight in the dining room. She ate the last baby carrot on her plate. That wouldn't be surprising except it was her second plateful of food. Single-handedly, she'd nearly devoured an entire head of broccoli, not to mention all of her generous pork chop. She caught Sam's amused grin as she put her fork on the side of her empty plate.

"So, Twin Number Two is still off for dinner with her intended, but have you seen Twin Number One since this morning?" he asked, pushing aside his empty plate. Six-foot-five and the man only had one helping. Go figure. She took another bite of her roll as she pondered it all.

"Lexa?"

"Sorry. No, I haven't seen Josh since he and Beck drove off together to Kevin's work site this morning. Unless I'm totally off the mark here, I imagine they'll both have big news when we see them in the morning. What?" she asked, seeing those smile lines deepen as she finished the roll. She loved her husband's smile, but his intense scrutiny at the moment wasn't welcome since she felt like a gluttonous pig. She couldn't seem to stop eating, and she'd gained a pound in the last week alone. She didn't want to think about the reason.

"Baby, you seem awfully hungry these days, not to mention a little forgetful."

"Trust me, if you had to nurse a baby countless times every day and run a catering business, you'd understand." Her eyes widened. "Sorry, that didn't come out right, and not to discount everything you do."

"You put up with a lot from both the men in your life."

She waved her hand. "Like you're hard to take, Sam Lewis. But, I will say our son is going to be a big, strapping cowboy like his daddy, based on the way he's draining me. And I mean that quite literally." She shushed him when he laughed. Getting up from her chair, she lovingly shoved his hands aside and positioned herself on his lap, inching her hands around his neck and kissing him the way she knew he loved best. "I love you, handsome cowboy."

"I love you, beautiful girl, but I think we'd better move this into the living room. Unless you'd rather finish up the dishes and go upstairs early?" He quirked a brow.

She teared up, and he tightened his hold on her. "I know I'm eating like a pig, and I can't help it. No two ways around it, I'm getting fat." She attempted to slide down from his lap, but he stopped her, pulling her next to him and holding on tight.

"You're not fat, but I *do* think you're pregnant again."

"Of course I'm not," she said. "Not that you don't do your part, but I'm not ready for that. Joe's still so young, and the business is just getting started . . ."

"Is that why you got so bent out of shape about that emergency catering job a few months ago?"

"No, that was legitimate panic," she said, laughing even as a tear slipped down her cheek.

"Shh. Then why the tears? You've already hired additional help, and you couldn't ask for a better partner than Winnie."

"Who will probably be expecting within six months herself," Lexa said, leaning her head against his chest. "I didn't think I'd get pregnant again since I'm still nursing Joe." She pulled back and lifted her eyes. "You're okay with it?"

"I'm more than okay. Remember, I come from a family with six kids. Plus assorted animals. I'm used to chaos and some would say I even thrive on it."

She giggled and moved her hand over his heart. How she loved sitting with him like this. "I'll try to keep the level of chaos under control. But, wait, you wanted to move so I don't break down this chair." She started to push away, but he held her steady.

"Stay," he said, caressing her cheek before moving his hand to her stomach. "Hello, little Lewis baby." He grinned when he saw the corners of her lips upturn. "It's awfully soon, yes, but the Lord knows best. Don't worry, Lexa. It'll all work out. Now," he said, standing with her in his arms, "I'm going to take you upstairs and tuck you into bed. I'll do the dishes and join you shortly. In the morning, if you're not too tired, you can make your delicious pancakes and we can share in everyone's joy."

"I don't want to detract from their news by saying anything yet. Not until we know for sure."

He nodded. "Agreed, but I know the Lord has blessed us again. Even though I'm prejudiced, we make beautiful babies together."

"As long as this isn't some crazy race between you and Marc. I don't want to be pregnant all the time, you know."

He laughed, climbing the stairs with her still in his arms. "Maybe we'll have twins this time."

"Sam, did you say anything to Josh and Rebekah yet?" she asked as he carried her into their bedroom.

"Not yet." Lowering her onto the bed, he winked. "That's tomorrow's big surprise."

CHAPTER FORTY-SIX

THE NEXT MORNING, they all sat around the dining room table, laughing and talking. Winnie had her hand in Josh's and she kept stealing glances at Beck and Kevin, their hands clasped together—whenever Josh wasn't sneaking kisses from her. They all had hearty appetites for Lexa's pancakes, both peach and strawberry.

"Lexa had a wonderful suggestion," Sam said as they finished breakfast. "If you're game, we think it's time for some Texas two-stepping tonight. I believe you're all here until at least tomorrow," he said, "so what do you say? Time to pull your partner close and share a few dances?"

"I've heard that can be dangerous for your wife," Josh said under his breath.

She giggled and shot a glance at Lexa.

"I'm willing to take my chances," Lexa said, planting a kiss on the top of Sam's head as she carried another empty platter back into the kitchen.

Winnie eyed her business partner. The last couple of weeks, she'd alternated between scarfing down her food or else turning a little green and excusing herself from the room in a heartbeat. Little Joe might be getting a little brother or sister sooner than later. Chloe would be ecstatic.

"Sounds like a great idea," Kevin said, bringing her back to the posed question.

Beck nodded. "We're game."

Winnie suppressed a smile. Josh's beautiful sister wouldn't care where she was, as long as Kevin was beside her. She was so happy for them, and they made a great couple.

Josh squeezed her hand. "So are we."

"Okay, how about we all meet here tonight at seven, and head out together," Sam said. He called to Josh and Rebekah as they got up from the breakfast table, asking for a word with them.

Winnie shared a glance and a shrug with Kevin as they gathered the breakfast dishes, following Lexa into the kitchen. Even though Lexa must know what it was about, she had the suspicion she wouldn't be talking. No doubt, they'd find out soon enough.

~

Something about his tone told Josh the TeamWork leader had something serious on his mind. "Come into the study. We need to talk privately."

"Yes sir," Josh said with a mock salute. Beck looked at him, a question in her eyes. He shrugged as Sam led the way, closing the door behind him as they took seats across from his desk and he sat down in the massive black leather chair.

"Have we done something wrong?" she asked.

"Relax. I have something I need to discuss with the two of you. I wanted to talk with you first so you can think about it before giving me your answers."

"What's on your mind?" he asked.

"Josh, have you and Winnie discussed your plans as far as where you'll be living and working?"

At least he got right to the point. "We haven't worked through everything yet, no, but we've talked about it. I know how important the catering business is to both Winnie and Lexa, and I'm not planning on asking her to break up that partnership. I enjoy my work at the firm, but mergers and acquisitions and the whole corporate thing—pushing numbers around to make everybody happy—isn't what I want to do the rest of my working life." He met his friend's piercing gaze. "It's not where my heart is."

"So you're at least considering a possible move to Houston?"

He nodded. "Definitely."

"Do you have any idea what you'd like to pursue? Are you talking about leaving your law practice entirely?"

"No. I've always wanted to practice in some capacity, but I'm thinking more along the lines of family law or something where I could work in conjunction with social services. I've done a lot of pro bono work in Baton Rouge, helping families get benefits and insurance payouts. Plus the TeamWork project in New Orleans has been great. I've prayed about it, and I believe the Lord's leading me in a different direction. I'm open to finding out what that is."

When Sam nodded, Josh couldn't miss his look of pleased satisfaction. Knowing Sam like he did, something was on his mind. He suspected he'd find out very soon.

"What about you, Beck?" Sam asked. "Have you and Kevin talked about where you're going to settle?"

She sighed. "A lot is up in the air right now since he's not sure how long he'll be here in Houston once the business is up and running. For the foreseeable future, except for frequent trips to Baton Rouge, it looks like he'll pretty much be stationed here."

"You sound like it's the military," Josh said.

"It sorts of feels like it," she said. "At least it's only temporary."

Sam sat up straighter and clasped his hands together on the top of his desk. "Let me tell you what I have in mind. As part of my position as Domestic Missions Director of TeamWork, I have the authority to appoint new positions within the TeamWork organization, both here in Texas and around the country. Josh, I'm in the market for a full-time general counsel. You'd need to take the Texas bar exam, but I know that wouldn't be a problem for you. Our current general counsel is retiring in about three months. There's no way I can promise you the type of salary I know you're accustomed to at the firm in Baton Rouge, but this is what I can offer."

Taking out a sheet of paper from his desk drawer, he pushed it across the desk. On it were printed facts and figures. Sam waited as he scanned it and noted the generous benefits package. That would be a big consideration with a wife and daughter, and hopefully more children in the not-so-distant future.

"I don't know what to say," Josh said.

"Don't say no right away. I know your future wife is making some decent money these days with the catering business, and it promises to take on even more clientele in the near future." He smiled. "People always need to eat, thank the Lord. You could work in the TeamWork office, from home or wherever you'd like."

"Do you have something in mind for me?" Beck asked. Josh shot her a grin. She sounded like a kid impatient to get her present at Christmas.

Sam's eyes softened as he looked at her. "As a matter of fact, yes. The woman who's the head of our school operations is leaving the organization to stay home and raise her children, so we have an immediate opening. You'd be able to work from home for now, or you can have a small space in the TeamWork main office, if you're willing to put up with me."

"What would I be expected to do?"

"You'd set up all the schoolroom operations for all the TeamWork missions around the country. It takes a lot of planning that most people don't understand. With your experience as a teacher, and with your past TeamWork missions, you understand better than anyone else the conditions and what's needed. You could scout out the locations, make recommendations, work with the TeamWork staff on curriculum, that type of thing. I know you've felt like you've been searching for something, needing to fill a void in your life. While Kevin is probably the answer to a lot of that, I know you've been seeking more professional fulfillment. I'm offering this to you as a possibility, combining your teaching expertise with TeamWork and doing the Lord's work."

It was Rebekah's turn to echo his words. "I don't know what to say."

"All I ask now is that you both pray about it, talk with Winnie and Kevin, and give me your answers when you're ready. I'm not in a hurry, but if possible, let me know your thoughts before you leave Houston. I'll be happy to answer any questions."

Josh looked over at his sister with raised eyebrows. As soon as he saw her smile, and felt the squeeze of her hand, he knew. "We accept."

CHAPTER FORTY-SEVEN

THEY ALL PILED into the Volvo station wagon after dinner, headed downtown for a fun night out of Texas line-dancing. They wore their jeans and boots, and the guys all wore Stetsons. Winnie caught Lexa's grin as Josh pulled her inside the back of the station wagon, practically on his lap. She smiled as Kevin stole a quick kiss from Rebekah before settling in beside her.

"I didn't know you owned a cowboy hat," she said to Josh, nestling into the curve of his arm in the backseat as they waited for Lexa to finish giving her instructions to the babysitter before joining them. Dottie was with Chloe, and being Josh's preferred sitter, she could rest easy for one night she wouldn't get the third degree.

"I don't wear it much, but I have the feeling I'll be wearing it a lot more in the future. I hear it's the first thing Marc bought when he got back to Boston after the Montana mission." Tipping it further back on his forehead, he laughed and caught it before it toppled off his head.

Winnie giggled. "There's definitely something about a man in a Stetson. Natalie learned that lesson in Montana, and Marc is a very wise man. I, for one, love it." She gave him a quick kiss.

"Watch it, buddy. This backseat can get dangerous," Josh said.

The comment made its mark when a slow flush crept into Kevin's cheeks.

"Now you see why I never double date with him," Rebekah said, rolling her eyes.

"Would you two please stop it over there?" Josh said, winking at his sister. "You're embarrassing me."

"Only if you do the same," Kevin shot back.

"I didn't know you had it in you," Josh said, laughing, winking at his brother-in-law-to-be. "Sarcasm and public displays of affection all in the same night." He planted a quick kiss on Winnie's nose. "What's the world coming to, anyway?"

"Well, I for one think God's world, and the TeamWork world, in particular, is absolutely fabulous about now," Winnie said. She smiled when he snuggled her even closer to him.

"We're pairing off quite nicely, don't you think?" Rebekah said. "Let's see, we've got Sam and Lexa, Natalie and Marc, Winnie and Josh, me and Kevin. Dare I ask who's next? Amy? Dean? Eliot, anyone?"

"Don't forget Marta and Cassie," Winnie said. "And Gayle."

"I'm sure some of us will marry outside the fold, so to speak," Josh said, his voice wry.

"Tell me Sam," Rebekah said, raising her voice so he could hear, "what is it about TeamWork that brings about all these romances, do you think?"

"First of all, I hesitate to use the word romance," Sam said.

Lexa laughed. "You're such a man's man, Sam Lewis. Okay, then, pick another more appropriate term. 'Relationship,' perhaps?"

"In answer to your question," Sam said, ignoring Lexa's barb, "I believe it's a case of the Lord planting workers where they're most needed among others of His choosing. Then He sits back and watches all the fun, shaking His head while we make fools of ourselves before we finally awaken to the great love He's blessed us with right in front of our eyes."

"My husband, thank you very much," Lexa said. "See what we started, Sam?"

"Yeah, and ain't it grand?"

Josh laughed and shot a look at Kevin. "Just serve my sister frog legs for every anniversary, and you'll enjoy lasting bliss the rest of your lives." He planted another kiss on Winnie's cheek. "I'll stick with my guppy."

She gave him a love swat and reached for Beck's hand. "Let me see that diamond again. It's gorgeous. You did very well, Kevin, and I'm not just talking about the ring."

"Don't I know it," Kevin said. He shot an amused look at Josh. "Guppy?"

~

"Maybe I should have stayed home tonight," Lexa whispered to Sam. She'd hired a young college student from their church to watch Joe, but she still worried as Sam drove them to the highway. She hated leaving her son at home, but knew it was important to get out of the house with their adult friends every now and then. "I feel like I'm abandoning our child." Crossing her arms, she stared out the window.

"You're doing it again." Sam reached for her hand, dislodging her crossed arms.

"Sorry. Old habits die hard." She squeezed his hand. Glancing over her shoulder to make sure none of their four passengers heard their conversation, she sighed. "I am. Pregnant again." The next minute, she wanted to burst into tears. It was a wonder the man put up with her.

"I love you, Lexa."

"Remember the night of the barbecue at church? We couldn't wait to get home. There was a lot of playfulness . . ."

"Well, that's pretty much a given with us." Sam chuckled. "We're getting a great start to our own TeamWork family. Kind of like TeamWork: the Next Generation. Has a nice ring to it, don't you think?"

"Sounds like a sci-fi TV show, but yes, it does sound very nice." She laughed a little, but then brought one hand up to her mouth.

"Are you okay?" He touched her arm. "Oh, oh. I remember that look. Breathe deep. In and out, in and out."

~

"So, tell us about the plans for your weddings," Lexa said a short time later, waving her hand as the bowl of nachos passed her by. Better not tempt anything. For the last couple of hours, her stomach had been a roller coaster. "You go first, Beck."

"Kevin and I are thinking of an early December wedding." When Rebekah reached for his hand, he looked at her with such adoration it stilled Lexa's heart. She'd been praying for them ever since the trip to Milestone Ranch in Montana. Sam nudged her knee under the table, reaching for her hand. He probably loved this as much as she did, hearing their plans, sharing in their joy.

"It doesn't give us much time," Rebekah said, "but I'm sure we can do it. I've always loved that time of the year, and it will brighten Mom's holiday season especially since it will be our first without Daddy around. I know she'll love helping with all the details." She darted a glance at her twin. "I don't want to be insensitive, either. Do you think that's too soon, Josh?"

Josh shook his head and cleared his throat. "It sounds perfect." His eyes were bright. "Mom will love it."

"You're giving me away, you know," Beck told him as Winnie tucked her hand in the crook of Josh's arm, leaning her head on his shoulder. "And Chloe will be the flower girl, of course."

Winnie brightened. "She'll love that. Thanks, Beck."

"Not to change the subject," Josh said, "but I think we need to hear these famous rules of marriage from our man Sam."

Lexa stiffened at the mention, but was surprised by her husband's broad grin.

"Since you all seem to know about those rules, anyway, I've started to write notes for a possible book," Sam told them.

"Really?" she asked, quickly echoed by Winnie.

Kevin laughed. "Have you told Marc yet? He'll be really happy to hear it."

"Not yet, but I will. He seems to think a lot of men, especially, might be encouraged by those rules. They're based on biblical principles and wanting God's best for our mate, so I'm willing to try. Just another adventure." Sam gave her a reassuring wink, and she nodded.

Josh smiled. "It's our turn to share you with the rest of the world. I'm with Marc on this one. It could be the start of something big."

"You know what they say," Sam said, "cliché or not, everything's big in Texas, my friends. And now, gang," he said, "it's time for some line-dancing."

"Wait a minute," Rebekah said. "We need to hear about Winnie and Josh's wedding plans."

"Oh, I thought they were eloping next week," Lexa said, shooting Winnie and Josh a grin. She'd been praying for *them* since Chloe's birth. "I highly recommend it." She caught her husband's amused glance at that comment.

"I tried that tactic, but Winnie wouldn't have it," Josh said. "Actually, Sam, we'd be honored if you'd give her away. What do you say?"

Sam's pleasure showed on his face. "I'd be honored," he said. "Like I told Marc when he wanted to remarry Natalie, just tell me when and where to show up and I'll be there."

"Since you're ordained in Texas, we were hoping you might do double-duty and perform the honors," Josh said.

"It would be very simple," Winnie added. "Maybe even in your lovely backyard . . ."

"Don't forget I have a gazebo, with hearts and everything," Rebekah said. "Which might have to be moved, anyway." She winked at Kevin and they both smiled.

"When?" Lexa asked.

"Late September sound okay?" Josh asked. He shot a look at Rebekah. "I don't think Mom will mind at all."

Rebekah's eyes were full. "She'll love it."

Lexa nodded, praying she could make it to the ladies room. "Great. Now, if you'll excuse me." She clamped a hand over her mouth and darted away from the table.

~

Rebekah watched as Sam stood up, giving Winnie a rare look of helplessness and a shrug. It was sweet seeing their strong leader humbled and at a loss to know how to help his wife.

"I'll go," Winnie said, rising from the table and hurrying after Lexa.

"Is she okay?" Kevin asked.

Bless his heart, he had no clue. Oh, what fun she'd have when the time came—in a few short years—to share the news with him that *he* was going to be a father. *All in good time.* Rebekah leaned her head on his shoulder and Kevin kissed the top of her head.

Sam sighed. "We didn't want to say anything yet—" He gave them a sheepish grin, another unusual sight.

"You're adding to the TeamWork crew again," Josh said for him. "That's great, man."

"Congratulations, Sam," Kevin said. "We're thrilled for you."

Rebekah squeezed Kevin's hand and whispered, "I think it's time for you to take me in your arms and dance with me, Mr. Moore. If you'll excuse us," she said to the others. Standing, she pulled him behind her toward the dance floor. She stopped abruptly and turned around; he almost bumped into her and she planted both hands on his chest.

Slipping one arm around her waist, Kevin captured her hand in his and led her to the dance floor, skillfully pulling her around to face him. He was taking charge, and she had the suspicion he was about to reveal another one of his hidden talents.

"You're really good at this," she said as he whirled her around the dance floor—laughing, exchanging a word here, a glance there, a kiss there, waving to Sam and Lexa each time they passed by them. At least Lexa didn't look so pale and looked like she felt better. "I'm getting dizzy here. It's like I'm on a merry-go-round."

He slowed them down for a moment. "Need to sit down?"

"No," she said, laughing, "and I never want to stop."

Josh came alongside with Winnie in his arms. "Cut in?"

"Not tonight." Kevin pulled his Stetson lower and ignored him. "No offense, Winnie," he called after them.

"None taken," she said as Josh twirled her in the opposite direction.

Rebekah watched her brother and his bride-to-be and released a sigh. "They make a beautiful couple, don't they?"

"They do, and Chloe makes three. God knows what He's doing. Not that I ever doubted it."

"Hmm," she said. "Since I don't think you'll run screaming in the opposite direction, how many little Moores would you like to see running around in a few years?"

"As many as the Lord wants to give us, sweetheart. Each and every one will be a blessing. How about you?"

She smiled. "We'll keep having them until we get at least one that has a loopy grin just like their handsome daddy."

He laughed. "You want us to have loopy children?"

"Oh, yeah," she said. "Lots of them."

A ballad began and their steps slowed again. "Have I told you lately how much I love you?" Kevin whispered as they moved together.

"Not in the last ten minutes or so," she said as they clasped hands, locked eyes and hearts. "I love you, too. All this time, I was under the impression I was waiting on you, but it turns out, you were waiting for me all along. My sweet lumber man."

He chuckled. "Not a problem. You're worth it."

"Kevin?"

His eyes swept over her face, settling on her lips. "Kiss the girl," he said, his lips hovering so close. "My pleasure."

"Wait," she said, putting one hand on his chest. "We're in a public place."

"You know, Rebekah," he said—his lips on hers—"I don't care. Let 'em talk."

~

"We're going to have to scramble to find a place to live, Josh." Winnie glanced over at Kevin and Rebekah dancing nearby. Those two were oblivious to everyone else, moving slowly to the country western ballad.

"Why? I thought we could camp out at Sam and Lexa's for a while. They wouldn't mind, would they?" Josh's grin was irresistible. "What are you thinking?" With his eyes trained only on her, he made her feel like the only woman in the room.

"I love your house in Baton Rouge. Maybe we could dig it up and move it here?"

Josh laughed. "I don't think so. I want a new house to start fresh with you and Chloe."

"But one with window seats and a special hiding place," Winnie said. "And, if it's not too much to ask, a state-of-the-art-kitchen?"

"Wouldn't build one without all those things. Here's an idea. I'll build you a house that's perfect, the way you want it. You'll be so cute running around, checking it out and making plans. I'll have a lot of fun watching you and Chloe as it's being built." Saluting Kevin as he danced nearby with Rebekah, Josh chuckled. "I'm pretty sure I can get a decent price on lumber and building supplies." His eyes met hers. "Winnie, I want to give you everything you've ever wanted. In the meantime, we can stay in your apartment, rent a bigger one, or we can ask Sam and Lexa if it's okay to stay with them."

"No, no," she said, laughing. "They need their privacy."

"We can always camp out in the Volvo in their garage out back." They both laughed.

"Seriously," she said, "Sam and Lexa practically have a revolving front door as it is. To tell you the truth, I'm afraid to even drink the water at their house these days."

"Yeah, I'm thrilled for them. That's not a bad idea, you know," he said, his voice low. He quirked a brow and gave her one of those dare-you-to-resist-me looks.

"Josh," she breathed, "we need a little time to ourselves first. Besides, Chloe needs time to adjust to having you around full-time." She smoothed her hands over the collar of his shirt before moving them to the back of his neck, a small smile playing about her lips. "She's already asked if you can come for sleepovers." Her smile grew wider when she heard his laughter. "Should we tell her?"

"That I'm her daddy?" His hold on her tightened and he pulled her close to his chest, whirling her around in tune to the music. "Put it this way: I doubt she'll be calling me 'Mr. Josh' much longer. I think if we leave it up to her, she'll be asking soon enough. I'm sure she'll ask before we marry, or we'll tell her then." He kissed her cheek. "Our daughter's very bright, you know." Josh rested his cheek against hers as he dipped her and gave her a sweet, soft kiss. Pulling her upright with him, he anchored his large, warm hand over hers.

"I know." Her eyes misted every time he made reference to *our.* "You're already her daddy in her heart, you know. I'm so thankful for the blind trust and love she's shown you." Winnie loved being this close to him. Protected. Cherished. *Loved.* Even a few months ago, she'd never have dreamed she'd be dancing with the father of her child like this, making plans for a future together where they'd share everything of life, from the heartbreaking sorrows to the exhilarating triumphs.

"Winnie," he said, his voice husky, "I promise you I'll be a faithful, loving husband and the best father I can be for all our children." He put his hands on either side of her face, his look intense, the passion undeniable. "I love you, and I'll spend the rest of my life proving it and thanking the Lord for bringing us together again."

"*Healed* our hearts, Josh. That's what the Lord did. He took the broken pieces and put them together in the way only He can." She patted her hand over his heart, giving him a smile through her happy tears. "Don't know about you, but I think we're in for quite the adventure."

His kiss was tender as he leaned his forehead against hers and they swayed together to the music. "You asked me once where I see myself in ten years. I have an answer now."

"Oh?" Winnie pulled back.

"I see us in bed," he said, chuckling as he heard her sharp intake of breath, "with several children and a couple of dogs snuggled together, watching *The Wizard of Oz.* Or *Veggie Tales.*"

"Add a cat or two, and I think you're onto something. By then, I'm sure we'll have Snickers and Kit Kat."

They laughed together before he planted a guppy kiss on her cheek. "The more the merrier, sweetheart. Bring it on."

~

"Just look at all our children, Sam. We are so blessed." Feeling slightly better, at least for the moment, Lexa leaned against him with a contented smile—her back to him, his arms wrapped around her—as they watched the twins and their partners on the dance floor.

"Feel like joining them?" Sam stroked her hair. She'd worn it down on purpose tonight, knowing he loved it as a change from her usual braid.

"Not tonight. I'm perfectly content sitting here with my handsome husband, if you don't mind." She eyed the bowl of chips on the table. "Sam?"

"Hmm?"

"I think I'm having my first real craving."

He shifted her to the side, kissing her temple and giving her a look that took her back to Maxie's, the coffee house in San Antonio, almost five years ago. "That's what got us here in the first place, you know."

She recognized that huskiness in his voice, adored the deepening smile lines. If possible, Sam grew more handsome every day. He was such a godly man, a wonderful father, the husband of her heart. "Are you complaining?" She put her hand on his jaw, resting it there.

"Never, my love. Tell me about this craving of yours, and I'll see what I can do."

She winked. "I'll give you one guess."

One brow quirked.

"Need a little hint?"

"It'll save time. Since you're a caterer, the possibilities are endless."

"Okay, then. Here goes. It's just like you—smooth and tough on the outside, tender in the middle, but with a rock-solid core."

Sam's laugh was deep and hearty. "That's quite the hint. I take it that's a compliment?"

"Trust me, I think you'll be very happy about this one. Be good, and I might share." With a giggle, Lexa pulled him close and whispered in his ear. "Peaches."

About the Author

Twin Hearts is JoAnn Durgin's third published novel in ***The Lewis Legacy Series***, following the popular ***Awakening*** and ***Second Time Around***. Get ready for romance, adventure, friendship, faith and family in each new installment of the series with Sam and Lexa Lewis and their lively TeamWork Missions volunteers.

JoAnn and her husband, Jim, live with their three children in southern Indiana. When she's not writing, she's a full-time estate administration paralegal in a Louisville, Kentucky law firm. As a member of the American Christian Fiction Writers (national and Indiana chapter), Louisville Christian Writers and Romance Writers of America, JoAnn's prayer is that her contemporary romantic adventures will touch hearts and lives with the redeeming love of Jesus Christ.

She'd love to hear from you at www.joanndurgin.com or on Facebook.

DAYDREAMS

A fun, wildly romantic adventure coming for the Christmas season!

It's early December 2002, and Amy Jacobsen is living the dream: a job she loves with a trendy New York City magazine, a Manhattan walk-up inherited from her grandfather, and a busy social life *without* the unwanted complication of a steady boyfriend. During dinner one evening with her Wall Street financier brother, Mitch, she spies Landon Warnick at the next table. He's one of the most influential, successful and youngest magazine publishers in the country—not to mention one of New York's most eligible bachelors.

After Mitch wrangles a meeting between the two, Landon wastes little time asking her to dinner. Usually wary of smooth men and romantic entanglements, Amy questions her sanity when they share a cozy carriage ride in Central Park and she comes *this* close to kissing him. Is it the joy and wonder of the Christmas season that's put stars in her eyes or the enigmatic, intelligent, challenging and incredibly handsome man?

The following weekend, she travels to Louisiana to be a bridesmaid in a wedding and a reunion with Sam and Lexa Lewis and some of her dearest friends and fellow volunteers in TeamWork Missions. Headed down the aisle at the wedding, Amy's steps falter. Standing at the front is a groomsman who flew into town only an hour before . . . She does a double take. What's Landon Warnick doing in *her* world, with *her* friends? Perhaps more important, why does he suddenly have a Texas drawl and a crescent-shaped scar on his forehead? Sharing a romantic dance at the wedding reception, she casts aside her better judgment and kisses him. She's lost her mind, and her heart might not be far behind, it seems.

Let the adventure begin! Is the Lord showing her the "right" man for her heart or is Amy in *way* over her head?

The *Lewis Legacy Series*

by JoAnn Durgin

A God-fearing man. A God-seeking woman. For Sam Lewis and Lexa Clarke, it proves a combustible combination. You'll keep turning the pages of this sweeping romantic adventure. With great characters, plenty of humor, enough emotion to make you shed a tear or two, and an ending that'll have you cheering, *Awakening* will leave you breathless. Hold on tight.

Paperback ISBN 978-1-926712-56-7

Newlyweds Marc and Natalie Thompson have it all, but two months after the wedding, Natalie suffers a horrible fall. Not only does she not remember their life together, but now Marc has a personal timeline to reconnect with her—seven months. You'll root for them as they fight against the odds to find their way back to one another... the second time around.

Paperback ISBN 978-1-926712-35-2

It's been more than four years since Josh was thrown out of the TeamWork missions camp, and he's still haunted by the bittersweet memory of his final meeting with another volunteer. When he also seeks her forgiveness, he gets the shock of his life. Could turning his deepest sin into his greatest blessing be God's answer for his hurting heart?

Paperback ISBN 978-1-927339-13-8

The ***Lewis Legacy Series*** is available in paperback and eBook at your favorite online retailer like Amazon.com

TORN VEIL BOOKS
Your Christian Book Publisher

Visit us on the Web at
www.tornveilbooks.com